THE BOY WHO DEFIED HIS KARMA

THE BOY WHO DEFIED HIS KARMA

A novel by

Michael S. Koyama

Mutual Publishing

Library of Congress Control Number: 2011930592
ISBN-10: 1-56647-950-9
ISBN-13: 978-1-56647-950-9

First Printing, October 2011
Cover design by Jane Gillespie
Cover composite was created using these photos:
Bay Bridge and San Francisco © Zhou Minyun | Dreamstime.com
Cambridge © Bjeayes | Dreamstime.com
Myanmar (Burma) © Rafał Cichawa | Dreamstime.com
Bangkok panorama © Dalibor Kantor | Dreamstime.com
Little boy walking in autumn park © Iurii Davydov | Dreamstime.com

Mutual Publishing, LLC
1215 Center Street, Suite 210
Honolulu, Hawaii 96816
Phone: (808) 732-1709 / Fax: (808) 734-4094
e-mail: info@mutualpublishing.com / www.mutualpublishing.com
Printed in Korea

Chapter 1

Bangkok and Japan, 1943

B UNJI HAD NEVER BEEN SO COLD. He shivered uncontrollably in his shorts and sandals as he stood on the deck of the *Bungo Maru* with his father while waiting to disembark in Sasebo. Even with his father's arms around him, his teeth were chattering. Bunji looked up at the moon, visible through a thin cloud, and wondered what karma had in store for him once they landed in Japan. Surely nothing could be as terrible as the long and trying journey from Bangkok, thought the nine-year-old boy. He bit down on his lower lip to keep from crying.

The nightmare had begun twelve days before when a Japanese army sedan with three *kempei*—military police— arrived at Bunji's house on the outskirts of Bangkok. The soldiers marched into the house and tramped through the rooms with their boots on until they found Bunji and his father in the study where Bunji was having a lesson in calligraphy. The sergeant ordered both to come with them immediately. Bunji listened to his father pleading to have his son left at home, but the *kempei* hustled them both out of the room and to the foyer. While Bunji was putting on his socks and sandals, Mama Cheung, their housekeeper, thrust at him a small bundle of clothing, including his dark blue jacket. She whispered, "Take this, you may need it. Follow your karma, Bunji." Bunji's last view of her, as the car pulled away, was of her alternately wringing her hands and waving, as she sobbed, big tears rolling down her cheeks.

The port was only twenty-five minutes away. Father and son were taken to the *Bungo Maru,* an old freighter that was to take them to Sasebo in Kyushu—their destination in Japan—his father told Bunji as they climbed the gangway together. Bunji wondered how such a small ship could make the long voyage. Docked alongside it was the *Hizen Maru,* another freighter of similar size that was to travel with them. Both ships were overcrowded with evacuating Japanese civilians, plus a dozen soldiers in uniform and carrying guns. A large black tarp covered what seemed to be a huge mound of crates piled up in the middle of the deck. Despite the strong wind, there was a pervasive odor of rotting vegetation on the ship. Bunji couldn't figure out where it came from.

At the crack of dawn the following day, the long journey began. Bunji couldn't stop his tears as the camouflaged green and brown buildings in the harbor grew smaller and smaller.

The twelve-day voyage on often rough seas was both the worst and best experience in Bunji's short life. The physical aspects of the voyage were almost intolerable. Twice, the ship ran into heavy storms; even in the crowded cabin below deck, Bunji could hear the crashing of waves as they swept over the deck. For the first two days, there were some fruits and vegetables, but these quickly ran out and meals became meager and tasteless, or worse. They were fed dried blackened bananas, military rations of tooth-breaking hardtack, and thin soup with grease floating on top. Portions were small and grew even smaller as the days went by. The toilets were used by far more people than intended, and even though the sailors emptied the contents into the sea frequently, the smell and filth were almost more than Bunji could stand. There were only thin, soiled futon and straw-mattresses that proved woefully inadequate by the time the freighter passed the southern tip of Taiwan. Bunji kept over his shoulders the worn gray blanket he had been issued when he boarded the ship, but it was so thin it offered scant protection from the cold.

Mindful of a possible attack from American submarines, the ships hugged the coast where they could, and ran at full speed only at night; smoke from the funnels had to be minimized during daylight so as not to give away their location. And the captain's fear was justified. It was at dawn several days into the voyage when Bunji was suddenly awakened by loud shouts and the sound of running feet."Hey! Look! The *Hizen Maru* has been torpedoed!" people were screaming.

Bunji scrambled up the stairs to the top desk and joined a score of people peering out to sea. Then he saw it: a burning ship that appeared to be listing. Within moments, he saw a flame shoot up into the sky; a few seconds later, he heard the sound of an explosion.

Someone yelled: "That ship has more than a hundred people on board! Aren't we going to rescue them?"

The *Hizen Maru* was several hundred meters away, so Bunji couldn't see if anyone had survived the explosion, possibly on lifeboats or swimming. He felt the *Bungo Maru* start to veer towards the *Hizen Maru,* but it quickly reversed course and moved away from the sinking ship. Late that afternoon, Bunji heard a shame-faced young sailor explain to a passenger: "The captain of the ship wanted to help. But the major in command ordered the captain to steam on because we have no space or rations to take on any more people...and the major was concerned that our ship might get torpedoed, too."

Overhearing this, all Bunji could think was that it was karma that he had been put on the *Bungo Maru* and not the *Hizen Maru*. He wondered if he could or should thank karma. Although Bunji was cold, hungry, tired, and felt dirty and cramped during the voyage, these were the best days of his life because he could be with his father all day every day, and, for the first time, his father talked to him as if he were an adult.

One of Bunji's first questions to his father was: "Why were you arrested by the *kempei*?" It was then that he learned that what he suspected his father had been doing when he so often disappeared from home during the past year was essentially accurate.

"Bunji, I have been doing my part to bring this war to an end as quickly as possible. And I want both Germany and Japan to return to being the kind of countries they once were. But both nations have started wars that are killing so many people...and why? It's because their people are led— deceived and coerced—in Germany by Hitler and the Nazis; and in Japan, by an ignorant and conceited group of military leaders, and a government controlled by foolish and weak politicians who are using the Emperor's name to justify their doomed war."

His father continued, "I was helping the British in Burma. A Colonel Wingate is in command of a 3,000-man brigade called the Chindits, who got trapped by the Japanese army in northern Burma. They are desperate for ammunition, medicine, even food. I was helping to supply them, but I made a mistake and took too many risks. Mr. Tsutsumi from the Japanese Embassy—you've met him, remember?—told me in passing where the Japanese soldiers were going to search for the locals helping the brigade, but he was deliberately giving me misinformation. I became a bit careless and got caught."

"But, Father, why are they taking me to Japan with you? Why didn't they just leave me in Bangkok?"

"I'm not sure, but my best guess is that the Japanese officers in Bangkok think that I should be questioned by the high-ranking specialist officers in Japan. And I think they are hoping it will be easier to break me if you are with me. But I may be entirely wrong. They could be taking you back because, in their eyes, you are Japanese. According to Japanese law, if your father is Japanese, you are Japanese too. And they wanted you on this ship because it's probably one of the last that can go back to Japan, given how the war is going....Would you have rather stayed with Mama Cheung in Bangkok?"

Bunji shook his head, but he felt he could not really answer the question. What would have happened to him if he stayed in Bangkok? What will happen to him in Japan? The answer, it seemed, depended on how the war went and on the karma Mama Cheung always said would decide his future.

Thinking of Mama Cheung made Bunji ask one more question.

"Since we're gone, what will happen to Mama Cheung... and to Anna?"

"Mama Cheung will be fine. I'm sure she'll go live with her nephew in Chiang Mai. Anna will be fine, too. Even if she hadn't been out shopping when the *kempei* came, they couldn't have touched her. After her husband died, she managed to get an Irish passport even though she's English. The Irish consul was most obliging because he didn't want her to be stuck with an English passport should the Japanese come to Bangkok. Remember, Bunji, Ireland is a neutral country—meaning it's staying out of the war. She will have enough money to live on because I deposited money in a bank for her. And she is a brave lady....She was working with me help the Chindits."

"I like Anna. I'm glad she'll be okay."

Father said nothing but smiled and mussed Bunji's hair. After twelve long days in deplorable conditions, the ship finally docked in Sasebo. The passengers shuffled down the gangway to waiting buses. A soldier tapped Bunji's father on the shoulder and handcuffed him. They were herded into a bus along with the others and driven to the train station. Despite the number of ships in the harbor—two large warships and a score of other smaller ships—and all the buses and military cars on the street, the night was so quiet that the droning of the engines sounded very loud to Bunji.

At the station in Sasebo, Bunji was separated from his father, and they were boarded onto different cars of the train that would take them to Tokyo. The two-day train ride was a sheer nightmare for Bunji. The trip should have taken no more than twenty hours, but the train made a number of unscheduled stops on the line for an hour or more, for what reasons Bunji didn't know. Bunji's car was jam-packed, mostly with soldiers, all of whom looked sick and emaciated. The soldier sitting across Bunji didn't have a right arm. They slept or stared vacantly into space and said nothing.

Bunji's car was cold; a bitter wind blew in through several windows that had lost their glass panes, and the doors opened all too frequently. He regretted that he had no long pants. He shivered under the worn and smelly blanket he still kept wrapped around him. At least he was wearing his jacket—the only one he had—which he had worn to western-style dinners with his father. But even the jacket and his extra underwear, which he thanked Mama Cheung for, weren't enough to keep him from feeling so cold even with three people crammed in a seat designed for two.

Three times during the two days, a corporal distributed what he called "rations from the Emperor" in paper sacks invariably containing two small cold rice-balls, made with far more barley than rice; a grilled, small, and very salty, dried sardine; and a few slices of pickled radish. The food was distributed irregularly, and there was nothing to eat when the train arrived in Tokyo in the early morning of the third day. If a middle-aged woman wearing *monpe*—baggy wartime pants—hadn't given Bunji a small bottle of water, he would have had nothing to drink because even the non-potable water in the toilet had run out on the first day.

Only the changing scenery kept Bunji from despair. He saw the calm Seto Inland Sea—unusual at this time of the year, he was told by the woman in baggy pants. He found Himeji castle beautiful. He was surprised to see how the cities, both large and small, followed one another almost in succession, and how densely packed the houses were compared to Bangkok. As the train neared Tokyo, he realized the air smelled of sulfurous smoke.

Tokyo station overwhelmed him. It was monstrously huge, noisy with constant announcements made on loudspeakers, and crowded with large numbers of soldiers, and a sea of sullen-looking and ill-clad people. He looked for his father as he stepped down on the platform but didn't see him anywhere. A sergeant, the oldest man Bunji saw in uniform, approached him and said that he was to be taken to an orphanage in western Tokyo.

"Where's my father?!" His frantic question elicited only a terse reply from the sergeant: "You will see him soon enough. He's being taken to Matsushiro in Nagano prefecture northeast of Tokyo."

Bunji didn't want to cry but the tears kept coming. He followed the sergeant, wondering when "soon enough" would be. Bunji had no way of knowing then that "soon enough" would turn out to be "never." Or that Matsushiro was where the Japanese were excavating a four-kilometer-long secret tunnel to supply military headquarters with food, weapons, and ammunition stores, and, if necessary, to house the Imperial household, all in anticipation of an Allied landing on Japan.

The sergeant drove Bunji to the orphanage in a drab green military car that ran on charcoal and emitted a smelly gray smoke. The morning air was numbing. The trip took nearly an hour, but finally, they arrived in a section of Tokyo called Asagaya. The car pulled up in front of a two-story square building that reminded Bunji of his school in Bangkok's foreign settlement; but on this cold gray day, this building looked older and shabbier. While Bunji stared at the building, the sergeant came around and hauled him out of the car, taking the blanket from Bunji's shoulders. "You don't need this dirty blanket. It makes you look like a beggar." With his hand on Bunji's shoulder, he pushed him toward the door and knocked hard on it. When a young woman answered, the sergeant said, "Here's the Koyama boy," and without waiting for a reply, he returned to the car and drove off.

As Bunji stood at the door, a smiling, gray-haired woman appeared behind the younger one. She was taller than all the Japanese women he had ever seen in Bangkok or after arriving in Japan. She turned out to be Michiko Shimazu, the head of this small orphanage in Asagaya, which housed some thirty children.

Mrs. Shimazu welcomed Bunji and took him to the dormitory he was to share with other boys. Though it wasn't yet noon, a nurse named Endo-san arrived with a tray of food for Bunji, a crumbly rice-ball made almost entirely of barley, some boiled pumpkin, and something called *chikuwa*, which Bunji had never seen before but which he later learned was made from steamed fish paste. It looked like a stick, but the inside was hollow. It was chewy and Bunji liked it immediately. He was so hungry that he rapidly devoured all the food and drank down a glass of water. As soon as he had finished, the nurse led him to the room where the children were bathed. She unceremoniously stripped Bunji of his clothing. Handing him a small piece of soap and a *tenugui*— a small towel he was to use to wash and wipe himself off with—she said, "We don't have any hot water now, but wash yourself really well as best you can." She left with his pile of dirty clothes, and, in a few minutes, returned with some used but clean clothes for him. Bunji put them on and began his new life.

ORPHANAGE LIFE WAS EXTREMELY DIFFICULT FOR BUNJI, but he soon learned that the war had made life hard for all the Japanese he saw. In the orphanage, the boys in his room slept on thin cots. In the winter, there were never enough covers, so they put newspapers between their blankets to make themselves warmer. The rule was that no heat was allowed in the dorm room unless the temperature was so cold that water in a glass froze on top. Only then was a small charcoal heater lit.

Bunji wasn't familiar with any of the food. Meals consisted of a thin gruel of barley and vegetables, mostly radish and green leaves. Once or twice a week, the children were fed sweet potatoes and some chopped-up grayish fish with very little flavor, food the staff called *gochiso,* though Bunji didn't see how anyone could consider such meals "feasts." The children were fed regularly, but all of them, whether aged two or twelve, were always hungry.

Exactly a week after Bunji arrived at the orphanage, Mrs. Shimazu called him to her office. When he arrived, he saw a tall, stooped, middle-aged army officer standing next to her. She didn't look at Bunji, and it seemed as if she was speaking to the ceiling:

"Bunji, this is Major Takamori from Matsushiro. The army didn't send him—he was kind enough to come a long way so he can give you some very sad news himself."

The major spoke up, his anxiety apparent in his voice: "I very much regret what I have to tell you. Your father died two days ago...."

Bunji was dumbstruck.

"You know your father was helping the enemy...the British army in Burma....He wouldn't give us any of the information we wanted, and he rejected our offer of leniency for what he did if he would take part in our effort to liberate Burma....So Headquarters had no choice but to carry out the punishment dictated in such a case."

"He's DEAD?? You KILLED him??" Bunji wailed. Then he put his lips tightly together, hoping that would stop him from bursting into tears.

"The execution followed standard procedure." The major did not elaborate.

"Can I see him? I mean...just to say good-bye to him?"

"No, he has already been cremated."

"Cremated? What does that mean?"

"He became ashes. In Japan we burn the bodies of dead people."

Bunji's mind went blank, as if something had hit him hard on the head. In a daze, he heard Mrs. Shimazu say, "Major, I think that is enough. I am sure Bunji understands, and neither you nor I need to prolong this....Thank you again for taking the long trip to come here."

But the major wasn't finished. He took a small metal box out of his pocket and handed it to Bunji. "I am here to give you this and a message from your father. These are your father's eyeglasses. He wanted you to have them and his watch as well, but we couldn't find the watch."

Numbly, Bunji extended his hand and accepted the dark brown, horn-rimmed eyeglasses his father always wore. Pressing his lips together didn't help anymore. He began to sob, and the tears would not stop.

The major, looking intently at Bunji, said quietly: "What your father did was wrong, but I think he was a brave man and he handled himself like a true samurai during the last few days of his life. I don't need to go into detail, but because of how he handled himself, I came here today to give you the message he wanted me to relay to you. I don't know what it means exactly, but here it is: He said to tell you, 'Mama Cheung is a good person, but she is not always right. You are a weak person if you do not believe you can change and improve your karma. You must believe in yourself.' That's it. I hope this makes sense to you."

Bunji, now crying uncontrollably, did not see Mrs. Shimazu escort the major out. She returned and led the sobbing Bunji back to the room he shared with the other boys. The following day, she gave him a boiled egg, a real treat given only to very sick children. For three days, Bunji spoke not a word to anyone.

Now Bunji was an orphan. His mother, a Thai woman from the northern part of the country, had died after giving birth to him. His father had left Japan as a young man and, after some years in Germany, settled in Bangkok, building up a thriving business as an importer of machinery, mostly from Germany. He was the only family Bunji had ever had, and now Bunji was totally alone. He was bereft.

Bunji thought back over his last conversation with his father. It was on the final day of their journey from Bangkok.

Now Bunji realized that his father knew then what was going to happen to him, and that these would be his last words to his son. His father faced Bunji, put his hands on Bunji's shoulders and, clearly enunciating each word, said:

"Bunji, it would be a lie if I told you that you will be well taken care of in Japan, and that you will have an easy road ahead. On the contrary, because the war will soon be lost, and most likely because of what I did to help the Chindits in Burma, you are going to have some very difficult years in Japan. I hope there will not be many. I wish I could promise to help you, but I cannot. So, let me say only this: *do whatever you must do in order to live fully.* Live at all costs! I do not mean 'exist' at all costs; I mean, take risks, and do not shy away from challenges. To always take the safe road is merely to exist. I've always believed to live is to meet and overcome challenges, and to never shrink from taking risks and new paths. Many people disagree with me, but this is what I believe and I want you to remember my words!"

Finally, recalling his father's words, Bunji once again began to speak and to take up his new life in Japan. Although it was years—decades—before he could talk about his father to anyone, he always tried to follow his last words of advice.

Chapter 2

Kobe, 1947–48

THE SLIDING DOOR OF THE FREIGHT CAR SCREECHED SHUT, plunging the three small boys into darkness. Fearful that someone might open the door again, they remained huddled under the foul-smelling tarpaper they had found lying on the floor of the empty car. As their eyes became accustomed to the darkness, they could see slivers of light coming through cracks between the car doors. Bunji had no idea how long they waited, but at last, the train juddered and began to slowly move. Then the freight train gathered speed, and they heard the rhythmic clickety-clack of the wheels on the rails.

Bunji was elated, though a bit anxious as well. There was no turning back now. At last, they were on their way to Sendai to see the orphanage nurse who had left to marry a dentist. When the very kind Nurse Endo left in March, her last words to Bunji were, "Someday, if you ever come to Sendai, look me up, okay? My fiancé's name is Nishio, like the leader of the Socialist party. He's a dentist. Look us up in the phone book and come see me."

Gradually the idea of leaving the orphanage had begun to take hold of Bunji. When the war had been over for almost a year and a half, Bunji thought life might become easier, but in early 1947, more children began to arrive. All were babies. The nurses said, "They were abandoned—their mothers couldn't afford to keep them and they are fatherless." Many of them looked, to Bunji, as if their fathers were either white or black GIs. The orphanage, already beyond its capacity, became even more crowded, and the older children like Bunji were often asked to wash the diapers of the newly arrived babies and clean up after them. Life seemed to be getting harder, not easier.

Bunji found almost everything about life in the orphanage intolerable. For half the year, he was always cold. The winter nights were worst, when he couldn't sleep for being so cold, though he soon convinced the other boys in his room to keep the glass of water on the windowsill where it would be most likely to freeze. Even when there was clear evidence of ice, the charcoal heater sometimes wasn't lit. There was just no charcoal or any other fuel.

The children, now numbering over forty, were always hungry, even after the war ended and some American soldiers began to periodically bring food to the orphanage by jeep. Very rare treats of Spam and oranges were nice, but they only reminded Bunji how starved he usually was. Sweet potatoes and the flavorless gray fish were still considered *gochiso*. Bunji spent much of his time doing chores that, in Bangkok, Mama Cheung had always done: washing pots and pans and cleaning floors and toilets. But he did as he was told because the staff at the orphanage was working far harder than the children were ever asked to.

At least the air raids had ended when the war did. There had been air raids when Bunji arrived, but these had intensified in 1945 when the firebombing of Tokyo by long-range B-29s began. At first, the raids had been carried out in the daytime in what Bunji often thought were beautiful formations of planes against the blue sky. They came first from China, and then from the Mariana and other Pacific islands as the Americans captured them. When the firebombing started in early 1945, the raids came almost nightly, raining incendiary and anti-personnel bombs on Tokyo, the prime target. On moonlit nights, Bunji could count thirty or more B-29s over the skies of Asagaya while being hustled to the shelter. He cringed each time he heard the warning sirens scream. He hated the nightly raids because they meant being waked up to rush to a dank and crowded air-raid shelter built under the orphanage's now empty storehouse. After seeing numerous houses in a nearby area bombed and burning for hours, he was sure Asagaya and his orphanage would be next. He fervently hoped his karma would protect him from getting killed by the bombs or the subsequent fires that swept through large swathes of the city.

Bunji had tried hard to adapt to his new life, but he couldn't forget his early childhood in what he would forever think of as Siam, when he was always warm, always had enough good food to eat, and was always busy with study or friends. Here in Japan, food was his major concern. By 1944, food had become so scarce that the head of the orphanage and the nurses were skipping meals. Exacerbating the food shortages were the intensifying American bombardments, which totally disrupted rail transportation, preventing the delivery of rationed supplies. Bunji often had a pain in his stomach from hunger. All the children in the orphanage spent more time talking about food or foraging for it than doing anything else. During the summer months and into the fall, Bunji and two of his friends—Shumpei Nomura, whose parents were killed in Taiwan, and Saburo Kim, whose Korean father had been arrested by the military police and who never spoke of his mother—went "hunting" in nearby vegetable patches where people grew tomatoes, peas, radishes, and cabbages. This was very risky because people kept a close watch on their precious garden patches. Bunji was afraid that the head of the orphanage knew what they were doing, but Mrs. Shimazu never said anything.

Saburo and Bunji also ventured out at night to the "rice distribution center"—the shop of the rice seller who, by now, distributed only rationed barley. They would "siphon off" some barley using a tube made of a piece of bamboo, one end of which Bunji had sharpened to make the stick penetrate the burlap sack. One night they were caught by an angry bow-legged night watchman, who mercilessly boxed their ears, and pelted them with questions. By the time the head of the orphanage was called, he was screaming, "I knew they weren't Japanese! I just knew it!" Mrs. Shimazu profusely apologized to the night watchman, and he reluctantly agreed not to report to the police "the attempted theft by foreign boys." Without saying a word, she led the two boys back to the orphanage.

When fall turned to winter, it was no longer possible for Bunji to scavenge for fresh vegetables, and the orphanage had to cut the already meager rations to the older children because the babies were starting to die from malnutrition. Bunji decided that he had to find a new way to get some food. He couldn't remember when he had last eaten meat and, after much thought, he came up with a plan. He convinced his two friends to kill and cook a cat, arguing that meat would fill their stomachs in a way "hunted" vegetables could not. His friends went along with the plan very reluctantly only because they were so hungry.

Using an old burlap sack, the boys managed to bag an unsuspecting neighborhood cat and securely imprison it, tying the sack with a piece of string. That hadn't been difficult, but the boys were surprised at how hard the large cat struggled to get free. None of them wanted to choke or club the animal to death, so they dragged the bag to a nearby drainage ditch and dumped the cat in. They watched the cat struggle even after the bundle had been thrown into two feet of water. The cat continued to writhe for what seemed like forever to Bunji. Then it suddenly stopped. The boys looked at each other. Shumpei looked as if he might burst into tears. A few minutes passed with none of the boys saying a word. Finally, Shumpei said:

"I'm going. You two can eat the cat." And off he ran. By this time, Saburo looked dubious, and Bunji, too, changed his mind. He had no idea how to skin or cook a cat, and he wasn't up to doing it by himself. So they left the dead cat in the ditch and scampered after Shumpei. For many weeks afterwards and even much later, Bunji dreamed of the cat's spasmodic movements in the bag, but he mentioned this to no one.

Then on August 15, 1945, a day no one in Japan would ever forget, Bunji and all the older children were told to gather in Mrs. Shimazu's office. There, they heard the tinny and almost feminine voice of the Emperor come over the radio. Bunji scarcely understood what the Emperor said, but Mrs. Shimazu, her eyes brimming with tears, said that Japan had accepted "all the terms of the Allies unconditionally." Bunji didn't think he understood what this meant exactly, but he knew that his father had been right: Japan had lost the war.

Bunji's hope that after the surrender life in the orphanage would improve was soon shattered. Instead, it grew worse. By March of 1946, the government was no longer able to provide even the meager grain-ration of 900 calories per day. Bunji was told not to go too far from the orphanage because crimes, both petty and serious, had become rampant—"the social order" was breaking down. Bunji knew this meant something very serious was happening in Japan.

In January and February of 1946, Bunji heard the nurses talk about the police carting away the bodies of people frozen to death in subway stations. The orphanage now had to buy its supplies of gauze, medical alcohol, enemas, and everything else sick children needed at exorbitant prices at the black-market near Shinjuku, several train stations away. It was also during this winter Bunji learned a new expression: 'onion living.'" He heard one of the nurses say, "Mrs. Shimazu is now getting our medical supplies and food for children by doing 'onion living.'" Baffled by what this meant, Bunji later asked one of them if he could do it, too, to get something to eat. The nurse hadn't realized she had been overheard.

"Where did you hear that? The phrase means to peel off to sell things...like you peel the outer layers of an onion...to sell anything valuable you have to buy the things you need. Bunji, you can't do it, you don't have anything to sell."

"Why an onion? Why not a cabbage? You can peel a cabbage too."

"But you don't cry when you peel a cabbage. See, it's called 'onion living' because you sell things you'd rather not, and you cry when you part with your kimono, chests, clocks...whatever...valuable things you had for years, things you cherish. Mrs. Shimazu even sold her grand piano...the one she used to play when she gave music lessons before the war. She managed to exchange it with the Americans for a lot of canned milk and Spam and some sheets. She said a high-ranking officer wanted the piano for the officers' club at his base." Bunji remembered seeing a military truck come to take away the piano, leaving behind a number of crates.

Even a year and a half after the war ended, life was wretched and seemed, to Bunji, to get worse. The more time passed, the more his life in Bangkok seemed more dreamlike, almost magical. He tried to remember the sweet fragrances of frangipani and night-blooming jasmine blossoming in his father's large garden, but the stench of the nearby sewers in Asagaya would fill his nose instead. Even preferable to the odors around the orphanage was the peculiar, slightly fetid smell of the Chao Phraya that flowed just west of his favorite temple, Wat Musang Khae, where he often played on the temple grounds with his friends who called him Kivet, a Thai nickname they had given him.

At night, crammed into a single room with seven or eight other boys all sleeping on uncomfortable cots, Bunji would lie awake thinking of his room in his father's large airy house where he slept alone on a hammock covered with mosquito netting. It was a spacious house in a huge compound, but the main building was home only to his father and himself, until the last year in Bangkok when his father brought Anna Wells, an Englishwoman, to live with them. Never was it crowded like the orphanage, which had only four dormitory rooms for all the boys, girls, and babies. He never got used to having so many people around him all day long, talking, crying, playing, clamoring for attention.

Bunji missed his life among the Thais, who seemed at once so carefree and so ready to smile. He remembered, one day, playing along the river with a friend when they both had to pee. His little Thai friend had said, "Let's pee over the bank into the river." Neither noticed a man fishing just downstream from them. But he was totally unperturbed, though Bunji had thought he would be mad. But his friend had explained, "It doesn't matter. Water cleanses itself when it flows, so he could even brush his teeth several meters downstream from us." The Thai boys' lives were so different from his own, without all the rules his father made him follow. Bunji always had to take his sandals off in the entryway, change his clothes long before anyone else would think them dirty, and he had no doubt that his father would have been furious if he had told him what he had done in the river. However, most of the rules applied only when his father was at home. During his frequent absences, Bunji lived the life of a Thai child, running around the neighborhood organizing games with the local boys, and coming back home to cadge a snack from Mama Cheung whenever he felt hungry.

When he thought about his early childhood, Bunji thought about the people he missed. He didn't miss his mother; she had died when he was born so he didn't know what it was like to have a mother. Instead, there was Nanny An-Yee, who was his amah. But one morning when he was about seven, he woke up to find her gone. His father simply said that Bunji was too big a boy to have an amah look after him all day long. After that, Mama Cheung was responsible for him when his father was away on one of his frequent business trips, but she was both cook and housekeeper, and too busy to bother with how he spent his time. Instead, she spoiled him with all sorts of little treats whenever he hung around her kitchen located in a detached building. He wondered if she had gone to live with her nephew in Chiang Mai, as his father had said she would.

Most of all, of course, he missed his father, who, when he was at home, spent hours with his son, teaching him everything from Japanese language to the classical music he had grown to love during his years in Germany. When he had business in Singapore and Hong Kong, he would take Bunji with him, and it was with his father that Bunji had had his first plane ride. But Bunji couldn't bear to think about his father for very long.

Among all his activities, he missed school and studying the most. His father had sent him to school in the foreign settlement located in the southwestern corner of Bangkok amid embassies and tall buildings housing foreign firms. It was about a 20–25-minute walk from Bunji's home. Because of its location, Bunji always called his school the "settlement." It was a German-run, kindergarten-cum-elementary school, which catered exclusively to children of diplomats and foreign businessmen. Classes were held in a two-story, redbrick building, impressive to Thais but ill-suited to a hot and humid climate. His teachers were two German priests, an old, retired German businessman, several Western-educated Chinese, and one American woman, Mrs. Michael Middleton, the wife of Bunji's favorite among his father's good friends.

At the settlement school, Bunji learned a mixture of things. He was taught both Thai and English alphabets, as well as some simple sentences and words in those languages. He learned a few German songs from one of the priests, but he had no idea what the words meant. Mrs. Middleton taught geography, one of the Chinese teachers, arithmetic. Because the pupils came from a variety of countries, most of the instruction was in elementary English.

However, Bunji's real education came from his father. His amah talked to Bunji in his mother's native Karen, which was spoken in northern Thailand; the cook spoke a Chinese dialect; his friends spoke to him in Thai or, more commonly, in a mixture of Thai, Chinese, and a few English words. His father, however, had always insisted that Bunji speak to him in standard Japanese, albeit in what turned out to be a somewhat old-fashioned style and vocabulary since he had left Japan so many years before. He taught Bunji everything from calligraphy and geography, to history and current events. His father imported textbooks, and also hired various Japanese—a former teacher working for a trading company in Bangkok, and well-educated Japanese wives living in Bangkok—to give Bunji Japanese language instruction so his son would have regular lessons even when he was away on business.

When his father was away, he let Bunji have free run of his study. He could peruse his father's library and listen to his wind-up victrola. Bunji was fascinated by his father's records, and spent hours playing them. He listened to his father's favorite German composers: Bach, Beethoven, and Brahms—the "3 Bs" his father called them. They remained the favorites of Bunji as well. His father had other kinds of records, too, and Bunji played them over and over, ending up memorizing the names of the first forty or so Emperors of Japan, and many comic *rakugo* and *manzai* dialogues by famous comedians. As a result of this rather odd early education, Bunji surprised his friends in Japan with his impressions of comic routines; at the same time, they were amused by his stilted, outdated Japanese.

All of these interesting experiences and contacts with people of varied backgrounds came to an end once Bunji landed in Japan. Although Japan had compulsory education laws, the local authorities denied entry of the orphanage children to the local schools with spurious excuses, such as lack of formal papers, or saying they weren't real residents of the ward because they had no families. Under the increasingly desperate wartime circumstances, financially strapped officials had more important things to contend with than enforcing the law to allow orphans to attend school.

None of the staff at the orphanage had time to give the children any schooling, though they knew they should have it. A couple of times Mrs. Shimazu called Bunji into her office and talked to him in English, showing him some books in English about New York and the college she had attended in the U.S. She lent him books, and one of the older nurses gave him a couple of used middle-school textbooks in mathematics and Japanese history, but no one had the time to sit down and answer questions he had about their contents. One nurse complained that Bunji went through the books they found for him far too quickly. Still, he kept on studying books every free moment he had. He was hungry for learning, and he couldn't stand to sit around staring into space like other children did. Reading took his mind off his empty stomach, and it kept him out of the trouble he got into when he was bored.

And get into trouble he did. One day, he amused himself by telling the younger children that eggs screamed with pain when they were cracked open. He considered it the nursery equivalent of the adult ghost stories that were so popular in Japan. A few days later, on a rare occasion when all of the children were given an egg to eat, the nurses couldn't understand why some five- and six-year olds refused this treat. Bunji was abashed to realize that this was his fault. He teased the slightly retarded cook, and pulled other pranks that he didn't like to even think about later. He knew it was because he was so bored with orphanage life and the lack of mental stimulation.

By 1947, Bunji began to feel that he had nothing to lose by leaving the orphanage. He had a constant nagging feeling in the back of his mind. He saw little hope of getting the education his father had always stressed was so impor-tant. He had once said that Bunji, who liked to swim and to "boss around other boys," should study hard so he could become an admiral in the Japanese navy; and here in Tokyo, he couldn't even gain admission to elementary school. He felt he would regret it if he stayed in the orphanage until his thirteenth birthday in August, when he was certain to be placed as an apprentice in a factory or shop where he would be expected to be no more than minimally literate. The girls were sent out to work by age ten or so, and all the boys by age thirteen at the latest. Last fall, one boy had become an apprentice in a small metal foundry that made pots and pans in Yokohama, and another became a helper in a large greengrocer nearby. Wouldn't the same fate await him if he stayed in the orphanage?

But if asked, Bunji could not have given a coherent answer as to what he expected once he had run away from the orphanage, or what he thought the kind Nurse Endo, now Mrs. Nishio, could do for him. Nor did he realize that Nishio was a common name, and that if he did manage to get to Sendai, he might have trouble locating his former nurse as all he knew was her husband's last name and that he was a dentist. Bunji had thought none of this out. He ran away simply because he felt he had to.

Once Bunji had decided to leave the orphanage, his immediate concern became how to get to Sendai. He had no money for a ticket, and he knew Sendai was a long way from Tokyo. The question of how to travel was quickly solved when he remembered Saburo saying that his father used to travel by hiding himself in a freight car. He talked to a nurse from Aomori, which he knew wasn't too far from Sendai, about how one went north by train, and he learned that trains for northern Japan left from Ueno Station.

Bunji didn't want to travel alone. He would be too lonely, and it would be useful to have someone else along. He would take Shigeo, a quiet, level-headed boy his own age, and also Junzo, a small boy a couple of years younger, who followed Bunji everywhere, always ready to do his bidding. It wasn't hard to convince them to leave—they seemed to feel that anything would be better than staying hungry much of the time, and considered it a great adventure. His two friends would take almost any chance of possibly getting more to eat than they did in the orphanage. As they discussed leaving the orphanage, their topics were the long train trip, the food they would eat in Sendai, and meeting their former nurse, not where and how they would live once they arrived.

Bunji knew it would be a long journey, and so he had them collect bits of food they could take with them—it had to be things that wouldn't spoil, such as *kanpan*, a kind of hardtack made of coarse grains, and dried meat that the American sergeant who brought it called "beef jerky." But accumulating a stash of food had taken some time, because the boys would store something for a few days, and then be so hungry they would give in and eat it up. In the end, Bunji had to hide the food from his friends.

Finally, just after breakfast, one morning in mid-May of 1947, the three boys put on all the clothes they owned— no more than two of any garment—and with a small bag containing the food and an empty vinegar bottle wrapped in a small towel to fill with water at Ueno, they quietly left through the back door of the orphanage while the nurses were busy with the babies. They walked the half-kilometer to the railway tracks, and then followed the tracks until they came to Asagaya Station a few hundred meters away. It was the morning rush hour, the platform was crowded with people going to work, and the station personnel were all preoccupied. When a commuter train pulled into the station, the boys had no difficulty in clambering up onto the platform undetected. They jumped into the last car of a train bound for Tokyo Station just before the doors closed.

This was the easy part of the trip. Tickets were checked only at the wickets, so the boys didn't have to worry about being asked for their tickets once on the train. They simply had to ride to the end of the line at Tokyo Station, and, there, follow the signs for trains to Ueno, just four stops away. But Bunji had no idea how he would find a freight train going north and then sneak aboard.

Ueno Station was huge and crowded with tired-looking office workers and people with packs on their back almost bigger than they were. Bunji was sure they were on their way to the country to barter for food. The freight yard was huge, noisy, and confusing. Unlike passenger trains, freight trains had no destination signs. After studying the situation for some time and getting nowhere, Bunji bravely went to talk to an old man in dirty clothes lying on a bench. When Bunji asked which train would be going north to Sendai, the man sat up, looked over at the rail yard, and pointed at a train.

Now the difficulty was how to cross the busy tracks and get to the train. The boys squatted and surveyed the railroad yard. It was scary, but, eventually, they managed to cross the tracks between trains pulling in and out of the station. They made their way over to the train the old man had indicated, and ran alongside it looking for an empty car. Hauling themselves up into the first empty freight car they came to, they sat down out of sight of anyone who might glance in. They stayed ready to hide themselves under the foul-smelling tarpaper covering the floor at the first sound of footsteps, indicating that someone might be checking for anyone trying to steal a ride.

Later, Bunji couldn't clearly remember how long everything had taken from the time they left the orphanage until it grew dark. Soon after they boarded the freight car, Junzo announced he was hungry, though it couldn't have been lunchtime. Bunji handed out a few *kanpan* with a bit of dried beef, and let each of them take just a swig of water from the bottle he had filled in the station. The sun moved across the sky, but to their surprise and disappointment, the train stayed where it was. To pass the time, the three began to discuss what they were going to say when they finally met Mrs. Nishio, and what food they would buy first when they got jobs and were paid. But time dragged. Junzo started to cry. Shigeo said, "Why don't we go back to Asagaya?" "Absolutely not!" Bunji said forcefully. "All we have to do now is wait until the train leaves and within a few hours we'll be in Sendai!" He handed out more *kanpan* and beef jerky and suggested they take a nap.

His two friends were soon fast asleep, but Bunji couldn't sleep because of the noise of the yard, the smell of the tarpaper, and the sunlight. He sat back against the side of the car and looked at the ceiling. He thought about his days in Bangkok playing by the river. His mind jumped to wondering why the major who came to the orphanage hadn't been able to find his father's watch, which he would have loved to have. Finally, as the light began to fade, Bunji was startled out of his thoughts by someone hitting the wheels of the train, making a metallic noise, so he woke the other two boys and they crawled under the tarpaper and held their breath as the trainman came closer and closer. At last, he reached their car, hit its wheels, and continued down the train.

Still the train didn't move. Finally, at dusk, the area around their freight car became noisier, and there were people about, so the boys again crawled under the smelly tarpaper. Within a few minutes, someone came and slammed the door to their car, making a huge noise as a latch clicked into place.

After the door to the car had been closed and it was clear the train was on its way, the boys urinated in total darkness, aiming at the bottom of the door through which came a faint line of moonlight, and then crept under the tarpaper for some warmth. Soothed by the rhythmical sound of the moving train, they soon slept.

The train groaned and came to a stop with a jolt, waking Bunji up. He shook Shigeo awake, and together they tried to open the door of the freight car, but it wouldn't budge. Their water long gone, they were by now very thirsty. It seemed like hours had passed by before Bunji began to see slivers of light seeping into the car, and then suddenly, he heard noises of people walking around. Within minutes, Bunji heard the metallic sound of the latch being pushed back, then the sound of footsteps retreating.

The three boys waited a few minutes, and Bunji and Shigeo fearfully tried to open the door once more. This time it slid open with a heavy, squeaky sound when they pushed on it with all their might. Bunji poked his head out of the car, but no one was about so they jumped down onto a station platform. Bunji looked around to make sure they were really in Sendai. To his amazement, he spotted a sign that read "Kobe." They hadn't gone north, they had come west!

"I'm hungry. What do we do now, Bunji?" Junzo cried.

Bunji needed time to think. "I smell sea air. Let's get a drink of water at the station and walk to the shore and eat what we've got left."

IT TOOK LESS THAN THREE DAYS to transform the three boys with vague hopes and delighted by their adventure into very young runaways from an orphanage facing the unforgiving reality of life alone in immediate postwar Japan. The three boys ate foul-smelling food they found in garbage cans, and stole what they could, but they still starved. They tried to sleep on park benches, but they were hard and the sea winds were bitterly cold after sundown. For three days, the boys wandered around like sleepwalkers.

The morning of the fourth day found the boys starving, desolate, and desperate. For the rest of his life, Bunji refused to talk about those three long days after he arrived in Kobe before the boys were rescued by a black-marketeer. All he would say was that, by the fourth day, he felt they had to do something, anything, and so he suggested they walk to Osaka, which his father had told him was a large, prosperous city, without knowing it was more than thirty kilometers away, and had been carpet bombed by B-29s.

As it was, the boys got only as far as Sannomiya Station in Kobe before Junzo refused to move another step. Bunji, too, was feeling weak from hunger and was often dizzy. The acute pains in his stomach had stopped several hours earlier, now he only felt dull aches and occasional spasms where he thought his stomach must be. Whenever the spasms came, his vision blurred. He had to squeeze his eyelids shut tight and open them quickly to focus his eyes.

The boys had walked toward some loud noises and found themselves in front of a row of black-market stalls under the elevated railway line at Sannomiya. They squatted on their heels and looked around. No one said a word, but each knew that the others were looking for an unattended shelf or unwatched boxes from which they could steal some kind— any kind—of food. There was no such shelf or boxes. Every black-marketeer was watching his wares like a hawk.

A man in his early thirties yelled, "Hey, you runaways from reform school! Don't think you can swipe anything here. If you're hungry, you can help me move these crates. I'll give you each a bun with sweet bean paste inside."

The boys stared at him uncomprehending. Realizing that they couldn't understand his strong Osaka dialect laced with underworld argot, the man repeated what he'd said in the standard Japanese spoken on the radio. Bunji nodded vigorously, and the boys followed the handsome man with a longish face to a nearby stall. Behind it on the pavement were some fifty small boxes. They weren't heavy, and together, the exhausted and hungry boys were able to carry them into the man's stall. The work took only fifteen minutes, but as promised, the man gave each of them a bun that was much larger than Bunji had expected. As the boys were happily devouring them, the man brought each a cup of tea.

When his mind cleared, helped by the bun and the tea, Bunji began to suspect the man's motive was to help the boys because the work involved was no more than he could have done by himself in the same amount of time. The man introduced himself. "I'm Ichiro Konishi, but my friends just call me Konishi." He said he was thirty-two and had had two younger brothers, but his entire family died in an air raid over Osaka. Konishi himself had been a typesetter in one of the largest printing shops in Osaka, but that, too, had been bombed out. Bunji also learned a few days later that Konishi was spared from military service because he had TB. He remembered Konishi adding:

"But don't worry, you won't get it from me. I decided to go into this business and eat well to cure myself of TB, and I think I have almost done it." However, Konishi coughed so much that Bunji was not sure what he said was true.

Konishi's "business" turned out to be selling anything he could get his hands on. Some of the things he sold came from the cars of the nearby railroad yard, others from "salesmen" who brought still rationed rice, clothes, and many kinds of meats and beans, and still others came from a place called "pee-ekkisu." Bunji had never heard of it, and only much later did he learn that the "pee-ekkisu" was PX, which stood for "post exchange," the stores for the American military found on all their bases.

No one was quite sure how or when it was decided that the boys would "live" in Konishi's stall. After the boys had finished their meal, Konishi had asked them where they intended to spend the night. Bunji had said they didn't know because they were on their way to Osaka to find work but had no money. Konishi looked at the three grubby waifs and told them they could spend the night in his stall. He fed them some noodles in broth, and told them they could bed down on some straw mats on the ground at the back of the stall. He brought some U.S. army blankets to cover them. The next morning before Konishi emerged from his little back room and while Shigeo was still asleep, Bunji and Junzo swept out the stall and the area around it, and then sprinkled the street in front with water to tamp down the dust, using a watering can borrowed from a neighbor who had just done the same. Konishi was both surprised and pleased and rewarded all the boys with "breakfast"—more tea and buns.

The boys hung around the area that day, reluctant to leave for the unknown, and Konishi didn't seem in any hurry to get rid of them. They very quickly learned how to make themselves useful running errands and unpacking boxes of wares, and in turn, they were fed noodles and the barley rice-balls that were still standard fare in Japan. Within days, Konishi found the boys reliable enough that he could start spending nights with his "admiring ladies." And so, they settled into working for Konishi in return for a place to sleep and enough to eat. Sleeping on straw mats laid on the bare ground wasn't very comfortable, but it was a minor discomfort the boys were most willing to bear for not being hungry all the time.

Although Konishi had certainly fed them the first time as an act of charity, possibly thinking of his younger brothers,

Bunji worked hard to earn his keep. He carefully erased "unnecessary" printed or stenciled labels on the merchandise Konishi's "salesmen" brought in. Bunji noticed that large items that came from the PX, such as furniture and bed linen, had a lot of labels and tags on them in English. Konishi wanted all traces of English eliminated from these goods. However, for items he could claim he had purchased from legitimate sources, such as canned goods, utensils, and clothing, he insisted that all English labels remain on the goods because "people will pay more when they see these labels." Bunji even learned to reseal canned goods using the solder and tools Konishi had, and following his instructions. Konishi soon called him an "expert solderer" because Bunji could make the resealing nearly impossible to detect.

Bunji quickly got the hang of life in Sannomiya, but he found he had to work hard to get Shigeo to put any energy into the work, and Junzo soon became unreliable, disappearing for hours at a time. Shigeo, never a voluble child, became quieter and quieter, sometimes going all day without saying a word. Then, several weeks after their arrival in Sannomiya, Shigeo suddenly developed a high fever and stopped eating. Konishi gave him some medicine, but it had no effect. He even managed to produce a large navel orange, but Shigeo wouldn't eat even that, and Bunji consumed most of it. Konishi then brought a nurse to see Shigeo, but he became hotter and hotter. Konishi promised to take Shigeo to the hospital the next day, but when Bunji awoke in the morning, his friend, sleeping next to him, was cold. Bunji screamed and then cried his eyes out.

A couple of months later, Junzo disappeared for good. After Shigeo died, Junzo took to disappearing overnight. He became secretive and wouldn't tell Bunji where he went. Always an excitable and active child, he now became hyperactive. He would eagerly start any project, but within a short time he would abandon it and start something else or disappear. Bunji could no longer rely on him and wondered what was going on. Konishi clued him in. He thought Junzo had met up with drug dealers and was taking *hiropon*, diluted heroin that makes you "happy" but not sleepy. "I know this happened to Junzo. Look at his eyes," Konishi said. Bunji tried to keep Junzo from sneaking away, but it was impossible. After Junzo had been gone for nearly three days, Bunji suggested to Konishi that they go look for him, but Konishi replied, "I think it's too late for that. If he's on *hiropon*, as I'm sure he is, then he's mixed up with yakuza—the really bad underworld guys—and the two of us couldn't possibly take them on. The main group in Kobe has ties to a bigger group in Osaka, and they trap young girls and boys by first giving them *hiropon* like candy, and when the kids are addicted, they make them take *hiropon* to their customers, and also force the girls to work as *panpan*—hookers."

Bunji felt sorry for little Junzo. For a long time Junzo's small pile of clothes remained in a corner at the back of the stall, but Bunji never saw him again. Now Bunji had lost both of the boys who had run away with him. For the rest of his life, whenever Bunji thought about the two friends he had asked to leave the orphanage with him, he felt culpable for what had happened to both of them.

Despite these tragedies, Bunji found life in Sannomiya far preferable to minding sickly babies and cleaning toilets in the orphanage, hungry all the while. Not only was he getting enough to eat—albeit mostly noodles and buns— he liked the work, the free time, and he could study now that he wasn't thinking about food all the time. In addition to doing whatever Konishi asked, he also tried to read the magazines in English that one of the "salesmen" of things from the PX gave him from time to time. He also borrowed textbooks from Minoru Wada, a third-year, middle-school student, whose parents sold second-hand clothes in a stall not far away. He spent quite a lot of time talking to Minoru about the books. And often, while working, he chatted with Konishi about what he had learned as a typesetter.

Konishi grew to appreciate Bunji more and more, not only for his hard work, but for his resourcefulness as well. Bunji even found a way to make money out of rotten fish.

One hot day at the end of summer, Minoru came running to him.

"Hey! On the way back from baseball practice, I was stopped by a truck driver, whose truck broke down on the street behind the station. He asked me if I could tell him the best place to get noodles for his lunch break and where he could find a telephone to call his boss—he has to ask him what he should do about the fish he said are going bad. I saw the load...it's leaking...most of the ice has melted. After he left, I opened a crate—they're full of whole salmon. They didn't smell too bad. Bring some containers and let's see if we can get a few fish that we can eat."

"Minoru, you said he went to eat, right? Do you know where he went?"

Minoru nodded and smiled. "I told him the big noodle shop on the other side of the station had the best noodles. It was the furthest shop I could think of."

"Good. That means we have enough time. We've got to borrow your father's pushcart. I'll get some empty cartons for the fish."

"What? That'll be way too many fish for us to eat!"

"We're not going to eat them. We're going to sell them," Bunji announced.

"That's stealing! I just thought we'd lift a few. What if we get caught?" Minoru suddenly panicked.

"Nah, we're not stealing," Bunji assured his friend. "We're just going to help the driver dispose of rotting fish. You said he was worried about what to do about the fish going bad. C'mon, we'll make some money!"

When Bunji saw the unmarked, battered old truck, he was almost certain that the load of salmon had been stolen and was headed for the Sannomiya black-market. He climbed onto the back of the truck and looked inside a crate. The salmon on the top were definitely beginning to rot and Bunji could see scores of maggots inside the fish, which had been gutted. But as they dug into the bottom of the crate, Bunji couldn't see any maggots.

There was no time to waste. The boys quickly transferred as many of the less maggoty fish as they could from the bottom of the crates into the cardboard boxes, and pushed the now heavy cart back to Konishi's stall where they stacked the cartons in the back room, dripping with sweat from their exertions.

Promising to pay Minoru some money later, Bunji asked him to help wash the fish and cut them into slices a little larger than those Bunji saw in the fish-shop. Then he got two paper sacks of salt on credit from a close friend of Konishi, who sold pickles and salt at a stall nearby. With that, the boys salted all the fish.

Next Bunji needed ice. Knowing that the nearby fish-market always had left-over ice at the end of the day, which no one wanted because it smelled of fish, Bunji took Minoru and the pushcart and brought back as many blocks of partially melted ice as the wheelbarrow would hold to cover the well-salted fish. By now, the entire stall and both boys reeked of fish, but Bunji didn't smell it anymore.

When Konishi arrived at his stall the next morning, Bunji explained why the backroom was filled with smelly boxes of fish, and what he wanted to do with them: "We need to get your 'salesmen' to sell all this fish directly to housewives in residential areas."

Konishi wondered if Bunji and the salesmen—three young men Konishi hastily rounded up—could sell all the fish, over 400 pieces. But 10 yen a slice was much lower than the price in stores and salmon was hard to come by. The fish literally flew away; housewives snapped them up everywhere. By nightfall, all the fish were gone and Bunji and Konishi counted the total take: 4,350 yen!! Even after paying for the salt, the "salesmen," and Minoru, the total profit was 3,100 yen.

Elated, Konishi gave Bunji 1,000 yen, saying:

"You know, you're not just a smart kid who spends all his free time reading English magazines the guy brings from the PX and those school textbooks you borrow from Minoru. You're very resourceful...let's call you that, even though other people might use different words. And you sure come up with some 'grand slams'!" After that, Konishi used to refer to Bunji's marketing exploits as "home runs."

Bunji wondered what "resourceful" really meant. His father had emphasized the need to be resourceful, saying: "As I found out in Germany, in life you run into situations in which your success—and even your survival—depends on being alert to any and all opportunities, and on deciding what matters in the long-run, not the short-run. You may have to hurt someone's feelings or even do things at times that make some people think you are taking advantage of others, but you can repay them or repay society if you become, in the long-run, a person people can respect, a person who can help others." But would his father really think that selling stolen, rotting fish was a good thing? Had his father done this sort of thing? Maybe in a pinch, but from what he had taught Bunji, he wouldn't consider Bunji's "home runs" an ethically acceptable way to make a living.

Occasionally, Bunji's "resourcefulness" got him into trouble. There was the time he suggested to Susumu, the not-too-bright boy at the tempura shop, that on a hot summer day, fried ice cubes were just the right treat. "Delicious...crisp on the outside but ice cold in the middle." Unfortunately, Susumu tried frying battered-coated ice cubes when he was alone minding the shop, and was rather badly burned by the splattering oil. Bunji had known the oil would splatter, but thought only enough to make the experiment interesting. A day later, Bunji ran into Susumu and was appalled when he saw the white bandages covering Susumu's arms. Bunji was much relieved when Susumu told him he never told his parents frying ice cubes was Bunji's idea.

After that, Bunji resolved to limit his "resourceful" acts to ones that made money and didn't hurt anyone. What happened to Susumu reminded him of the last time a prank had gone badly wrong, but that time, it was he himself who had been hurt. In fact, he had nearly lost an eye. Bunji so often got into scrapes back in Bangkok that one timid little boy had stopped playing with him after the incident with the elephant.

It had been a hot afternoon and, a bit bored, Bunji and his friends, Monyakul and Gong-Suk, had gone down to the shallow tributary of the Chao Phraya that flowed near Wat Musang Khae. The boys had finished eating some bananas Gong-Suk had brought when they heard the undulating bellow of an elephant. Walking north along the tributary to follow the sound, they soon spotted a mother and her baby wading in the tributary, grazing on the grass on the bank. The boys had stopped about twenty meters away and watched the pair placidly feed. What ensued had started as a discussion about when elephants would chase people and how angry they would have to be, and ended with Bunji deciding they should throw stones at the elephants to find out the answer.

Monyakul was petrified at what might happen, but Bunji convinced Gong-Suk to pelt the baby with stones. If the mother chased them, they could run to a nearby grove where the trees were too thick for an elephant to enter. As could have been predicted, the mother elephant had gone after the pair as soon as they managed to hit their target and the baby started to howl. The boys were taken aback by the speed with which the mother elephant climbed up the bank and took after them. They ran with all their might, reaching the grove barely ahead of her. When the boys disappeared into the trees, the mother had turned back to the river and her baby.

Something hit Bunji's face with force as he ran head-long into the grove. He was momentarily stunned. He had run into a branch hanging down from a tree and a twig had pierced his right eye. He felt a sharp pain. When he put his hand up to try to touch the eye, he felt the twig instead. He yanked the twig away from his eye and, as he did so, he felt another jolt of sharp pain. He touched his eye and his right cheek. Both were slippery and when he looked at his palm with his left eye, he saw his palm red with blood. He had screamed both from the pain and fright, but he had managed to get Gong-Suk to guide him to the nearby French Embassy while Bunji held onto his right eye with his right hand and to Gong-Suk with the other. From there, the boys were driven by a young secretary to a Chinese doctor who knew Bunji's father.

The mustachioed Chinese ophthalmologist in a white coat told Bunji that he had been very lucky because had the twig penetrated his right eye four millimeters more to the right, it would have penetrated the pupil and he would have lost the eye. The doctor covered his right eye with several layers of gauze and had them secured with a long gauze strip that diagonally encircled the top of his head.

Bunji arrived home in the Ambassador's car just before four in the afternoon. When Mama Cheung saw Bunji jump down from the car, she raised both hands to the sky and shook her head to and fro, a wailing gesture that Bunji saw every time she was unhappy with him. Mama Cheung once told him she wondered what kind of karma Bunji had that got him into trouble so often, but kept him alive to get into more mischief almost immediately.

Bunji had almost forgotten this incident, though the scar was still visible in his right eye for the rest of his life. Nor did he often think about his old life in Bangkok very often these days. He was too busy. With the coming of autumn, Bunji's life settled into a regular pattern. The work for Konishi, reading the PX magazines with photos and descriptions of American life, studying Minoru's textbooks—the English textbooks were not difficult, but the math textbooks were challenging—and tending to the chores of living, such as washing and eating, made the days fly by.

Bunji also very much enjoyed his conversations with Konishi, who surprised him by knowing so many difficult Chinese compounds necessary in reading newspapers and more advanced Japanese books, and by being able to discuss politics and the social issues of the day. Bunji recalled Konishi saying: "I went only through middle school, but you learn to read and learn a lot when you set type day after day. Read, Bunji, read! That's much more important than you think."

Bunji wanted to read, to study, to go to school. He knew that school was free for any child, but he already knew from his life in the orphanage that the authorities could find ways to keep children out and thereby lower the amount of money they had to spend on education. He wondered if he could go to school during the day and work for Konishi early and late in the day, as well as on weekends. He could do as much work for him in those hours as he was doing now. But Bunji learned that it wasn't as easy as it seemed. It wasn't that Konishi wouldn't agree to such an arrangement, but the authorities certainly would not.

Since Minoru lived on the street of stalls and attended school, Bunji had thought he could too. But Minoru's parents had a legal occupation selling second-hand clothes, and they were registered residents of the ward. They were also a family unit. Bunji didn't come out and ask Konishi his status, but he gradually realized that Konishi was essentially a squatter with no legal status. In fact, he had set up his stall so as to make it possible for him to flee at a moment's notice should the police or the American military come to investigate him. There was no way Konishi could register Bunji in school, and, in any case, Bunji wasn't any relation to him and had no identification papers.

Bunji began to think about his future again. He couldn't go to school here in Sannomiya, and if he stayed and worked for Konishi, he would face a future at the edge of the underworld. Life was better here than in the orphanage, but thinking of the future, surely it would have been better to become an apprentice than the seller of dubious goods in the black-market. Bunji was well aware by now that he was engaging in conduct he knew ranged from mendacious to felonious. Konishi was always just one step ahead of the authorities, and Bunji didn't want to risk being sent to a reformatory.

And so before a year had passed after his arrival in Sannomiya, Bunji began to think of moving again.

Bunji had no idea where he would go, but he was sure he should leave in the spring so he could get settled while the weather was still warm. This time, he would prepare himself with more than a change of clothes, some snacks, and a small towel. He didn't tell anyone what he was planning, but he started to collect supplies: a thick blanket he purchased from Minoru's parents; a pair of sneakers from Konishi's stock; and some canned goods.

His decision about where to go came about by accident. One evening, he was chatting with Minoru at a nearby Buddhist temple. The two were sitting on the narrow veranda of a building that had been shut up for the night, dangling their legs as they talked. Minoru mentioned that he was going with the baseball team to Ashiya to play the team from the middle school there. He was looking forward to the excursion because the town was in a nice residential area with lots of trees and a sandy beach. What interested Bunji most was Minoru's off-the-cuff remark, "The schools in Ashiya have a great reputation."

Bunji was silent, and Minoru changed the subject. But the germ of an idea had been planted in Bunji's mind. A week later, on a Monday in late March when Konishi's stall was closed, Bunji jumped the wicket at the Sannomiya station when the agent was busy, and rode to Ashiya, twenty minutes from Kobe. He had heard of this city, but he'd never been there before. He walked down to the shore from the station and found the beach Minoru had told him about. Behind the wide, sandy beach was a large grove of pines just a few hundred meters inland from the sea. The streets were cleaner, the shops seemed to be stocked with better clothes and food, and unlike in Sannomiya, there were no beggars. He scouted the area. He liked it very much. When he went into the pine grove, he found a few likely places under the dense cover of branches where he could sleep...at least for a few days or possibly even for a few weeks until he figured out what he would do next.

And so, just eleven months after he ran away from the orphanage in Tokyo, Bunji ran away again, this time alone. He packed his few belongings and the supplies he had collected in a large *furoshiki* wrapping cloth, wrote a short note to Konishi thanking him, but telling him he would not be back, and left early in the morning before the stall owners opened up.

This time, at four months short of fourteen, he was full of apprehension. He was now totally alone. He thought of how his father had taught him to swim. He had pushed Bunji into the slow-flowing river, and standing on the bank, his father had held out a long stick, saying: "If you can't swim, grab onto the stick. But even dogs can swim, so you should be able to paddle your way to shore." Bunji had managed to somehow swim back by himself. But he had known that his father would rescue him if necessary. Now there was no father with a stick. And no Konishi. How long could he feed himself on his small savings? Where would he sleep when the June rains came? Was he foolhardy to leave Sannomiya?

But he had to leave! He couldn't live the way he had in Sannomiya if he wanted to go to school. He had to do more than just survive. He had to "live by taking risks!" as his father had exhorted him. And Bunji had swum to shore without grabbing the stick!

Grasping his unwieldy bundle, Bunji made his way to the entrance of the train station. This time he paid the fare and struggled up the long flight of stairs to the platform. A well-dressed lady sitting opposite him on the train stared at this little ragamuffin with the huge bundle at an hour when children should be going to school. Bunji stared back.

Both of them got off the train at Ashiya. Bunji stopped to reorganize his bundle and retie the *furoshiki*. Then he set out on the long walk along the Ashiya River to the pine grove near the beach. The spring breeze was cool on his cheeks. As he trudged on, he was becoming more determined to face his karma head on. He had no choice—he had to.

Chapter 3

Ashiya, 1949-53

THIS WAS THE SIXTH OR SEVENTH TIME since he had arrived in Ashiya that Bunji had stood on the same spot beside a large pine tree just outside the grounds of Ashiya High School. He rested his hand on top of the chest-high, chain-link fence intently watching the school's baseball team practice. Today, he had been there for over half an hour, fascinated by how very good the team was. He tried not to think how desperately he wanted to be inside the fence instead of looking in from outside.

Bunji had arrived in Ashiya almost a year and a half before, in April of 1948. He was now well settled in with two jobs and a place to sleep at night. It had been two and a half years since he left the orphanage in Tokyo, very long years fraught with uncertainty, anxiety and, of late, an increasingly strong foreboding. Three months ago, he turned fifteen. Although he no longer had to worry about getting enough to eat, he was no closer to going to school, and so he stood looking at these happy high school students without any real hope of becoming one of them.

Bunji asked himself: "Where will I be three years from today?" The most likely answer was: "Still working and not in high school even if I study all the textbooks I can borrow." Had it been a big mistake to leave the orphanage? If he was destined to work on jobs he could get without even going to middle school, wouldn't it have been better if he had become an apprentice in some trade like the other boys who left the orphanage when they turned thirteen? The head of the orphanage, he was sure, would have found him the best job she could.

He had known when he moved to Ashiya that getting into high school would be a very long shot, if possible at all. Since he wasn't now enrolled in middle school, he wasn't eligible to take the high school entrance examinations. He didn't even have a "legal" residence registered with the city, nor did he have any papers proving he was Japanese. He knew these were all necessary for admission to a Japanese public high school. He was now increasingly resigned to believing that going to high school was an impossible dream. But it didn't prevent him from hoping for a miracle.

He tried to console himself that at least he was better off than he had been in Sannomiya, and certainly his life was better than his first summer in Ashiya when he lived by himself on the beach. He thought back to his arrival in the spring of 1948....

From the Ashiya train station, he had trudged to the pine grove near the beach with his bundle of belongings, which, meager though they were, seemed awfully heavy long before he reached his destination. At the grove, he had set about making a "camp" for himself under some thick branches. He had made a bed from sand that he lugged from the beach in a rusted bucket he found. The "sand bed" proved to be more comfortable than he had expected, justifying his investment of effort in making a score of trips with the heavy bucket. Some nights his blanket wasn't warm enough, especially just before dawn, so he had put several layers of newspaper between his body and the blanket just as he had done in the orphanage.

He soon discovered that three other people were also sleeping in the grove. One was a man of about thirty with heavy glasses, who reminded Bunji of Mr. Tsutsumi from the Japanese Embassy in Bangkok, the man who had deliberately given misinformation to his father, causing him to be arrested by the Japanese military police. But this "Mr. Tsutsumi" looked so shy that Bunji was not afraid of him. The other two people were an older couple who kept to themselves. Bunji had a brief talk with "Mr. Tsutsumi" and learned that police rarely came to the grove, and even when they did, they didn't ask anyone to leave.

Bunji explored the immediate area. He found that a little further inland, people kept small vegetable patches where he could "hunt," as he used to in Tokyo, for tomatoes, cucumbers, and other vegetables he could eat with a little salt. He made sure that he "hunted" carefully so that no one lost so many vegetables that they would lie in wait to catch the culprit. On the fourth day, he made his first purchase: a loaf of dark bread that tasted like the sawdust he was sure it contained.

It was during the following week that he found a part-time "job." One morning, he approached a large group of fishermen on the beach. They were divided into two groups, each group pulling in a very long rope at the each end of a net almost 100 meters long and 40 meters wide and laid deep into the ocean. One of the fishermen, wearing nothing but a red loincloth and a sweatband around his head, called out to Bunji:

"Hey, boy! Join us and pull...we can use all the hands we can get."

Bunji first thought the fisherman was joking, but quickly realizing he was not, he joined the men and helped pull the rope in. This "job" turned out to be for two or three times a week. A boat would take the nets out into the ocean, changing the location from the shore each time, and then the fishermen would pull them in. The group repeated the process two or three times every day. Bunji joined the fishermen and pulled on the rope with all his might, becoming sweaty and bruising his hands from gripping the thick, coarse rope for half an hour at a time. But the "job" was a "paying" one; after the net was in for the last time, the head fisherman would give Bunji a bucketful of fish. How many and what kind of fish depended on the catch of the day.

Bunji couldn't eat all the fish so he became a trader. He would take his bucket and go to nearby food shops. When he found shopkeepers who wanted some fish, he traded his fish for the goods they had to offer. He bartered for potato croquettes, bread, tofu, eggs, and other things he liked. Thanks to bartering fish and "hunting" vegetables, Bunji found that, on most days, he didn't need to spend money out of his scant savings in order to eat.

With a place to sleep and enough food, the weeks passed without his realizing how many nights he had slept in the grove. He found he could wash his clothes by "borrowing" water from one of the two faucets in the vegetable patches. He hid his few belongings: his change of clothes, a dictionary, half a dozen books, several cans of food, a can-opener, some soap, a pair of chopsticks, and two empty cans used as all-purpose containers. First, he wrapped everything in newspaper, and stowed it all in a discarded oilcan that he had laboriously cleaned. Then he buried the oilcan in a hole he dug near the pine tree where he slept. When the mound was covered with a little sand and pine leaves, no one but he could find it.

For a toilet, he used several half-buried large earthen jars that the owners of nearby vegetable patches kept to "age" human waste; the owners followed the long-established Japanese farm practice of using human waste for fertilizer after "aging" it for a few weeks. The only problem he had was occasional rain. But he found that he could keep himself dry on a rainy night in the common shed used by the people who worked the small vegetable patches. The padlock was easy to pick and then relock the next morning. He didn't know why, but the smell coming from the earthenware jars stored next to the shed bothered him little when it was raining.

Most days passed without incident, but one day, something happened to force Bunji to spend what was to him a large sum of money out of his precious savings. One morning when he returned to his camp from his early morning "hunting trip," he found a large, feral cat busily gnawing at one of his sneakers. Unless it was raining, he usually took these trips barefoot and left his sneakers near his "bed."

"Hey, what are you doing? Get away!" yelled Bunji. But the cat went on chewing the sole of his shoe. Bunji scooped up a handful of sand and threw it at the cat. It gave Bunji a derisive look, pulled hard at the edge of the sole with its mouth, and detached it from the sneaker. Before Bunji could grab the cat or the sole, the cat ran away with the sole in its mouth.

Bunji was angry at the cat. Now with his only pair of shoes ruined, he had to buy a new pair. But despite his loss, he quickly began to see the funny side of the incident. The cat wanted the sole of the sneaker because it was made of dried squid, which Bunji had painstakingly fashioned into a new sole and inserted in his left shoe to patch it when his cheap black-market sneaker had sprung a leak. Bunji had mended it using the method he had learned from an old man in Sannomiya. He now realized he should be complaining to that old man instead of being furious with the cat.

By mid-August, the peak season for fishing was ending as the waves were becoming a little too rough for the large nets. Bunji realized that his "job" wouldn't last much longer. He needed to come up a new way to "earn" some food. He had seen on the beach a university student who sold popsicles, called "ice candies," during the hot summer months. Bunji had said hello a few times, so one day in late August, he approached the student to ask how to sell ice candy. The student didn't seem too happy to have a new competitor, but told him where he could find the ice candy maker who would sell him the candies at wholesale, and let him borrow a small portable icebox to carry them.

The next day Bunji purchased a supply of ice candy, and trudged along the beach with the small icebox hung from his shoulders in front of him. However, he found few customers, and under the hot sun, both the ice and the ice candies melted much more quickly than he had anticipated. He tried to salvage a few by eating them himself, thereby blowing any profit he might have made. By early afternoon, he gave up, his neck and shoulders sore from the band holding up the box and his remaining wares too melted to sell. He decided to try one more day as it would be a Sunday and there were sure to be more people on the beach. But again, he lost money. On his way to return the icebox, he ran into the student and asked how he could make money when Bunji found it impossible.

"Well, as you can see, I have a bicycle and so I can quickly move to where people are. And I have regular customers as well. Also, look, I keep most of the ice candies wrapped up in newspapers so they don't melt so fast. But why do you want to peddle ice candies at your age? Don't your parents give you enough spending money?" The university student was curious.

Bunji told him that he had no family and was living alone in the pine tree grove nearby, and that the fishing season was ending and he needed money. The student was surprised by all of this.

"I'll tell you what. My aunt is starting a bakery this fall, and I think she could use someone like you to help around the shop. I doubt she can pay you much of anything, but it would certainly beat losing money trying to sell ice candies."

Bunji couldn't believe anyone would hire him, a 14-year-old boy without any formal education or training in bread-making, but the student, Hiroshi Takeda, told him to meet him the following day at ten in the morning. True to his word, Hiroshi took Bunji to his aunt's new bakery in the mid-town shopping district. Bunji liked the aunt, a very pretty lady in her early thirties who had beautiful large eyes like those of a Chinese actress he had once seen in a movie at the settlement in Bangkok. She was a small lady, and from the way she spoke to him, Bunji knew at once she would be kind as well as forthright. Hiroshi had told Bunji to call her Mrs. Nitta, not her real name, but the name of the man who had put up the funds for her venture. He also told Bunji that she was a *mekake*, but it was some time before Bunji learned that a *mekake* was a sort of "second wife."

Much to Bunji's surprise, Mrs. Nitta offered him on the spot a "job" in her bakery, which was to open in just a few days. He was to do everything she and the baker asked, and maybe he might also learn to bake bread. His "wages" would be "a reasonable amount of bread" for Bunji to eat, which delighted him as he liked bread, and this would insure that he always had a full stomach. And she acceded to his request that he be allowed to stay overnight in the bakery. When

Bunji, who always disliked being cold at night, was told he could have his wish and sleep in the bakery's oven on the condition that he clean it every day, he was delighted.

A very happy Bunji came to work at the bakery at the beginning of September. It quickly became a going concern because the baker, Mr. Maekawa, made better bread than his nearby competitors. Bunji's work was laborious but not difficult, and neither Mrs. Nitta nor the baker was a hard taskmaster. Bunji's jobs included sweeping the floor, washing the vats and large boards used by the baker, chopping wood for the oven, waiting on customers when Mrs. Nitta was away for meals or on errands, and cleaning the oven after it had cooled down. The oven was large enough so that he didn't feel claustrophobic, and with a bottom futon Mrs. Nitta provided him with, it was warm and comfortable on winter nights. Although it wasn't part of the bargain, Mrs. Nitta frequently gave him something she had cooked, and the baker fed him miso soup full of vegetables every morning.

Bunji, however, still had one big problem. Although he had enough to eat and a warm place to sleep, he had no money to buy clothes, shoes, notebooks, or any of the other things he needed. He decided to take on a second job delivering newspapers every morning. When Bunji approached the owner of the delivery station across the street, the owner immediately agreed to hire him because he could assign Bunji to a hilly route older men didn't want. Bunji's route was in the northern, more affluent part of Ashiya delivering to 135 houses, each of which subscribed to one or more papers. Sorting and delivering the papers would take nearly two hours, but within two weeks he had figured out how to revise the route to save him a good fifteen minutes a day. Though he had to get up before four every morning, he would earn 800 yen a month.

At last Bunji had a regular source of income. It wasn't close to what anyone could live on, but now he could afford to buy a toothbrush and toothpaste, which he much preferred to the salt he had been using. He could go to the public bath instead of taking a "bird bath"—using a wooden bucket in the bakery's back yard. But he had to be as frugal as possible on his meager earnings. When he went to the public bathhouse, he made sure to remember to pick up still usable slivers of soaps other customers had left behind. He collected inserts from newspapers and flyers and used the blank backside to take notes. So for months at a time, the only things Bunji had to buy were fruit, occasional bowls of noodles, toothbrushes, and toothpaste. His experience in Ashiya taught him habits that for the rest of his life made him hate to spend money on "things."

Bunji didn't spend all of his time working. He started to make friends in Ashiya. In December, he began to have conversations with Isamu Kameyama, a senior at Ashiya High, who came regularly to buy bread. Isamu lent Bunji his textbooks just as Minoru had done in Sannomiya, and seeing Bunji's interest in English, Isamu promised to borrow some books in English from his older brother who was studying English at Osaka University. A week later, Isamu made good on his promise and brought an English book entitled *Gone with the Wind*. As he handed the thick book to Bunji, Isamu said:

"It's a story about the American Civil War and what happened to the people in the South. My brother said it's a good story...he's very skeptical whether your English is good enough to read it."

But Bunji could understand enough to motivate him to read as much of the long novel as he could. Night after night, he pored over it in his oven with the light of a small flashlight he bought. He had to constantly consult a small English-Japanese dictionary he had bought in Sannomiya, but many English words in the novel were not in his small dictionary. Some sentences were so difficult that all Bunji could do was guess at what they meant. Mr. Maekawa was puzzled and Mrs. Nitta amused by the effort Bunji was making to read this long English novel. But for Bunji, it was an intellectual challenge as well as something akin to tugging an emotional string that led back to "the settlement" where he had learned simple English words and sentences, and to Anna Wells, who had lived with them and read aloud and explained, all in English, the children's stories she borrowed from her friends.

As he read *Gone with the Wind* and encountered descriptions of historical facts or events he didn't know, he often thought of what his father had done for him: read aloud articles from months-old English and sometimes American newspapers, and then translate them into Japanese. Often, his father spent more time explaining the events described in the articles than translating them. Bunji could read no more than a couple of pages of *Gone with the Wind* a night, but he plowed on with determination night after night, wondering what the plantation called Tara really looked like in the southern state of Georgia, which Bunji incorrectly concluded was named after an important woman.

The work at the bakery, his job delivering papers, Isamu's old textbooks, and the novel kept Bunji very busy. And by the early spring of 1948, Mr. Maekawa began to show Bunji how to make bread. He was impressed by Bunji's ability to accurately gauge the weight of the dough to apportion it into loaves without having to weigh it. He even taught Bunji how to prepare the "chocolate" filling for some of the buns. This was a secret Bunji was not to share with anyone as the chocolate was actually a dark brown paste Mr. Maekawa made by mixing flour, chemical sweetener, dye, and only a few pinches of chocolate powder, which was still very expensive. Bunji enjoyed his busy life and began to feel more secure. Although he got through only 115 pages of *Gone with the Wind* in the two months before he had to return the book to Isamu's brother, he managed to borrow other books to study. He often thought of his father, and also of Mama Cheung and Anna, but he decided he was happy, and that he would be happier still if he could sleep a little longer every morning. But in the back of his mind, he still dreamed of somehow going to high school.

So on this late November afternoon in 1949, Bunji made still another "visit" to the high school, going to his usual spot near the tall pine. He had only an hour before he had to start cleaning the mixing bowls and baking pans the baker had used that day. In one of his hands was a first-year geometry textbook for high school students, which Isamu had just lent him. With his other hand on the fence, he watched the baseball practice in full swing. He had no idea at all that this afternoon would change the course of his life.

Although Bunji was absorbed in the batting practice, in his peripheral vision, he saw someone slowly approach him. As the man neared, Bunji turned to see a man so emaciated that it was hard to tell how old he was. He could have been in his fifties, maybe even younger, but his obvious ill-health made him look old. The man had thick graying hair; he was wearing a very worn "people's uniform," a wartime high-necked, light brown suit. As he neared Bunji, the man smiled and motioned to Bunji to walk towards a small bench about five meters away.

"Here, come sit next to me. I just want to have a little chat with you," the man said. Seeing his kindly smile, Bunji silently obeyed.

"My name is Iguchi; I am a mathematics teacher at Ashiya High. I've seen you here...standing at the exact same place...several times. You seem to come even when there isn't a team practicing. I have been wondering what brings you here."

"Sir, I come here just to see what Ashiya High School students do, though I do like to watch the baseball team practice."

"I didn't think you were a student here. If you don't mind telling me, why do you want to see what the high school students do? I should think for a young boy like you there are a lot more interesting things you could be doing." The teacher saw the book Bunji was carrying. "Isn't that our geometry text? Why are you carrying it?"

"Yes, Sir, this is the first-year geometry textbook. A friend loaned it to me so I can study it."

"How do you have time to study high school geometry in addition to doing your work for middle school?"

Bunji's answer that he was not in school though he was planning on studying high school geometry surprised the teacher; he asked Bunji more questions. Bunji gave him an abbreviated account of his life, why he had come to Ashiya and was now working at a bakery. So many people had sad wartime stories like Bunji's, and it wasn't unusual for children in the early prewar years not to be attending school, so that part of Bunji's account didn't seem to strike the teacher as unusual. Nor did Bunji's statement that he really wanted to go to school. What did elicit a look of astonishment was hearing how Bunji was spending his spare time—studying everything from high-school math to a difficult English novel.

The math teacher was skeptical that an unschooled boy could really get anything out of a high-school geometry textbook, despite Bunji's insistence that he was sure he could understand it. He asked Bunji some questions about math. When it was clear that Bunji could easily answer virtually all of his questions, he went on to other subjects, since Bunji said he had studied textbooks on other subjects, such as English and Japanese. He asked how Bunji had acquired his knowledge without having been to school, so Bunji told him about the settlement school in Bangkok, how his father had taught him and even hired tutors to come in twice a week to teach him Japanese. And how he had studied everything he could while in the orphanage, Sannomiya, and, now, Ashiya.

Mr. Iguchi nodded thoughtfully. "So now I know why you come here so often. From all what you just told me, I certainly think you should go to high school, but I suspect it will be pretty nigh impossible since you say you don't have any official documents to establish your nationality and, more importantly, you are not attending middle school now."

The math teacher slowly stood up. He looked like a man thinking of something else while bidding goodbye to Bunji. Bunji was glad he had a chance to talk to this friendly high school teacher, but as he walked back to the bakery the words that his chances of getting into Ashiya High were "pretty nigh impossible" played over and over in his mind. He was crushed. Though he had known he had only an outside chance, he had hoped against hope that somehow, he would be admitted.

Bunji was surprised when, two weeks later, the teacher phoned the bakery. He asked Bunji to meet him at the bench outside Ashiya High the following day at four in the afternoon. Bunji was astonished that the teacher even remembered the name of the bakery that he had mentioned only in passing. He wondered why Mr. Iguchi wanted to meet him again.

When Bunji arrived at his usual "spot," he found Mr. Iguchi and another man waiting for him. Mr. Iguchi introduced the man as "Tsuji Sensei," using the title of respect given teachers. This second teacher, a specialist in Japanese classical literature, taught Japanese at the high school. In contrast to the math teacher's humble and kind demeanor, this teacher seemed rather haughty, as though he had done Mr. Iguchi and Bunji a huge favor in giving up half an hour of his time to meet Bunji.

Mr. Tsuji quizzed Bunji on a number of subjects. He seemed impressed that Bunji had learned the names of the first 40 Emperors in correct order, and had memorized the beginning of the great classic, *The Tale of Heike.* However, Bunji could tell from the look on his face that he seemed to find Bunji's knowledge of Japanese language and history wanting. This didn't surprise Bunji, though he was disappointed. He felt as if he had failed a test. He plodded back to the bakery wondering what the math teacher had in mind in having him meet the language teacher.

What with his increased workload in December, when the bakery made more varieties of breads plus imitation European Christmas cakes, Bunji put his meeting with the high school teachers into the back of his mind. Then, at the end of January, Mr. Iguchi visited the bakery. Mrs. Nitta called Bunji, who had been cleaning the vats, out to the shop to meet him. The teacher had news—earth-shaking news for Bunji:

"I am here to tell you that you are being admitted to Ashiya High, to enter in April with the other first-year students."

Bunji just stood and gaped at him. The math teacher smiled at Bunji, and he could see Mrs. Nitta beaming behind him.

"Yes, it's true. Admittedly, it's all very extraordinary, but these are extraordinary times for Japan. You are way ahead of the entering students in math and English, and a bit behind in language and history, but Mr. Tsuji says you should be able to catch up quickly. So I met with the principal, Mr. Toda, and told him about you and your circumstances. He agreed to admit you if we could get the necessary paperwork in order."

Bunji, still speechless, stared unbelievingly at the teacher, who continued:

"I contacted your orphanage in Tokyo. The woman in charge—a Mrs. Shimazu—was very pleased to hear what I had to say about you and immediately sent a letter confirming that your father was a Japanese citizen and, if necessary, she knows how to get an official document proving your citizenship. The education section of Hyogo Prefecture said that under the circumstances, they would accept her letter, properly notarized, as proof of nationality. The people in that section said they have accepted dozens of such letters since the end of the war. And Mrs. Nitta here has solved the final obstacle to your admission by supplying you with a formal place of residence here in Ashiya. On paper, you are to live with her."

Iguchi told Bunji that he was very lucky because by next year, when the transition to the newly introduced, American-style education system was completed, no one would have the authority to admit a student merely at the request of the principal, who was relying on the recommendations of a couple of teachers. A year later, Bunji learned how accurate the math teacher had been when the prefecture instituted a mandatory entrance examination that could be taken only by students in their final year of middle school.

At the end of February, Bunji received an official notice of admission to Ashiya High School, and two weeks later,

Mrs. Nitta surprised him again. She called him into the shop just after the bakery closed. There, he found with her both the baker and the owner of the newspaper delivery service. Mrs. Nitta and Mr. Maekawa gave Bunji a high school uniform, and the owner of the paper delivery shop presented him with a pair of brand new trainers "to keep you running on the routes of the papers and your life." Bunji was overwhelmed by these gifts. He could hardly wait for school to begin in April.

April of 1950 came and Bunji finally realized what he had thought had been an impossible dream. He was determined to get the most out of this opportunity. Even though he had little time to spare, he signed up for the ESS—the English Speaking Society—and for the rugby team. He would have loved to go out for baseball, but he knew he was neither good enough nor big enough to make the team. So he settled for rugby, which he had seen played in Bangkok, and which he was told didn't have as many hours of practice as did the baseball team. However, he didn't last long in either extracurricular activity. He cracked the left side of his collarbone during one of the early rugby practices, and he found the level of English in the ESS well below his own. And he really didn't have time for these activities, particularly during his first year when he had to make up for what he had missed by not attending middle school.

Although Bunji had no trouble keeping up with his studies in class, his classmates were astounded to learn that he had been admitted to high school without having learned so many things that they had learned in middle school or earlier. They quickly found that he really didn't know the Japan creation myths, children's stories, and some very famous people in Japanese history. They often teasingly said they put Bunji through middle school while he attended his first year of high school. With all of this, Bunji's life was so full that his mind scarcely registered the fact that the Korean War had begun in June.

Bunji couldn't be happier at achieving his dream, but life was by no means easy. In addition to attending classes and keeping up with his schoolwork, he still had both his work in the bakery and his job delivering papers. He got up before four to be at the newspaper delivery center by 4:15. There he sorted the various papers he had to deliver, set out running at 4:45, and finished his route by a little before six. After a quick breakfast of bread and miso soup prepared by the baker, he helped him for an hour—adding the final flour to the dough, and kneading and cutting the dough for the bread to be baked later that morning. By now, Bunji was doing far more than just cleaning up.

Bunji was tired much of the time. He usually managed to get to high school an hour early, and stayed an hour after classes were over in order to study, but he had to get back to the bakery shortly after four to sweep the shop, wash up after Mr. Maekawa, and clean the oven. After a break for his evening meal, he studied until his eyes refused to stay open, usually sleeping before ten. There were only three days a year when no newspaper was published, and the bakery closed only twice a month, so Bunji worked virtually every day. He went to school on Saturday until noon, and on Sunday he had to wash his clothes as well as study. Occasionally, he even got up in the middle of the night to study, and sometimes he worked for a few hours late at night if Mr. Maekawa was making something special. Once or twice a month, on a Sunday evening, he would just collapse and go to sleep right after supper.

After Bunji began this hectic life with never enough time to sleep at night, he tried to nap during the day between various tasks, but found he couldn't sleep in daylight. Mr. Maekawa called Bunji's sleep problems "the most unfortunate congenital disorder." No matter how sleepy or tired he was, Bunji simply could not take a short nap. Although he didn't know it then, this "disorder" was to plague him for the rest of his life.

Though Bunji was constantly short of sleep, he didn't have to worry about getting enough to eat. Rarely did he have to buy food. In addition to the "reasonable amount" of freshly baked bread he was allowed to eat daily, a few times a month he was given a bit more bread—rolls and buns— when these remained unsold. He sometimes bartered bread for croquettes made of potatoes, a bit of meat, and vegetables from the shop next-door. Then there were the dishes that Mrs. Nitta would give him, and the leftover fruits and other unsold food that neighboring shopkeepers would give him at the end of the day. Bunji longed for meat, but, very occasionally, a classmate whose family owned a nearby butcher shop gave Bunji some scraps of meat. These Bunji cooked on the edge of the oven, being careful to clean it all up so that it didn't affect the taste of the bread.

After Bunji began school, he saw that a number of students didn't have enough to eat. Sometimes when he had extra bread, he gave it to classmates he knew went hungry. One of the most frequent beneficiaries was Tetsuo Takenaka, a short, angular boy who always sat alone at lunch, far from his classmates. Carefully watching Tetsuo as he "ate" and having once or twice hefted the lunch box left on his desk, Bunji concluded that Tetsuo's lunch box was often empty. Feeling sorry for the boy who was forced to pretend that he brought lunch to school like everyone else, Bunji occasionally gave him a large bun, saying that it was "going to waste" as he had eaten all he wanted. Every time Bunji did a "good deed" to help a hungry friend, he was keenly aware that he, too, was the beneficiary of the same kindness by the green-grocer down the street who frequently asked Bunji to "dispose" of "unsold" bananas; and Mr. Maekawa, who often left candy, rice crackers, or baked sweet potatoes by the oven for Bunji to find when he cleaned it in the evening. Though Bunji never went hungry, he knew his diet was lacking in protein. He had watched the smallest children in the orphanage die from malnutrition, and both Konishi and his teacher, Mr. Iguchi, had contracted TB, basically the result of poor nutrition. Also, Bunji missed the taste of the milk that he had grown up on in Thailand. When he began his paper route, he noticed that many affluent families took up to three or four bottles of milk daily. Since milk was not part of the traditional Japanese diet, it was sold in small bottles about a cup in size. These the milkman left in a wooden container outside the gate of each house.

Bunji found that he could take a bottle, gulp it down in seconds, and either replace it as an empty bottle that hadn't been collected or leave it at another house. He was careful not to take milk again from the same house or surrounding houses for a long time, so that the missing milk would just be considered the milkman's mistake or a minor theft not worth bothering about. He never took milk from the poorer houses on his route, or when only one bottle was delivered and it might mean a child went without milk. He could only justify his behavior to himself by reminding himself that his father had exhorted him to do whatever he had to survive, and Bunji knew that he could not afford to get sick.

Though Ashiya was known as a wealthy city, it was actually divided into two different communities: the well-to-do lived *up* on the mountainside while the poor and working classes lived *down below* near the ocean. Many students' families, not just Takenaka's, had no money to spare. Bunji experienced a likely consequence of this fact the hard way. He saved up to buy a new cotton shirt, but shortly after purchasing it, he took it off and left it with his schoolbooks on a bench to keep it clean while playing ball with friends. When he went to retrieve it, the books were there but the shirt was gone.

But by and large, people were very generous. The owners of the local bathhouse would give Bunji underwear and other items they said people had forgotten. One of his classmates, a girl named Morita-san who lived on the mountainside of Ashiya, brought a pair of very new-looking sneakers to school and gave them to Bunji, saying that her brother had bought them but they really didn't fit him very well. He was puzzled that anyone would buy shoes that didn't fit, but he gratefully accepted them. Some months later, he saw her with her brother, who was tall with very big feet. He then realized that she had purchased the shoes especially for him and had tried to spare him any embarrassment.

The sister of one of his friends bought Bunji his first pair of glasses. One day, he went to study with Okagami-kun at his large house. The two boys took a break and played catch. His sister came out and watched. "Koyama-kun, you squint all the time. You must be near-sighted. You ought to get eyeglasses," she said. A few days later, she came to the bakery and took the surprised and protesting Bunji to an eyeglass shop where, with her pocket money, she bought him a pair of glasses from the shopkeeper's ready-made selection. The shopkeeper told her, "These glasses are as close as I can get to what he needs without paying for prescription lenses." The glasses did wonders for Bunji.

One of the gifts he was to remember all his life was being taken to see his first film in Technicolor. Mr. Okuda, his English teacher, learned that Bunji had read over 100 pages of *Gone with the Wind* in English, and when the movie came to a theater nearby, he took Bunji to see it. Bunji was overwhelmed by the most exciting movie he had ever seen in unbelievably beautiful Technicolor because all he had ever seen before were short educational films at the settlement school in Bangkok, and a few black and white movies after coming to Japan.

One gift caused some trouble for Bunji. He had been helping Fukuda-kun with his physics, and one day he presented Bunji with some remnants of white cotton knit material from his family's dry-goods shop. It was knit in tube form for making underwear and T-shirts. Shirts were expensive, so he didn't wear one under his high-necked uniform during the warm months. But during the winter months, Bunji needed to wear something underneath for warmth. Thus, he was delighted with the gift and set about to make some T-shirts.

However, Bunji had not the slightest idea how to make a T-shirt nor did he know how to sew. He cut off a piece at the right length and then basted thread around one end, scrunching it up to make it narrower for the neck. Sleeves proved to be beyond him, so he just cut slits in the sides of the tubing for his arms. These undershirts proved to be rather useful though they looked very odd. Bunji had no problem as long as he kept his uniform jacket on. Then one very warm day in late spring when Bunji was fooling around with a ball with some classmates, they all got hot and his friends took off their jackets. Bunji kept his on, though he was obviously sweaty. Finally, he gave in to his friends' jibe and took off his jacket, exposing the "T-shirt." One boy remarked that Bunji looked like a scarecrow and they all roared with laughter.

School became less stressful when Bunji caught up with his classmates in history and Japanese. And despite the long hours he spent working, life wasn't without its pleasures or lighter moments. He could recall organizing an excursion or two up Mt. Rokko, when he and his friends would hike up the mountain, make a bonfire, and cook lunch in large, old military lunch boxes made of aluminum. In summer, he would go to the beach and swim with friends. He was occasionally invited to friends' houses, especially at New Year's. He also served on the student council when he was elected at the end of his first year.

Because Bunji didn't belong to any of the clubs at school, he was rather surprised when, in January of his second year, he was approached by a group of his classmates who asked him to run for student council president for his third and final year of high school. The leader of the group, Noriko Nakano, one of the best students in the A class, comprised of the top forty-plus students, spoke for her "delegation":

"We've already talked to a lot of students in the ESS, the science club, the music and other clubs, and we all think you ought to run for president. Your opponent will be Amaya-kun who will be supported by most of the sports clubs. But we think you have a very good chance of winning because even some people in the sports clubs won't vote for Amaya. After all, you are our top student, already a member of the student council...and many students think you are a natural leader... they like you because you are serious but also amusing as we know by all the funny things you say and do...like your imitation of Tsuji Sensei!"

Noriko was referring to one of the mimicking routines Bunji did to amuse his classmates. At times when Bunji knew his classmates were highly stressed because of up-coming tests or after a few consecutive hard classes, he would go to the blackboard and "become" Mr. Tsuji, imitating his exaggerated Tokyo accent, his strutting from one end of the blackboard to the other, and the way he glared over the top of his glasses at any student who couldn't answer a question. Within a few minutes, his classmates were invariably in stitches. After mimicking Tsuji Sensei, his classmates often asked Bunji to imitate Kodama Sensei, the bow-legged vice-principal who taught physics, lecturing very slowly in a droll intonation unique to him. That Bunji would sometimes almost get caught by the arrival of a teacher for the next class made it all the more entertaining.

At first Bunji was hesitant to accept his friends' request to run for president, wondering if he would have enough time to perform all the duties. Not only would he have to preside over weekly school-wide meetings attended by all the students and make the weekly announcements by megaphone out on the school grounds, he would have to act as liaison between students and faculty, and deal with various financial and other problems in the sports and all the other clubs. But Bunji thought he could manage and accepted the challenge. He started to campaign with the help of his supporters. He even made several speeches in various clubs.

Soon, Bunji became aware of a rumor going about the school against his candidacy. He asked a couple of his supporters to tell him specifically what was going on. He was so insistent that one friend finally told him that some of his classmates' mothers had sent a "petition" to the principal of the school, saying something to the effect that Bunji was not "a suitable candidate" and he should withdraw his candidacy. Bunji asked why.

Hesitantly, the friend replied, "I heard that some mothers of our school are saying that you are not a real Japanese... you are an *ainoko*—a half-breed born to a Japanese father and a Filipina or some other Southeast Asian woman—and not fit to represent our school."

"I'm going to go see the principal," Bunji announced and immediately went off to the principal's office.

As soon as the principal saw Bunji, he invited him in. "I thought I might see you soon. So, you've heard about the petition?"

"Sir, what does it mean I am not suitable to represent Ashiya High?"

"It's all nonsense. These people are ignorant....Don't worry about them. I also think that the fact that the father of Susumu Amaya, your opponent in the election, is a city councilman and a very rich man has something to do with this. Mr. Amaya is buying the uniforms for our baseball team, but he can keep his uniforms if he thinks he can bully me this way. We are now living in a democratic society, and if you are elected, you will become president. You don't have to withdraw…I am not going to change my mind."

Bunji had no intention of withdrawing. But what he heard made him think more of what he had been increasingly feeling, if only vaguely. During the past few years, as he began to have more dealings with adults at work and school, and as he heard gossip among the customers of the bakery, he had become aware that Japan was—he did not know the right words—"closed"; that is, the Japanese were less accepting of people who were different from themselves. Society was well ordered at the cost of intolerance, not only of foreigners, but also of other Japanese who deviated even slightly from the accepted ways to speak, to behave, or even to dress.

Bunji had long been aware that he, too, was considered different. Other boys wondered why his skin became so dark so quickly under the summer sun. And they were puzzled by the strange way his hair looked. In fact, Bunji was cutting his own hair to save money, and he couldn't see what he was doing, which resulted in some very odd haircuts. But when Bunji told the boy who asked why his hair looked so funny that it was because he was half Thai, his answer was readily accepted as fact. He had heard whispered questions about his background in the bakery.

Though Bunji was considered Japanese when he lived in Bangkok, it didn't always seem to be the case in Ashiya. The Thailand that Bunji remembered was very different from Japan. He could play with anyone, whether at the settlement school or in his neighborhood. Though his father was a very well-to-do foreigner, Bunji played with the son of his father's Thai gardener and the son of a Chinese shopkeeper. One's place in society seemed to be less significant there.

The petition made Bunji think of Japanese prejudice against people they considered "outsiders." A very pretty girl at Ashiya High was only grudgingly allowed to join the Drama Club, which put on a play at the annual school festival. However, she wasn't given any speaking roles because she was a *burakumin*. She belonged to a group of "outcast" Japanese who had been discriminated by other Japanese for centuries. Discrimination continued even after the Meiji Restoration of 1868, when the *burakumin* were made legally equal to all other citizens. Scholars debated the origins of the *burakumin:* whether they were people who had engaged in "unclean" trades, like butchers or undertakers; whether their ancestors were defeated in the battles fought in earlier centuries; or whether they were the descendants of immigrants from Korea and China. But whatever the origin of this group, it seemed impossible to stamp out the prejudice against anyone even suspected of belonging to it, though *burakumin* were indistinguishable from other

Japanese. However, no one wanted to admit to prejudice. Instead they said the girl was "too pretty like a bar hostess" or "too young to be given good roles." Bunji remembered that when he heard this gossip he felt sorry for the girl and angry as well.

Nor could he forget how often he had heard subtle or not so subtle pejorative remarks against Korean-Japanese, most of whom were born and had lived their entire lives in Ashiya or nearby, had adopted Japanese names, and spoke native Japanese. Bunji would never have known they were Korean-Japanese if someone hadn't made an insulting comment.

And hadn't Bunji himself often wondered why some local merchants or customers at the bakery were so curious— overly curious—about his birthplace and parentage? Had he not felt, more than a dozen times, uncomfortable, and even angry, when he had to answer what he believed were highly intrusive questions about his "non-Japanese" mother?

Could he ever feel at home in such a society? More important, did he want to? Could his feelings of ambivalence be because he was still too young to really understand Japanese society?

Bunji went on to win the election by a comfortable margin and became the president of the student council, who was in effect the president of the student body. He enjoyed his position and the perks it gave him. Students automatically let him have the warmest spot in the library, next to the heater. And best of all, it enabled him to participate in the national baseball championships, which Ashiya High was playing in after becoming the prefectural champion.

As president, Bunji appointed himself head cheerleader and led the students of his high school at the Koshien stadium in cheering for the school's team. At first the students laughed when Bunji led the cheers by imitating the moves of

Thai dancers, but in no time, all the students were cheering enthusiastically and lustily, following Bunji's rhythmically moving hands. Ashiya High won the national championship! It was one of the highlights of his high school years.

However much he enjoyed serving in student government, his studies were Bunji's primary concern. Once again, he had to consider his future. He had achieved his goal of going to high school and was within months of graduating. What should he do next? Being at the top of his class, going on to university seemed the logical choice. Could he manage it? While he was mulling over his future, he was called into the principal's office where he received a startling offer.

"Koyama-kun," the principal began, "Mr. Noda, the president of the Bank of Osaka, has proposed that you become his adopted son. You know that his daughter, Kazuko, is a first-year student here. He has no son; Kazuko is his only child, so he has no one to carry on his family's name. If you agree to his proposal, he will pay for all of your expenses at university, both tuition and living expenses. When you graduate, you will be given a position at his bank. Of course, this means taking the name of Noda and eventually marrying Kazuko, but she's a very nice girl, and your future would be assured. You can concentrate on your studies without worrying about money or your future. Isn't this a wonderful offer?"

Bunji was taken aback. He said he would have to think about it. Obviously a little miffed, the principal responded, "But do get back to me in a day or two. It would be rude to keep Mr. Noda waiting on his very generous offer."

Bunji had known immediately that he would turn the offer down. It wasn't just having to marry Kazuko, who was rather plain and a mediocre student. He barely knew who she was. But the basic reason was that he didn't want to have someone else decide his future for him. Nor did he want to be at the beck and call of the Noda family, forever having to act grateful for what they had done for him. He went back to the principal and tried to give the least offensive reason he could come up with for his refusal to become Bunji Noda.

"I appreciate Mr. Noda's offer, but I have decided I can't give up my father's name...," he said.

"Koyama-kun, have you really thought this through?" the principal asked him sternly but kindly. "Your father is no longer alive. You have no one to support you through university, and as our best student, you should certainly go on to earn a university degree. And remember, in Japan you may have a difficult time getting a top job with your...um, background."

But Bunji held his ground. He felt rather sorry for Kazuko, who soon left Ashiya High. A classmate told Bunji that she had gone around bragging that she was going to marry the president of the student body, and when he turned down the offer, she was mortified. Bunji never saw her again as she changed schools.

But Bunji was too busy to think about the Nodas. He had decided to take the entrance examination for the University of Tokyo, ranked by everyone as the best university in Japan. He thought he should be able to manage financially with the help of the national scholarship fund, which provided tuition and a small stipend on a competitive basis to needy students who were admitted to the top universities. He also planned to work part time. If he could manage high school, why couldn't he manage university? So, encouraged by several of his teachers, he put "all of his eggs in one basket" and applied only to the University of Tokyo.

At the beginning of February 1953, Bunji and Masao Yamashiro, a good friend and competitor for the top grades in all their classes, went to Tokyo to take the entrance exam. After three weeks on tenterhooks, finally the day of the announcement of the examination results arrived. In the bakery, the two waited for a call from Hideo Ishida, who had graduated from Ashiya High School two years before and was now attending Tokyo University. He had promised to call with the results as soon as they were posted.

The call came at 10:40. Ishida said Bunji had passed but Yamashiro-kun's number was not on the list. Hearing the news, Bunji patted the shoulder of his friend, whose eyes were beginning to brim with tears, and said: "You can try again next year; losing a battle doesn't mean you've lost the war." Downcast, Yamashiro-kun left without saying a word.

Graduation soon followed. Bunji was asked to speak on behalf of his class. This was an emotional time for him. He could only marvel at how quickly time had passed since the days when he stood at the fence of Ashiya High envying the students who were studying there, and now he had fulfilled his dream and was graduating from this very high school. After the ceremony, he spent a few busy weeks going around to the people at the bakery and the newspaper delivery shop and many of his friends to thank them and bid farewell. The only thing that marred these hectic and euphoric days was his knowledge that Mr. Iguchi, who had gone to so much trouble to get him admitted to high school, and whose classes he had enjoyed so much in his second year, was now in an isolation ward in a hospital at the foot of the Rokko Mountains, not far from Ashiya. His TB had grown worse over the winter months and he was not expected to live much longer.

So Bunji moved once again, but this time without fear or trepidation for what he might encounter. He was neither being forcibly repatriated nor running away. Instead, he was sent off with the well wishes of friends, teachers, and neighbors to face his future as a student of the top university in Japan, and with a scholarship as well. One morning in late March, Bunji took his small blue suitcase—a gift from Mrs. Nitta—packed with his few worldly possessions, purchased the very cheapest ticket, and boarded a train that would stop at every station on the long journey from Ashiya to Tokyo. This was a journey that he was sure his father would strongly approve of. And as the train left Kobe heading for Osaka, Bunji eagerly looked forward to the karma awaiting him in Tokyo.

Chapter 4

Tokyo, 1953

BUNJI WAS EUPHORIC UPON HIS ARRIVAL IN TOKYO. Signing up for his university courses made him realize that he had indeed been admitted to Tokyo University, the pinnacle of all Japanese universities. He was beginning a new, glorious chapter in his life. And he knew that his father, who considered education so important, would have been so very proud to have his son studying here.

He found university life even more satisfying than he had expected. He enjoyed the lectures and meeting other students. Walking around the campus, Bunji scarcely noticed how dilapidated all the buildings were, or how tall the grass and weeds were on the neglected grounds.

Bunji had chosen economics as his major, a decision Japanese college students are required to make even before they take their university entrance exams. Hideo Ishida, the third-year economics student who had been president of Ashiya High's student council two years before Bunji, had recommended this major. "Modern economics is an analytic study of the economy making use of theories and logic with the aid of mathematics and statistical analyses." He emphasized that knowledge of this discipline would be "essential in helping our war-torn economy recover."

But far more important to Bunji was that he believed economics would be a potent tool to help him understand why poverty persisted—the reason for hunger and all the other suffering he had seen in many parts of Bangkok, again in Kobe, and in the southern part of Ashiya. In all of those places, he had seen the dire poverty of many that sharply contrasted with the affluence enjoyed by a few. He thought that economics would prepare him to do what he could to reduce such disparities in income and wealth. And so, Bunji signed up for introductory courses in both micro and macroeconomics.

After a few weeks, however, Bunji's feet gradually touched ground again as his finances began to seriously worry him. He had known that, at some point, he would need to take a part-time job because the living stipend he received was not generous. He had thought he would manage on that plus his meager savings until he could find a suitable, well-paying job. However, he had not counted on prices in Tokyo being higher than in Ashiya, and he had never before had to buy all of his food. He had gone to the university's service center, but there were no jobs he was qualified for that didn't conflict with his class schedule. As the days passed and his finances became ever more precarious, hard economic reality gradually smothered his euphoria.

He had to do something soon. But what?

Bunji thought about his largest expense: his lodging. When he arrived in Tokyo, he quickly found near the campus a small 4.5 *tatami*-mat room, just nine square feet, on the second floor of a rather dilapidated house owned by a gentle war widow. The *tatami* was old, the bedding worn but clean, and the location meant that he would have no transportation expenses. For what he was getting, the rent was reasonable, and it was not possible to find a cheaper lodging of the same quality and convenience. So he couldn't save money on lodging.

Bunji had put off buying the university uniform. Instead, he had attached to his old Ashiya uniform the Tokyo University's metal badge on which was imprinted the university's gingko leaf insignia. He was buying only the textbooks that were absolutely necessary, and living very, very frugally. He ate *natto* (fermented soybeans) as his principal source of protein, often skipped lunch, brushed his teeth with salt, and even tried to shave with the edge of a piece of broken glass. He couldn't be any more frugal than he was already and remain healthy.

He reached the inevitable conclusion befitting a budding economist: if he couldn't reduce the demand for money, he had to increase its supply. Since the student service office still had nothing suitable for him, he made the rounds of local bakeries, thinking that one of them might like a part-time helper who had had three years of experience. But they all said they had apprentices to do what Bunji was capable of, or that the family's labor was sufficient.

His only alternative was to take one of the jobs offered on notices posted on bulletin boards around campus, a job moving beer kegs onto trucks at a large warehouse located twenty minutes north of the university. From the fact that the job paid better than others available, he knew it would be hard work; but the hours wouldn't interfere with his classes. The major disadvantage was that he wouldn't be paid until the end of the fourth week.

The work at the warehouse proved to be more punishing than he anticipated. Six days a week, from five to eight in the evening, Bunji and three other students struggled to move heavy metal beer kegs over the concrete floor of the warehouse, which was wet from having just been washed and made even more slippery by beer spilt from the aluminum kegs as they crashed against each other or the side wall as the boys worked. The boys had to roll both small and large kegs—some weighing nearly ninety kilos—across the floor and hoist them onto waiting trucks. Even though the temperature in the warehouse was cool in the May evenings, Bunji's shirt was soaking wet within an hour. By the end of the evening, his fingers were blistered and his shoulders ached badly. But he stayed on the job for the four weeks, regretting the hours stolen from study, but thinking of the 3,240 yen he would receive at the end of the fourth week.

Even though Bunji wouldn't be paid until the end of the contract, finding a job meant that he could stop worrying about money for food. A small restaurant near the campus gave him credit, allowing him to eat simple dinners—a bowl of barley mixed with rice and a few small, yellow pickles along with a side dish of broiled fish with some green vegetable, or on some days sautéed cabbage with bits of pork. The owner, a middle-aged man with a bad leg, who told Bunji he was a communist, had said, "Okay, you can eat on credit until you get paid. But don't forget the poor people like us when you become rich and famous after graduating from Tokyo University."

As soon as work ended on Saturday of the fourth week, Bunji and three other students gathered at the edge of the loading dock to wait for their wages. They waited nearly an hour as it gradually grew dark, save for a weak light coming from the window of the small administrative office. Finally, Bunji suggested that they go over to the office. He knocked on the door. A tired-looking man with thinning gray hair opened it.

"What do you want? I'm trying to finish my accounts."

Bunji spoke for all of them: "We have being waiting now for almost an hour to get paid. Mr. Kaneda said he would give us our wages tonight."

"Aah, Kaneda…." Bunji's heart sank at the tone of the man's voice, but he plunged on.

"Yes, Sir. We are waiting for Mr. Kaneda, who hired us for four weeks of work. When he signed us up, he told us to wait for him tonight at the loading dock until he came with our wages. He's a short fellow about thirty years old. He wore a leather jacket with the picture of a dragon on the back."

"Oh, you're describing Kaneda all right. Mr. Goto, the assistant manager, always has trouble getting enough help for the evening shift, so against his better judgment, he used Kaneda to act as a temporary recruiting agent. I handle the pay only for regular employees, so I can't help you. But Mr. Goto said something about giving Kaneda the money for the students' wages earlier, so you should have been paid by now."

"What? Kaneda has the money for our wages? Then where can we find him?" Now Bunji was truly alarmed.

"I have no idea. Frankly, I wouldn't be surprised if you never see Kaneda again. Since he hasn't come with your pay, the only thing you boys can do, I think, is to go to the police."

The bookkeeper shook his head as he closed the door of the office saying, "Sorry boys, but I can't help you."

Bunji was in near despair. Although he had just received his monthly stipend, he had used it up to pay his rent and to repay the restaurant owner for most but not all of his meals. All the cash he had was two ten-yen coins.

Bunji had had no lunch that day and had managed to get through the three hours of hard work thinking about the good meal he would treat himself to once he was paid. He knew he couldn't go back to the restaurant owner still owing money and with no job in sight. Utterly disconsolate, he went to bed with a very empty stomach.

Sunday, Bunji woke with a pain in his stomach from hunger. He was so hungry he couldn't think. He decided the first thing he would do was to spend his twenty yen on food. The most filling thing he could buy with it was a bowl of noodles with a few vegetables and half a boiled egg. The soup would make him feel full, at least temporarily.

After he had eaten, he decided his next step was to go to the university police, though he was not confident that they could find Kaneda. The officer he talked to said that anyone could post a notice on one of the boards around campus and he had no knowledge of Kaneda or the job he had advertised. But the officer did agree to make inquiries with the city police. From the way he spoke, Bunji feared the officer was likely to make only a half-hearted effort, so he decided to investigate on his own.

Bunji made the rounds of all the bulletin boards on campus to see if Kaneda had posted any more notices. Nothing. Nor were there any jobs immediately available. The service office wasn't open on Sunday so he couldn't ask about another job, and he didn't see anyone he knew who might lend him the price of a meal.

He dejectedly wandered around campus, wondering what to do. He thought of the 385 yen still remaining in the bank account he had opened so that his stipend could be paid to him. But banks weren't open on Sunday, and in any case, Bunji had no intention of touching his paltry savings. If he withdrew them on Monday, he would spend the money within a few days, and then what would he do if he couldn't find a part-time job, or in a real emergency, such as having to go to a doctor? He couldn't use the money now when he hadn't gone even a day without eating anything. Finally he went to the library and tried to study, but he was too tired and hungry to concentrate. When the library closed, he sat on a bench and tried to figure out what to do, but he was too depressed and no longer thinking straight. Long after dark, he crept back to his room and went to bed.

Bunji couldn't get to sleep because he was so hungry. The acute pain in his stomach made him remember going through trashcans for edible remnants of food during the three days he and his two friends had starved after arriving in Kobe from Tokyo. Before he finally dozed near dawn, the thought came to him that he might have made a grave mistake in not accepting the offer the rich banker in Ashiya had made to adopt him and pay for his university education.

On Monday morning, Bunji got up feeling desperate. He went to his macroeconomics class, which he didn't want to miss, but he found he couldn't follow the lecture because all he could think was whether he would go to the bank and withdraw 150 yen, or possibly sell his blood, which he had heard some of his classmates were doing. In the end, he decided to do neither, convincing himself that he wasn't *that* desperate. Somehow, he would find a way to get a decent meal and would then think.

He came up with a plan. Though feeling weak from not having had a filling meal since Friday night, he walked a kilometer to the back of a mid-sized department store and rummaged for a large, still usable paper shopping bag and enough discarded wrapping paper to fill the bag. This he took with him to a good-sized restaurant nearly filled with customers. He ordered his favorite pork cutlet that came with a lot of thinly sliced cabbage, a bowl of *miso* soup, and a larger bowl of rice. He began to devour his meal, but slowed down so people wouldn't stare, and because he knew that he shouldn't eat quickly after not having anything to eat for so long.

When Bunji had finished every morsel, he asked the middle-aged man eating at the same table to watch his shopping bag while he went to the toilet. But once in the narrow hallway, Bunji made for the back door and got away from the restaurant as quickly as he could without running. As he walked back to campus, he tried to justify to himself what he had just done: "I'm only following my father's advice. I did what I had to do to survive. It would be a great waste of a life if I become malnourished and contract TB like Konishi in Sannomiya and Iguchi Sensei in Ashiya." But he knew full well that what he had done was criminal, and he didn't want to become one like Kaneda. He had to find another solution. But what? He couldn't think of an immediate solution, so he went to his German class, and, by evening, he was hungry again and went to bed with his stomach empty.

Tuesday morning, when Bunji bumped into his landlady in the hall, she took one look at him and realized something was wrong. Bunji realized he must have looked tired and depressed, and when she so kindly inquired what the matter was, he told her part of the story. She led him into her little sitting room and, there, fed him some leftover rice with hot tea poured over it, a small bowl of boiled vegetables, and a few pickles. He ate it all very gratefully, particularly since this was most likely her lunch he was consuming.

Bunji went back to the university police, where an officer reported: "The local police located a man named Fujio Kaneda and questioned him, but he said he didn't know anything about any wages for any students. The police said you could file a formal complaint. But the officer who contacted us also noted that Kaneda is known to belong to a local yakuza gang, and I got the impression the police didn't want to get involved with yakuza for anything this minor.

Are you sure you want to file a formal complaint against a local gangster?"

Desperate as Bunji was, he decided not to file a complaint. He knew there was only the smallest chance of getting any money, and it was not worth risking certain retribution from the yakuza group. He went back to the student service office but found no job he thought he could get.

That afternoon, in a fog of hunger, Bunji went to his microeconomics class and plopped down as usual next to Yasusuke Murakami, whom he liked and respected for his exceptional ability in mathematics. Murakami looked over at Bunji a couple of times because Bunji's stomach kept growling. When the lecture was over, Murakami commented on Bunji being "uncharacteristically subdued." In a concerned voice he asked, "Aren't you eating?" At his wit's end, Bunji told Murakami the whole sad tale and his dire financial situation.

Murakami listened without saying a word and then reached into his hip pocket and took out his wallet. He withdrew two one-thousand-yen notes and handed them to Bunji saying, "Take this. Pay me back when you become somebody. Don't worry, you will." He added with his lopsided smile, "And when you do, be sure to add interest, calculated using the competitive market rate for non-secured loans and adjusted for the rate of inflation." Murakami was joking to put Bunji at ease. Bunji was so relieved and grateful that he could barely manage to hold back tears, but Murakami pretended not to notice and turned the conversation to what had been discussed in class.

However, Murakami's money was just a stopgap. To make ends meet, Bunji now had to take on any part-time odd job he could find. The only condition he had for the jobs he took was that he be paid daily. He was in no position to quibble about low pay. He took any job he could get: unpacking and stacking books in a bookshop; helping a grocer unload his wares; inserting advertisements in newspapers; and even helping to clean up construction sites. None of the work lasted more than a day or two, so he had to continually look for new jobs. All the while, he regretted the amount of time earning money took from his studies. Life in Tokyo at Japan's top university even on a stipend was turning out to be more difficult than earning his way through high school in Ashiya.

While Bunji was doing his best to come to grips with hard reality, Mori from his English class said to him one day: "I saw a notice on the bulletin board in English stating that an American foundation is looking for candidates for a scholarship to study in the United States. It says the foundation will pay for the passage to America, tuition, and living expenses. It's an amazing offer! The notice says candidates must be able to speak and comprehend English sufficiently to pursue a university education in the U.S. You've said you wanted to study abroad someday, and your English is much better than mine. You might have a chance. Why don't you go take a look?"

Bunji immediately went to read the notice. It said that a Mr. Elliott Siegrist from something called the William Foundation would interview students who wished to compete for a four-year scholarship to study in the U.S. In addition to English ability, the conditions included an interest in "promoting mutual understanding among the peoples of the world" and being a student in good standing at a "top university" in Japan.

Bunji didn't even think twice. He immediately called the telephone number on the notice and was given a day and time when he was to go for an interview at the Imperial Hotel. *I hope my karma is improving*, he thought.

Two days later, Bunji arrived at Tokyo's most famous hotel. As he entered the lobby, he wondered which of the half dozen foreigners he was there to meet. Then his eyes lit on a man in his sixties, slender with gray hair and gold-framed eyeglasses, Bunji's idea of an elderly American professor or doctor. The man noticed Bunji, the only young Japanese in the lobby, and waved him over. It was Mr. Siegrist.

Mr. Siegrist shook Bunji's hand and asked him to sit down. As Bunji handed him his university ID card, Mr. Siegrist began the interview by bluntly saying, "This interview will be conducted entirely in English. Please reply to my questions in English. To my disappointment, I've seen too many students who can read English but not speak it. I hope you will be different."

Mr. Siegrist quickly found that Bunji was different. He had no difficulty responding in English to questions about his parents, his academic background, and why he wanted to study in the U.S. The interview was scheduled for half an hour but lasted for more than forty-five minutes, both because Mr. Siegrist found that Bunji could speak English, and because he was so interested in Bunji's unusual background. It ended with Mr. Siegrist saying: "All right, Mr. Koyama. I'm putting you on my short list. Most students seem to come to see me only out of curiosity—they aren't really willing to leave Tokyo or any other top university because they know when they graduate, they can get a good job in a big company or with the government. But you seem to be genuinely interested in studying in the U.S. even if it means leaving this good university just after entering it."

Bunji waited on pins and needles for four days, until he heard from Mr. Siegrist. He hadn't told anyone what he had applied for. There was no point in talking about what was such a long shot. Mr. Siegrist was interviewing a number of students from Tokyo University, and he said he planned to interview students from other universities as well. But finally, a telegram arrived at Bunji's lodgings asking him to meet Mr. Siegrist again, this time at the American Embassy. Did this mean Bunji had the grant, or was this just another stage in the selection process? He spruced himself up and cut two lectures to be at the embassy at two o'clock the following day as requested in the telegram.

Mr. Siegrist warmly greeted him in a small office, which Bunji was sure the American had borrowed from someone. After asking only a few questions, Mr. Siegrist broke out in a smile and announced:

"I'm happy to award you one of the two scholarships the William Foundation will give to Japanese students this year. Congratulations!"

Then, Mr. Siegrist said in a more serious voice, "You may think you are able to tell me now whether you will accept the grant, but I don't need a written letter of acceptance until the end of next week. So think carefully about your decision, because this could change your life. Consult anyone who may be able to advise you. When you are very sure of your decision, send your letter to me in English, care of Mr. Dennis Abercrombie here at the American Embassy." Mr. Siegrist handed him a slip of paper with the name and address on it and continued, "After he gets a letter of acceptance from you, he will start processing the necessary papers."

Mr. Siegrist shook Bunji's hand and beamed at him. Bunji wanted to say something but he was so happy he couldn't find the words. All he could do was firmly shake Mr. Siegrist's hand and beam back at him.

Bunji returned to his small room, scarcely aware how he got back from the embassy. He couldn't believe his luck. All he could think of was, "I got the scholarship! I'm going to America!" He was so overjoyed in the first few hours after getting the news that he couldn't study and had difficulty falling sleep. But by the following morning, he had calmed down a bit and thought that maybe he had better follow Mr. Siegrist's advice. He knew in his heart of hearts he would go to the U.S., but he couldn't shake the feeling that his decision might be based more on an inchoate emotional reaction than on reasoned judgment. He decided to seek the advice of his classmates and acquaintances during the next few days just to make sure he wasn't making a big mistake.

The opinions Bunji heard were sharply divided between strong opposition expressed in no uncertain terms and wholehearted support mixed with undisguised envy. After his English class, he announced to three of his classmates that he had been awarded the scholarship. Mori clapped him on the back, saying, "See, I told you. You had a chance! When do you leave?"

When Bunji told the small group that he had been told to seek advice from people, and only then decide whether to accept the offer, all three began to speak at once. They couldn't get over what they considered his good fortune.

Hattori, who had worked with Bunji in the beer warehouse, said: "'You hit the jackpot' is the English expression. No more dreadful part-time jobs at a slave wage. When you come back with an American degree and fluent English, you can get a plum position. And if you can go on to graduate school, you could even become a professor!" Mori said emphatically: "Only a fool would turn down the opportunity to go to the richest country in the world. Someone told me that Japan's per capita income is still only 5 percent of America's!"

Uchimura urged Bunji to "become a real cosmopolitan in America. Our generation is suffocating under our country's rigid traditions and customs. You can have a real influence when you return—indeed *if* you return."

Virtually all of the other classmates he told about the offer were also enthusiastic about his going to the U.S. Like most Japanese, they were fascinated by the nation that had defeated Japan less than eight years ago, and they knew a lot about America. They saw newsreels about the U.S. whenever they went to the movies, and there were articles about the U.S. in every magazine and newspaper. Anyone who had graduated from high school could recite the major geographical and historical facts of the U.S. and knew who Washington, Lincoln, and Roosevelt were.

But not everyone thought Bunji should accept the scholarship. Strong opposition came from a classmate in his German class, from the communist owner of the restaurant, and from a regular customer of the restaurant who was a third year student at Tokyo University and also a leader of the Zengakuren, a national federation of committed Marxist students.

Naito from his German class gave Bunji a long emotional argument against accepting the scholarship: "America is the country that defeated Japan by dropping the atomic bomb and killing hundreds of thousands of Japanese only eight years ago. Even though we've finally signed a peace treaty, Americans are keeping many of their military bases in Japan, and their impudent soldiers are all over our country, seducing and raping innocent Japanese girls. Might justifies everything. And now Japan, vanquished and impoverished, is doing everything it can to ape American 'democracy' from adopting a constitution the Americans drafted to watering down our excellent education system. But soon the Japanese economy will grow rapidly and Japan will become powerful once again. Then you'll see the current fever to mimic everything American will cool down. We'll rediscover the true value of our distinctive culture and institutions and become confident again as a people. Don't you want to be a part of this?"

The owner of the restaurant didn't mince words: "Today the only thing that matters in Japan is that we rebuild our economy and let the working people live a better life. Koyama-kun, you've always said that the life of the poor is miserable and what the politicians and big companies ought to change. So what you must do is to graduate from Tokyo University and get a responsible job that can help change Japan for the working class. If you go study in America, you are running away. I don't like the U.S., which is behaving like a suzerain toward Japan. But what I'm telling you has nothing to do with how I feel about America." Bunji thought that the restaurant owner had a more logical argument than his classmate.

The radical student leader, Takamatsu, told Bunji in an angry voice, "If you go to an American university on money from an American foundation, you are going to be 'brainwashed.' You'll completely sell out to the capitalists." He went on and on, but Bunji had trouble following his logic and thought it came more from slogans than reasoning.

After listening to their arguments against Bunji going to the U.S., he came to the conclusion that their "reasons" were based on their ideological convictions, rather than practical considerations. However, Naito did say one thing that Bunji knew he should keep in mind: "You'll come back Americanized, and because you'll speak good English, you will be someone useful in dealing with foreigners, but you'll find yourself sidelined and will never become a leader in government or business here in Japan."

Much to his surprise, Bunji's landlady was also dead set against his going to the U.S. She admonished him almost tearfully: "Please don't go. You think you want to go but you don't know America. There, you'll be someone who comes from a country that was an enemy only eight years ago and... you are not a white person so you will be subjected to racial discrimination which I hear is rampant over there. You'll be wretched. If you were my son, I'd never permit you to go. But if you graduate from Tokyo University, you'll be respected; you'll get a very good job everyone envies."

Bunji appreciated her concern, and what she said next made him seriously think.

"I'm worried about your making a hasty decision. Look how hard you worked to get into the university ranked number one in Japan. And now, when you've barely begun your studies here, you're thinking of chucking it all up and leaving. *Mottai nai,* what a waste! If you want to study abroad, why not first get your degree here and then think about further study abroad?"

Bunji decided he needed a more objective opinion about getting a college degree in the U.S. and made an appointment with Professor Sakaguchi, who taught his macroeconomics class. He wanted to ask him about the study of economics in the U.S. When Bunji arrived in his professor's office, he found him in a talkative mood. Though Bunji didn't understand everything he was told about the state of economics in the U.S., even many years later, he still remembered some of the things his professor had said—things Bunji learned later were very accurate.

"The study of neoclassical economics, which we call modern economics, has developed rapidly in the past half century since the time of Alfred Marshall. And there is no doubt whatsoever that the U.S. is at the cutting edge of our discipline. Joseph Schumpeter, a leader in economic history, although he is from Austria, started the American econometrics society based on neoclassical economics. And Paul Samuelson wrote a Ph.D. thesis that made major inroads in integrating micro and macroeconomics and became an instant classic. In contrast, in Japan most regretfully we still have many Marxist economists who exert power and influence in many universities, including our own Tokyo University." He concluded his advice with the strong recommendation: "You should go. You are very fortunate to have this opportunity."

But even the people who strongly supported Bunji's going to America advised him not to withdraw from the university, but to take a leave of absence so that if "for any reason you decide to come back, you can resume your studies here." None of them came out and said Bunji might have language problems, or face some other obstacle that might force him to return to Japan without a degree. Bunji decided that taking leave would be the sensible thing to do and would cost nothing.

So after three days of seeking advice from virtually everyone he knew, Bunji stood leaning against the wall of his room watching the sun slowly set over the roof of the house next door and pondered what everyone had told him, and examined his own reasons for applying for the scholarship.

He had both read and heard that racial discrimination against Negroes was a serious problem in the U.S. But he didn't believe that he would be subjected to discrimination because he wasn't Caucasian. Neither did he believe Americans would discriminate against him because he came from a country that was an enemy until recently. Look at how the Americans had set out to feed the Japanese right after the war, instead of letting them starve. Even the sergeant who brought food to the orphanage had been nice to Bunji, and if a soldier who had fought against the Japanese was being so kind to the Japanese people, what did Bunji have to fear from Americans? And look at how they had done so much to try to help rebuild Japan and its economy instead of behaving punitively toward the nation they had defeated.

The main reason Bunji was not overly concerned about any racial discrimination he might face in the U.S. was because of the various Americans he had met through his father. There was his father's close friend, Mr. Michael Middleton, a big man from somewhere in the American Midwest, who, like his father, had imported machinery. Mr. Middleton was always affable, kind and outgoing, and had gone out of his way to chat with Bunji. Bunji thought of several other Americans he had met in Bangkok and couldn't recall anyone he had met either there or while traveling with his father to Hong Kong and Singapore who had discriminated against him because he wasn't Caucasian.

Bunji well remembered what his father had told him about the U.S. and the Americans he had met when he went to New York and Chicago on a business trip in the late twenties. "I couldn't be more surprised by the booming economy and how advanced the American machine-tool industry was, in many respects more so than in Germany. Even more surprising was that I found Americans magnanimous—I mean generous, big-hearted and kind."

Although Bunji thought he was being objective and rational in analyzing the probability of his being subjected to racial discrimination in the U.S., he failed to consider that the handful of Americans he had met as a child were already predisposed to like Asians or they would not have chosen to live in Bangkok or other Asian cities. And he was unaware of any real discrimination in the U.S. except against Negroes. So his conclusions about discrimination were reached on very incomplete knowledge. Only much later did he learn of the severe discrimination against Chinese immigrants, the anti-Asian immigration laws passed by the U.S. Congress in the twenties, and the internment camps for American citizens of Japanese ancestry during World War II. He wondered then had he known all this back in 1953, whether this knowledge would have affected his decision to study in the U.S. But he rather thought not, for two reasons.

One was his father's admiration for Westerners and Western civilization. He had considered the Nazis an aberration that would pass. And second, balanced against any possible discrimination Bunji might face in the U.S. was the discrimination he had seen in Japan as well as what he himself had experienced. When he was in the orphanage in Asagaya, people in Tokyo had called him "a foreign brat" more than once. In Ashiya, he had seen discrimination against anyone who was not considered fully Japanese. Bunji hadn't faced the kind of discrimination inflicted upon the *burakumin* and Koreans, even those who were born in Japan and spoke only Japanese. Still he had been called "not fit to run for the office of the president of the student body" because he wasn't pure Japanese. Even with a degree from Tokyo University, he wasn't at all confident that he would escape discrimination in the future because of his Thai mother, and because of the way his father had died. From all he knew, he was sure his background would affect his chances of getting the job he wanted, and possibly permission from the parents of a girl he wished to marry.

He didn't believe the criticism accurate that he was being "blinded" by the American scholarship because it promised an escape from the harsh financial situation he faced at present. Who wouldn't want to live in the richest country in the world? This was clearly an attraction, particularly for Bunji who had no family ties in Japan and hadn't even lived here until he was nine. But he was under no illusion that he would have an easy time financially in the U.S. because Mr. Siegrist had said the living stipend was set at a basic level, with the expectation that the recipients would have some help from their families, and of course Bunji would have to rely entirely on the scholarship.

After hearing what Professor Sakaguchi had to say, Bunji knew he was thinking how wonderful it would be to study economics in the U.S. where this discipline was "at the cutting edge." He wasn't naïve enough to believe that studying economics alone could help alleviate poverty around the world, but he was sure it was important. He definitely didn't believe he would become a reactionary, let alone "a puppet of imperialism."

Bunji considered what his landlady had said about this being a hasty decision. On the surface, it did seem like it: to have suddenly applied for a scholarship for study in the U.S. when he had only just entered Tokyo University. But Bunji now realized that all along he had been a latent candidate for emigrating. And Japan wasn't Bunji's first or only home-land. In Thailand, he had lived in a much less "order-bound" and vertical society, one that had felt to him much less regi-mented, less insular, and without all the extreme concern for face and protocol. Thais seemed to do what they pleased, not what was socially expected. From the very first, he had found life in Japan "confining." And this feeling had grown over time.

Moreover, he had a "role model" in his father who had taken the risk of leaving Japan, first for Germany, and then

Thailand. And his father had always pushed him to accept challenges, whether it was studying more hours every day than Bunji wanted to, or learning how to swim. And his last advice to Bunji had been to take risks to live a full life, to challenge the unknown.

Bunji briefly analyzed whether he wanted to leave Japan because he couldn't forgive how the Japanese army had executed his father. He knew that his father hadn't believed in the war and was convinced what he was doing was right, and Bunji, as his son, thought he agreed with him. But by the time Bunji was in high school, he clearly understood that from the Japanese viewpoint, his father had committed treason and that was why his father had lost his life. It was simply the war. No, his father's execution wasn't the reason that Bunji wanted to leave Japan and go to the U.S.

But while Japan was "pushing" him away in various ways, as it had his father, Bunji found the U.S. "pulling" him toward it. He both admired and envied the kind of country he thought the U.S. was, and he wanted what it could offer him. He wanted to experience its open and democratic ways, in short, to live the American dream.

As the setting sun now touched the neighbor's rooftop, Bunji came to a realization: there were in fact two Bunjis. One was cogitating about what he had heard and considered during the past three days, and the other was silently yelling at the top of his lungs, "Sure, listen to all the opinions. But above all listen to your own heart. You want to go to America not because of some calculation of pluses and minuses for your future employment, advancement, let alone income... but because you still hear what you father said: 'live fully taking risks, don't take a familiar or easy road...what you need to do to truly live is to be adventurous, unafraid of challenges!'"

Hadn't Bunji followed his father's advice when he left the orphanage? And a year later, in Sannomiya? Didn't his seemingly foolhardy risk-taking get him into Ashiya High and then Tokyo University? Why not take another risk and go across the Pacific? Bunji scarcely noticed that the sun had set and his room was growing dark. He smiled to himself. He had made his decision and was now feeling an odd mixture of resolve and exhilaration.

The next morning Bunji carefully wrote an acceptance letter in his best English. He sent it by Special Delivery to Mr. Siegrist care of the man at the American Embassy with the strange long name of Abercrombie.

A FEW DAYS LATER, BUNJI RECEIVED A SHORT LETTER asking him to come to the embassy as soon as possible to process his application to enter the U.S. When he arrived, Mr. Abercrombie, a rather plump man in a too-tight shirt, asked him to fill out several forms and sign most of them. Bunji had to borrow a dictionary to understand some legal words and phrases, such as "affidavit" and "domicile of origin," as well as the names of diseases he could have had. He signed in Roman letters, imitating what he had seen his father do many times. Next, he had to go to a hospital near the embassy for a chest X-ray as people with TB were not admitted to the U.S. However, the doctor who saw Bunji's X-ray pronounced it, "Clean. No problem."

But a major problem did arise that same afternoon. When Bunji returned to the embassy clutching his X-ray, Mr. Abercrombie told him that it didn't look like it would be possible for Bunji to get a visa in time to start school in September. Only a very limited number of student visas was available for Japanese, and the quota had already been filled. But Mr. Abercrombie was very sympathetic with what Mr. Siegrist was trying to do and said he would do his best. He asked Bunji more questions about his background, and asked him to call him in three days.

Bunji was anguished. Just as things seemed to be going so smoothly, there was this obstacle. Would Mr. Siegrist give him a grant a year from now if Bunji couldn't get a visa for the coming autumn? Bunji went back to his studies to make up for what he had missed with all his interviews, but it wasn't easy with his mind full of worry about the possibility that he might not be able to go to the U.S.

Three days later, on pins and needles, Bunji called Mr. Abercrombie's office from the public telephone in the student union. He was nervous about what the news would be. Could Mr. Abercrombie really do anything to get a visa for him? But to his delight, Bunji was told that Mr. Abercrombie thought the problem had been solved and asked Bunji to come to the embassy that afternoon.

When Bunji reached Mr. Abercrombie's office, it was explained to him that the officer in charge of visas had concluded that Bunji might be qualified to get a visa from the underused Thai quota for immigration visas to the U.S. under the new Immigration and Naturalization Act of 1952. Bunji had trouble understanding the long explanation of the procedures the U.S. officials had gone through, but he did grasp that the visa officer had called the Thai Embassy, which in turn had telexed Bangkok, and the result was that the Thai Embassy had informed the American officials that, "We've established Bunji Koyama's father was a legal, alien resident of Bangkok and his mother was a Thai national." Bunji was told that it would take a few weeks to get all the documents in place, but all Bunji cared about was Mr. Abercrombie's statement: "This means you are qualified to enter the U.S. using one of the immigration visas allotted to Thai nationals." Bunji let out such a long sigh of relief that Mr. Abercrombie smiled at him.

More paperwork had to be filled out, so that Bunji was late in arriving at the Chinese restaurant in Akasaka where Mr. Siegrist was treating Bunji and the second scholarship recipient to dinner. Mr. Siegrist has just returned to Tokyo from a week in western Japan and had been a bit worried when Bunji didn't appear in time. However, he was relieved to learn that Bunji would be able to go to the U.S. in time for the beginning of the 1953 academic year. He thought a minute about what Bunji had told him and remarked:

"This means technically that you can stay on in the U.S. and become an American citizen. It doesn't matter to me on what visa you go. The most important thing is that you can now start school in September. But remember that when you go on an immigration visa, you are liable for military service as soon as you graduate. However, you won't have to worry about that because you'll be coming back to Japan."

Then Mr. Siegrist turned to the other person in the small private room of the restaurant and introduced him to Bunji whom he had now started to call by his given name. "Bunji, this is Fumio Shimada, who goes by his English name, Peter. He is a third-year student at Tokyo University. I gather you haven't met. Peter was born in Canada and returned to Japan with his family just before the war started. He wants to study sociology at the University of Chicago which, he says, has the best sociology department in the country."

Bunji responded to the introduction and then turned to Mr. Siegrist. "I have been thinking about my name, I mean my first name. I've decided I want to be called Michael. My father had a good friend named Michael. I liked him...and I like the sound of the name. I thought of keeping Bunji, but

I know Americans will pronounce it, 'Bun,' like the bun we eat. I can't offhand think of an English word that has 'un' and is pronounced as in my name. The only one that comes to my mind is a German word 'Bundestag.'"

"I understand," responded Mr Siegrist. "'Michael' will make things easier for you in the U.S. So now I have Peter and Michael."

Then a waitress entered the room with a large platter of cold hors d'oeuvres and the sumptuous meal began. Bunji hadn't had Chinese food like this since he had traveled with his father to Hong Kong, and he hadn't seen so much food for three people ever in his decade in Japan. But he couldn't just sit and relish the meal as Mr. Siegrist was plying him with questions, and he had to concentrate on his English.

Mr. Siegrist's first question was: "So Michael, what do you want to study in the U.S.? I know you are pursuing an economics degree at Tokyo University. Do you plan to continue with the same major in the U.S.?"

Bunji had anticipated this question and was ready with an answer. "I want to study economics," and went on to make a long speech explaining that there was too wide a gap between the rich and the poor, that the poor suffer from many disadvantages and hardships, and many changes were needed both in politics and the economy to create a fairer society, and he wished to help make the needed changes. He concluded, "I know a knowledge of economics is crucial to understanding how to make changes in the economy, and my professor at Tokyo University says that America is the most advanced country in the study of economics."

When Bunji finally finished, Mr. Siegrist, a little over-whelmed by the passion he sensed in his words, responded, "Goodness. You certainly know what you want to study. My next question is where you would like to pursue these studies. Do you have a university in mind, as Peter here does?"

Bunji was no longer on sure ground. He hadn't forgotten a paragraph he had read in the William Foundation's description of the scholarship: the foundation would pay the tuition of each recipient during the regular academic year, it would pay the cost of travel by ship from Japan to the U.S., and it would provide a living stipend that was intended to supplement the funds each recipient was currently spending on his education in Japan. This would be generous because the cost of living was so much higher in the U.S. than in Japan, but it also meant that any travel expenses within the U.S. would be born by the recipient. But Bunji, of course, would have no money for living except for the grant because he had no family to depend on, as Peter did. So now he answered Mr. Siegrist's question with another question: "To which port will our ship go in the U.S?"

Mr. Siegrist replied with a slightly puzzled look on his face, "San Francisco."

So with some assurance, Bunji said he would prefer to go to a university in California. Mr. Siegrist declared forcefully:

"Then Berkeley would be the best choice for you. That's the campus of the University of California located just outside San Francisco. It's one of the best universities in the U.S. I know it isn't an easy school to get into. But we should be able to get you admitted. After all, you got into the University of Tokyo.

As the various courses continued to arrive, all three began to relax, and Mr. Siegrist at last revealed what the William Foundation really was. He explained that it was a foundation in name only, established for tax purposes. He had provided all the funds because he wanted to do something in memory of his son, William. "I am the president of one of the largest feed and grains wholesaling companies in Chicago, and William was my only son, my only child." With his voice full of grief, he told them that William had been a doctor who was killed while tending to wounded GIs in the outskirts of Cologne only two months before the war ended in Europe.

Bunji never forgot what Mr. Siegrist said.

"William was killed by a mortar shell. That's why I don't want to see another war. To prevent wars, I decided to spend our money...my wife is with me on this 100 percent...to help the bright young men of our former enemies...Germany and Japan in particular...become peace-loving, international citizens by getting a good education in the U.S. I promise to do all I can to help you guys so long as you keep your grades up. All in memory of William."

AFTER DECIDING TO GO TO AMERICA, and filing with Tokyo University his request for a leave of absence of one academic year, the maximum permitted, Bunji stopped attending most lectures. Instead, he did as much part-time work as he needed to make ends meet, and the rest of his time he spent reading books on American history, politics, and economy, which he checked out of the university library. He scarcely noticed when summer vacation began.

Just when Bunji had resigned himself to a series of grueling, poorly paid part-time jobs until his departure for America, a totally unexpected piece of good luck came his way. Ishida, the student from Ashiya High who had recommended that Bunji major in economics, contacted him out of blue and said, "For family reasons, I have to go back home for the summer. Would you be interested in taking over my part-time job during the university vacation?"

The job turned out to be "assistant secretary" to a first-term Liberal Party member in the Upper House of the Diet. The title "secretary" was in fact a misnomer as the job was really that of a factotum who was willing to show some initiative and was not afraid of long hours. Jumping at the opportunity, Bunji immediately went to the Councilor's office in Nagata-cho where the Councilor's gaunt, forty-ish secretary perfunctorily interviewed Bunji and hired him on the spot. Bunji was told to start work the following day at a daily wage more than double what he could earn from doing anything else.

The next day, Bunji was shown to a small desk in a corner of the secretary's office. He threw himself into the work, which was so much more interesting than any other job he had ever held. He was to read newspapers and magazines and clip out any articles that the Councilor, who was serving on the Agriculture Committee, "should read," summarize the longer articles, man the telephones when needed, write some letters and file papers, send inexpensive gifts to "people who mattered in the electoral district" when anyone in their family or their close relatives married, died, graduated from a school, received noteworthy honors, etc.

Near the end of his first week, the Councilor, impeccable in a fine suit, sauntered into the office and, without any greeting, said to Bunji: "That summary on the subsidies for rice was well done. Keep it up."

A few days later, the Councilor handed several pages of notes to Bunji with the request: "This is what I plan to say at the session of the Agriculture Committee. If you think you can add anything that could be useful to me, write it down and give it to me within three days."

Bunji read the notes carefully and went to the National Diet Library where he spent nearly four hours researching the issues raised by the Councilor. On the morning of the third day, he sent his comments to the Councilor. Within two hours he was summoned to the Councilor's office where he was told, "Reading your comments is like walking through a freshly mown field of hay. Smells green. But I must admit you made a few good points. So go back to the library and dig up some data to make the points of yours I've marked more persuasive."

Bunji returned to the Diet Library and spent the hours until it closed searching for the data. For a few days after he handed the data back to the secretary, he heard nothing from the Councilor. But for the next month, he received a dozen requests, one after another, all of which meant more trips to the library. A number of times he had to stay till it closed. He was so busy that he had little time to read books on America, but he consoled himself with the thought that these requests from the Councilor meant his work was proving to be useful. And the generous weekly pay he received was a godsend, for Bunji no longer had to worry about where he was going to find the money to eat, and could begin to think of buying a set of new clothes for his journey.

At the end of July, as a reward for Bunji's being so helpful, the Councilor included him in the small party he took to see the American movie, "Singing in the Rain." Bunji understood most of light-hearted and amusing dialogue between Gene Kelly and Debby Reynolds, and enjoyed the fast-paced and entertaining singing and dancing. He paid close attention to the depictions of American life, but he realized that they probably weren't terribly realistic in this romantic musical. Even so, how different was the standard of living in this movie from the life Bunji saw around him in the Japan of 1953!

Also near the end of July, Bunji received a letter from the embassy containing a formal letter of admission from Berkeley, and a message Mr. Siegrist had sent from Germany which read: "The two fellows from the William Foundation will depart from Yokohama on the President Line's SS *President McKinley* on August 17, arriving in San Francisco via Honolulu on September 1." So Bunji learned that he was to be a student at Berkeley and would leave for America on his nineteenth birthday!

On August 10, the Councilor called Bunji into his office and handed him "a farewell gift" saying, "I'm going back home for the Obon festival to see my parents and pay respect to my ancestors, so I'll give you this now." Bunji was very surprised to find three crisp new 1,000-yen notes in the envelope the Councilor handed him. The extremely generous gift was as big as the sum of the wages he had been cheated out of for his work at the beer warehouse!

Bunji worked until Friday and then got ready for his long journey. He sold all his textbooks at the student cooperative. He threw away his ragged high school uniform and tattered underwear. He washed his one decent pair of pants, frayed a bit at the bottom, but they didn't look too bad after he borrowed his landlady's iron. These he packed into the blue suitcase Mrs. Nitta had given him when he left for Tokyo. He added an extra shirt and an extra set of underwear. He would wear a new pair of pants and shirt along with his new sneakers, all of which he had purchased with the gift from the Councilor.

Though he debated a little, he put in the copy of the Japanese translation of *Das Kapital* by Marx—a gift from the restaurant owner "to prevent Koyama-kun from becoming an imperialist capitalist." Still, the suitcase was far from full, but these were all of Bunji's worldly belongings he considered worth taking to his new life in the U.S.

On Saturday, he made a long distance call to Okagami-kun to tell him he was going to America. His friend gave Bunji two very sad pieces of news. One was the death of Mr. Iguchi, the math teacher who had gotten him admitted to Ashiya High. The other was the death of Yamashiro-kun who had gone to Tokyo with Bunji to take the entrance examination for Tokyo University but failed. Okagami said, "I think he jumped in front of a train even though his family said he was pushed by someone. The poor guy, I heard, had a nervous breakdown while attending a cram school." Bunji couldn't help but think how deplorable and meaningless Yamashiro-kun's death was, just because he received a few points less in the entrance examination than Bunji had.

On his last night in Tokyo, Bunji took the remainder of the Councilor's gift and treated Mori to dinner in thanks for telling him about the notice about the scholarship. It was meant to be a happy occasion, but Mori was morose at the thought that he was being left behind in a Japan where "a lot of people still live in shacks without adequate heat or even running water, and eating food you don't want anybody else to see," while Bunji was going to enjoy living in "the golden state of California." Mori listed the wonders that Bunji would enjoy, ranging from dinners of beefsteak to flush toilets and running hot water. "And you'll even have what they call central heating, though I don't understand how you can make an entire house warm without big stoves or fireplaces." Far from celebrating, Bunji had to spend their time together trying to cheer his friend up.

SHORTLY AFTER 6 ON THE MORNING OF MONDAY, AUGUST 17, with a cloudless sky promising a beautiful summer day, Bunji boarded a commuter train headed for the port of Yokohama. His mind was a jumble of thoughts. Why had Americans elected a former general for their president? What kind a town would Berkeley be? After Stalin died in March, the Japanese stock market had crashed and now, with a ceasefire ending the fighting of the Korean War, the Japanese economy was heading for a serious recession. What's going to happen to Japan now?

But by the time Bunji arrived at the port and was walking toward the pier where the SS *President McKinley* was docked, he was scarcely aware of the fresh sea breeze and was no longer thinking of the American president or the future of the Japanese economy. As he came in sight of the giant ship, he became so exhilarated that he thought his heart would burst. He really was about to embark on what he was sure would be his life's most decisive adventure far across the Pacific Ocean. He was almost dizzy with so many dreams and a vague anxiety.

Chapter 5

Berkeley, 1953-57

B UNJI FELT AS IF HE HAD ARRIVED IN THE U.S. the minute he stepped aboard the SS *President McKinley* and was welcomed in English by five smiling ship's officers in white uniforms who were lined up on the deck. The *President McKinley* was certainly not the *Bungo Maru*. The huge ship seemed at least ten times as large, and the cheerful, voluble, and confident passengers, most of them American military and their families, were very different from the dispirited and silent Japanese fleeing for home back in 1943. And the food! It reminded Bunji of sumptuous Western meals he had once eaten with his father at a very large hotel in Hong Kong, where his father had gone on business and had taken Bunji along to celebrate his sixth birthday. It was nothing like the meager, unappetizing and watery fare on the *Bungo Maru!* All this despite the fact that he was traveling third class.

As third-class passengers, Bunji and Peter had bunks in a large cabin down in the bowels of the ship. It contained four bunk beds of three tiers each, and Bunji made sure he got a top bunk. Lockers were located at one end of the room, and there were two small, round portholes no larger than a person's face. They opened inward to let in fresh air, and at least it was possible to see whether it was day or night, stormy or clear. Though spartan, the quarters were clean, and Bunji was surprised when, halfway through the voyage, the sheets were changed. No one he knew in Japan changed sheets after only a week.

Like most other people, Bunji became seasick from the rolling of the ship, but he ate very little so he wasn't rushing to the lavatory like other people. By the third day, he found he could eat again and began to enjoy himself. Three times a day he made his way along a bridge next to the ship's engines to the mess hall for third-class passengers. There, served on china plates, was all the food that Bunji could consume. At almost all meals, he ate so many juicy California oranges— once as many as five—that the steward finally plunked an entire bowl of them in front of Bunji. In the final days of his two weeks at sea, Bunji realized that he had gained at least two, possibly three kilos, from eating—overeating—so much bacon, sausages, grilled pork chops, and white bread. After almost ten years of suffering from almost constant want of food and even near starvation, Bunji understood why he was rather piggish. He could count on one hand the number of times he had eaten until he was overfull in Japan.

At the same time that Bunji began to feel normal, he realized he had time to himself—leisure he had not had in years—and he was eager to find something to do. He found the small dayroom for third-class passengers full of people reading old magazines and paperbacks. Most of the others in his cabin were older Japanese in their thirties and forties and Americans of various ages who clearly had little interest in talking to him. So Bunji spent most of his time talking to Peter, sitting together on Peter's bottom bunk.

Both boys went up to the open deck during the hours of the day they were allowed there. They could use the second-class passenger deck for two hours in the morning and another hour in the late afternoon. They carried on their most serious discussions in Japanese, but up on deck where nearly all the people around them were talking in English, Peter spoke mostly in English to Bunji.

Bunji found talking to Peter stimulating, but their conversations also revealed to him how much he had to learn. Peter was a Quaker born near Vancouver, where his family had a dairy farm. His father gave up the farm and returned to Japan in 1939, shortly after the Germans invaded Poland, because his father believed "it was only a matter of time before Japanese, the citizens of an Axis Power, would become unwelcome in Canada." Peter had gone to middle school and high school in Kyoto, then to Tokyo University. Bunji was sure Peter was a genius. His English sounded to Bunji's ears like that of a native speaker, and Bunji learned that Peter read books in French as well. Bunji was fascinated when Peter spoke of the works of French sociologists, which had inspired him to become a sociologist.

But Bunji found he could hold his own with Peter when they debated the main causes of and possible solutions to serious social problems, especially the poverty of so many people around the world. Peter firmly believed that poverty was the outcome of innate disadvantages in intellectual or physical abilities, lack of education, inadequate self-discipline, and various misfortunes. Thus, poverty could not be eliminated, but only be mitigated by education, both moral and utilitarian, and the goodwill of society in the form of increased individual charity, plus public policy to provide various types of "safety nets" for the poor. Bunji found Peter's view superficial and condescending to the poor, saying that Peter blamed poverty on the poor themselves.

Bunji argued that poverty, more often than not, resulted from political-economic realities, such as the exploitation of workers, unequal educational and other opportunities, and tax and other policies that favored the rich. Thus the solution for eliminating poverty and its attendant social ills required not only improved educational and occupational opportunities for the poor, but also the adoption of much more progressive income and inheritance taxes than those found in rich countries. Bunji said Peter wanted only to mitigate poverty, not eradicate it as much as possible. In one heated session he went so far as to accuse Peter of seeing poverty only from the perspective of someone who grew up in a comfortable middle-class family with no real comprehension of what it was like to be poor.

These arguments on poverty frequently turned to a discussion of political economic systems, or Marxism versus Capitalism. In these discussions, the better-read Peter could frequently present more articulate analyses of the strengths and weaknesses of both ideologies than Bunji could. Peter said he was aware of the excesses of capitalism—monopolies and "big business always trying to buy government'— but he abhorred even more the excesses of Marxism—"what happened under Stalin and what is happening today in China." Bunji responded that while he didn't consider himself either a socialist or a communist, he did think capitalism had gone too far and argued that capitalists already controlled the supposedly democratically elected governments of the U.S., the U.K., Japan and other industrialized nations.

But Bunji and Peter didn't spend all their time debating political and economic issues. Leaning on the rail and looking out over the sea to the horizon, they would talk about their dreams and hopes for the future. Peter was conflicted about what he should do when he completed his studies in Chicago. Should he return to Japan or go back to Canada where he had been born and lived as a child? "I know Mr. Siegrist hoped we would become internationalists, but he also seemed to assume that we would return to Japan. But I'm not sure I belong in Japan. And I left Canada when I was so young that I'm not sure I belong in Canada either."

Although Bunji hadn't really thought about what he'd do in the future, he was increasingly aware that he was thinking of the possibility of staying on in the U.S. and not returning to Japan. He thought his having an immigration visa could be a sign that karma was giving him leeway to decide whether his future would be in Japan or in the U.S. He had no idea how he would live after graduating from Berkeley and what he would do if he did stay on. But he thought a lot about his future while on the ship.

One of the highlights of the voyage was their arrival in Honolulu on the eighth day. From the deck, Bunji could see green hills in the distance. At last, he was going to see America, but as the ship drew close enough for Bunji to smell the fragrant warm air, he was reminded of the days when he went running on the bank of the Chao Phraya, which the boys just called *menum*, meaning "river."

Japanese nationals were not allowed to disembark because they were to undergo immigration procedures to enter the U.S. in San Francisco. Several people who looked Japanese went down the gangway, but Bunji was told they were Japanese-Americans who lived in Hawaii. That night at dinner, Bunji had his first taste of real American ice cream, which had been loaded along with other supplies. He loved the rich coconut flavor, which he hadn't tasted since he left Bangkok.

A couple of days out of Hawaii, a Japanese-looking woman—slender and attractive—surprised Bunji by suddenly addressing him in English: "Hi, I just boarded in Honolulu, and I heard you and your friend talking in English. He was speaking like a native speaker and you were making yourself understood, though you often searched for words and, at times, mangled English grammar. Not bad. In no time, you'll do fine. Where did you learn to speak like that?" So began the first of a number of chats Bunji had with Lisa Higashiguchi. From her English and her straightforward manner, he wasn't surprised to learn she had been born on a sugar plantation on Maui. Her parents had named her Hanako, but in school, she had renamed herself Lisa because "Hanako is such an old-fashioned name." She was now on her way to Oakland to meet her fiancé who was starting a dental practice there.

In one of these "chats" with Lisa, she asked how much money he had in dollars. Bunji had to tell her that he had none, and only a couple hundred yen. Even though he was to be met when the ship docked, she worried about his having no money even to make a phone call or take a bus to Berkeley should something go wrong. On the last day of the voyage, she handed Bunji five dollars "just in case." Bunji gratefully accepted the very first American money he had ever held in his hand. Looking at the face of President Lincoln on the face of the five-dollar bill, he knew he was ever closer to the U.S.

THE SITE OF THE GOLDEN GATE BRIDGE UNDER A BLUE SKY glittering in the morning sun was simply spectacular. Loudly blowing its whistle twice, the *President McKinley* docked at Pier 57 in San Francisco. American passengers, some of them shouting at the top of their lungs to friends and family members on the pier, descended the gangway first, and then about 30 Japanese followed. The Japanese were led to a separate room for processing, and within half an hour, Bunji and Peter had their documents checked and were welcomed to the United States by an immigration officer.

On September 1, 1953, Bunji walked out into a bright California day with his future before him. He wanted to say something to Peter, but no words came out. He was too overwhelmed by the realization he was now in America.

A tall, blond man in his late twenties walked up to the boys and introduced himself. "My name is David Mathews. I'm helping Mr. Siegrist. He sent me your photos, so you must be Peter Shimada, and you...Michael Koyama."

The switch from being called Bunji to being known as Michael punctuated the feeling that he had begun a new life.

David said that he was to take Peter to the train station to put him on his train to Chicago, and then drive Michael to Berkeley. After dropping off Peter, David, Mathews, and Bunji set off for Berkeley. When Bunji, now Michael, addressed the American as Mr. Mathews, he was corrected. "Call me David. We think first names are friendlier."

In later years, when people asked him what surprised him most about the U.S. when he first arrived, his reply was, "Everyone calls everyone else by their first name. Even if they have just met, and even if one person is older than the other." In Bunji's high school, no one but his closest male friends had called him by his given name. To his teachers and most students, he was known as Koyama-kun.

Arriving at the International House in Berkeley, David handed Michael over to a tall Indian student in a turban and bade him goodbye. The student showed Michael around the large two-story building known as "I House," where about an equal number—about fifty each—of foreign and American students lived. After sternly warning Michael never to go into the girls' section, he took Michael to his room.

Though the room Michael was assigned was small by American standards as he later realized, it had a bed, a small desk, a chair, and a lamp, plus one window. He was delighted, thinking how much better it was going to be sleeping on this bed than in a cramped bakery oven in Ashiya, or on the thin futon on the *tatami* of his room in Tokyo. With a door that locked, he would have his own private space, something he had not had anywhere in Japan, certainly not in the orphanage dormitory nor even in the lodging in Tokyo where only a thin sliding door separated his space from his landlady's. Suddenly the realization that he was in America to study hit him. His father had always said to study was the most important thing in life, and it was what he himself so passionately wanted to do. He sat down at his desk and looked out the window where he could see a single cloud in the sky. Everything that was happening was almost too amazing for him to take in. Almost in a daze, he stared at the cloud as it moved across the sky.

At dinnertime, reality set in. Michael went down to the cafeteria and through the line. The server asked which vegetable he wanted, and Michael replied, "pea." The server put exactly one pea on his plate, saying, "as you requested." Michael was perplexed. Then, smiling broadly, the server added a generous spoonful to Michael's plate. This brought home to him that plurals really were important in everyday English, not just on English exams. What a nuisance! Japanese, like Thai, had no plural forms to worry about.

Michael had been fairly confident about his English ability before his arrival in Berkeley. Hadn't he learned how to hold simple conversations in the settlement school and with Anna, read a good chunk of *Gone with the Wind* on his own, excelled in English in high school, and passed the English exam for Tokyo University? Even Lisa Higashiguchi had praised his English. He knew he couldn't converse the way Peter could, but he had expected to have few problems with English in everyday life. However, in the days following his arrival, Michael found the English spoken by people he met in shops and even by other students was very difficult to understand. He now realized that on the *President McKinley,* the staff and others he had spoken with were speaking to him carefully, knowing he wasn't fully fluent. Years later, he still remembered his first encounter with slapdash American English at a lunch counter in Berkeley:

"Whaddayawan, Mac? You gonna have da special?"

Not really comprehending the question, Michael had tried to order spaghetti with meatballs, but much to his surprise, an enormous hamburger topped by a fried egg was plopped down in front of him in a portion so large that it could easily have satisfied three undernourished students at Tokyo University.

Michael soon realized that not only did he have a language to learn, but a new culture as well. The America he faced daily in Berkeley was very different from what he had imagined from what his father had told him, what he had learned from books and the mass media, and from the Americans he had known in Thailand. And his new cultural experiences included one that was quite unpleasant. He was introduced to hard liquor.

Some residents of I House—two Americans and an Icelandic student—said that Michael should see something of San Francisco, and he joined the three of them in an excursion to the city. The four took a bus in and toured such places as Fisherman's Wharf and Ghiradelli Square, ending the evening in a bar. One American student ordered a Manhattan—how could a geographic location be a drink, Michael wondered. Another ordered a whiskey. The only alcohol that Michael had ever tasted was beer and some ceremonial sake at New Year's. He was leery of hard liquor, so when the Icelandic student ordered an Irish coffee, Michael ordered the same, thinking it sounded safe. He found it delicious. Feeling very good, he had a second. Then the whiskey hit him. Michael had no idea there was any hard liquor in the coffee drink. It didn't take long before Michel began to feel like his head was exploding and his heart beating like a drum played by a crazed drummer.

The next thing Michael knew was that it was daylight and he was curled up in the bottom of a tall, narrow box with windows. He felt dreadful. He looked up and discovered that he was in a telephone booth. Somehow, asking many questions about where to catch buses and ending up taking a circuitous route, he made his way back to Berkeley and I House. Later in the day, the Icelandic student came to his room to find out how Michael was and to apologize. He was newly arrived himself and he had been astonished at the effect what he considered a small amount of whiskey had on Michael.

"We were all surprised how you got so drunk on so little alcohol. Matt and Doug decided to leave you in the telephone booth to sleep it off. I felt bad but I had to agree—you were so out of it that we couldn't possibly get you back to Berkeley on the bus and so we tried to put you someplace where you would be safe until you woke up." Neither of the American students ever apologized or mentioned the incident.

Then classes began. Michael signed up for required courses in English and science—he chose chemistry—plus economics and German. The lectures were nothing like listening to the English spoken in one-to-one conversations on an expected or everyday topic. To Michael's ears, they came in a torrent, giving him no time to puzzle over unfamiliar words or concepts. During his first two semesters, he found he could pretty much follow lectures in mathematics, chemistry, and economics, because the professors wrote equations, technical notations, diagrams, and tables on the blackboard, but, very frequently, lectures in philosophy, the social sciences, and history left him wondering how much he really understood of what the professor had said. His first year was the most difficult because of all the hours he had to spend preparing for lectures and examinations, which robbed him of sleep, just as working in the bakery and delivering newspapers once had.

As time passed, he became aware that learning in English was becoming easier, almost exponentially, and he enjoyed his final two years at Berkeley enormously. He always took the maximum number of credit hours allowed without paying additional tuition—18 units. As he completed the required courses in English and other subjects, he took more and more classes in his major, economics. He found particularly stimulating a professor of macroeconomics, Dr. Solomon Minsky, from whom he took three courses. In addition, he took courses in political science, history, and philosophy, plus some Russian—a popular language because of the Cold War. He also continued to study German, and by his senior year, he was reading on his own Goethe's *Die Leiden des Junge Werthers,* hoping someday he would meet someone like Werther's Charlotte who would become the love of his life.

Although Michael spent nearly all of his time studying as hard as he could during his four years at Berkeley, he also learned about life in America. Every time he thought he now understood American culture, something would come up that baffled him. During his freshman year, it was the McCarthy hearings that perplexed and even worried him. He watched some of the hearings in the Common Room at I House, most often with Stuart Stein, a graduate student in political science. All but a few of the American students watching with him were very critical of Senator McCarthy, but Stuart was particularly vehement in his criticism.

"He's a fascist! That's what he is. He blames all the policy failures of the U.S and the rising strength of the USSR on Americans he calls communists without any evidence! What happened to the Bill of Rights?"

Most Berkeley students were as appalled by the hearings as Stuart and Michael, but from what Michael read in the newspapers and from what was said in the hearings, he was afraid that many Americans supported the views expressed by Senator McCarthy and his allies. Michael thought there was the danger, as had happened in Germany and Japan, that people might be persuaded to "support" leaders who would turn the U.S. into something like a fascist country. He fervently hoped that he was wrong, but what he heard on television gnawed at him for months.

One day Michael ran into Stuart on Telegraph Avenue near Sather gate. Stuart had an invitation for him: "Next Monday, those of us who are against the McCarthy hearings and what the House Un-American Activities Committee is doing are holding a meeting. Why not join us? You don't like these fascists, so you might enjoy meeting my friends."

Michael was curious but he was still struggling to prepare for his classes and so declined the invitation, but Stuart insisted on getting his room number and the number of the telephone on his floor of I House so that he could contact him for future meetings. Michael gave Stuart the information he asked for, an act he was to regret four years later.

BY MICHAEL'S SECOND SEMESTER, he had another concern besides his schoolwork and American politics. The scholarship allowance, calculated on the assumption that each fellow would receive supplementary help from his own family, was inadequate. And most worrying, he wasn't able to save the money he would need to tide him over the summer months when he wouldn't receive the monthly stipend. Though he had an immigration visa and was legally permitted to work, he didn't know who would want to give him a summer job, and there were few available in the early fifties. He ate the simplest possible lunches, often buying bread and fruit at a grocery store, with only the occasional indulgence of a nineteen-cent hamburger, but his few clothes were nearly worn out, and there were always books he wanted to buy. He needed more than his $100-a-month stipend.

One spring day, while he had been racking his brain about how to make some money, he was on his way to his German class, which was held outside the main campus area. As he walked down a residential street, Michael saw a plump, gray-haired lady struggling to mow the lawn in front of a large three-story house. Suddenly he had an idea.

"Excuse me, Ma'am...I wonder if I could help you. If I said I would mow your lawn for, say a dollar an hour, would you be interested?"

She stopped, looked at him somewhat suspiciously, and said, mopping her forehead. "My son used to do this, but he went away to medical school." She looked long and hard at Michael and finally said, "Okay, I'll try you out. For one dollar an hour, and weed the flower beds and trim the bushes as well in two hours max."

A few days later Michael came on a Saturday morning and tended Mrs. Samuel Pritchard's yard in less than two hours. She pronounced herself "very satisfied" and hired Michael on a regular basis.

Within a few weeks of starting what Michael thought of as a simple weekly work-cum-exercise session, his enterprise took an unexpected and profitable turn. Mrs. Pritchard told her neighbors and friends at church how pleased she was with her "Japanese gardener." One thing led to another. These friends had their own friends, each of whom wanted Michael to mow her lawn on a regular basis. Some of them also wanted Michael to weed, trim bushes, and even plant some flowers. After finding it impossible to handle more than four yards per week without seriously compromising his studies, he decided to "hire" three "Japanese" gardeners: one Japanese and two Chinese acquaintances from I House. Michael was very much aware that Mrs. Pritchard and her friends wanted Japanese, known in California for being good gardeners and farmers, but he also knew that few of his customers could tell the difference between Japanese and Chinese. All of the students agreed to work *with* Michael for eighty cents an hour.

Michael had thought that getting twenty cents for each hour that his "employees" worked would be a nice easy profit. As a child, he had helped his father's gardener in Bangkok, as he was fascinated with the mower and liked to trim bushes. But his three "employees" had all grown up in large cities and had no idea how to care for a garden. He found he had to teach his employees how to tend a yard, and check up on the work, and do the more difficult tasks himself. He learned that an entrepreneur makes money by earning it.

An incident one Saturday taught Michael another lesson about American society. Mrs. Pritchard asked Michael, "Before you start mowing, please move the Chevy so I can get the hose out of the garage."

Michael went to the back of the house and searched for a "sheh-vie," both in the garage and all around it. His best guess was that it was some kind of a tool he had never heard of. After ten minutes of an unsuccessful search, he reported his failure to find the "sheh-vie."

"What do you mean you can't find it?"

"I looked for it all over, even behind the garage."

"The car is gone?" Mrs. Pritchard was shocked.

"The car? A sheh-vie is a car?"

She gasped and let out a huge laugh of relief. "Oh, dear, you didn't know a Chevy is a Chevrolet?" Then she dissolved into laughter.

Michael had never considered that anyone would ask him to move a car. Why would she think that he knew how to drive or had a license? He learned that Americans thought everyone knew how to drive. And that they were willing to let someone else drive their expensive automobiles.

Michael's "Japanese Yard Service" flourished, and he continued it until the end of his junior year when he sold it to a Japanese graduate student, who was the son of a landscape gardener in Shizuoka. Michael had decided that he needed extra time for his senior thesis on the economic growth of Asian countries, which he was writing under Professor Minsky. By then he had sufficient savings to see him through his final year at Berkeley, and the student agreed to buy "the business rights of the Japanese Yard Service" for fifty dollars, which made the decision to give it up easier.

MICHAEL'S FIRST SUMMER IN THE U.S. was such a hodgepodge of experiences, that in later life he couldn't remember when he had done what. He took a camping trip around California with two friends from I House, the Icelandic student and a German student who had an old beat-up VW. Michael enjoyed seeing the redwoods, Sugarloaf Mountain, and a number of other places whose names he couldn't recall. Sometime during that same summer, Michael also spent a week at a Bible camp.

Jim Sanders, an American graduate student living in I House, had invited him to the camp. Michael was attracted by the opportunity to visit the beautiful coastal city of La Jolla, and the fact that he would be fed and housed for free, as much as by the opportunity to learn more about the importance of Christianity in American life and culture. He was also curious because he knew Jim's religion was important to him in a way no religion was important to Japanese university students.

During the long drive down the beautiful, coastal highway, Jim talked knowledgably but almost continuously of how Christianity was the religious foundation of Europe and the U.S., and how it had shaped their culture. Although there was much Michael learned from Jim's erudite talk, Michael wondered if he ever thought of other parts of the world, or about Buddhism and Islam. To Michael, Jim's tone often sounded arrogant, and this feeling grew stronger during the retreat where Jim was clearly in his own milieu.

The retreat was attended by nearly forty people ranging from college students to people in their fifties and older, but everyone except Michael was Caucasian. The days were filled with prayer sessions, Bible reading and discussions, testimonials, sermons, hymn singing, and simple meals eaten in a warm and congenial atmosphere. Everyone was very friendly toward Michael, but they were also very persistent in trying to find out what he believed, and when he admitted that he wasn't a Christian, the older among them did their best to persuade him to "accept the Lord as your Savior."

Michael spent the days at the camp feeling strange and even detached because he didn't really have a religion. His father hadn't believed in any religion, his amah had taught him a little about Buddhism in daily conversations, Mama Cheung believed in karma, and the German priests, who ran the settlement school, had made no attempt to convert him to Catholicism. What he found in Japan was that people practiced the rites of both Shinto and Buddhism without any feeling of conflict. Moreover, he had had no friend at either high school or university who was religious.

But at the retreat, Michael was told that the only true religion was evangelical Christianity. Though he was impressed by the sincerity of these people, he was a little surprised by their passion in "bringing God to all corners of the world." Why did these Christians expect people to reject all other ways of thought or religious experience? Why should all the Thais and Japanese he knew be consigned to a Christian hell?

It was also during that first summer in the U.S. that Michael decided he had to decrease his living expenses so he could worry less about earning money. He would have two more summers without a living stipend but with rent to pay and food to buy. And the season for yard work was mostly from May to October, so he couldn't count on that money in the winter. He asked around, and in the same way that he found the notice in Tokyo of the William Foundation's scholarship, so did he find a new place to live by a friend telling him about a posting on a bulletin board.

A small residential hotel near the campus, the Ivanhoe, was looking for someone to act as a residential manager in exchange for a room. Michael applied and, somewhat to his surprise, he was accepted, but the owner told him that most Berkeley students didn't want to handle trash disposal, sweep the front sidewalk, and call a plumber when necessary. The job suited Michael as it took very little of his time and got him a room that was larger and less spartan than his room at I House. It even had two windows.

One unexpected bonus of living at the Ivanhoe was the people he met who stayed there. One was Miss Heath, a retired English teacher living in the hotel. She took Michael under her wing and helped him with his English in the essays and term papers he was assigned. She gave him an English dictionary, which he used for years until it finally fell apart. He also remembered having a number of conversations with the famous Chinese educator and former Ambassador to the U.S., Hu Shih, who was giving a series of lectures at the university.

MICHAEL EXPECTED HIS SECOND SUMMER TO BE MUCH LIKE HIS FIRST, but in April of his sophomore year, an invitation came from the Siegrists to spend the summer in Chicago with them. Mr. Siegrist's letter said the invitation was a "reward for the stellar grades" Michael earned during his first three semesters at Berkeley. Michael gladly accepted the invitation, and Mr. Siegrist mailed him a round-trip train ticket from San Francisco to Chicago. Michael arranged for a student from Hong Kong to take over his job at the Ivanhoe for the summer.

Michael set out for Chicago on the two-day train ride. As he traversed nearly two-thirds of the American continent, through interminable fields, over the Rocky Mountains, and along the Mississippi River, Michael recalled what his father once said: "America is a large and rich country. Japan cannot hope to win a war against such a country."

Mr. and Mrs. Siegrist were most kind and put Michael up in the second-floor room that had been their son's. Michael was awed by the posh lifestyle of the Siegrists, though they thought of it as merely "comfortable." In fact, it was much more luxurious than his father's in Bangkok. Like his father, they had a large house with live-in servants, though the grounds were smaller. The Siegrists' house not only had central heating which was standard in Chicago in the fifties, but also central air-conditioning, wall-to-wall carpeting, and two full bathrooms plus a powder-room, which Michael knew was not the norm for middle-class families.

This was the first time Michael had lived in an American home. He was well aware that the Siegrists' standard of living was higher than average, but still it shocked him at times to see how they lived. He couldn't see why anyone would want such thick carpeting. He couldn't understand why lights were left on in rooms with no one in them, and he was almost appalled by the amount of food that was thrown out. The American lifestyle seemed wasteful to Michael's eyes.

Michael very much enjoyed his stay with the Siegrists. Free from studies and yard-work, he had all the free time he could ever wish for. To his delight, Mrs. Siegrist took him to the local library and got a card for him so he could take out all the books he could carry. Mr. Siegrist took him to see the main office of his feed and grain business, and invited him to a dinner party they were hosting at their country club. He proudly introduced Michael to his friends, saying:

"This is Michael Koyama, one of our boys. We are very proud at how well he is doing at Berkeley. When he reported his grades to us after his first semester, he told my wife that he had gotten a B in English. She said, 'That's wonderful. I hope all your other grades are almost as good.' And do you know what he told her? 'Yes, I got two As and one A-.' And now he's getting straight As."

Michael was embarrassed at this introduction, but pleased that he was justifying Mr. Siegrist's decision to grant him a scholarship.

The Siegrists' country club was an entirely new experience for Michael. Located on the shore of Lake Michigan, it had two very large dining halls, a tennis court, a large pool, and a room full of leather furniture that Mr. Siegrist called "the smoking and card room." If the elegance of the clubhouse and the lavish dinner served surprised him, what shocked him was something no one thought he would even notice.

All of the waiters were Negroes, whereas the members of the club were all white. It didn't surprise Michael that the employees were Negro, but what did shock him was how the club members treated them. Even Mrs. Siegrist, whom Michael found so considerate and warm, was curt and almost haughty in addressing the waiters, and Michael could hear others at nearby tables speaking to the servers in arrogant, condescending tones. In the conversation in the lounge following dinner, one of the topics was "the Negro problem" but the discussion was carried out in code so the conversation wouldn't sound offensive, at least to their own ears. Negroes were referred to as "those living on the South Side" or "the new arrivals"; they couldn't help what they did because of "their southern tradition or upbringing"; and "their blood" determined how well they waited on tables.

Michael couldn't help wondering how this could be. Hadn't a century passed since the end of the Civil War that he had read about in *Gone with the Wind?* The members of the country club were professional, well-educated, and, he thought, good and respectable people. But there was absolutely no denying that, without anyone of them being self-conscious or even aware of it, they were racists. Michael wondered if Mrs. Pritchard in Berkeley spoke of her "Japanese gardeners" in a similar fashion using a set of code words. But the Japanese in Ashiya had talked about the *burakumin* and Koreans in much the same way white American talked about Negroes. He remembered how his landlady in Tokyo had warned him of the racial discrimination he would find in the U.S. He began to realize that discrimination and racism were deeply rooted in the history and culture of every country and that any comparison of the treatment of minority groups in the U.S and Japan had to be made very carefully.

Michael was suddenly aware that he had not thought about discrimination and racism since he had arrived in Berkeley mainly because his life there—both at I House and on campus—was removed from the real world. I House in particular, and the university as a whole, had a large number of foreign students of all races and ethnicities. True, students from the same country or the same race tended to congregate, but Michael had never thought of this as a manifestation of discrimination or racism that somehow had an ugly or sinister intent. Michael decided that he wanted to learn more about race relations and how the Negroes lived.

He began to spend time at the country club where he had guest privileges, courtesy of the Siegrists. But instead of lolling around the pool, he made friends with the waiters by helping them move tables and otherwise set up for events, and he gave a hand in the kitchen as well. The manager—Mr. Hogg, whose name Michael thought so funny—took a liking to what he saw as a helpful boy and after a couple of weeks suggested that Michael work for pay as a temporary employee when they needed extra help. Michael was delighted as it meant that during the coming academic year he wouldn't have to debate between buying a book he wanted or eating better. The mostly Negro staff enjoyed having him help, particularly as none of them had even met a Japanese before Michael. They turned out to be as curious about him as he was about them, but they quickly got used to this boy with an offbeat sense of humor who had originally volunteered to help without any thought of pay.

Michael never felt an object of curiosity in Berkeley with all its foreign students and living in California with so many Asians, but he was finding the Midwest different. One Saturday Mr. Siegrist invited Michael to accompany him when he went to collect a side of beef from the tenant of a farm he owned in southern Illinois, and do some other business. They left at five in the morning for the long drive across the state. While Mr. Siegrist went to check on a grain supplier in the small town of Keokuk, just across the border into Iowa, Michael wandered around the center of town, deserted in the midday sun. Suddenly he heard giggling behind him. He looked around and saw three little boys and a smaller girl, all no more than seven or eight.

One boy shouted: "Are you from China?"

Michael answered, "No, from Japan."

"You don't look like the Japanese I saw in my father's magazine. They all have very thick eyeglasses and all their upper teeth stick out. Like this," and he gestured with his fingers behind his front teeth.

Michael told the children that that was wartime propaganda, and then he had to explain what propaganda was. "I am what Japanese really look like."

The children nodded and Michael waved goodbye and walked on. He recalled seeing around 1944 some posters of American military men on the walls of the Asagaya train station. In one poster, a soldier and a sailor with bloodshot, wicked-looking eyes and unnaturally long noses were pictured thrusting their bayonets into the four Japanese islands painted at the upper-left corner of the poster. Two characters, which read *shin-koku,* "God's Nation," were superimposed on the islands.

That evening, when Michael was enjoying the juicy steak that the Siegrists cook broiled for them, he thought back over the day with the ride through endless plains, like an ocean of corn and soybean fields, and the enormous cows on the farms. He reflected, "No wonder the American soldiers I saw in Tokyo were so big and well fed!" He looked over at the Siegrists' faces and saw amusement on Mrs. Siegrist's. She remarked:

"I never thought you would like steak so much. I thought we would have to buy fish especially for you—that's what we were told Japanese eat."

Rather to Michael's surprise, he ended up spending a second summer in Chicago. One of Mr. Siegrist's neighbors, a Mr. John Bloemveld, offered Michael a summer job at his large flower shop on State Street in the downtown "Loop" area. He had heard about how helpful Michael had been at the country club, talked to Mr. Siegrist, and phoned Michael, telling him, "We can use a hard-working young man who comes from a country of flower lovers just like Holland, where my grandfather was born." The Siegrists readily agreed to let Michael stay with them for another summer. Mr. Siegrist had said, "You were certainly no trouble. Either you were out of the house or in your room with your nose in a book."

Michael never knew why, but he always remembered everyone who worked at Bloemveld's Flowers and all their names, long after he had forgotten the names of many professors and friends. At the flower shop, he had been assigned to the Wedding and Banquet Team, consisting of four employees. Michael's job was to help Mrs. Lucille Marshall, who was an expert corsage maker and head of the team. There were also two "flower arrangers": Miss Edna Harrison, a spinster in her late thirties and attractive but somehow pale and "wilted," and Otto Bremmer, thirty-four years old, always smiling and humming, and weighing, Michael guessed, no less than 300 pounds. The final member was Rufus Washington, a fifty-ish, reticent black man who did all the "heavy lifting" and deliveries.

Michael quickly fitted into the team and enjoyed the work. On his third day in the shop, Lucille, while constantly chatting about her grandchildren, taught him how to make corsages for a big wedding she was working on. By late afternoon, she found that Michael could already turn out corsages made with calla lilies, alyssum, and white roses.

Rufus said little in the shop, but Michael had many conversations with him because Rufus was "assigned" by Mr. Bloemveld to pick him up from the Siegrists' each morning and take him back after work. By the end of Michael's third week, he was frequently eating lunch with Rufus. As the weeks passed, Rufus became less reticent and surprised Michael by telling him that he had a son attending the University of Kansas, and that during the war, he himself had served in Italy as a sergeant.

One day at lunchtime, Michael got up his nerve and haltingly asked Rufus:

"Rufus, you are the first person of your race I have become well acquainted with...I mean talked to and became friendly with...so, I hope you will permit me to ask you something without taking offense...Don't you get angry knowing if you were white, you could've had a different kind of a job, a better job? I mean you are intelligent and hard working, but the kind of work you do here...."

Rufus was silent for a while. Then he answered Michael in a quiet and deliberate voice. "I understand your question only too well. You mean if I was not a Negro, I could've had a better job, so am I resentful? I don't think about it...I stopped thinking like that many years ago. This is the way it's been for a long time and will be for many more years to come. The Supreme Court decision a couple of years ago, Brown v. The Board of Education of Topeka, saying that educational segregation is unconstitutional, is a start. But it's only a start. Do I resent discrimination? You bet I do...all the time...but I don't let it bother me too much...there's no point."

Michael and Rufus became good friends and regular lunch buddies. Midway through the summer, Lucille obliquely suggested to Michael that he should have lunch "with us" more often, not always with Rufus. Michael chose to ignore her suggestion. Several times Rufus invited Michael to his home on the south side of Chicago. Michael kept in touch with Rufus until the mid-sixties, when Rufus suddenly died after suffering a major heart attack.

DURING MICHAEL'S FIRST FOUR YEARS IN THE U.S., he worked harder than at any other time during his life. Berkeley was the premier university in California, admitting only the top high school graduates in California, and still the failure rate was 20 percent. Here was Michael, competing with extremely bright and well-prepared students with native English, and he could barely understand many of the lectures in his first two years. Furthermore, if he was going to keep his scholarship, he had to have not just passing grades, but a B average. And flunking out was not an option; he would not receive his fare back to Japan, and after his first year, he would no longer be able to go back to Tokyo University. Shocking him was the suicide of a science student from Kyoto University who couldn't make the grade at Berkeley and had hung himself in Strawberry Canyon. Michael knew he had to succeed.

When Michael looked back on his college years, he realized he hadn't made any close friends, had spent almost no time in leisure activities, and hadn't had a girlfriend. He had enjoyed some lighthearted moments, such as the evening at I House when he had won five dollars in a bet that he couldn't eat at one go an entire stick of butter, a quarter of a pound. That had been a nice windfall if rather hard on his digestion. But even at I House he knew he was considered a "grind," studying every hour of the day and long into the night. He used to sleep a few hours, get up, and study in the wee hours, and then sleep a couple more hours, a habit he continued the rest of his life.

Michael would rather have liked to have a girlfriend, but he had neither the money nor time for dating. Nor had he had a girlfriend back in Ashiya because Japanese high school students didn't date in the fifties. And in the U.S. in those years, it was the boys who asked out the girls, and it would have been up to him to find a girlfriend. When he listened during dinner at I House to students talking about dating, he came to the conclusion that the social mores and "rules" of dating were more difficult to comprehend than differentiating complex mathematical equations.

What might have been Michael's introduction to a romantic experience turned into a misadventure. During Michael's sophomore year, he met in his German class Priscilla Molsberger, a senior whom he frequently came across at the library. Priscilla suggested they review together, and so they met a few times during the semester. Then several days prior to the final exam, she suggested that Michael come to study at her apartment. The evening started off as usual, with a review of recent lessons, but Priscilla kept moving closer to him on the couch as if to better see what Michael was pointing at in the textbook. Next, he found her hand on his knee.

Warning bells started to go in Michael's head as Priscilla crammed herself next to him. Michael had absolutely no idea how to handle the situation he found himself in. He realized that Priscilla was coming on to him, but he had no desire for a relationship with her beyond studying together, and he didn't know how to extricate himself. When Priscilla jumped up, announcing that she would just go into the bedroom to "slip into something more comfortable," Michael made a dash for the bathroom to escape the only way he could think of. The apartment was on the ground floor, so Michael was able to crawl through the small window and jump to the ground without being seen. Priscilla never spoke to him again.

The long hours of study and self-discipline paid off. Michael received an A in every class he took except for the English class in his first semester. He was scheduled to graduate as "an academic senator"—the recognition given each year to the three students graduating with the highest grade point averages. With this academic record, everyone said that it would easy for Michael to continue his studies in graduate school.

And Michael very much wanted to go on in a Ph.D. program in economics. So he had a problem that kept surfacing in his mind, even as he spent every spare moment on his senior thesis. It was the draft notice that was sure to come because he had come to the U.S. on a Thai immigration visa, and had been required to sign up with the draft board for possible service in the army. In early May, a month before graduation, the notice arrived. Michael knew immigrants couldn't get waivers for going on to graduate school, which is why he hadn't applied to any Ph.D. programs. But even though he had expected the draft notice, its arrival was somehow momentous.

Should he serve in the American army? What would he have to do as a soldier? He had no idea, but America wasn't at war, and the Cold War didn't seem likely to turn into a hot one, so he didn't think he would have to worry about being killed. Serving would take two years from his life, but what would he do if he didn't serve in the army? He would have to leave the U.S., availing himself of the William Foundations' promise of a return ticket. But he now knew he didn't want to return to Japan. Returning to Thailand wasn't even a consideration. This being the case, the debate he was having with himself was meaningless.

When he thought about it, he realized that the idea of staying on in the U.S. had been in his mind almost from the moment he had been told he would be going on an immigration visa. If he went back to Japan, he knew he could find a good job almost anywhere with an American degree in economics. But he didn't want to go back because by now he was convinced that American society was more "open" and "welcoming" to him than Japanese society was ever likely to be.

What would his father have expected him to do? In a real sense, he would be following his father's footsteps if he took the risks to live the life he wanted to, just as his father had done, though it meant living in a country his father couldn't have imagined he would. Yes, he would follow his father's exhortation, "Live taking risks." Why not go into the army? He couldn't imagine what army life would be like for him, but it seemed the only path to his future. And he finally, and decisively, made up his mind.

Michael went to talk to a young man in the I House office who counseled students on their visa and immigration problems because his draft notice ordered him to report to Fort Ord two days before the graduation ceremony where he was to receive special recognition as a "senator." He very much wanted to attend. He asked if his induction could be postponed just long enough for him to attend graduation. The young man was anti-war and anti the draft, but familiar with draft notices. Michael thought he might help him. After giving Michael a long lecture on why Michael shouldn't serve in the army, he finally said he would call the draft board and Michael should come back in a day or two.

The young man did something Michael hadn't asked him to. Since he knew that Michael had entered the U.S. on a Thai immigration visa, he called the Thai Embassy. He learned that Michael could, if he chose, go back to Thailand to avoid the American draft. However, he would be required to serve in the Thai army, which conscripted males between the ages of 20 and 31. "But you would be a major because of your American B.A., and you'd be issued a pair of fine leather shoes. And you wouldn't have to worry about going to war for the U.S."

Michael politely explained his decision to the young man: "I want to go to graduate school in the U.S. so I will elect to be a private in the U.S. Army rather than a major in the Thai army, and I don't need shoes." He added, "By the way, if I were to go back to Thailand, I'd also have to serve in the military—what's the difference between that and the U.S. draft?"

Unfortunately, the young man hadn't followed up on Michael's request to have his induction postponed for a few days. And so Michael missed his ceremony. Sadly, he learned later that an extension of up to one month would certainly have been granted him, allowing him to join the next group of inductees.

And so, two days before graduation and after a farewell party of beer and chips at I House, Michael boarded an early morning bus to Fort Ord with fourteen other recruits. As the bus lumbered on to the beautiful Monterey Bay Peninsula, the sun began to shine through the windows of the bus. Michael had absolutely no idea what karma was awaiting him and, had he hazarded a guess, he would have been very wrong.

Chapter 6

Fort Ord, Fort Benning, and Fort Dix, 1957-58

R EAL BULLETS WERE FLYING ONLY A FOOT OR SO ABOVE MICHAEL'S HEAD. He could hear the whizzing sound of the bullets over the horrible, loud mechanical staccato rhythms of the machine guns a few hundred feet away. He was near exhaustion, and for the third or fourth time since "the real bullet exercise" had started at five that morning, he muttered, "What a dreadful karma this is." His shirt was soaking wet from sweat and his pants clung to his thighs from running through tall rain-soaked grass.

At the first sound of the bullets, he had thrown himself flat onto the damp field. Now he was inching on his elbows and knees towards the machine guns mounted on a raised concrete base. His progress was slowed by the heavy M-16 rifle he was cradling in his arms and by the sixty-pound backpack that weighed him down. His shoulders were in agony because every time he moved, the straps of his backpack ate into them. He felt a sharp pain in his knees as he crept forward on the ground and knew they must be bleeding. Did a Thai major have to go through this kind of experience?

Horst Heiduk crawling up behind him said: "Hey, Michael. You okay? Hang in there!" Michael numbly answered: "Yeah...."

In the morning, before this exercise had started, Captain Ingram, the CO of Michael's company, had said: "We end the seventh week of training giving you your one and only experience of getting shot at by live bullets. We want you to know what to expect if you ever end up on a real battlefield. This will make men of you guys. If you live through it, you'll have only one more week of Basic Training."

For Recruit Koyama, the past seven weeks had been a blur. When he arrived at Fort Ord, he had been issued a set of fatigues, underclothes, and a pair of military boots; a barber cut his hair so short his skull became visible; and he was assigned one of twenty-four bunks in a barracks. A new life had begun for him. It was one that nothing had prepared him for, not even all the hardships he had experienced in the orphanage, in Sannomiya, or in Ashiya.

The daily training tested how much Michael's body could stand. At the beginning, he had been confident that he could easily do everything the drill sergeant demanded of him. He thought himself physically fit thanks to running eight kilometers every morning to deliver newspapers while in high school, and in Berkeley, he had walked everywhere to save bus fares. Then on weekends, he had mowed lawns. When his high school had held ten-kilometer runs, Michael had always finished in the top six, even if earlier that same day he had run his paper route, which included some steep roads on the mountainside of Ashiya.

He very quickly found how badly mistaken he was. All this running had been too far in the past, and for the last four years, he had spent too many hours sitting in class and in the library. And the training programs, Michael came to believe, seemed to have been designed for the bigger and sturdier young high school grads, Americans 5'10" tall and weighing 180 pounds, not for someone like Michael, barely

5'7" and 135 pounds. The training was so punishing that Michael could sympathize with the recruit who snapped and went AWOL, only to be caught in a bar in Oakland almost dead drunk, eventually ending up in the brig.

But Michael had grimly persevered. He ran, climbed ropes, swam, did calisthenics, engaged in all types of "field exercises"—fighting mock battles and drilling in formation. He even managed to survive a ten-mile march "with full gear"—M-16 rifle and sixty-pound backpack.

However, when a second, even longer march was scheduled, this one for twenty miles, again with full gear, Michael knew from his experience of the last march that it would be foolhardy for him to attempt it. This time his "resourcefulness" had to intervene to prevent this impossible march his karma had come up with. As soon as he got up on the morning of the march, he ate two large Hershey bars. He ended up in the infirmary with a severe nosebleed that wouldn't stop and had to be excused from the march for medical reasons. He didn't tell the nurse captain that he had always been allergic to chocolate.

Michael also learned how to use an M-16, but he remained a poor marksman despite much practice and help from Horst Heiduk, a former policeman from Mannheim. This was the one test Michael was worried about failing, and he was extremely nervous on the morning of the test. He hoped to make the sixty points he needed to pass, but when the scores were read out, he had a solid seventy-six. Michael was so relieved that he gloated a bit in the mess hall that evening. "Horst, I got only fourteen points less than you. But what happened to you? I thought you would make 100 or at least 95?"

Horst replied, "How do you think you got a seventy-six? Were you so nervous that you didn't notice I was shooting next to you? After I was sure I had my ninety, I shot into your target. Instead of gloating, you owe me a *danke schön!*"

Michael returned the favor by explaining to Horst the pamphlets and books they were assigned to read for the lecture sessions on military justice, "the potential enemy"— meaning the Warsaw Pact nations—the identification and uses of military ordnance, and other subjects. Their conversations were in an ad hoc mélange of German and English they both enjoyed using.

In many ways, what surprised Michael most about the army was the life in the barracks. He was fascinated by the diverse group of young men assigned to his barracks, ranging from college graduates, including one with an M.A., sixteen high school grads, and one recruit who didn't want to talk about his schooling so everyone surmised he was a high school drop-out. There were twelve whites, eight blacks and three Chicanos, plus himself. Michael was fascinated most not by the racial composition of his fellow recruits, but what the different groups talked about and how they talked. Many of the conversations in the barracks were crude, but the topics were discussed with unabashed openness. This shocked him, as did the constant misuse of simple grammar, and the incessant swearing, much of which Michael heard for the first time. But as the time passed, he gradually learned that crude topics, curses, and four-letter words were often used by youths anxious to be accepted by others and meld into what they felt was "the culture" of the barracks.

What Michael heard in the barracks was only one indication of how little he still had to learn about American life. He thought that his four years at Berkeley and his summers in Chicago had given him an understanding of Americans. He also thought that he had become fluent in American conversational English, at least to understand it if not speak it perfectly. However, the army, he was discovering, was an entirely new world.

Michael's first inkling of how different the world of the army was from university life came when he was issued his dog tags. The sergeant taking down the information got Michael's name, rank, and serial number and then asked: "Religion?"

"What do you need to know that for?" was Michael's response.

"In case you get killed in combat, we need to know how to mark your gravestone—whether with a cross, a Star of David, whatever."

"Oh, in that case, put down atheist or agnostic…no, just put down 'agnostic,'" Michael replied.

The sergeant wanted to know what kind of religion that was. Was it some kind of sect or cult? Some obscure Asian religion?

Michael assured him that it was nothing like that. "The chaplains will know what it means."

"If you say so. Just spell if for me." The sergeant wasn't going to waste any more time on Michael.

He recalled one equally unlikely late night conversation after "lights-out." Michael had been on his bunk looking up a word in a small dictionary by the light of a flashlight.

"So what word are you looking up tonight?" The question came from Don Morrison, a linguist with an M.A. who had lost his student deferment and been drafted.

"Nincompoop," Michael replied. "The drill sergeant called us a bunch of nincompoops this morning. It's not a four-letter word, so I don't think it's swearing, but I can't find it in this dictionary no matter how I try to spell it."

Don laughed. "If you want a dictionary of the words you hear in basic training, you are going to have to compile your own. But I can actually answer your question. A nincompoop is probably a corruption of the name Nicodemus, a Pharisee who asked Jesus stupid questions. It means simpleton or a stupid person."

"Hey, you two nincompoops, shut up already!" called a voice from a few bunks away. "Reveille is at five in case you college boys can't remember."

The big surprise of his eight weeks of basic training came on Sunday morning at the beginning of the fifth week. Michael was enjoying the rare quiet of the barracks, when the overweight black sergeant in charge called out:

"Hey, Koyama, a call from the CO's office. You've got a visitor...she's waiting for you there. On the double!"

Michael was totally puzzled. A female visitor? Who could that possibly be? He ran, as ordered, and arrived to find Captain Ingram waiting for him with a female captain in her mid-thirties, her curly brown hair cut short.

"Oh...Koyama. Come in. This is Captain Glennys Young from the Pentagon. She's come to talk to you. I'm going to church, so we agreed that she will interview you here in my office."

Captain Ingram nodded to them and left his office. Turning to Michael, Captain Young said:

"Recruit Koyama, thanks for coming. Sorry to break in on you on a Sunday. But I was sent to the West Coast to interview several recruits with very high scores on the Battery A and B tests as well as those with some special talents. With your scores and the languages you listed you speak, you ended up on my list. Captain Ingram told you I'm from the Pentagon, actually I'm from G2—I trust you know what G2 people do?"

Michael liked the captain's voice and her engaging smile.

"Yes, Ma'am. G2, we were told, is Army Intelligence.'

"Right. G2 wants to get the best talent that meets our needs, men and women who are highly intelligent and enterprising, especially people with fluency in certain languages. I got into G2 because I speak Russian, but we are now interested in getting more people who can handle some Southeast Asian languages. Your test scores and your Thai...plus your Japanese...and you've taken German and Russian in university, which shows you like to learn languages. These facts and your interesting background got you on my list. Col. Lund, my superior at G2, asked me to ask you some questions so we'll know more about you than what's in your 201 file. Okay?"

Michael nodded, thinking a G2-related assignment after basic training could be interesting. For the next hour, Captain Young asked questions. It was easy to see why she asked some of them, but the reason for others Michael couldn't fathom. She asked questions about his parents, education, and health. Then she probed into his life in Bangkok and the Tokyo orphanage, and how he managed to survive in Sannomiya and Ashiya. She even wanted to know the details of the devious and dubious "commerce" Michael had engaged in while in Sannomiya.

Finally Captain Young stopped questioning Michael and asked if he had any questions for her.

"Captain, I'm not assuming that I'm going to be assigned to G2, but what does it mean if I am?"

"Well, first you have to become an officer and go through Officer Candidate School. That would be before you got any training in intelligence."

"And if I go to OCS, I have to stay in the Army three years instead of two? Right?" Michael asked.

"Yes. But for the extra year, you'll get a lot of training which I'm sure someone like you will enjoy and benefit from immensely. More important, I can guarantee you'll be sent abroad and given some challenging assignments. In my book, becoming an officer and working for G2...even though it adds a year to your service...is a smart choice. What you learn at OCS and then at Fort Dix, where we give G2 training, and then the experience of living somewhere abroad...all this will be invaluable."

"Captain, if I don't want to become a G2 officer, the Army might not be interested in sending me to the OCS and I will serve two years as a soldier. Is this correct?"

"I'll be frank. Yes, you're right. If you don't want to become a G2 officer, that's what will most likely happen. We already have enough officers in infantry and you don't have the background needed to be an officer in the more specialized branches such as engineering or law."

Michael's mind was made up as soon as her heard the captain's answer. He said quietly, "Captain Young, I would be honored if I could become a G2 officer."

She smiled and said, "*Ochen horosho*. You will hear from us soon through your company commander."

Michael returned to the barracks feeling a little unsettled. He wondered when he might hear from G2. In the meantime, his grueling daily regime continued, and when he hadn't heard anything for a couple of weeks, he began to feel resigned to spending the rest of his time in the army in either demanding but boring infantry duties or doing a lot of tedious paperwork. Then, in his seventh week of basic training, Michael was ordered to report to the company room by Captain Ingram. When he arrived, he found a major whom he had never seen before standing in front of the captain's desk.

Captain Ingram said, "Come in, Koyama. This is Major Simon from battalion headquarters. He is the officer in charge of OCS candidates, and he has something to discuss with you."

The captain left the room, vacating his chair for the major, who said, "Recruit Koyama, the personnel office at HQ told me that you did exceptionally well in both the A and B Batteries—you remember the exams you took during the first week? I'm told that your scores were among the highest in the past dozen years for a non-native speaker of English. Also, the people at headquarters are pretty impressed by the languages you know. Most important, G2 wants you. So I'm here to talk to you about applying to OCS. How about it?"

"Sir, one of my barracks mates is applying to OCS, and he said you had to be an American citizen to apply. I'm a legal immigrant but I'm not yet a citizen."

"Yes, strictly speaking you're right, of course. But we know you're a legal immigrant and the Army can be flexible when we spot the talent we need. What I mean by that is we—the government—can waive the five-year residency requirement. It's done whenever the U.S. finds some special talent it wants, such as an Olympic athlete or a scientist for a classified project. In your case, we need to reduce the residency requirement only by a year since you came to the U.S in 1953. Of course, we'll have to do some special paperwork and go through the proper channels, but the Pentagon will do that if you want go to become an intelligence officer."

Major Simon wanted to make sure Michael understood fully what he was telling him. So he added, "You do know that if you become an officer, you will stay in the service three years, not two?"

Michael responded, "Yes, Sir, I do."

The major continued. "Good. If you agree to become a G2 officer, then we will apply for your residency requirement to be waived. After you complete the course at OCS, a naturalization ceremony will be arranged for you. So at the end of the 14 weeks at OCS, you will become a citizen and a second lieutenant at the same time."

Signaling that the meeting was over, the major stood up. "So, Recruit Koyama, do you need to think about it, or shall I tell Col. Howard that you are willing to go to OCS and then G2? It could change your life."

Michael, who had come to the CO's office half expecting a reprimand by Captain Ingram for missing the long march, was astounded and delighted by the offer. He had already decided to accept if one was made, but he had thought it unlikely that anything would come of his interview with Capt. Young because of the citizenship requirement. He immediately accepted and added his thanks for the honor and the opportunity.

In his final week of basic training, Michael thought a lot about becoming an American citizen, not just going to graduate school in the U.S. He had considered it for several years now, and it was why he was willing to spend two years doing anything the army assigned him. But he hadn't thought the opportunity would come so soon. At one level, his decision was a simple process of elimination. He knew he would never really fit into Japanese society despite his Japanese blood and the decade he had spent there. And he didn't speak Thai well enough to function in the country of his birth, certainly not in any occupation that required a college education.

Michael knew he was still "smitten" with what life in the United States had to offer. He still had trouble in articu-lating what it was...the openness? The "American dream?" Or an indefinable societal ability to "embrace" an outsider like himself? He knew in his heart of hearts he wanted to belong to this country with its capacity to welcome an immigrant like himself where he could hope to realize his dream of continuing his education.

So Michael would go to OCS and become an American. He had no idea how prophetic the words of the major— "Going to OCS could change your life"—would prove to be.

MICHAEL ENJOYED THE LONG TRAIN RIDE to Fort Benning in Georgia where he was to get his training to become an officer. His only problem came when he changed trains in Chicago. He had found a phone booth in the station from which he could call the Siegrists. His duffle bag was too large to fit into the booth, so he left it just outside. As he to talked to Mr. Siegrist, he saw from the corner of his eye the bag move a couple of inches. He thought someone had pushed it aside to stand in line outside the booth. But when it disappeared from view, he became slightly concerned. However, Michael was crammed inside the phone booth and in conversation with his benefactor. He couldn't just hang up on Mr. Siegrist, so he ended the conversation as quickly as he could, got out of the booth and looked around for his duffle bag. It was nowhere in sight. Why did anyone want a soldier's gear anyway? Luckily, his temporary duty orders, which also served as his train ticket, were in his pocket.

Michael searched the station for a good fifteen minutes, thinking the thief might have dumped the duffle bag somewhere after finding nothing of value in it, but in the end he had to give up or he would miss his train. He was bewildered by the theft and annoyed at the inconvenience and the expense the loss of the bag would cause.

When the sergeant signing in the new candidates for officer training at Fort Benning found that Michael had arrived with no luggage, he said, "I've seen men who travel lightly, but you're the first one to arrive without even a tooth-brush!" Laughing, he sent Michael off to the quartermaster to get outfitted and told him where the PX was so he could buy a toothbrush, razor, and other personal items.

Michael thought that some officers or sergeants at OCS might show some indication of their awareness of Michael's non-citizen status, but no one did. As for the training, unlike during the past eight weeks, very little of what happened during the fourteen weeks at Fort Benning surprised him. He had little difficulty with "the fitness tests," but he survived the "full-gear" twelve-mile marches only with the help of Henry Moss, the biggest man in his platoon. Henry carried in his backpack Michael's heavier gear—a shovel, a bayonet, iron pins for a "pup tent," and the like—in exchange for his bulky pup tent. He did this on condition that Michael help him in the engineering course, one of ten required "academic" courses.

Michael also managed to get through, if only barely, the water survival training, believed to be the hardest of the physical tests. Neither his experience in his Thai river nor in the ocean off Ashiya had prepared him for swimming with a heavy pack on his back. Six trainees at a time jumped into a huge pool at the command of a sergeant. Michael hit the bottom with his feet, but when he tried to surface, his forty-pound backpack, filled with heavy metal gear, kept him under water. Panicked, he had to bend his knees and shove his body upward and, at the same time, move his arms frantically in order to surface. It was far worse than when his father had pushed him into the river near their home in Bangkok and told him to swim.

Michael found life in the barracks at OCS quite different from during basic training. At night, the barracks were quiet because all twenty-four candidates were busy preparing for the next day's classes. Conversations were muted and the expletives Michael heard were limited to a few four-letter words that Berkeley students also used. Since most of their training was in the classroom, the men had the energy for sports on Sundays. Michael liked to swim and went to the pool almost every Sunday.

Soon after Michael arrived at OCS, he became friends with another immigrant, Jack Landauer, who was originally from Strasbourg. Jack was in a different platoon but sat alongside him in Terrain Reconnaissance and Map Reading. Michael learned that Jack had been told by his American uncle "to spend a few years in the Army to get Americanized." When Michael found that Jack was fluent in German as well as French, he tried out his college German on him. Jack corrected Michael's German pronunciation and grammar when the two began to chat in German after class. Michael returned the favor by helping Jack calculate map coordinates through triangulation, which at times required some higher math. On a few weekends, they went to nearby Columbus for the *vin rouge* Jack insisted was the only civilized drink.

Michael enjoyed the academic side of his OCS training, but he had trouble believing in the usefulness of much of what he had to do under the guise of "officer leadership and discipline" training. This training consisted mostly of giving simulated orders at the top of one's lungs, plus continuing the same tasks assigned in basic training: cleaning the barracks to an absurd standard; making up the cots as rigidly prescribed; and dismantling, cleaning, and reassembling rifles at maximum speed. But eventually, the tasks involved became routine. However, Michael never did come to understand why so much time and energy were expended on these basic tasks instead of on the academic courses he was sure would have been more useful. When Michael voiced this view to Jack, he was told: "Ever heard of 'the right way, the wrong way, and the Army way'? And 'your duty is to obey, not to question'? My uncle told me to keep these maxims in mind while I'm in the Army."

Michael had two surprise meetings just prior to the end of his training at OCS. The first one slightly unnerved him. He was suddenly called out of a lecture one afternoon and told to report to a Major Lawson whom he had never heard of. He entered the small interview room to find the major seated at a small table. He had a folder in front of him, which Michael could see had his name on the tab.

"Koyama? At ease, and sit down. I'm Major Ken Lawson. I'm in charge of clearing you for G2 training. Our people dug up something for which I need a bit of explanation because we have to clear you to at least the Secret level, and possibly in time to Top Secret." He paused and looked down at his notes. "Do you know a Stuart Stein?"

Michael replied almost immediately, "Yes, Sir, he was a graduate student living in International House while I was at Berkeley."

"How well did you know him?"

"How well? We used to watch the McCarthy hearings in the Common Room at I House during my freshman year and I discussed these with him."

"What were his opinions?"

"He was more critical of the hearings than anyone else I talked to, and since most American students were critical—I was too—so I guess you could say that he was on the extreme side. He called Senator McCarthy a Fascist."

"What other contact did you have with him?"

"I moved out of I House, so after my first year, I saw him on campus only to say hello."

"Did you go to any meetings with him?"

"No, Sir. I was too busy." Michael was finally figuring out where the questions were leading. "But he did invite me to attend a meeting that discussed the HUAC—the House Un-American Activities Committee."

"Did you go?"

"No Sir, I did not. It was during my freshman year and I was too busy."

"You never had dealings with the Trotskyites in Berkeley?"

"The Trotskyites? I know who they are—'the internationalist Marxists.' No, Sir. Stein asked me to attend a meeting but he never said specifically what the group was. Just that they were going to discuss the HUAC. I declined, Sir."

"Did you ever attend any meetings of Marxist or any other leftwing groups while you were at Berkeley?"

"No, Sir. I didn't join any groups and I didn't attend any leftist meetings."

"So how do you think your name got on our list of people who attended Trotskyite meetings?" The major looked hard at Michael.

Michael was silent for a moment as he thought. Suddenly he remembered his last conversation at I House with Stuart. "Sir, I remember that when I turned down Stein's invitation, he asked for my room and phone numbers at I House so I could be contacted about future meetings. But no one ever called me. I can't think of any other way my name could have gotten on the list."

"I can't reveal the details, but yes, your explanation fits. Your name on that list really raised eyebrows for a time, but we couldn't find any other evidence that you were involved with the group. This isn't the first time this sort of thing has happened. Okay, you're dismissed."

Michael was very surprised that G2's "people" could get hold of such a list with his name on it. What a thorough process the Army was going through to get him cleared for the "Secret" level!

The second surprise came in the week before graduation. On November 1, Michael was told to report to the CO, Captain Schwartz. As he entered the CO's room, he found Captain Schwartz and an older ruddy-faced man waiting for him.

The captain introduced the visitor: "Koyama, this is Judge Morton Spencer, the U.S. District Court Judge from the Middle District of Georgia. He's here to conduct a naturalization ceremony for you. Judge, should I call someone in? Don't you need a witness for this?"

Judge Spencer was a little amused. "This isn't a wedding. You already have what we need for this ceremony...an American flag...right behind you. I have all the papers I need. Of course, if you call in a few people, like the soldier sitting at the desk in the anteroom and some others, it would be more like the usual naturalization ceremony...."

Captain Schwartz also thought it a good idea to have a few people attend and asked the company clerk in the anteroom to "witness the ceremony" along with any "volunteers" he could readily "rope in." The clerk, plus a corporal and two sergeants on duty in the company office thought this might be interesting and joined them. Judge Spencer thanked them for coming and promptly began the ceremony to grant citizenship to one Bunji Koyama. He gave an obviously oft-made three-minute talk on the "privileges and obligations" of becoming an American citizen and administered the oath of allegiance.

Michael—legally Bunji—raised his right hand and repeated after the judge: "I hereby declare, on oath, that I absolutely and entirely renounce and abjure all allegiance to any foreign prince, potentate, state...I will support and defend the Constitution and law of the United States of America against all enemies, domestic or foreign...I will bear arms on behalf of the United States when required by law...I take this obligation freely without any mental reservation or purpose of evasion, so help me God."

The judge, now smiling, shook hands with Michael and said: "Congratulations. You are now an American citizen. Within a few days, you will get a fine-looking, official document stating so. By the way, it's customary to ask at this point if you would like to change your name in any way. It's not necessary, but if you have been thinking about it, it can be done now without any cumbersome legal procedures to go through. Just let me know what name you would like to have on your citizenship papers."

"I am usually called Michael here in the U.S. But I don't want to give up the name my father gave me. Could I become Michael Bunji Koyama?"

"Sure, why not. Most Americans have middle names."

The short ceremony completed, Michael found himself alone. He now had a new legal name as well as a new country. He found himself thinking, "I have just sworn allegiance to the United States and become an American! But I don't feel any different than when I got up this morning. What is this really going to mean to me?"

Because of what his father had done for him—hiring educated Japanese living in Bangkok to tutor him in the Japanese language, buying elementary textbooks and records of Japanese songs, and teaching him calligraphy himself—Michael had grown up thinking of himself as Japanese. Also, the fact the he had lived in "the foreign zone" of Bangkok had reinforced this belief. But once in Japan, he found that he wasn't "Japanese" like the people around him. Somehow, he was different. However, he certainly wasn't Thai, even though he had been born in Thailand of a Thai-Karen mother and had come to the U.S on the Thai immigration quota. For Michael, becoming an American meant that legally, he was neither Japanese nor Thai anymore, but how should he feel now he was an American? He decided he would figure it out later as now he was late for the last map reading exercise.

As "graduation" neared, rumors became rampant among the men who were nervous about what their assignments would be. Michael had joined the army thinking that there was no war in the offing, but his fellow candidates were concerned about the likelihood of war in Vietnam, and they all recalled the international crises of the year before, the Hungarian Uprising and the Suez Canal Crisis. Michael knew he would be assigned to G2, but he thought that much of the unease among the others was undoubtedly due to the fact that they had no idea what their assignments would be, or where they would be posted. But he found the jittery mood of his classmates infectious, and so, like the other men nearing the end of their officers' training, Michael, too, grew excited and slightly apprehensive about what awaited him.

Finally November 9, the day of the graduation cum commissioning ceremony, arrived. The brigadier general in command of the base opened the ceremony with a congratu-latory—and hortatory—speech. After two more speeches, a commissioning certificate was handed out to each candidate. The ceremony ended with music played by the base's band. As the last note was played, the newest lieutenants in the U. S Army all let out a whoop and tossed their hats into the air.

Before the newly commissioned lieutenants disbanded, NCOs from each company distributed the orders of duty assignments. Despite the earlier rumors, most were given leave and told to report to various posts around the country immediately after Thanksgiving. However, Michael had orders to report immediately to Fort Dix in New Jersey for "further advanced training."

That evening, Michael and Jack went to Columbus to celebrate and to have their farewell dinner. At Jack's insistence, they went to the only "continental" restaurant in the city where they ordered *boeuf bourguignon* and red table wine. Jack asked Michael what his orders were, but Michael was evasive, saying only that he had been assigned to Fort Dix, as he assumed that G2 didn't want him to broadcast that he was to get training in intelligence. He then asked Jack what the army had in mind for him. Jack said that he had also been assigned to Fort Dix for "further training" because he had been selected to work for G2. They looked at each other and broke out in laughter. "So this isn't a farewell dinner after all!" Jack said with a broad smile.

Both the food and wine proved to be extremely mediocre, but the two new lieutenants barely noticed what they consumed. They were slightly intoxicated by the wine and their speculations of what awaited them at Fort Dix and why they hadn't been granted any leave.

JACK AND MICHAEL ARRIVED AT FORT DIX on a cold and rainy Thursday two weeks before Thanksgiving. Everything in the northeast—the style of the houses, the kind of trees, and even the look of the streets—was new to Michael. The cold reminded him of his first winter in Tokyo. Jack, who had spent eight weeks at the fort for his basic training, knew his way around. They checked into a TDY-BOQ—a temporary-duty, bachelor officers' quarters. Waiting for them was a note for each of them from a Colonel Lund ordering them to report to him on the following Monday, November 18. The note also said that two other lieutenants, Anthony Blando and Winston Taylor, would be joining them at the TDY-BOQ, "thus I suggest that all four of you meet and get acquainted before you come to my office at nine on Monday morning."

Seeing the name of Colonel Lund, Michael recalled that he was the G2 officer at the Pentagon with whom Colonel Howard at Fort Ord had discussed Michael's applying to OCS. Michael surmised that the note from Col. Lund meant that he, Jack, and the two others the colonel mentioned were about to begin training together to become G2 officers.

Lieutenants Blando and Taylor both checked into the officers' quarters by five, and the four met for dinner to get acquainted. And get to know each other they did. Though they didn't know it then, they were cementing a friendship that was to last into the next century.

The four were very different in background and appearance, but they bonded almost immediately. Tony Blando had dark hair and a Roman nose. He was very solidly built at 5'10". His father was an Italian immigrant and his mother an Italian-American from Chicago. His father, who had finished only middle school in Sorrento, sold hot dogs at the White Sox baseball stadium where his mother ran a concession. They did odd jobs during the winter and money was always tight. Tony had gone through the University of Illinois on a football scholarship and wasn't sure what career he wanted to follow, though he knew it wouldn't be sports and would involve making money.

Jack Landauer could pass as French because he had been born and lived his early years in Strasbourg where he had been Jacques. He was fluent in three languages—French, German, and English. But he ruefully said that his English still bore traces of an accent, and his German was what

Berliners call '*Elsass-deutsch*' or Low German. The tallest of the four at 6'2", he had blond hair and deep-set blue eyes. He had gone to Boston College where his uncle who sponsored him to come to the U.S. taught law. Like Michael, he was in the army because he wanted to stay in America. He intended to go to law school after he got out.

Winston Taylor was an African-American, but in the fifties, he was classified as a Negro. He had golden skin—lots of white ancestry was apparent—and Michael was sure that in many foreign countries he would be considered Caucasian. His father was a doctor in New Orleans and his mother a piano teacher. Winston had graduated from Stanford with a double major in Classics and Greek. His career goal was to become a novelist. But first, he thought he needed more knowledge of the real world. And besides, he said, he didn't have much choice because writing novels was not a "reserved occupation." So he had ended up in the army and was very excited about G2 work. Everyone who met Winston was quickly charmed by his free spirit and large, smiling brown eyes.

At 5'7", Michael was the shrimp of the group, the only Asian, and with the strongest accent, plus he had a tendency not to observe all the rules of grammar in the English language. With his glasses on, he looked Japanese, but when he took them off, no one could be sure. He had an earnest way of speaking, and asked lots of questions, so at first meeting he seemed very serious. But a year later, Jack would remark, "Michael always surprises us with his innovative and improbable ideas, and amuses us with his quirky sense of humor and love of multi-lingual puns."

Despite their differences, the four had much in common. Each knew well at least one culture in addition to American, even Winston who could both read and speak Greek and had spent a summer in Greece. All were adept at languages and fluent in at least two, if not more. All had graduated from college with high honors and were avid readers. Most important, all four proved to be resourceful, especially when caught in tight spots. As it turned out, all were to have distinguished careers: Tony as an investment banker, Winston as a writer, Jack as an international corporate lawyer, and Michael as an economics professor.

After a weekend of getting to know one another, the four new lieutenants found themselves on Monday morning in front of the office Colonel Lund used when he came up from the Pentagon. They stood, spic and span in their new uniforms, looking at the name on the door of the fourth-floor office of the headquarters building, which read: "Col. Lund G2, EXO," meaning, an executive officer of intelligence at the G2 office in the Pentagon. Michael took a deep breath and knocked.

A deep voice said, "Come in." The four entered to find Colonel Lund sitting at a large desk piled several inches high with dossiers.

The colonel, even taller than Jack, stood to greet them. "Good morning. He pointed to four chairs arranged around his desk. "At ease and sit."

As they sat down, Michael took a good look at the colonel. He was his idea of a high-ranking officer: sharp, almost handsome features, short graying hair, and a trim physique with no excess poundage. The colonel came around his desk and leaned back on it, half sitting, and addressed the four new lieutenants.

"To start off, I would like to welcome the four of you to army intelligence. I hope you will consider serving as a G2 officer a privilege. I know a lot about each of you because I have been reading your 201 files, which include the assessments from your interviews with G2 people as well as what the officers from your basic and officer training have reported about you. In fact, as soon as we saw your scores in Batteries A and B and your linguistic abilities, we got busy."

Col. Lund stood up, walked back around his desk, and picked up a sheet of paper, which he glanced at before continuing.

"You are going to be surprised. I hope 'delighted' surprised and not 'disappointed' surprised. Your training will begin in exactly two weeks, on Monday, December 2. For the following sixteen weeks, you will be attached, technically at least, to a training group for intelligence officers. You will learn some basic techniques and skills relating to information gathering, transmittal, self-defense and uses of some weapons, and so on. There are fancy names for them, like torture tolerance, coding-decoding, and the use of directional electronic receivers and silenced small arms, etc. but I know you will do fine. Of course, the specifics of what you learn are classified, so you will not discuss with anyone what you study during the next four months. Understood?"

The lieutenants nodded wordlessly. Seeing their assent, the colonel went on. "When you have finished the training, each of you will be sent to a different European city."

He looked directly at Jack and spoke to him. Michael realized that Col. Lund knew each one of them from the photos in their files.

"Lt. Landauer, you will be going to Berlin. Don't look so shocked. We will let you know later what your specific assignments are and at which unit of the army in Berlin you will find your bed. One of your assignments will be learning to talk as much like a Berliner as possible. We know you speak fluent French, but your German gets you placed right in Alsace."

Then the colonel turned to Tony.

"Lt. Blando, you will be going to Rome. I am thinking of attaching you to our embassy but you won't work at the embassy. You'll simply get your assignments there. You are to polish your Italian and get rid of your Americanisms so you can pass as a Roman. It would be a good idea for you to also read a French paper daily to improve your French."

Next, the colonel looked at Winston.

"Lt. Taylor, you will be heading to Athens to see if you can learn to talk like an Athenian rather than someone who has majored in Greek. I hate to admit that we have so few officers who are fluent in that language. We've got bases in Greece, as you know, and we will tell you what we want you to do after you finish our training."

Winston couldn't hide his excitement and said in a loud voice, "Wonderful! Sir, thank you, Sir."

The colonel laughed saying, "I'm glad you think it's wonderful," and turned to Michael.

"Now, Lt. Koyama. You will be going to Paris. You wonder why not Japan, Thailand, or Germany because of your languages. We know you do not speak French. But trust me...I know what you are capable of...you'll learn French quickly. Do your best to become functional as soon as you can. We will attach you to the HQ of USEUCOM, that's the US European Command, at Camp de Loges near Paris. But you will live in Paris among the French and away from the BOQ at USEUCOM so that you can learn French as quickly as possible. You will be given your assignment after you arrive in Paris."

A look at the faces of the four new lieutenants revealed that all were "delightedly" surprised. Michael could scarcely retain what the colonel said after, "You will be going to Paris." He was flabbergasted and at the same time delighted.

Never had he dreamed that he would be going to live in Paris! But the colonel wasn't finished.

"Before I turn you guys over to the G2 Training Officer, there is something I have to tell you. You are being good junior officers and have not asked *why* I am sending you to those cities. I cannot, at this point, go into all the details, but I can tell you this much. We have a very fluid situation in Western Europe, as you must know. Let's just say that the situation is unsettled because of what de Gaulle is up to, the rising political strength of communists in France and Italy, the continuing flow of refugees from East Germany, the formation of the Warsaw Pact, and that darn Sputnik going up in October. All this, plus the fact that the economies of Western Europe have many problems that worry Uncle Sam. These factors and more will affect how we change the deployment patterns of our manpower and ordnance, and a lot of other things I don't need to go into now."

Taking a deep breath, the colonel added:

"Because of all this, the Secretary of Defense, the Secretary of the Army, and G2 had talks about what we could do to get more info, and do so more informally and expeditiously without writing proposals in quadruplicate and getting them approved at five or six levels on the command chain. The upshot—for which I don't mind taking some credit—was to create a couple of teams of guys like you... bright, linguistically talented with useful backgrounds and knowledge...to act as floating short-stops to plug the big hole between second and third base. You may work alone or as a group, sometimes only two of you together. Your job is to do what I ask of you: get information, write analyses, and, possibly, do something that needs to be done quickly and as covertly as possible." The colonel paused. "Any questions so far?"

More than a little overwhelmed, they remained silent. So the colonel continued.

"I see the period from early April, when you arrive at your posts, to the end of the year as one of warming up. You will undertake some general work at each of your postings and become proficient in the language you've been assigned. Then, toward the end of the year, I am hoping to come up with some G2 projects that will make the best use of your talents. You men are a sort of experiment. If you and the other team—I cannot tell you who they are—work out, we may maintain in the future similar teams on a long-term basis, getting officers who will stay in the service longer than you four plan to."

By now, Michael wanted to ask some questions—why Paris, exactly what the assignments would be and more—but he didn't speak up because none of the others said a word. The colonel stopped a moment and then smiled.

"To change the subject a bit, none of you has asked, but you are probably wondering why you were told to report here today only to be told your training won't begin for two weeks. That's because I want the four of you to get to know one another well enough to be able to work together as a team. I hope you enjoy this but also make good use of the time. You will have no assignments during that period so you can bone up on your languages and read up on the places to which you will be posted. That's all for now. Good luck, and I'll see you when your training has been completed."

The four lieutenants quietly left Col. Lund's office, but once outside the building, they broke out in exuberant exclamations over their great luck in postings. None of them was going to be a very junior "gofer" officer in a large divisional or battalion headquarters or an assistant to a company commander at a small base somewhere in the United States or Germany, where the largest number of the army bases abroad were located. Delighted as Jack, Tony, and Winston were with their assignments, they thought they made sense given their backgrounds and knowledge. But they all agreed that why Michael was being sent to Paris was a real mystery. "But Paris, how exciting," they all said.

The four enjoyed their two weeks of freedom. Their only "duty" was to show up for morning reveille, at which a duty officer perfunctorily called out their names. They established a routine of going to the gym before nine when it was sure to be empty, and then spent the rest of the day studying. Michael combed the base library for books on France, and a helpful manager at the PX obtained for him a map of Paris, a college textbook for French, a history of modern France, and a guidebook to Paris. At the end of the two weeks, he had learned a lot but felt overwhelmed by how much work lay ahead of him.

The four men took nearly all their meals together. They talked about their lives, their hopes for the future, and what might be in store for them when they reported for their G2 training in December.

Michael found his new friends well informed. He was especially impressed by Tony Blando who could lucidly discuss almost everything related to the stock market—the reasons for the recent sustained 'bull' market and "buying long" and "selling short"—and the financial responsibilities of the U.S. as "the provider of global liquidity." Winston, Michael found, had some very endearing qualities about him. And not only could he speak lucidly with a rich vocabulary, he also was extremely knowledgeable of many things Michael knew little of, including Greco-Roman history and culture, and modern painting. Michael discovered that Jack, whom he thought he knew better than the others, not only had a sharp analytical mind, but could discuss many political and legal topics as well as had the advanced graduate students who had lectured in his political science and history classes at Berkeley. Michael later remembered not having been as open as he could have in discussing his life in Thailand and Japan, and especially about his father, but something—perhaps his unwillingness to divulge what he then believed was shameful or too painful to discuss—had held him back.

Michael never discussed the content of his G2 training in any detail with anyone. He had had to sign a document before it began that the content of the training was not to be discussed except on a documented "need to know" basis. What the four lieutenants learned during their sixteen weeks of training was both highly instructive and severely tested both their mental and physical abilities. On the rare occasion when the subject of his G2 training came up, Michael would vaguely mention handgun practice, field exercises after being deprived of sleep for forty-eight hours, and how interesting decoding and various electronic devices were. He never spoke about several types of training he received, which few people outside G2 or who were not engaged in other U.S. clandestine activities would know about or even imagine existed. Nor did he ever mention the lectures by CIA officers.

The four months of training ended at the end of March. Michael received an order telling him to go to nearby McGuire Air Force Base and take a MATS flight—a flight in the military air transport system—to Paris via the Azores.

So on the last day of March in 1958, Michael found himself on his way to Paris. How different this flight was from his first, which had been an exciting, scary twenty-minute ride over the Gulf of Siam in a Thai Royal Navy plane, which looked like an elongated box that made a constant and infernal rattle, very different from the sleek, much quieter plane he was now flying in. His father had said that the newly crowned King Rama VIII had purchased six planes from Japan, but no one could interpret the instructions so his father had been brought in to translate them into English. Giving the two a short ride in the plane was the way thanks had been expressed to Michael's father.

But this flight was taking Michael to Paris, a city he never dreamed of ever going to. He still didn't know why he was being sent to France. All he knew was it was "the army way." As he listened to the heavy drone of the airplane's engines, he thought Mama Cheung would undoubtedly say "the Army way" was part of his karma.

Chapter 7

Paris, 1958

MICHAEL WAS FEELING DISCOURAGED. It didn't help that his feet hurt from all the walking he had done the past few days in the new shoes he had bought just before he left for Paris. It was now Friday, and he was getting nowhere in finding a place to live, and Colonel Lund's orders were for him to live in Paris, not in military quarters.

He had arrived on Tuesday, and on Wednesday morning, reported to Colonel Henderson at USEUCOM—the U.S. European Command. The colonel was a large man, big-boned, and a little overweight. He had been brusque but welcoming.

"At ease, at ease. Never seen such a strange order from the Pentagon. When you skip the standard stuff about the transfer of station, the pay grade, et cetera, and translate the whole Army-speak into ordinary English, it says the following: You are to work with us up to three days per week—only three days!—doing whatever we ask of you. God almighty, I've never seen a part-time assignment in this business. And you are authorized—meaning, you will if you have any sense—to find your own lodging in Paris and live among the locals 'for reasons already communicated to the lieutenant.' I hope you know what these reasons are. So be it. They outrank us. Captain Burns—Charlie Burns, our G1 officer who oversees all our personnel matters—will give you your first assignment. He's down the hall, third door on the right. And welcome to Paris, Lieutenant."

Michael had no trouble in finding Captain Burns' office. He was a very ordinary looking man of about thirty with light brown hair, but on his desk was a mug decorated with a picture of Mt. Fuji and cherry blossoms. The captain was very helpful.

"I have your order. Here is a list of six places you can look over for possible lodgings in Paris. They all rent to Americans. If you don't like them, more apartments will turn up in time. Take a couple of days and come see me for an assignment on Monday. Your office...sorry, it's more like a cubicle...is further down the corridor, 308B. It's not locked and the keys should be in the top drawer of the desk. Any questions?"

Michael asked how to get into Paris. Burns told him he could take the subway—"there's a shuttle bus between USEUCOM and the subway station." He added, "I expect you speak some French, since you're a G2 officer, and you've been told to find housing in the city." His tone made it clear he expected the answer to be "yes."

Michael had to admit that he didn't. The surprised captain responded, "Well, if you run into trouble and need an interpreter, come see me and I'll get you some help from a lieutenant who's fluent. Okay, see you on Monday. Good luck."

Michael walked down the corridor and located 308B immediately. He entered a tiny office with one small window facing north and looking out on two large eight-story-high USEUCOM buildings. Beyond these was visible the building housing The Supreme Headquarters of the Allied Powers, always referred to as SHAPE, and beyond that he thought he could see a forest. He opened the window to let the fresh spring air in and sat down on the only chair...a swivel chair... to gather his thoughts.

Since it was Wednesday morning, Captain Burns had, in effect, given Michael five days to find a place to stay and settle in. From his inside pocket of his jacket, he pulled out the large, folded map of Paris he had bought at the PX in Fort Dix.

Based on what he had read about Paris, Michael decided to start with the two apartments on the Left Bank where students and working class people lived. He would start with the apartment located on rue Dante near the Sorbonne and across the Seine from Notre Dame Cathedral. Having been told that going into Paris wearing a uniform was "strongly discouraged" except when on "official business," he changed some money at the finance office, and went back to his temporary billet and put on civvies. Then he took the shuttle bus to La Défense, where he got the Métro into Paris. He got off at Saint-Michel and consulted his map again.

He had no trouble finding the first apartment on rue Dante. The building was a two-story, brownstone building with a small, untended garden in front. He rang the bell, and, after a minute or two, a middle-aged man with a two-day beard and wearing an open shirt and leather vest opened the door. He took one look at Michael and said, "*L'apartment est seulement pour les Françaises.*"

Michael was puzzled, and it must have shown on his face. The man spoke again, this time in English. "No Vietnam people." And he turned away, went inside, and slammed the door in Michael's face.

Michael wondered what the man would have said if he had said, "I'm an American army officer and not Vietnamese." But it didn't matter because he was sure he wouldn't have liked to live in an apartment owned by that man. He went on to search for the second apartment on the list, only a few streets away. A middle-aged lady in an apron was very polite to him but said in English that she had rented the apartment only the day before. She must have thought Michael looked skeptical because she added, "See, the *A louer*—for rent— sign is no longer in the window."

Michael tried two of the other four apartments on the list, but they were too expensive. He didn't bother with the remaining two because they were located in the eastern part of Paris, which would involve too long a commute from his office. So he purchased a small dictionary and traveled back to USEUCOM, had a very late lunch at the mess, and then walked back to his billet in the annex. Determined to find an apartment on his own, he took out his new dictionary and his French textbook and spent the evening constructing sentences in French he thought he might need in looking for a room in Paris. Then he memorized them.

Thursday morning he had gone back to the area around the Sorbonne and wandered around the narrow streets searching for windows with a "For Rent" sign in them. He had rung several doorbells, and he had used his memorized questions when someone came to the door. Sometimes his questions weren't understood, but, more often, he could ask his question but couldn't fully understand the reply. He eventually saw three apartments, but one was too dingy and the other two were far too expensive. Totally disheartened, tired, and footsore, he returned to USEUCOM.

The best part of the day had been lunch. He had purchased a baguette, some ham, a packet of mustard, and a bottle of orange drink. The drink tasted like it came from a chemistry lab rather than an orchard, but the sandwich was delicious. As he ate sitting on the bank of the Seine and looking over at Notre Dame, he knew he would really enjoy Paris if only he could find a place to live! He determined to try at least one more day before he went back to Captain Burns and asked for his help in finding lodging.

Friday, Michael set out again, walking down streets he hadn't been before, but so far, he had had no luck. Despite the map, he began to get confused, and it was now after one. Not only did his feet hurt, he was also very hungry. Finally, he recognized that he was near the Parthenon, and he decided to walk downhill toward rue des Ecoles to find something to eat that he could afford. He hadn't been on this street before. It was totally uninteresting, but to his right he came across a small side street, quiet and quaint-looking. On a whim, he turned into it. Within moments, he found himself in front of a cozy and inviting restaurant: "Chez Maman." Michael decided that it was time to splurge a bit and have a real French meal.

The restaurant was small but clean with no more than ten tables. Only six customers remained. As Michael hesitated in the doorway, a tiny, attractive woman, perhaps in her fifties, and a little on a plump side, appeared from behind a curtain and greeted Michael with what sounded to him like a torrent of French, none of which he could understand. Nonplussed, he finally managed to say in English,

"Sorry, Madame. I don't speak French."

The woman laughed good-naturedly and responded in heavily accented but good English: "My apologies. Do come in. What would you like to eat?"

Michael liked the lady —Brigitte Varsonne, the owner of the restaurant as it turned out. He ordered an *omelette aux champignons* and a green salad. The omelet tasted as if a magician had made it!

As he was eating the last bite, the owner, whom everyone had been calling "Maman," appeared again and asked if he would like coffee. By now, he was the only customer, so when Maman brought his espresso, she sat down opposite him to chat. She asked him if he was a student. "Or maybe a tourist, since you don't speak French?" She was so friendly and interested that Michael opened up and told her he was a lieutenant in the American army, and today was the third day of trying to find lodgings in Paris.

Maman, surprised to hear what he said, was very sympathetic. "This is the wrong time of year...the good affordable rooms are all taken by students. But you must live in Paris if you are going to enjoy the city and learn to speak French!" Maman was most emphatic about that. "*Ecoutez moi bien,*" she said, interjecting a phrase Michael was to hear her use often. "Listen to me well, I will ask around my regulars tonight and some friends as well and see if anyone knows of a nice vacant room that isn't expensive. Can you come back tomorrow?"

His stomach full from his delicious omelet and with his hopes raised by the bubbling Maman, he promised to return the next day. He decided to stop searching for now and went to look around Notre Dame. Although he had seen it from a distance the day before, up close, the Gothic cathedral, with its magnificent flying buttresses and sculptured façade, was even more breathtaking.

Michael was so hopeful that Maman would find him a place that he spent Saturday morning studying his French textbook, and then went back to Chez Maman at lunchtime. Today he was served a beef stew made with red wine that was even more delicious than yesterday's omelet. He realized now how inferior the same dish had been at the French restaurant near Fort Dix, which he had gone to with Jack. Again, after all the customers had left, Maman emerged from her kitchen and came to talk to Michael.

"Everyone knows of possibilities for you in the summer when students go home. But that doesn't help you now, so I talked to my night waiter. If you don't mind sharing, Jean-Luc would be happy to let you live in his small apartment. It's really not an apartment, just two rooms with a toilet and shower. He will rent you the smaller room. It has a bed in it, and Jean-Luc says he can move in a table you can use for a desk. Jean-Luc doesn't speak any English, but that should help you learn French more quickly, don't you think?"

Michael thought this was well worth looking into. So Maman asked Michael to wait until she closed the restaurant for the afternoon, and she would take Michael to meet Jean-Luc in the apartment. By then, Jean-Luc would be back from his noon job at a cafeteria.

The apartment was located at the opposite end of the short rue Laplace from Maman's. It proved to be as small as Maman had said, but the room offered to Michael was almost the same size as his room at I House in Berkeley, and the toilet and shower were clean enough. From the window of what would be his room, Michael could see across the street a Chinese restaurant with four large Chinese characters that read Gentle Wind Restaurant.

Jean-Luc was tall with curly dark hair, very handsome in a gypsy-like way, and Michael was sure he was popular with the ladies. He was eager to economize by sharing his small apartment and, with Maman as interpreter, they agreed that Michael would pay half the rent and take turns cleaning the toilet and hall. The only drawback was that there was no kitchen, not even a hot plate, because Jean-Luc, who never cooked, managed to get a bargain rent for rooms without any kitchen facilities.

Maman had a solution to this problem, as she seemed to have to everything. "You can eat breakfast and lunch anywhere around here. We have many coffee shops nearby and, naturally, we can arrange for your evening meal at Chez Maman—I'll give you a monthly rate. What do you think?"

Michael needed no coaxing. The monthly rate Maman offered him was more than reasonable. It was agreed that he would move in on Tuesday evening, the day Chez Maman was closed and Jean-Luc would be free. Michael was delighted and, three days later, moved in with his few belongings.

Jean Luc proved to be amiable and easy-going. Because their schedules were so different, they rarely met. The only complaint Michael had was the lingering odor of the Gauloise that Jean Luke often smoked in the toilet. As Michael quickly learned to use the Métro system and the USEUCOM shuttle bus service, commuting between his room at rue Laplace and USEUCOM became routine. His lodging problem solved, Michael began work on his "part-time" assignments and to study French.

Michael found that dividing his time between living in Paris and working at USEUCOM made him feel he was dividing his time between two worlds. France was his second new country in five years, and he wondered how his life in Paris would compare to his first year in the U.S. He knew no French upon his arrival, and so he couldn't immediately become part of the society. Nor could he immerse himself in this new culture because he spent at least three days a week at USEUCOM working with American military personnel, and when work was pressing, he stayed overnight in transit quarters. USEUCOM was also a new culture to which, as a newly minted second lieutenant, he had to try his best to adjust. So he felt as if he was constantly moving back and forth between two different worlds with separate cultures and languages.

Michael resolved to learn to speak and read French as quickly as he could. He borrowed half a dozen books the small library of USEUCOM had for American personnel and began to study them with dogged determination. The French secretaries at USEUCOM, Maman, and the customers of Chez Maman helped Michael as if his learning French was their joint project. He started reading newspapers with a Larousse, and began to listen to the newscasts on the radio that followed the songs of Edith Piaf, who became his instant favorite. And his crash "course" with native speakers worked. Michael never mastered French grammar and his French spelling was worse than his English, but he learned to speak Parisian argot in such a genuine accent that for the rest of his life, the French were puzzled how he learned their language.

In mid-July, Michael succeeded in making an arrangement for French lessons three times a week with one of the regular customers of Chez Maman. Georges LaMont was a part-time lecturer of French literature at the Sorbonne and a teacher at the Lycee Voltaire four blocks away from the restaurant. For Michael, with his military pay, the lessons were easily affordable, but he knew they provided a welcome supplement to Professor LaMont's income. For each lesson, Michael read a dozen pages from the works of famous French authors, Gide, Balzac, Zola, and others. Professor LaMont also helped him read French newspapers. Michael quickly learned that the professor was a communist, but it mattered little because he was an excellent teacher.

The meals at Chez Maman were always superb. When not too busy, Maman would prepare anything Michael asked her to make. She even managed to find a bottle of Japanese soy sauce somewhere near the Métro Station Jasmin so she could make Michael a Japanese-style omelet. Gradually,

Michael learned the sad facts of Maman's life. Her only son had been just sixteen when the Nazis killed him. He was caught after curfew carrying false identity cards and passes for the Maquis, the underground resistance groups. Then her husband ran off with "a waitress half his age" and she hadn't seen him since. But she had managed to make the restaurant a success on her own. Michael thought Maman had a lot of spunk to make a success of her small restaurant after these losses. She lavished so much attention on Michael that, at times, he felt a bit abashed.

Sundays, Michael explored Paris. He walked everywhere. He sometimes strolled from his room on rue Laplace to the Arc de Triomphe, crossing the Seine over one of the many bridges, then, walking the length of the Champs Élysées, where he would stop for coffee at one of the cafés. Once, sipping coffee and enjoying the view of the grassy boulevard and all the passers-by, he recalled something his father had said to him about his days in Berlin. Michael now thought he knew what his father had meant when he said, "Nothing like it...walking down the boulevard called Unter den Linden. You think you are soaking up the culture." Michael had been only seven or eight at the time, and very baffled, he had asked, "What do you mean by soaking up the culture?" His father had replied, "It's difficult to explain. It's something like getting an appreciation of who the Germans are and what they've accomplished."

Three days a week, Michael reported to Captain Burns at USEUCOM. The assignments he received were interesting and highly "educational." Michael's first assignment was to assist two captains who were preparing to defend accused soldiers in Summary and Special court martial cases of lower-ranked enlisted personnel, mostly soldiers below the rank of sergeant. The captains were lawyers as well, and Michael's job was essentially clerical, despite his title of "co-consul." Many of the cases involved petty thievery, jogging Michael's memories of what he had done while in the orphanage and living in Sannomiya so many years before.

Toward the end of summer, as Michael's spoken French was becoming functional, he was asked to "evaluate" and make recommendations regarding the requests for permission to marry that were submitted by soldiers who came under the command of USEUCOM. His job was to determine whether the prospective brides were communists, prostitutes, either currently or in the past, had such legally designated diseases as syphilis and gonorrhea, which would bar them from entry to the U.S., and whether they were legally marriageable, that is, single, divorced, or widowed. Michael duty was to "recommend" to Captain Burns whether or not permission should be granted.

The work involved interviewing the prospective brides, checking with the French police and the prefects of the regions where the prospective brides resided, and ascertaining the accuracy of the statements and facts in the requests, including those in the medical records. Some cases were time-consuming, but Michael found the work interesting and useful, at least from the standpoint of learning colloquial French and finding his way around some of the seedy districts of Paris.

In close to half of the requests, Michael was asked to evaluate, he found that the prospective brides had been arrested for "soliciting" or that the statements of the doctors who examined them were suspiciously vague or inconsistent in order to avoid reporting diseases that would prevent the women from immigrating to the U.S. He recalled with distaste the number of times he had had to tell incredulous soldiers that their "beloved fiancées" had a long arrest record for solicitation, and/or had a venereal disease and they had better see a doctor themselves.

In most cases, it was very clear to Michael whether the French fiancée should be admitted to the U.S. or not. In only one case did he use his discretion and admit a bride who had an arrest record. The documents sent to Michael troubled him from the start. The CO of Corporal Jay Trent, twenty-two years old, had approved his request to marry Theresa Boussant, twenty-seven years old, stating, "I interviewed the young lady and found her to be a respectable woman, if a few years older than Cpl. Trent." She was listed as working in a souvenir shop. However, in the form letter from the Gendarme, a clerk had checked a box for "Arrest for Solicitation." The date of the arrest was 1955, and she was listed as "unemployed." Michael was puzzled by the discrepancies and decided to look into the case.

First, he interviewed the corporal, who he found to be a straightforward young man, a mechanic who had already save $1,500 to take his fiancée back to his home in Milwaukee. Next, Michael visited Theresa in her dingy, walk-up apartment. He found not a fast-talking, street-smart prostitute past her prime, but a fresh-faced, serious young woman with a sad story. When Michael questioned her about the arrest, she broke down in tears. She had been raped at her mother's boarding house in the industrial city of Clermont Ferrand, and had run away to Paris. There, she gave birth to a boy and supported him by working as a waitress. However, at age five, little Anton developed a high fever, and in a desperate attempt to quickly earn the money needed to buy the expensive medicine—something called penicillin, which the doctor said Anton had to have—she went on the streets. But being a novice, she was immediately spotted and arrested. Her son died. She said Cpl. Trent knew all about her son, but not her arrest. She tearfully pleaded with Michael not to destroy her future.

As Michael looked at the weeping young woman, he thought back to his own postwar experiences. How much harder life must have been for a girl, either in postwar Japan or France, than it had been for him. Under the rules in effect, Michael was required to reject a request involving anyone having an arrest record within the past three years, despite a CO's endorsement. Since the Theresa's arrest had been in 1955, Michael decided to assume that the arrest had occurred early in the year, and, thus, more than three years ago. He decided to recommend that Theresa Boussant and Cpl. Trent be permitted to marry and find a future in the U.S.

While Michael didn't mind and often enjoyed his "part-time" assignments, as his French became functional, he began to hope for a "real" G2 assignment. As if Colonel Lund could read his mind, Michael got his wish in mid-September in the form of a long order that began:

"You are assigned to work in G2, SHAPE for the next three months to assist Captain Ray Logan in his analysis of the current Algerian crisis in France. You are to carry out any tasks he asks of you relating to his assessment of the Algerian independence movement, its impact on French politics, and the effect it is likely to have on U.S.-Franco relations."

Included in the large envelope were a number of articles in English and French and some documents intended to give Michael the background he needed.

Living in the heart of Paris, Michael was aware of the "café wars" in Algeria and Paris, which had killed almost 2,000 café patrons and passers-by since 1954. Members of the two factions supporting Algerian independence were not only targeting their "enemies"—the French military and members of their rival faction—they were also terrorizing the general public by throwing Molotov cocktails into cafés. The almost daily acts of violence were a major reason why members of the American military were forbidden from going into Paris in uniform except on "official business."

Michael was intrigued by this assignment and wondered what it would entail. He reported to Capt. Logan, a tall and owlish-looking captain in his mid-thirties. The captain turned out to be a very bright "desk" man who knew French politics inside out. However, much to Michael's surprise, Capt. Logan spoke almost no French and was relying on translations of reports and interviews. He needed Michael to go to newspaper offices and interview reporters, as well as go to police stations and get information, all of which required the use of the French language. He also needed Michael to get out into the city and do some interviews, and get the feel of the situation on the streets and in the cafés. The captain specifically asked Michael to have "chats" with demonstrators. While he would try to help Michael as much as he could in obtaining contacts, much of what Michael did was going to be up to his initiative.

Capt. Logan also needed Michael because he wasn't immediately identifiable as an American. Because of the "café wars" and frequent "demonstrations"—marches by thousands of supporters of the Algerian independence, including many Communists and Socialists—USEUCOM often made Paris "off-limits" to all American military personnel. But Michael could easily get about the streets of Paris because no one would know who he really was. He was beginning to figure out that was at least one of the reasons why he had been sent to Paris.

For this assignment, Michael suggested that he be a Japanese graduate student researching French and Algerian history and politics, to which Capt. Logan readily agreed.

This meant that Michael needed to be somewhat disguised. He was given the kind of eyeglasses and shoes worn by many Japanese. Although Michael wondered how and where G2 at SHAPE managed to get all of these Japanese things only a few days after he made his request, he didn't ask. Since Michael had been a Japanese university student, this identity wasn't hard to assume. The only thing he had to be careful about was not to use American mannerisms or speak English too well.

Before he could begin this assignment, Michael had to become completely immersed in the facts of the Algerian crisis. While France had granted independence to its former colonies of Tunisia and Morocco, it was dragging its feet in granting independence to Algeria. And this was fanning the anger of the Algerians who wanted to be liberated as soon as possible. The French army in Algeria often mounted merciless military actions against the Algerian independence movements, and at the same time, bloody conflicts continued to flare up between the two major, ideologically irreconcilable independence movements, each contending for control of the country once independence was granted.

The largest group working for independence was Le Front de Libération Nationale, known as the FLN. This group was supported by Algerian professionals, the middle class, and even by the larger labor unions in Algeria. The FLN was well funded, and had become increasing able to mount major assaults against the French army and its installations in Algeria. The supporters were anti-Communist, and envisioned an independent Algeria co-existing with the Muslims within their midst.

The second smaller, but more violent, group was Le Mouvement National Algérien, called by everyone the MNA. This group was supported by the French communists and by Algerian workers and the Algerian unemployed, many of whom lived in poverty in France, mostly in Paris. They were willing to fight for an independent, anti-capitalist Algeria that would not be ruled by the FLN. *Le Monde*, a conservative French daily, suggested that more than 90 percent of the terrorist acts in Paris were committed by the MNA.

Le Monde might have been correct, but this didn't mean that the FLN was non-violent because, in fact, it had instigated a "crisis" on November 1, 1954 with coordinated attacks on ports, warehouses, and other facilities in Algeria. These assaults had continued, and the violence had spilled over into France. A major difficulty in assessing the situation was that it was changing so rapidly: the French army in Algeria, commanded by General Salan, was ruthlessly attacking the military wing of the FLN with massive search and destroy missions which included bombarding villages. And the FLN was, in turn, systematically massacring the guerrilla units of the MNA all over Algeria. At the same time, de Gaulle was raising the hopes of the French colonials and the French army in Algeria with his vague statements that he "understood them."

In order to get around Paris as his assignment required, Michael requested and was provided with a velo. This was a cheap bicycle with a small motor, a type of vehicle used all over Paris. He enjoyed his work—what he called "being a wild Japanese student 'veloing' around Paris to observe everything." During late September and through October, Michael criss-crossed Paris on his velo to see various demonstrations, and to get as many as possible of the pamphlets being handed out by various groups of demonstrators. He also went to the Police Nationale, the Ministry of the Interior, and the Gendarmerie to ask officials questions a Japanese graduate student could reasonably ask, such as about the "café wars" and the immediate security concerns relating to the increasing influx of Algerians and returning *colons,* the French farmer-colonialists who numbered one-million strong.

As Captain Logan and Michael discussed how the report to Colonel Lund should be written, their problem was: how to accurately assess the extent of the "crisis"; how many supporters the various groups had; how those on the sidelines were likely to line up; and, most importantly, who was likely to take control in Algeria once freedom was granted. From the documents sent to them, they knew the Pentagon assumed that independence would come sooner or later, and its concern was whether the FLN or the strongly communist-leaning MNA would control an independent Algeria. If the MNA took control, it would be pro-USSR, and this could pose a threat to NATO, thus requiring possible changes in the deployment of American forces.

Michael's most difficult task was finding the right people to interview. He decided to ask Prof. LaMont for help. The professor willingly offered to introduce his Algerian friends at the Lycee Voltaire and the Sorbonne, plus other people supporting either the FLN or the MNA. LaMont was sure that, "They will talk to an American officer, but they will be more frank with a student from Tokyo University, so far away." Although he never needed to use it, LaMont even got him a student library card from the Sorbonne in the name of Bunji Koyama.

One of Michael's first interviews, one that made a very strong impression on him, was his interview with Emil Gascone, a short, homely man who limped visibly. It was Maman who told Michael where to find him—he had been a communist friend of her husband in the resistance movement during the war. Still an ardent communist, Emil had become "a dedicated supporter of the MNA because I myself was an agricultural worker—a *colon*—working alongside the poverty-stricken Algerian day-laborers." Michael found him to be a man with a strong sense of justice. Michael met Emil in a cheap restaurant in Montmartre.

"Why is the Communist Party supporting the MNA?" Michael asked him.

"They want an independent Algeria for the working people and not for the upper crust. I couldn't get a job after the war, so I went to Algeria and became a *colon* near Saida, not very far inland from Oran. There I saw what the French army and many *colons* were doing to the poor Algerians. Did you know the military forced many to relocate and they ended up having to beg? "

"No, I didn't. I understand why you support the MNA, but the FLN is much bigger and can fight against the French more effectively than the MNA can."

"If Algeria becomes independent with the FLN controlling the government, Algeria will be for the rich and for the Muslims—that is, the Arabs—and not for the working people who are the original North Africans. So we need to help the MNA in Algeria become stronger."

"Then why did you come back to France?"

"You can do more in Paris to get more money for them. They are desperately short of money. If you believe in justice, you've got to be a communist and help the MNA, it's that simple."

As the conversation continued, it became increasingly evident that Gascone had an unyielding and laudable but naive view of the world. He reminded Michael of the communist restaurant owner in Tokyo, who had limped like Gascone, and the student radical who was his regular customer, both of whom were guided more by ideology than by a critical assessment of a situation.

Michael found extremely useful some of the things Gascon said, often proudly, about the networks and monthly expenditures of the small groups of MNA members in his part of Paris. When he put these together with what he learned from other interviewees, he was better able to estimate the total number of MNA supporters in Paris and the magnitude of their financial wherewithal.

The second interview that Michael never forgot took place in a sleazy bar on rue de Lancry, two blocks from Gare de L'Est. A young Algerian—a former student of Prof. LaMont's close friend at the Sorbonne—agreed to meet Michael there. The slim, good-looking young Algerian with shrewd eyes, who Prof. LaMont said had dropped out of the Law Faculty of the Sorbonne after only a year, came with a very attractive young Algerian woman with lovely olive skin.

"My former professor said Prof. LaMont's friend is also his friend and I should see you. My name is Abdul Rahman, although I am Alphonse Riboux at the restaurant where I work as a waiter."

Rahman-Riboux was cordial. Michael introduced himself and said: "Very happy to meet you. Thanks for seeing me. Prof. LaMont said that he understands that you are a strong supporter of the FLN. I am hoping you can tell me why, and what you think will happen to Algeria in the next few years."

The three sat down at a table near the door and ordered red wine. The young Algerian first queried why Michael was asking the question. Michael told him that he was a Japanese graduate student in France to study the history of French colonial policy. Appearing satisfied with the answer, the young Algerian said:

"Whatever de Gaulle and other French political and military leaders say or think, the days of the French possession of Algeria are numbered. Any reasonable and objective person looking at what has been happening around the world after the war cannot deny this. We—the FLN—have documented at least 100,000 killed by the French Army and the *harkis*— the Muslim Algerians fighting alongside, or even as a part of the French Army. The FLN is like George Washington's army fighting against British colonialism. We want our independence first, and we'll worry about what kind of a government we will have later."

Rahman-Riboux was obviously very intelligent and even eloquent at times. As Michael listened to him, he knew he had to guard against being unduly swayed by the strong pro-FLN view he was hearing. At the same time, he felt ashamed by the realization that until he had interviewed several Algerians, especially this young man, he had been influenced by the popular French image of Algerians. The view that they were all poor, ignorant, and dirty was in need of radical revision.

Michael thanked Rahman-Riboux for his time and stood up. Still seated, the Algerian said:

"Sit down, please. I want to ask you something…to do a favor for us."

"A favor? What is it? I shall be happy to do anything I can."

"About what I'm going to ask you, I must ask you to keep it strictly *entre nous*. Can you promise that?"

Totally perplexed, Michael asked: "Yes, I can...but what is it?"

"After talking to you, I made up my mind that you may be just the person we are looking for."

"For what?"

"The *flics* of the Police Nationale have, we are very sure, bugged most of our telephones, and it has become very difficult for us to communicate. And several of us are constantly watched by the *flics,* and a couple of our runners have been caught. So we need someone they would never suspect who can help us communicate...maybe sometimes carry a few things, mind you, nothing heavy or big, from one of us to another in our group. Will you do that?"

Michael realized that Rahman was asking him be a courier for the FLN. He was surprised to hear that the FLN, supposedly less involved in the café wars than the MNA, was being so closely watched by the French police. He thought Rahman must be pretty desperate to ask him, but thinking that working for the FLN would enable him to learn more about their activities, he quickly agreed. "Yes, I'll do that, provided I don't need to take much time from my studies."

Michael carefully chose his "dead drop," the secret hiding place for the clandestine messages he was to receive: the underside of a stone bench near the statue of Diana à la Biche at the west end of the Jardin de Tuileries. He was rather amused at practicing the "spy craft" he had learned at Fort Dix, but it was essential that he receive Rahman's messages at a dead drop, and not in the mailbox of his apartment on rue Laplace. His dead drop was a place where there usually weren't many people, and which he could easily get to on his velo. He told Rahman to place a few stones at the edge of the base of the statue of the mythological Greek huntress whenever he left a message taped under the bench.

Michael saw stones for the first time on Monday, five days after his meeting with Rahman. When he checked the bench, he found an envelope and a small metal box taped to the underside. The envelope contained two light beige colored sheets of paper. One was addressed to him and said in good French, "Mr. K, please give the other note and metal box to the tall young man wearing a blue and white checked shirt who will be at the west entrance to the Métro station Passy between 7 and 7:15 p.m. on Wednesday. He answers to the name 'Bernard.' Thanks, R."

The note to "Bernard" seemed to be in gibberish because the letters of alphabet looked as if they had been randomly transposed. Realizing the coded message must be in French, Michael went back to his room on rue Laplace to see if he could decipher the code. To his surprise, he quickly found the code involved only a simple transposition of letters. Because Rahman made the amateur cryptographer's mistake of using the same words more than once—in the case of *flics* three times—Michael was able to break the code within an hour without resorting to any of the complex methods of decoding he had learned at Fort Dix. The message read in part, "Attack the enemy of Algerian independence at Café Balzac near the west entrance of the Métro station Trocadero," and gave a time and date when Michael was sure the café would be crowded.

When Michael carefully pried open the metal box, he found four miniature firing pins for explosives. He could clearly envision what these pins would do to the customers of the Café Balzac.

Michael took the deciphered note and metal box to Captain Logan and asked his opinion as to what he should do next. Capt. Logan advised him, as Michael had expected, to report what he had found to the anti-terrorist unit of the Ministry of the Interior, housed at the headquarters of the Police Nationale on Quai des Orfevres. When Michael went to the headquarters and identified himself to a policeman at the gate, he was immediately escorted to the office of the unit. Michael was cordially received by Major Marc Garmond of the French army, who had been seconded to serve as assistant head of the anti-terrorist unit. Michael explained why he had come, and found Major Garmond extremely grateful. The major explained that it was easy for the terrorists to obtain explosives, but it was more difficult for them to get their hands on these advanced firing pins, which was probably why they were being so careful in getting them to their intended destination.

After some discussion, Michael and the major agreed that Michael should continue to pick up the notes from Rahman and deliver whatever he was told to, after determining what it was. "We would like copies of all the notes you decipher, but it's too dangerous for you to come here again. Please call and we'll send an undercover man to collect the information from you. Remember that you are dealing with murderers," the major said. "But we promise to try to keep an eye on you so that you won't be harmed in any way for helping us."

Rahman continued to send notes to the dead drop every few days. Michael deciphered each, and turned them over to Major Garmond's courier, who met Michael dressed like a student whenever he called the major. All the notes directed various members of the FLN to "attack the enemy of Free Algeria." Major Garmond sent word that, "These notes and all the names, even though they are in code, tell me that we should worry more about the FLN and not be so focused on the MNA and the communists in looking for the people terrorizing Paris."

When Michael went to see if there was a seventh delivery from Rahman, he found three scruffy-looking, young Algerians standing not far from the statue. Michael had been pedaling his velo as motorized vehicles were banned inside the park. He stopped some distance away, but before he could turn around, the tallest of the three ran toward him and in a loud, threatening voice yelled:

"Hey, stop! We want to express how we feel about your reporting us to the police."

Michael knew he had to brazen it out: "What are you talking about?"

The tall leader shot back: "You're a traitor! The *flics* have been waiting for us too often lately, so Rahman sent a false message to you the other day. And sure enough, the *flics* were at the place mentioned in the message."

Michael made an instant decision. He jumped back on his velo and, with no time to try to start the motor, he quickly pedaled past the three and out of the park. The three pelted after him. He wasted seconds trying to unsuccessfully start the motor, and then a dozen pedestrians on the rue Rivoli hindered his progress. Michael managed to dodge two girls and swerved into a small side street. This made him lose his balance, and he almost fell off the velo. When he regained his balance and looked back, he could see the three Algerians no more than ten meters behind. There was no one else on the side street, narrow and walled in by three-story buildings. Michael pedaled furiously as he tried to start the engine on the old bike.

"*Arret*...or I shoot." The leader of the three yelled. Michael didn't believe the leader would shoot. He wasn't far from rue Rivoli, a busy street in the center of Paris, and he didn't think the Algerian even had a pistol, so he kept on going.

Within seconds he heard the sound of a gun going off and virtually simultaneously a bullet whizzed by his left ear. It was so close he almost felt it. He had never forgotten the sound of a bullet flying close to his head in basic training.

He had to get out of range. Almost without thinking, he turned right and swerved into the first side street he saw and the next thing he knew, there was no ground beneath him. He was falling through air. Then his velo landed, making a huge noise as it hit a hard surface, jolting Michael and throwing him off the bike, his right ankle twisted under it. His head hit the wall hard and stunned him, making him dizzy.

An agonizing pain shot thorough his right leg. He gripped his ankle and grimaced. It hurt so badly that he wasn't aware of any other bumps and bruises.

As his vision cleared, Michael began to look around him. Where was he? He was well below street level. He was sitting on a concrete floor and three sides of the hole he had fallen into were concrete as well, the fourth, an iron grille through which he could see what looked like cases of wine. He must have fallen into an underground loading room at a back of some business, most likely a restaurant, he thought.

He suddenly realized that he was trapped. If the trio came after him, he was a sitting duck. He looked up but didn't see anyone looking down into the loading room. He hoped that the three Algerians hadn't seen him fall into this underground area. Or had the three decided not pursue Michael for now? Were they only trying to scare him? Surely the gunshot must have attracted attention. Michael had no idea. He sat numbly on the cold concrete floor, his right ankle throbbing with intense pain.

Suddenly, a short overweight man wearing a chef's hat, a white jacket, and an apron opened the grill from inside.

"*Alors*, I heard a big noise. That must have been you... did you fall in here, riding that infernal velo? Look at it! Looks to me like it's headed for the junkyard," the chef said derisively.

"Someone was chasing me and I didn't see your open loading room. Please, please, would you call a taxi for me? I've hurt my ankle and can't walk," asked Michael politely, hoping the pain didn't make his voice sound whiney.

Michael saw that the chef's attention had turned upward. Looking up himself, he saw two French policemen looking down into the cellar area.

"Aha! You are escaping the *flics!*" the chef accused Michael.

Michael was now hurting so badly that he couldn't think straight. But one of the policemen dispelled the chef's suspicions. "This young man has been chased by criminals we are currently investigating. We arrived too late to prevent this accident, but we are here to help him now." The policemen managed to get Michael out of the cellar, and up through the restaurant to the street. Then, at the chef's insistence, they hauled the velo up onto the street using the ropes used for goods, and abandoned it for the time being. One of the policemen asked Michael where they should take him for medical treatment, for they realized that he couldn't bear weight on his right foot. Michael asked to be taken to USEUCOM. The chef looked puzzled but the policemen, who knew who Michael was, understood immediately.

Michael was taken back across Paris in a police car. The ride seemed to take forever, even though Michael's pains had subsided to dull throbs as he rode in the back of the car with his foot up on the back seat. When they arrived at USEUCOM, the guard at the entrance took one look at Michael, told him to stay where he was, and called the nursing station. In a few minutes the duty nurse arrived pushing a wheelchair. But after hearing about his foot, she said she would have to send him over to SHAPE headquarters where they had an X-ray machine and a doctor on duty. Michael's foot, and now his head too, were aching so badly that he offered no resistance.

Michael's foot was X-rayed, and after a long wait, a tired-looking doctor told Michael that he had a broken ankle.

"Nothing serious, but you can't walk on it for a month or more. We're also concerned about the bump you got on your head and so we're going to keep you here overnight. First let's get your foot strapped and your scrapes attended to. I'll give you some pain killers, and in a month or two, you will forget this every happened."

Michael spent a bad night, despite the painkillers. As he woke in the dark with no idea what time it was, he told himself he was lucky that despite all he had been through in his nearly a quarter a century of life, this was the first time he had ended up in the hospital or with a broken bone. No, wait, this was the second time he had broken a bone—the first was when he was playing rugby in high school and had broken his collarbone. He hadn't gone to the school nurse because he was ashamed that his teammates might find out he had fractured his collarbone so soon after he entered the rugby club. And he hadn't gone to a doctor because he didn't have the money, and so he just stopped playing rugby and waited for his shoulder to heal. It did eventually, but as his friends noted, it left one shoulder permanently lower than the other. No, his real scrapes had been in Thailand.

Which was the worst? Probably, when he chased elephants and nearly lost an eye. But was that worse than being eaten by those silver fish? He couldn't recall their name. He had been swimming in a lazily flowing tributary of the Chao Phraya with friends when he had run into a huge school of them, and they started pecking at the softest part of his body. He could still remember how badly it had stung. Luckily, when he started screaming, he had been pulled from the river by a fisherman.

So he had a scar in his eye, one shoulder that drooped, and scars in his groin, but at least he wouldn't have any physical reminders of his fall into the cellar. Little did he know that contrary to what the doctor told him, Michael was to be reminded of this incident the rest of his life whenever the weather turned cold and damp, for his ankle would throb in bad weather.

A week later, after Michael had hobbled back to his small office on crutches from a meeting with Capt. Burns, there was a gentle tap-tap on his door. When Michael half-shouted that the door was open, Major Garmond walked in.

"I was told that you were here. I came to say thanks on behalf of the anti-terrorist unit. You took some real risks for us, and you deciphered their messages as well. The messages plus the firing pins will be important evidence in the trial against Rahman and the guys who attacked you. By the way, those FLN thugs working for Rahman won't bother you again. Our back-up officers caught them as they came running into the rue Rivoli. I'm sorry we weren't able to prevent your accident. Our officers were watching for you, but you sped away before we could stop you."

"Did you always have someone watching the statue?"

"Not always," Major Garmond replied, "but you told us your schedule for checking for notes."

"Thanks. Now I don't need to worry about them anymore, I hope. I sure don't want to get shot at again!"

With Michael on crutches, his cover blown, and his velo destroyed, his days of speeding around Paris came to an end. But the holidays were at hand, and Michael found his mind occupied with how he would spend them. Colonel Lund had notified the four lieutenants they were all being granted ten days leave over Christmas and New Year's. After training so intensively together, they had then been apart since they had left for their separate posts in Europe. All four had been delighted when Col. Lund notified them that this leave was conditioned on their spending it together, wherever they liked. With three weekends added to the 10 days, the leave would give them sixteen days altogether, and meant they could travel some distance for their holiday.

The four had sent numerous messages back and forth with suggestions for exotic locations, but after Michael ended up on crutches, Jack, Tony, and Winston all decided that it would have to be Paris. Michael was the only one who was disappointed by the decision because he had longed for a warmer climate, and before his accident, he had all but persuaded the others to spend their leave in Barcelona.

However, since none of the others had ever been to Paris, except Jack who had spent a few days there when he was too young to remember much, they were excited at spending two weeks in "Gay Paree" as Winston put it. They figured they had an excellent guide in Michael who had already spent more than six months there. Michael was realistic and resigned to losing the opportunity to travel, but he cheered up when he thought about spending two weeks with his buddies.

Maman recommended that Michael's friends stay at the small and inexpensive Hotel St. Jean-Louis. The rooms turned out to be tiny with well-worn furniture and shared showers and toilets, but the price was right and the location was superb—on a narrow, winding street off Saint-Germain and just a short walk to Notre Dame, the Sorbonne, Luxembourg Gardens, and Michael's room on rue Laplace.

So on Saturday, December 20, after Michael had his foot checked prior to going on leave, he moved out of the transient quarters at USEUCOM where he had stayed after being discharged from the clinic, and moved back to his room at rue Laplace. He was still on crutches, but the doctor told him the ankle seemed to be healing nicely and he could gradually start putting weight on his foot. Later that same day, Tony,

Winston, and Jack arrived one by one and checked into their hotel. And at seven, there was the grand reunion at Maman's.

Maman warmly welcomed the four with a meal requested by Michael to give his friends their first taste of real French cuisine: Maman's locally famous *boeuf bourguignon*, accompanied with a rather expensive but superb Bordeaux wine, and followed by her special *crème caramel.* The four were in high spirits—from their reunion, their leave in Paris, and three bottles of wine. The other customers were puzzled by this diverse group of young men in their early twenties: a tall blond Nordic fellow, a solid-looking dark Mediterranean man, a slightly-built Asian, and a fourth, whose race and ethnic group they couldn't make out. Not Algerian, maybe Arab, but impossible to tell. But they were all conversing in American English, and their high spirits were infectious, particularly since they insisted on pouring glasses of wine from their bottles for everyone in the small restaurant.

Maman was pleased to have the four so obviously enjoy her meal. She hovered over the group whenever she could leave her kitchen, and by the end of the long evening, she had dubbed the foursome, *Les Quatre Copains*—"The Four Buddies." The name stuck, and for the next five decades, this was what the four friends called themselves.

Their leave was a huge success. Michael showed them all over Paris. For the first few days, they shared taxis as Michael hobbled about on crutches. At the Louvre, they borrowed a wheelchair and pushed him through the galleries. But as he practiced walking and his foot mended, he was able to lead them around the back streets near the Sorbonne and to his favorite haunts on the Left Bank. Winston was openly envious of Michael's experiences collecting secret messages for terrorists and being shot at. The others thought this hilariously funny for none of them thought risking one's life and ending up with a concussion and a broken ankle was anything to want to experience. But then, they weren't planning on becoming novelists.

On most nights, *Les Quatre Copains* ended up back at Maman's. They reveled in her wonderful bistro cooking, while they exchanged stories about their various experiences in Athens, Rome, Berlin, and Paris—at least the parts they felt they were allowed to relate. And again, as always, they speculated on what lay ahead. They celebrated the New Year with toasts to Colonel Lund who had given them such fascinating eight months in Europe, and to 1959 for what lay ahead for the four of them.

At midnight, the four friends exchanged wishes for a *Joyeux Nouvelle Année* with Maman and the regulars of the restaurant. With his wine glass held high, a very happy Michael just knew he was in for another wonderful year.

Chapter 8

Paris, Fôret d'Orléans, and Munich, 1959

THE HOLIDAYS OVER, Michael settled into the kind of quiet routine enjoyed by Parisian office workers. He was finding the cold of Paris less onerous, partly thanks to his new heavy, gray woolen overcoat—the most expensive item of clothing he had ever owned—purchased from the very "bourgeois" Printemps department store. No longer did he have to wear the thinner and drab khaki one that screamed, "Look at me, I'm a GI!" The purchase was to celebrate the notice he received in early January informing him that he had been promoted to First Lieutenant, an unusually "fast promotion" according to Captain Burns. He justified the expense of the overcoat by not having traveled to Barcelona, and in any case, the pay raise would almost cover the cost of the coat in six months.

In January, Michael had stayed in temporary quarters in the annex of USEUCOM to help heal his injured foot he had rather overused during the holidays. He worked in his small office on two reports assigned by General Lund, just promoted from colonel. Finally at the end of the month, the doctor pronounced his foot healed. Michael was pleased because it meant he could once again get new assignments that would take him out of the office. He went back to living in his room on rue Laplace, again enjoying daily dinners and lively conversations at Chez Maman. Michael couldn't be happier when Maman said, *"Alors*, you will be talking like a Parisian very soon."

His flatmate, Jean-Luc, maintained "an active social life" with waitresses and shop girls. He told Michael that he needed a girlfriend and offered to find him one. Michael declined the offer, saying he was too busy and his schedule unpredictable. He felt envious when he saw couples obviously in love walking along the Seine or on the Champs Elysees, but none of Jean-Luc's girls was anything like Michael's image of his "Charlotte."

In the meantime, he wasn't short of social life. Prof. LaMont, with whom Michael had resumed his French lessons, invited him almost weekly for gatherings of his students who came to discuss French literature, and to share some cheap red wine. He went to dinners and concerts a few times during the winter with a few young, bachelor officers working at USEUCOM. Captain Burns and his Japanese wife, Michiko—"Michi is the best thing that happened to me in Japan"—treated Michael to excellent "faux-sukiyaki" dinners, cooked using substitute ingredients except for beef and soy sauce.

Early in February, Michael found a surprising telegram waiting for him when he arrived at his office in USEUCOM. It was from Mr. Siegrist, informing Michael that he and his wife were coming to Paris on the tenth and would Michael please contact him at the Hotel Bristol. Michael was pleased that he would see the Siegrists once again, but bowled over by their invitation. Their travel agent had made a reservation for dinner at Maxim's for the three of them.

Dinner at the world famous restaurant—Michael wasn't sure whether to use the adjective "luxurious" or "garish" to describe its décor—proved to be an unforgettable occasion, and Michael was at last grateful to his father for all the painful lessons in Western table manners. Dinner took the entire evening, as course after course was served, along with a different wine paired with every course by the maître d'. Michael soon realized that dinner at Maxim's was not a meal, but rather a drama with many acts, directed by the maître d', and performed by the diners, one overly attentive waiter per guest, and with a photographer and a scantily-clad "cigarette girl" appearing in the later acts. The food, far too copious and mostly very rich, and the wines, all of them superb but far too expensive—Michael saw Mr. Siegrist wince when the bill finally came—were the props in the play. By the end of the evening, Michael was very certain that participating in this performance once in a lifetime was quite enough for him.

But he much enjoyed seeing his benefactors. Though, Mrs. Siegrist was as he remembered her, Michael thought Mr. Siegrist had aged considerably since he had last seen him in Chicago prior to his senior year at Berkeley. Both were interested in his life in Paris and asked him numerous questions. Mrs. Siegrist was taken by the romance of the city and wanted to know if Michael had found his "*mademoiselle*" yet. He blushingly said, "Not yet," while thinking of the dark-haired beauty who was frequently on his Metro train when he traveled out to La Défense to catch the USEUCOM shuttle.

Michael continued writing intelligence reports for General Lund and carrying out assignments for Captain Burns. He found his work satisfying, but he did think an assignment that got him out of the office would make a nice change. He got his wish in late February, but in a very unexpected way, when he received a message from Gen.

Lund telling him to meet on February 25 a Lt. Col. Thomas Symington from the office of the Inspector General at the Pentagon. The lieutenant colonel, waiting for him at a small conference room in the USEUCOM headquarters, was a slim, graying officer wearing near Coke-bottle eyeglasses who got right down to business.

"I am looking into pilferage...no, more like organized thievery...on our European bases. As you may know, we have three quarters of a million military personnel and more than forty-five bases all over Europe. In Germany alone, we have eight large and twenty-two smaller bases. You can easily surmise that we spend millions every month just for food."

Michael had no idea where this was going, but he listened politely.

"The problem I want to talk to you about concerns at least a dozen bases in the countries under the purview of USEUCOM. Simply put, food is systematically being stolen from the storage areas. In Fôret d'Orléans, not far from Orléans, we have reason to believe large amounts of eggs, bacon, ham, and other foodstuffs are being stolen month after month."

"Bacon and eggs?" queried Michael without thinking, and then tried to suppress a smile.

"Bacon, eggs, and *ham*, Lieutenant!" said Lt. Col. Symington with vehemence. "Our office has estimated that we are losing at least 5 percent, possibly more, of our total requisitions in a dozen or more bases. The costs at some of our bases are so out of line that we are certain wide-scale thievery is going on. At Fôret d'Orléans, the total loss of eggs, ham, and bacon comes to about $8,000 a month, close to what I make in a year!"

Michael wondered where he would come in. Surely missing food didn't come under G2's purview.

"It sounds like a real problem, Sir. But why is this a job for intelligence? With people at the Inspector General's office working on this as well as the Criminal Investigation Command...and doesn't the military police deal with thievery?"

"You are right, Lieutenant. But the bottom line is this: both the IG and the CIC have more work than they can handle, and neither has staff familiar with local conditions or with the language capabilities needed to investigate this problem. And the MPs on the bases where we are losing the foodstuffs haven't been able to catch the thieves."

If none of the units responsible for preventing thievery had been able to catch the thieves, Michael wondered what he could be expected to do, but he said nothing and Symington went on.

"Coming back to the base in Fôret d'Orléans, we have looked at the assignment records of the personnel who work in the mess halls or have access to the storage areas, and there have been so many turnovers in the past year that we think it unlikely the thefts at this base involve military personnel. Rather, it seems more likely that locals are involved. And if local civilians working on the base are involved, we have to have hard evidence in order to request help from the local authorities."

"Sir, what exactly do you have in mind? Are you suggesting I investigate the base at Fôret d'Orléans and see how it's losing eggs and other supplies?"

"Precisely. The idea of asking you to look into this problem came from Gen. Lund. He thought you would be ideally suited for this job because you are 'smart and not unfamiliar with the ways of filching things'—his words, not mine. And with your looks, you should be able do the job without alerting the thieves. Don't get me wrong, Lieutenant, all I'm saying is that, out of uniform, no one would suspect you are in the U.S. Army. Oh, yes, Gen. Lund also told me your French should be more adequate for the job."

Michael was still a bit perplexed. He didn't understand exactly what the colonel had in mind. This was nothing he had been trained for.

Symington resumed his disquisition. "We are starting with the base at Fôret d'Orléans for two reasons: the first is that the losses are so large and growing; and second, Captain Flowers, the S4 officer in charge of the mess halls has written to us of his concerns over all the additional requisitions he has to make. Capt. Flowers arrived only three months ago and can't figure out why he needs so many extra supplies, primarily for meat and eggs. Naturally, he has checked the stores on a regular basis, and all the crates that are supposed to be there are there. That means the thieves aren't just hauling off foodstuff by the crate. The thieves could just be greedy local employees, but possibly an organized gang, and we don't know for sure that no military personnel are involved, so be careful about your cover."

"Sir, will Capt. Flowers be helping me in this investigation?"

"Yes, he will. And General Lund is seconding a Lieutenant Anthony Blando to work within the base, ostensibly as an S4 officer on temporary duty to learn the ropes of overseeing a mess hall. He will arrive in Paris on Sunday so we'd like you to start your investigation next week. With him on the inside, and you working as a local, I am sure the two of you can come up with a plan to handle this assignment."

"Sir, if we manage to find the thieves, what should we do?"

"Depends on who is doing the stealing. If the thieves are locals, we'll turn them over to the French authorities, but if our military personnel is involved, the CIC and the MP will deal with them."

Michael still thought this was a very strange assignment for a G2 officer, but he thought it could be interesting to work as an undercover detective. The colonel stood up, apparently concluding that Michael's last question constituted his acceptance of the assignment. He left the conference room after saying, "Lt. Koyama, call me if you need any help our office can give you. Good hunting!"

It was now Wednesday, so Michael went to see Captain Burns, who just sighed when Michael said he would be on special assignment starting on Monday.

Michael decided that going out to Orléans would be a good way to spend his Sunday. An hour by train from Gare de Lyon, Orléans was a beautiful city with its magnificent cathedral and in the city center a life-size statue of Joan d'Arc mounted on a horse. After a pleasant lunch in a café called Le Duc, Michael went to a bookstore and thumbed through a tourist guide. From it he learned that the Fôret d'Orléans covered over 3,000 hectares, and for generations had been the hunting grounds for elk for French nobles. "At the southwestern corner of the forest is a large American base," the section on Fôret d'Orléans concluded.

Michael asked the proprietor of the bookshop where the "working people" of Orléans area lived. Looking at Michael closely, the proprietor said:

"Some live near the Loire in the northern part of this city, but most live in Blois, about 30-40 minutes from here by bus. Nearly all of your people also live in Blois, where rooms and apartments are much cheaper than here, Monsieur."

Michael knew exactly what he meant by "your people": the immigrants from Vietnam who had come to France after the end of World War II. What the proprietor had said also meant that many of the French who worked at the base were also likely to be living in Blois. Michael looked at his watch and realized that a trip to Blois would have to wait as Tony was arriving in Paris in less than two hours. He returned to the Gare de Lyon and met Tony's train.

The pair immediately began to mull over possible strategies. They continued their discussion at Chez Maman over dinner and red wine. Tony drank most of it, though only Michael turned red. By ten, they had come up with a plan.

Tony's role was to be the straightforward one the lieutenant colonel had assigned: he would be "a novice" S4 officer working under Capt. Flowers. The only people who were to know Tony was a "plant" were Major Couch, who was the CO of the headquarters company, and Flowers himself. Tony would spend his time checking the mess hall records on requisitions and personnel, and learn what he could by talking to the people who worked there, under the guise of learning what an S4 officer should know.

Michael's role was trickier. Despite what Symington had said, it wasn't going to be easy to make the locals trust him enough to talk to him. He hoped that, with his Asian features, his French haircut, and the wire-rimmed eyeglasses that many Vietnamese and other Asians in Paris seemed to prefer, no one would ever suspect him of being an American military officer. Given their experience in World War II, Vietnamese might be reluctant to talk to someone they might think of as a former colonialist, so he wouldn't go as a Japanese. Instead, when he questioned locals, Michael would pretend to be a Chinese student from Hong Kong studying at the Sorbonne and conducting interviews for his sociological research. Tony dubbed him Johnny Wong. "It sounds like a Chinese gangster in San Francisco who's a bit of a dandy."

The pair arranged to meet regularly at the café in Orléans where Michael had had lunch. "It's too expensive for the locals working on the base to patronize," Michael reassured Tony.

The next morning Tony reported to Captain Flowers. Michael decided to first check out the base and then monitor the locals going in and out. From the information Lt. Col. Symington had given him, he knew that there were only two entrances to the base, which was surrounded by a high wire-mesh perimeter fence. The main entrance was the only one accessible to vehicles. This was guarded at all times by MPs who checked traffic going into and off the base. There was a second gate at the northwest corner, a back entrance for foot traffic kept open for use by local employees because the bus from Blois stopped there. Michael decided he would first check out this entrance.

From Orléans Michael took a bus going to Blois and got off at the stop called "Caserne," meaning barracks, which was located at this back entrance. From the bus stop, he could see the roofs of several tall buildings. On the gate was a notice in French: "Admittance Only for Military Personnel and Base Employees." But there was no guard and the gate had no lock on it. Michael peered through it. A paved path ran from the gate at least as far as the nearest buildings. No one was in sight and the two nearest structures were without windows, so obviously used for storage. He toyed with the idea of entering the base and looking around. But he decided against doing so because of the sign on the gate. He didn't want to risk getting caught before they'd even begun the investigation.

Next, Michael walked around the base to the main entrance to see how heavily guarded it was. An MP stared suspiciously at him, so he asked him in fractured English how one went about getting a job on the base. In simple, clear, and very loud English, as if speaking to a child, the soldier told him to go straight ahead and into the first building on the left where he would find an office with application forms. Michael had no intention of applying for a job but didn't want to seem suspicious so he went and picked up a form. Then he left the base. So far, he had learned that it was very easy for a stranger to gain access to the base but little more.

Michael decided to watch the local employees when they left the base after work, but in the meantime, he would check out Blois, where he was sure most lived. He walked back to the Caserne stop and, after a twenty-minute wait, caught the bus to Blois.

In contrast to Orléans, Blois was a small shabby town where he saw almost an equal number of French and poorly clad immigrants from Algeria, Vietnam, and elsewhere, some wearing sandals despite the cold. Near the bus station were several restaurants and cafés, all of which had seen better days. But it was now well past lunchtime and there was nowhere to eat near the base, so Michael picked what looked like the best of the shabby cafés and ordered what he considered the safest item, a cheese sandwich. He still had several hours before the local employees would leave work, so he looked around Blois, but the only thing he learned from this visit was that Blois was a depressing place to live.

Michael took the bus back to the Caserne stop and plopped down on a rickety bench. He had a long wait ahead of him, but he reminded himself that an instructor during his G2 training at Fort Dix had said: "A good G2 officer must be patient."

Just after seven, the workers began filing out of the gate, heading for the bus stop. Michael could see three or four young men and nearly twenty very young girls. The only exception was an older, dark-complexioned, and stunningly beautiful woman with a slight limp. He approached the workers and in a heavy accent asked them how one applied for a job on the base. The beautiful, older woman pointed the way toward the main gate and told him to apply there during normal working hours. Many of the girls were very pretty, but what surprised Michael was that they all seemed very well built, "stacked" in current slang. Rarely did one see so many voluptuous, young women even in Paris. The girls seemed to be walking awfully slowly. Perhaps they were tired from their day's work. But he also noticed the peculiar gait some of the women had. They almost waddled.

When the bus to Blois arrived, he boarded after the women. He hoped to glean something from listening to them. But the conversations were very subdued and sporadic, not what he would have expected from a group of young women released for the day from their uninteresting jobs. Several stole glances at him, and when they realized he saw them, quickly averted their eyes. He got the feeling that the women didn't much want him on the bus with them, but he put it up to his looking Vietnamese in an area where the local French thought the Vietnamese were taking jobs from them.

Michael went back to Paris for the night. As he lay in the dark in his small room, he kept seeing in his mind the attractive young women with such prominent breasts. At first, he thought he was envisioning these sexy creatures the way any young man would, but something kept niggling at him. The way they were *all* stacked. And the fact that none of them seemed to want to be on the same bus with him. And why the strange walk for such young women, waddling as though they had fat legs, though none of them did.

Suddenly Michael sat bolt upright. "No, it couldn't be!" He chuckled to himself. He thought a few minutes more, seeing the scene at the bus stop play in his mind like a film. "It's got to be!" he decided. He lay back down, planned what he would do in the morning, and finally fell asleep.

Since Michael knew that the women working on the base had to check in by ten, he got up early and managed to arrive at the bus station in Blois ten minutes before the 9:15 bus left to take workers to the Caserne stop. He stood at one edge of the station and watched as the passengers arrived. The first to board the bus were the beautiful dark-complexioned woman and two younger companions. As he watched them cross the station and climb up the steps, he thought, *I was right on the mark!*

Just before the bus pulled out of the station, Michael got on and walked to a seat in the rear. Other girls got on along the way, also going to the Caserne stop. When all the workers got off at the back gate to the base, Michael peered intently at them as they walked to the gate and then through it. This morning, all of the young women looked perfectly ordinary, and not one of them walked with even a hint of a limp or waddle.

Michael stayed on the bus until the terminus in Orléans where he phoned Tony, calling himself Colonel Michael Winston. Tony, surprised that Michael wanted to meet him so soon, agreed to come to Le Duc in Orléans about two, bringing with him any information he could on the French women working on the base. Michael also suggested he bring Capt. Flowers if possible.

Tony arrived with the captain in tow. After recovering from the shock of learning that the Asian in the well-worn jacket and un-ironed pants was the lieutenant he was to meet, Tom Flowers greeted Michael warmly and said "Call me Tom," despite the fact that he outranked Michael. As soon as the men had been served coffee, Michael quietly announced:

"I think I've learned how some of the foodstuff is leaving the base."

Tom narrowed his eyes but said nothing. Tony, who looked surprised, said, "You must be kidding. How could you? We've only just begun the investigation and you aren't even on the base!"

Michael explained, "No, I'm not kidding. Last night I watched the girls who leave by the back gate walk to the bus stop. They had a peculiar gait, sort of a waddle—the way someone who has very fat legs walks. And the older, dark-haired woman had a slight limp. Some were very young and slender, but every one of them had big boobs."

Tony grinned and started to say something, but Michael raised his hand to stop him.

"This morning, I went to Blois and got on the same bus these workers take to get to the base by ten. I watched the girls as they boarded the bus, and again when they got off at the base and walked through the gate. All of them walked normally, and all the girls looked quite ordinary... no noticeably large 'headlights.' A couple looked down-right flat-chested."

Flowers was agog. Tony burst out laughing. "You can't mean they're carrying cold bacon in their bras?"

"More likely eggs," Michael said, "though I'm not sure how they do it so the eggs don't break. And from the way they walk, my guess is that they're hanging ham and bacon from their waists and the packets get between their legs and hamper the way they walk. Why don't we go look at them tonight when they leave the base so you can see for yourselves?"

"We've got to be careful," Tony said. "Assuming that the women are walking out with foodstuffs on their persons, we don't know who's orchestrating this. So much is missing that the ham and eggs the women take out with them can't be just for their own use; someone must be buying the goods from them."

Tom was aghast. "How could I have missed this for the three months I've been here?... But come to think of it, I'm almost never in my office at seven when they go off duty. One of the mess sergeants stays until after the local staff leaves and locks up after them, but their office is not near the back exit." He paused and then added in a tone heavy with self-reproach, "No wonder Monique has been so helpful— the sergeants say that she always goes to report when the kitchen staff has left so they can lock up. And I'll bet that on the days I stay late, Monique spreads the word and they don't take anything."

Tony and a very chagrinned Tom Flowers returned to the base. At six, both left the mess hall after Flowers informed the mess sergeant on late duty in earshot of several Frenchwomen that he was leaving so he could introduce Lt. Blando to the officers who hadn't yet met him. After changing into dark civilian clothing, they went to meet Michael, who had sneaked in the back entrance and was waiting for them behind a couple of large sycamore trees not far from the gate.

Shortly after seven, the local employees, nearly all women, came around the storage unit and headed toward the gate. It was nearly dark, but the small lights along the fence clearly illuminated the employees. Their silhouettes were visible, if not always their faces.

Tom started. "I don't believe this! Michael is right. Those girls...Monique, too...they do have something in their bras! Look. And the skinny girl just behind her is Yvette. She's sixteen and just started working at the base after I was trans-ferred here. No way does she have tits like that!" He went on to identify several others by name.

Their vigil had proven Michael's suspicions correct, so the next morning, Tom, accompanied by Tony, went to Colonel Bowles, the base commander, whom Tom characterized as "domineering but not all that able." They told him everything—who Tony really was, why he was on the base, and what they had seen the previous evening.

At first, the base commander was furious at Tom. He loudly chastised him for "going behind my back and writing to the IG in the Pentagon about your suspicions" and "colluding with Major Couch to have Lt. Blando on my base without informing me." The captain did his best to try to mollify his superior officer.

"I simply wrote in my monthly report that I wondered why I had to make such a large additional requisition every month. The IG had similar cases of food disappearing and decided to start their investigation with this base. They were the people who told me to tell no one on the base about the investigation. And, Sir, Major Couch thought you wouldn't be interested in knowing he had assigned a very junior officer in his company on a short TDY, temporary duty."

Finally the colonel calmed down after he realized that the two officers in front of him were informing him that they thought they had found the thieves, and that it wasn't anyone in the military. In the end, he granted their request to send four MPs to help them "nail" the thieves as they left the base that evening.

At 6:30, Michael, Tony, and Tom joined the MPs to await the departure of the French staff. Again Tom had left early after informing the staff he was departing for the day. Two MPs along with the three officers sequestered themselves behind the trees, while two more MPs waited outside the gate, out of sight of anyone on the base. It was drizzling, unpleasant weather for a stakeout. The three officers consoled themselves that the rainy night made it more likely the French women would fail to notice the MPs until it was too late.

Shortly after seven, they saw the mess hall employees head toward the back gate. The three officers looked at them intently. Yes, the women were generously endowed and waddled. Tom called the MPs outside the gate on the field phone he carried, "It's a go. They've got the goods."

As soon as half of the group had stepped through the gate, the MPs confronted them and told everyone to stop and face the fence. Two young men and the older woman tried to break away and run toward the trees near the bus stop, but an MP yelled, "Stop or we'll shoot," and the three immediately halted. The entire group was herded back onto the base by the MPs and Tom announced that all had to be body searched.

One of the youngest girls started to cry, and then two others burst into tears as well. The entire group, wet and bedraggled with tears and rain, was led back to the dayroom for soldiers in the headquarters building, which became a makeshift brig. The MPs searched the two men and WACs were called in to search the women. Altogether seventeen women were found with eggs and ham hidden under their clothes. The three young women who had nothing on their persons and the two men were released. Michael and Tony were very sure the two men were somehow involved because they had immediately run when they saw the MPs, but the lieutenants had no evidence to hold them.

Questioned by Flowers and Michael, the youngest girls confessed between their sobs. They had been given special pouches to attach to their bras to safely carry the eggs, and the meat was hung between their legs. They didn't dare carry anything in tote bags, thinking they might be searched on their way out, as happened very occasionally before Colonel Bowles took command of the base several months before. Asked why they were stealing, one girl said truculently: "Our wages at the base are very low and we need this food. You may laugh at us, but you don't know how poor we are compared to you Americans."

Michael and Tony were convinced that neither the quantities of foodstuff that was missing nor the organized fashion in which it was being taken could be accounted for by these girls taking a few eggs and some ham back to their families.

Seeing that Tom looked exasperated as he questioned Monique in a corner of the room, Michael wondered if he could trick her into confessing. He walked over with Tony and said, "We've just been told that all of the younger girls work for you. If you admit to being the mastermind behind all the losses, we promise to make things go easier for you with the base commander, and more importantly, with the French police. Why not admit to this and make things easier for yourself?"

Monique looked at Michael and said nothing for a long minute. He wondered if his trick would work, but finally she said quietly, "If I do as you request, will you also make it easier for all the young girls?"

Michael and Tony nodded and Michael said, "Yes, we are here to stop the thefts, not to make life any harder for all of you."

Monique stared at Michael, and then in a resigned voice, began to speak. "I saw you on the bus this morning. How could I know that you were an American officer? All right, *Monsieur Le Lieutenant*, what do you want to know?"

She began to confess, speaking in a level tone. With a frozen expression on her exotic face, she admitted that the thievery had begun about two years before, a year after she began working on the base. It had started on a very modest scale. "I took home a few eggs and occasionally some bacon and ham to feed my small son better than I could on my meager wages. No one would have missed the amounts I took."

But two things happened to cause Monique to begin stealing larger amounts and more systematically. Her son had several bouts of bronchitis and pneumonia, and in his undernourished condition, the doctor feared he would develop TB if he didn't have a better diet and a warmer home. At the same time, she learned that her Algerian husband had been killed in the outskirts of Oran by the French army. Her brother had been trying to persuade her to work with him for Le Mouvement National Algérien but she had resisted doing anything so illegal and dangerous. However, upon hearing of the death of her husband, she was so furious that she agreed to join her brother in fighting for Algerian independence.

Tony interrupted her: "And your brother started to work for the base as well. One of the two men we let go was your brother." He stated this as fact, not as a question.

Monique looked at him with her mouth open. "How did you know that? We have different names."

Tony replied, "You kept looking at him after we arrested you, and your eyes are the same as his."

Tom took over the questioning at this point, taking down the details for his report. Monique admitted designing and sewing the special pouches to hold the eggs and meat, recruiting new girls as they were hired—really coercing them to join her group but also offering them a cut of the stolen goods from the monthly amount they had to supply her with. But she was evasive when asked to whom she sold the goods.

"My brother's friends sold them for us somewhere in Paris. That's all I know."

On the following day, Colonel Bowles summarily fired all the young women and turned Monique over to the gendarmerie in Orléans. Michael was glad when he heard that all the young girls would go free. While listening to the sobbing girls tell why they were stealing, he had recalled all too vividly his years in the orphanage in Asagaya when, constantly hungry, he and a couple of boys had frequently gone "hunting" for food, taking a carrot or two out of one field, a few tomatoes and radishes from another.

MICHAEL WENT BACK TO HIS ROUTINE of working on intelligence reports for General Lund and on assignments from Captain Burns. Then, at the beginning of June, Michael received a call from Lt. Col. Symington asking Michael to go to Munich to help Jack Landauer with an investigation of mess hall losses at a large base there. As he had in the Fôret d'Orléans case, Michael was to go under cover. He took a train to Munich, checked into a small, rather dingy hotel where Jack had reserved a room for him.

The following morning, Jack picked him up at nine, and, as soon as Michael got into the motor pool sedan, Jack began to brief him, almost without stopping for breath.

"Michael, we've got a big problem here. Huge losses in everything, especially meat. But unlike at the Orléans base, here we have pretty good security, and General Applen, who's in charge, is giving me all the help I need. When Symington first gave me the assignment, I asked if I could get you. He agreed on the spot because of your success at Orléans. As to the plan, I'm here in the guise of an efficiency expert to advise the base on its mess hall procedures. I suggested that you be undercover and stay off base in case we need to investigate locals. The locals here wouldn't expect an Asian to speak German any better than you do."

"Thanks a lot!" Michael interjected.

Jack smiled and continued, "This is a big outfit—over 3,000 men. I've been here now for two days, but I have barely started looking at the records. Gen. Applen is letting us use the dining room in his house—it's off the base—so you'll have a place to work, and we can meet there as well since his wife is in the U.S."

Jack went on to describe the base to Michael. It was located just outside the city limits of Munich and occupied almost 300 hectares of flat grassland with a forest on the west side. There was a perimeter fence running around the entire base, and sentries guarded both the main gate on the east side of the base and the side gate for military and delivery trucks on the south side.

Jack's monologue turned to the investigation.

"Gen. Applen runs a tight ship here. There's no way you could have here the kind of thievery you found at Fôret d'Orléans. The two S4 officers have all the doors of the four cold storages secured every night, all the keys are kept by the officers, and they are responsible for whoever signs the keys out. Everything taken out of storage is monitored by a mess sergeant, and the comings and goings of the local mess employees are all carefully watched."

"However, despite these security measures, food is missing in large quantities?"

"Right. The S4 ends up making additional requisitions practically every month and not for small amounts either. Though I've only gone over the records quickly, I've come to the conclusion that the loss rate is usually around 5 percent. And that's adjusting for what I think is a reasonable extra amount for these big infantry boys to eat, over what the Army thinks is a normal amount."

"Have you looked at the fronts of the *Fräuleins* working at the mess when they go home?"

"I knew you'd ask that. Yes, I have. But I haven't seen many of these women with outsize boobs. And no one walks like a duck. Even if some of them are willing to suffer cold eggs in their bras and carry meats between their legs, that wouldn't begin to account for the losses we're seeing here. "

After showing Michael the base from the outside, Jack drove him to the general's home in a lovely wooded neighborhood nearby. A German housekeeper let them in. The records were already on the dining room table.

While Jack conducted interviews on the base, Michael scrutinized the monthly records of the foodstuffs, item by item, over the past two years. He found Jack was right— the monthly losses were large, starting about a year ago, despite the security at the gates to the base. After examining and reexamining the tables, Michael became frustrated at not finding any clues for solving this mystery. He sighed, thinking, "This is like one of Edgar Allan Poe's stories of a murder committed in a locked room—there must be a clue hidden in plain sight."

Michael's concern was with meats and eggs, most of which were transported from Denmark, the Netherlands, and northern Germany, to Stuttgart where a truck from the base collected them. He decided to draw a graph showing the amount of requisitions of these foodstuffs over the past eighteen months, and by each date he wrote in the name of the officer who had made the requisition and the receiving officer. He had no information about the civilian drivers or base workers who handled the unloading.

The graph showed no consistent pattern in the amount of the requisitions, other than a slowly rising trend, nor could Michael see any pattern in which officer made the requisitions. Then he looked at who signed for the requisitions when they arrived. Sometimes it was a Capt. Baum and slightly less often, a Capt. Evans. Did anyone who signed for the requisitions have any correlation with the losses? Although the evidence was circumstantial, the number and amount of extra requisitions tended to be higher after the dates when Capt. Baum signed for the shipments. Was it possible that he was signing for less than full shipments, that somehow part of the shipment was being diverted?

But where and how were the shipments being diverted? Was the captain the mastermind or only a part of a ring of thieves? This could be tricky to investigate.

Jack arrived just after five to compare notes on their investigation. Michael greeted him with, "I think I may have found a clue as to what's happening." After going over the records with him, Jack had to agree. But getting hard evidence to prove Captain Baum's culpability and nabbing all of the miscreants working with him could be difficult. After some discussion, they settled on a plan to have Jack find out what he could about the routing of the truck bringing the foodstuffs from Stuttgart to the base.

The next morning, Jack went back to interviewing personnel at the mess hall, but today he made sure the senior truck driver, Josef Fischer, was among them. Fischer had been working for the base as a driver for a decade, long before the losses began. Jack questioned him very carefully, not knowing if he was involved or not. He said that he was on the base to introduce efficiency measures into the running of the mess hall, and this included how foodstuffs were transported. His concern was with the long drive to Stuttgart and back, usually with an empty truck on the drive north.

Jack reported to Michael that "Herr Fischer was both nervous and almost obsequious, so I started out by making him detail everything they did en route. It was like pulling teeth." Then, Jack added, smiling, "But I finally figured out how the thefts must be taking place. And the amazing thing is that I don't think the drivers have a clue."

Michael was intrigued. "So what's going on?"

"The key is what happens on the trip back from Stuttgart to the base. It turns out that on some of their trips they are told to make an extra stop north of Munich to pick up eggs at the warehouse of a Johannes Berger, who, Fischer says, is one of the bigger wholesalers of many kinds of foodstuff, even though he started his business only after the war. Herr Berger has his own men load the eggs and kindly lets the two drivers have supper at the canteen for his employees. The driver thought I was concerned about the amount of time their stop for supper delayed the return of the truck to the base, and insisted that they ate quickly while the eggs were being loaded. Two things are significant: the drivers are out of sight of the truck during this meal break and—wait till you hear this—the base does *not* purchase eggs or anything else from Berger!"

"Okay, I got it! And on the days that the men are told to stop at Berger's, the officer signing for the shipment is Capt. Baum, right?"

"Right on, Michael. Baum must be signing for a full shipment, when in fact part of it was offloaded at Berger's warehouse. To make sure the drivers aren't suspicious when they open the truck and see the load, on the days the truck makes the extra stop and so it arrives late at the base, Fischer says the 'considerate' Capt. Baum tells the drivers to go home and has a couple of mess hall employees do the unloading."

Michael asked, "Who are the employees who unload for Baum?"

"Aaron Heineman and Reuben Mandel, two German employees who do odd jobs in the mess halls. Interestingly, both were hired after Capt. Baum arrived on the base.

Michael and Jack were now convinced that Captain Baum was involved, either as the mastermind or a key player in the ongoing theft. They went to present "the evidence" to Major Williams, the provost marshal of the base. Although the major thought their "evidence was inferential rather than solid," he nevertheless agreed that, "We've got to see. Nothing to lose." After checking the requisition record and the duty roaster of S4 officers, the three found that, in two days, Capt. Baum would be on duty to sign in a large incoming shipment of foodstuff coming from Stuttgart. The three decided they would be there when the shipment arrived.

Two days later, at 6:30 p.m., Michael—now in uniform— Jack, Major Williams, and an MP, sat quietly in one of the day rooms where off-duty soldiers came to play cards or ping pong or to watch TV. The loading dock was visible from the window. The four waited with the lights out for the arrival of the truck from Stuttgart.

Just before seven, the large army truck arrived and backed up to the loading dock. Capt. Baum immediately appeared, followed by the two Germans, Heineman and Mandel. The captain motioned the two men to open the back of the truck and unload, and went over to the two drivers. After briefly talking to Fischer, he signed the papers the driver handed him. Then the two drivers left.

Michael could see the crates begin to pile up on the dock as the captain watched, but oddly, he made no attempt to check them against the bill of lading.

At this point, Major Williams said, "Let's go," and the four men dashed out of the Day Room, through the storage area, and onto the dock.

"Captain Baum. May I see the copy of the papers you've just signed?

But before Baum answered, the major ordered Michael and Jack to verify the shipment. The two men who had been unloading the trunk tried to slink away, but the major called, "Halt!" and ordered them to help Jack and Michael move crates.

Captain Baum, who looked visibly shaken, silently handed over the documents. Major Williams gave Jack the bill of lading.

It took less than fifteen minutes for Jack and Michael to cross check the number of crates against the amounts listed on the papers. They matched exactly. Jack looked puzzled, but Michael said, "Let's open the crates and check the contents."

Major Williams ordered the two German employees to cut the metal straps from around the crates of meat while Michael started opening them. Capt. Baum watched what was happening in silence without moving a muscle.

With the help of two Germans, Michael and Jack went on to open nearly thirty crates at random, and all contained what the label said they did. Everything seemed to be in order.

Jack was taken aback and clearly flustered. This was not what he had expected. He started to apologize: "Major Williams...sorry, Sir. Looks like...."

Suddenly, Capt. Baum interrupted: "Major Williams, I have to oversee my men and get this stuff stored, and it's getting late. Is this nonsense over?"

Michael saw the relief on Baum's face and jumped in. "Wait a minute. I have an idea—please bear with me for a minute."

He went over to an opened crate of ham. He removed the top layer of meat and then the piece of cardboard separating that from the next layer. Next, he pulled out not more packages of ham, but something wrapped in newspaper. Captain Baum's expression froze.

Wordlessly, Michael unwrapped the newspaper to expose a log of firewood. Jack joined Michael, and the two unpacked crate after crate. Half of the crates they opened contained just what they should, but the two lieutenants soon discovered that the crates that had been nearest the rear door of the truck and unloaded first, contained more firewood and paper than they did foodstuffs, with just a layer or two on top in case anyone opened them to check.

All the while the crates were being checked, Baum sat on the steps of the loading dock, his eyes shut.

After some twenty crates were found to contain firewood, Major Williams told Jack and Michael they could stop their search. "We'll have S4 personnel check it all against the bill of lading." He then called Gen. Applen, and after a short conversation, he and the MP took Capt. Baum to the base brig. Jack and Michael stayed and oversaw the storage of the shipment in a corner of the refrigerated storeroom by the two German employees.

When the job had been completed and the door locked, Jack said, "Well, we've missed dinner at the mess."

"Let's go into the village and have some real German food. I'd rather have some German beer and knackwurst with sauerkraut instead of army fodder in any case," said Michael.

Later, with a stein of beer in front of each of them, Jack asked: "Why did you think of searching below the top layers. It never occurred to me that they would put a layer of eggs and meat in the crates to fool us. To think to examine below the top layer takes a devious mind. Are you even more devious than I give you credit for?"

Michael replied, "Thanks for the compliment. I think Baum is a careful man. He wanted to make sure he could go on stealing. So he wanted to minimize the risk of getting caught should he have been called away and someone else had to check in the shipment. I also think the two German guys who did the unloading are in on it. But we had to let them go because at this point we don't have any evidence. But Baum had to have someone take the firewood out and dispose of it.'

"Yeah, I agree with your logic, but my question is, why *did* you think to look beneath the top layers?" asked Jack.

"Well, there are some things about my dubious past you don't know about. Even though the statute of limitations kicked in a long time ago, I'm not sure I should let on to something that might be considered felonious," teased Michael.

"Come on, give," Jack demanded. "As you've said, the statute of limitations has passed and I won't tell anyone else!"

Michael took a large gulp of beer. "Well, there was the coffee can caper...." He grinned at Jack.

"Okay, okay, I'll buy dinner. Now tell me about it."

"Okay, you knew that after I ran away from the orphanage in Tokyo, I ended up 'working for' a small-time black-marketeer named Konishi near Kobe? What I did involved a lot of things that were definitely unethical, if not downright illegal, such as removing labels from goods that I realized later almost all came from a nearby PX. We also repackaged things—to do that I even learned how to solder."

"What does soldering have to do with why you looked under the top layers in the crates?" persisted Jack.

"The coffee can caper," answered Michael. "Someone brought to Konishi from the PX a dozen large cans of American coffee. He was just going to sell them as is, but I had another idea...I'm not sure I should admit to this," Michael said, and dug into his sauerkraut.

"You can't stop now," Jack insisted.

"Yeah, well, I thought we could make more money if we could sell more than just a dozen cans of coffee. So I went around to the best restaurants and bars in the area, many of which catered to Americans and other foreigners and to Japanese black-marketeers. Most were happy to let me have their empty coffee cans. I also 'rescued' some cans from garbage bins."

"Rescued? Anyway, go on."

"Well, after carefully cleaning the fifty-two cans I collected, I filled them with sawdust I found at the back of a lumberyard, and lugged back to Konishi's stall in his wheel-barrow. I didn't fill the cans up to the rim with sawdust but left about one inch at the top. This last inch I filled with real coffee from the twelve cans the salesman had brought. I filled the salesman's twelve cans the same way. Now there were sixty-four cans of coffee—more accurately, sixty-four cans of which only the top inch or so was coffee."

Jack's face registered first astonishment, then amuse-ment, as Michael continued his tale. "It took me full two days to solder all the cans. If I may say so, thanks to the experi-ence in soldering I had acquired by this time, no one but an expert could tell the cans had been opened and re-soldered. But I played it safe by having Konishi tell his 'salesmen' to market the coffee to unsuspecting housewives in the evening when it was getting dark....No giggling, Jack...and not to sell to restaurants, which were used to seeing new cans of coffee. My 'coffee' sold extremely well; all sixty-four cans, each priced at one-third less than the going price, were sold out over two evenings."

Jack could no longer contain his laughter.

"I was told there was only one very old lady who was suspicious and asked that the cans she was buying be opened. But after she saw the coffee and smelled its aroma, she was so pleased that she bought three cans. So that's why I thought there might be something other than foodstuffs under the top layers of bacon and ham," Michael finished. He took a swig of beer and sat back.

"Lt. Landauer, now please pay the bill and take me back to my hotel in Munich," requested Michael. "I have a long train ride back to Paris tomorrow."

IN THE CAVERNOUS HAUPTBAHNHOF—Munich's main train station—Michael, seeing all the people waiting for the express train going to Paris, regretted not having a reserved seat. When the train doors opened, he joined the crush of people waiting to board a second-class car and, as people began to get onto the train, he was shoved from behind and fell against a dark-haired young woman laden with a suitcase, a basket, and other belongings. She staggered. Michael braced himself with his small case against the side of the open door and grabbed her suitcase with his free hand, enabling her to regain her footing. He helped her onto the train, apologizing in his inadequate German. He helped her into one of the last empty seats, stowed her suitcase on the overhead rack, and then looked around for a place to sit. By now, only one seat, next to hers, remained empty. Michael hesitated, wondering if he could take the seat without appearing "too forward."

"*Bitte,*" the young woman said and patted the seat next to her. Michael put his own small case on the rack and gratefully sat down next to her. Then he took a good look at her. Simultaneously, the two recognized each other. "You're the one from the Metro," they both said in French. Then they looked at each other and laughed.

"Is your foot okay now? I saw you limping." The young woman spoke first.

"Yes, thank you. I had an accident on a velo and broke it," Michael replied. Since she seemed willing to talk to him, he asked, "You always seemed to be memorizing something whenever I see you on the train. What are you studying?"

She answered, smiling and showing evenly white teeth. "I'm studying to be an opera singer, but when I'm on the train to La Défense, I review for my Italian lessons. My Italian teacher lives very close to the La Défense station. What do you do out there?"

Michael thought that when she heard what he did, the conversation would come to an end, but he might as well get it over with. "I'm in the U.S. Army. I live in Paris but for my work I go out to USEUCOM—the headquarters of the U.S. Army in Europe. There's a shuttle bus from La Défense."

"Aah, now I understand. I thought you might be Vietnamese, but you don't quite look like one...and you're not wearing the metal-rimmed glasses they like. You have what I'm sure is a French overcoat, but those clunky shoes the American soldiers wear. I wondered what you were."

Michael was both embarrassed and pleased that she had checked him out so thoroughly while seemingly engrossed in her Italian. She asked Michael if he would mind switching to English, as her English was still better than her French. He readily agreed, and the two chatted a bit about what it was like to live in Paris as foreigners. Gradually, their conversation became more personal. Michael asked her about her studies in Paris and learned that she was taking private lessons under a former opera singer, Madame Wolkonskaya.

Becoming bolder, Michael asked, "What were you doing in Munich?"

"I went back to audition for a position as an understudy-apprentice in an opera company in Munich. My mother isn't very well and my parents would really like to have me come back home to live next year. But I'd like another year in Paris even though it means that I am terribly busy as I earn my lessons by serving as companion-cum-secretary to Madame Wolkonskaya."

Michael rather hoped she would stay in Paris as well. A cart came down the aisle with drinks and snacks, and he offered the young woman coffee. She accepted and then opened the large basket sitting on her lap. "My mother insisted that I take all kinds of goodies back, both to eat on the train and as gifts for Madame. How about some strudel with the coffee?"

Somehow balancing the hot coffee containers and dealing with the gooey strudel made Michael lose any lingering shyness he had. The two talked on and on as the train sped through the countryside. Cocooned in the crowded railway car, the two felt apart from the ordinary world and both revealed facts and feelings they rarely talked about in their daily lives in Paris. Michael thought this was what was often referred to as "chemistry," or when someone said two people "clicked." He knew he thoroughly enjoyed the conversation with her—he could even admit to being enthralled by her.

But he didn't yet know this was the beginning of an over-powering as well as all-consuming love he was soon to have for this young woman whose name was Alissa Weidenfeld and whose life had been molded no less than Michael's by the accident of birth and the madness and inhumanity of war.

Michael learned that Alissa was Jewish. Her father was a journalist and her mother had been a choral director at a *gymnasium*, a German secondary school. Moshe Weidenfeld, an international correspondent for *Suddeutsche Zeitung*, had been assigned to New York in the thirties. Alissa had been conceived while he was on a home visit in 1936, but Moshe wasn't able to persuade his wife to leave Germany when she could have, and then it was too late. Gertrude Weidenfeld "gave" her baby daughter to her best Christian friend the night before she "disappeared," though everyone knew she had been rounded up by soldiers along with other Jews.

Alissa spent her childhood in Fussen, a small town thirty kilometers south of Munich, thinking she was Alissa Meyer, the daughter of Peter and Angela Meyer. In 1946, when she was ten, her parents came and "reclaimed" a very shocked Alissa. She was told only that her mother survived because she had been "teaching piano to the camp commandant's daughter who was your age." Alissa never asked for the details of her disappearance and life in the camps because "I gradually realized mother had been through a ghastly ordeal."

Michael told Alissa that he too belonged to a racial minority. When she looked puzzled, he explained: "People who are half Thai and half Japanese are so rare in Japan, it felt like I was in a minority group of one person." And he went on to tell her that he had been born in Bangkok to a Thai mother, who had died at his birth, and a Japanese father, who was executed for treason by the Japanese military for

227

his opposition to the war and aiding the British in Burma. Michael smiled wryly and said, "The war transformed my life from that of a privileged child living in a sub-tropical paradise to a badly dressed orphan, almost always cold, and with never enough to eat."

When she heard Michael's story, Alissa said in a tone Michael thought was caring: "Compared to you, I am lucky. I have my parents, in fact two sets of parents, while you lost your mother at birth and your father was killed by the Japanese Nazis."

Michael decided it was time to change the subject and asked her about becoming an opera singer. Though he had heard arias on his father's gramophone, he had never seen an opera.

"I've always wanted to be a singer, but my family doesn't have the money to send me to a famous music school, like the Juilliard in New York. So I was lucky when Madame Wolkonskaya heard me in a school performance and agreed to tutor me. She's an excellent teacher but very demanding, both during lessons and after." And Alissa made a face.

"I hope you have a bit of free time," Michael ventured. "I really would like to see you again." The train was nearing Gare de L'Est and he couldn't bear the thought of not seeing her again, except across a crowded metro train.

Alissa responded instantly with a shy smile. "That would be nice. I usually have Sunday off and Wednesday evenings." She fished in her handbag and came up with a small piece of paper on which she wrote Madame Wolkonskaya's address and phone number. Michael was elated but tried not to show it.

It was dark when the train pulled into the Gare de l'Est. Going to the metro station together, Michael escorted Alissa as far as Chatelet where she had to change trains. She was insistent that she could manage from there on her own. She wouldn't think of Michael going out of his way to go any further with her.

Michael reluctantly agreed. As they were parting, he had a momentary thought of hugging her and kissing her cheek as a few couples were doing. But he couldn't quite muster the courage. Instead, he thrust his hand out, saying, "Thanks to you, it was a wonderful trip." Alissa clasped his hand and responded, "The same...thanks to you. I'll see you soon? *Au revoir*, a lieutenant who would like to be a professor."

After she disappeared down the passageway, Michael emerged from the station into the well-lit square from where he could see the silhouette of Notre Dame. He crossed the bridge to the left bank, with the Seine shining in the moonlight. Life couldn't be more perfect. "I've finally met my Charlotte!" As he walked uphill toward rue Laplace, the cobblestones under his feet felt more like air.

Chapter 9

Paris, 1960

NEW YEAR'S 1960 FOUND LES QUATRE COPAINS IN BARCELONA, the trip they had had to postpone the year before when Michael broke his ankle. The buddies all came with great anticipation because none of the four had visited Spain before. Michael had mistakenly looked forward to a warm vacation with perhaps some balmy Mediterranean breezes. Instead, he found the brisk winter winds too cold for his liking. And the hotel they had booked was rather run-down—the low rates should have made him suspicious.

"Jack, you told us your uncle said this was the best place he stayed in all of Spain," said Michael rather accusingly, as he tried to move his patio chair a bit more out of the wind.

Looking a bit chagrinned, Jack replied, "Well it was decades ago. And you'll have to admit it's cheap. And the food is great. Here, put on my windbreaker," and he tossed it over to Michael.

His friends laughed as Michael donned the jacket of a man a head taller and at least fifty pounds heavier, but Michael was happy to be a bit warmer. He'd have brought his French overcoat if he'd known how cold it was going to be.

"Okay, okay, I'll grant you that the food is great. I never had *paella* before—it's fantastic!" And with that, he stopped complaining and decided to make the best of this chilly vacation and two weeks away from Alissa, who had gone home to Munich for the holidays.

And as the days passed, Michael agreed that the proprietor and his staff were treating them royally, though from the questions they asked, they seemed to think the four a very odd group: four young men who all looked as if they came from different parts of the world. But the four came with U.S. military ID cards, and Michael was sure the staff could see they were very good friends. Certainly, they were appreciative of the delicious meals they were fed. So Michael didn't mind the smiles as he ordered Serrano ham again and again—it was even better than the *jambon de pays* he often ate in Paris.

Last year in Paris, the four *copains*, full of their new experiences in Europe, had talked of nothing but their experiences in the cities to which they had been posted. But this year, with less than six months to go before their tours of duty in Europe were up, their conversations focused on the future. While enjoying fishing expeditions off the coast and a visit to the Parc de Montjuic, a large national park just up the coast, they talked about what they wanted to do after their return to the States.

Jack wanted to go to law school and had applied to five, but Michael could tell that he had his heart set on getting into Harvard Law. Tony planned to go into business and hoped to be admitted to the Columbia Business School. Winston still wanted to be a writer but had come to the conclusion that he had better get some experience and earn a living before he set out to "write the novel that will earn me a Pulitzer or a Nobel," he said with a grin.

Michael had thought fleetingly of staying on in Europe because of Alissa, but French universities didn't teach the kind of economics he wanted to study. And with so little savings, he would be hard put to find a way to support himself, let alone pay for graduate education in France. It was simply not possible to stay on in Europe; his future lay back in the United States. He had applied to three American universities with top-notch economics departments, with the encouragement of and strong recommendations from Professor Minsky, who had not forgotten "the student who wrote the best paper I'd seen in some years but in the worst English I can remember." Michael's first choice was Berkeley, though he knew that students were encouraged to go for a Ph.D, at a school other than where they had received their B.A. And he would have to go to the university that offered him the most financial support. Going back to the U.S. meant parting from Alissa, certainly for some time. But Michael decided that there was no point in worrying about all this now. He would enjoy his two-week holiday.

On the third night after arriving in Barcelona, Michael, along with Tony and Jack, regaled Winston with stories of what they called the "bacon and egg investigations," stories they could tell because they weren't G2 investigations and which became more amusing with each telling.

Winston was instantly envious because he hadn't been part of an experience that he thought would make such great material for a novel. "But it would be even better if you knew why that captain had concocted his devious scheme to steal on such a large scale. I understand why the French women were stealing, but why would a career army man risk his career?"

"We did find out," Jack said. "It was another sad story. The captain was Jewish, and his relatives managed to get out of Germany just before the war, but his aunt stayed on. She was married to a Catholic man and she was sure he could protect her. But he was killed in Stalingrad in 1942, and then the aunt was rounded up and sent to Belzec, a concentration camp near Lvov in Poland. That camp had the highest rate of deaths of all the camps, but she miraculously survived. After the war, she returned to Leipzig, and then the poor woman found herself in what became East Germany. Eventually she was able to contact her relatives in the U.S. and they desperately tried to think of how they might get her out and over to the States."

His three listeners were fascinated, including Michael, who hadn't heard this before either.

"This woman's brother was Captain Baum's father. He contacted his son who had just been transferred to Munich. Baum began to search for a way to get his aunt out. He went to the newly rebuilt synagogue in Munich and someone there introduced him to Johannes Berger, a food wholesaler. This guy had organized a small group called 'Der Freiheit Eilbus'—The Freedom Coach—and they were spiriting East Germans out for profit. But they also had expenses as they had had to purchase cars in East Germany and buy the gas, pay the guys who worked for them across the border, and rather handsomely as this was a risky operation. The captain didn't have the money to pay for getting his aunt out, even though he was offered a 'special Jewish price.' So, he came up with a plan to 'earn' the money by selling American army supplies to Berger at a discounted price. Anyway, Baum got his aunt out and then kept on with the scheme because there were other Jews who needed to get out. It bothered his conscience less to steal from the army than to leave these people under East German rule."

"What happened to the captain?" asked the always-curious Winston.

"Oh, he's already been court-martialed. But given the circumstances, I'm very sure he won't spend too many years behind bars. I don't know what punishment the West Germans gave the wholesaler, but I heard the Freedom Coach was disbanded."

Michael wondered about all the people whom the Freedom Coach would have helped to escape from East Germany if it had stayed in business.

ALL TOO SOON THE LEAVE WAS OVER and the four parted. Michael's life returned to his old routines. He was now working full-time on reports for General Lund. For more than a year now, he had had assignments relating to the deteriorating situation in Algeria and how the independence of the former French colonial possessions in Africa was affecting French domestic politics. At the same time, Michael was also keeping track of and assessing the changing views seen in the major newspapers on the increase in the number of Communist mayors and municipal councilmen, and on French perceptions of the U.S. forces in France. Michael was finally beginning to grasp the breadth of the problems faced by staff officers in G2 at the Pentagon.

To carry out these assignments, Michael had to read a voluminous amount of articles and papers G2 sent, along with French papers, ranging from the Communist Party's l'Humanité on the left, to Le Monde on the right. He also had to go through articles and books by French journalists and scholars. As he became increasingly efficient at scanning materials in French on subjects he was familiar with, he had hoped his workload would become lighter, but the number of assignments grew because General Lund seemed to anticipate his growing abilities.

While Michael enjoyed his work, the highlight of his week was Sunday, when he almost invariably spent the day with Alissa. They had been meeting regularly since last summer. While the weather was warm, they had wandered around Paris, visiting the most famous museums and tourist spots, and ending up for dinner at Maman's. Then as the weather grew colder, they had taken to spending long after-noons in Michael's small room on rue Laplace.

Being with Alissa was so engrossing that while he was with her, he was taken up with the moment. He never knew what she was going to do or say next, and he was totally enchanted by her. When alone in his room or in his office, he found himself seeing her smile, hearing her English with a tinge of a German accent, and reliving those exquisite and soul-shattering hours they spent making love.

Then when the bitter north winds stopped blowing through Paris and the yellow and blue crocuses began to open their buds in the Jardin des Tuileries, Michael received two letters from California and another assignment all on the same day. He tore open the first letter to find he had been admitted to the Ph.D. program in economics at Berkeley with a fellow-ship. The second letter was from Prof. Minsky congratulating Michael on his acceptance into the Ph.D. program, and adding that he had managed to secure for him a research assistantship in addition to the fellowship. Michael was about to realize his dream of going to graduate school in economics in the U.S!

While he was still in a state of elation, he received a phone call summoning him to meet a General Bains at the Supreme Headquarters Allied Powers Europe (SHAPE), located a few hundred meters from USEUCOM. The general's office was the largest Michael had seen on any Army base, and with a magnificent view of the woods, behind which Michael knew lay Versailles.

General Bains was in his early sixties, a distinguished-looking man with salt and pepper hair, but he talked to

Michael almost as an equal. He started by saying: "Lieutenant Koyama, I have a very troublesome and delicate situation here that Gen. Lund said you might be able to help us with."

As Michael listened to the general, he felt as if he had had almost the same conversation a year ago when he was asked by Gen. Lund to help Lt. Col. Symington investigate the loss of ham and eggs at the base near Orléans. Only this time, the problem concerned the leaking of highly sensitive military information to the Russians. Michael thought this was a far more important assignment for an intelligence officer than finding who was stealing food. And this assignment was definitely quasi-G2 for it involved NATO.

General Bains outlined the problem: "During the past six months, whenever we've conducted divisional exercises in the eastern part of Turkey near the Georgian and Armenian borders, we found the Russians waiting for us, watching us from their side of the border. And when we've moved a dozen or so big bombers into or out of our airbases in Turkey—Incirlik, Adana, and Istres—we've had confirmation that locals, whom we surmise were local communists, were waiting to snap photos, as if they knew when these changes in our air force strength would occur."

Seeing he had Michael's full attention, the general went on.

"After six months of looking into this, we now are fairly certain that information is being leaked about NATO exercises and the movements of our bombers. And by process of elimination, and the fact that the leaks primarily concern Turkey, we think the leaks are by one of the two Turkish officers who attend our 'top secret' meetings. I don't know if you are aware of it, but we are required to have officers from Turkey, a NATO ally since 1952, at meetings to discuss NATO exercises and movements that will take place in their country. But we can't proceed further because we don't know which officer is doing the leaking—we have no evidence against either."

Michael nodded, and the general continued.

"The two Turkish officers in their G2 office here at SHAPE are Col. Adem Yilmaz and Major Resat Osman. The colonel is almost sixty and the major is in his forties—it seems the Turks promote their officers much more slowly than we do. What I'm going to ask you to do is to try to find out if either does anything suspicious. We don't want to use our own people because they could possibly be recognized, and we want to avoid any link between our office in SHAPE and this investigation. We can't risk anyone, especially journalists, finding out that one NATO country is investigating the officers of another. Our people are covering the Russian and other East Bloc countries' embassies pretty closely, and they don't think that either of the two Turkish officers has any contact...at least direct contact...with anyone from these embassies. We also know that no information is being electronically transmitted from the SHAPE headquarters building."

Michael was surprised: "Our people? You mean G2 is monitoring all communications by the Turkish officers at SHAPE?"

"Just leave it 'our people.' But, as I've said, we now need an outsider to investigate the two Turkish officers. If you don't mind my saying this, I have to agree with Gen. Lund that if anyone sees you out of uniform, they are unlikely to think you were an American officer."

Michael thought: *Another assignment because no one would suspect someone with an Asian face to be an American officer.* It finally made sense why he had been sent to Paris. But he was in no way unhappy with this assignment. He was thrilled with what sounded more cloak and dagger than most of his assignments. Though he was slightly apprehensive, what he was being asked to do didn't sound very risky, let alone dangerous.

The general looked pleased when Michael agreed. He said:

"I'll leave it up to you how you do this job. Contact Colonel Howell, my exec, for whatever you need. He will give you any reasonable amount of cash for your expenses. He has the official info about the two Turkish officers, their postings, their addresses in Paris, etc., and their photos. Okay, you're dismissed. And good luck."

Michael had a lot of thinking to do. But first, he needed to know whom he was investigating. He checked in with Col. Howell, and after receiving a packet of information, Michael asked him if it would be possible to get a glimpse of the two Turkish officers, if only from a distance. Photos were fine, but there was nothing like seeing real faces. The colonel understood the reason for Michael's request and he himself accompanied Michael to the fifth floor. He said with a mischievous grin:

"Just walk slowly from here to the end of the corridor, and look through the glass windows that give onto the corridor into the second office on your right. So many people walk by the office that they won't even look up. Wait a couple of minutes at the end of the corridor, and turn and walk slowly back. The officers should be sitting at desks next to the windows to the outside of the building, but the windows onto the corridor will give you a good view of both of them."

Michael went slowly down the corridor. He saw through a window a female secretary sitting at a desk next to the door and the two officers at desks on the other side of the office. He glanced at their faces, trying not to stare. The older officer, Col. Yilmaz, stocky with gray hair and a big nose, was reading what looked like a report, and the younger officer, Maj. Osman, who was typing, had black hair, a thin face, and finer features. On neither of the "passes" Michael made did any of the three in the office even look up.

Michael spent much of the weekend on some needed work on his reports, and planning how he could possibly get information the American SHAPE officers didn't already have. He did take Sunday afternoon off to walk with Alissa up the steps of the Sacre Coeur, one of their favorite excursions. She was somewhat annoyed that he couldn't meet her until lunchtime, and then commented on how preoccupied he seemed to be. Michael apologized, saying he had a new assignment, but couldn't say more.

In planning his strategy, Michael decided to follow the advice of a civilian—Michael guessed he was from the CIA—who had come to Fort Dix to give a lecture on surveillance while Michael was training to be an intelligence officer. "First, never forget that surveillance is inherently very boring. Second, you may think it pointless to begin your investigation by making a surveillance of the target individual in his habitat—where he lives. But you learn a lot about an animal by seeing where it lives...the same is true with the human animal. Be sure to try to answer the questions: Does the target seem to live within or beyond his known means? Does he keep a predictable routine, and if not, why not? Who visits him, men or women, and what do they look like? You get the idea. You'll be surprised how much you can learn about the target by casing his habitat even for just a few days."

Michael spent two evenings in a fruitless vigil of Col. Yilmaz's second-story apartment in an expensive-looking, nineteenth-century building two blocks from the Arc de

Triomphe. On both nights, he watched the apartment and the front door of the building from 6:30, when the colonel returned home, to a little after ten in the evening. He was fortunate to find in this largely residential area a small restaurant that gave him a view, albeit an oblique one, of the building's front entrance. At least, he didn't have to be overly concerned about being seen, but the meal was very over-priced, and he had to leave a ridiculously large tip on the first night so he could come back to a window table the next day.

But all his efforts were in vain. From the vigil over the two nights, he learned only two things. First, nothing happened at the colonel's apartment. No one came to visit him and he went nowhere. On both nights, all lights on his apartment went off exactly at ten. And second, the CIA man was right: surveillance was excruciatingly boring.

Michael decided that before he spent any more time observing the colonel, he would pay a visit to Place Léon Blum to see where Major Osman lived. He arrived shortly after six and had no trouble finding the address. It was in an old building on rue Roquette, just a few minutes from the Place Léon Blum metro station. Osman's apartment was on the third floor, according to the list of names by the door-bells. Michael had figured it would be in a mixed residential-commercial area, but what surprised him was finding several restaurants and shops with Russian names and specializing in Russian food and other goods. Many signs were in Cyrillic. Michael was in the Russian quarter of Paris. He hoped that this vigil would be more promising.

The buildings in the block were mostly apartment buildings with commercial establishments on the ground floor. The best place to keep tabs on the major's comings and goings was a small Russian restaurant just across rue Roquette. Michael went in and sat down in a corner near the window, hoping his Asian face wouldn't be noticed from across the street. Seated on an uncomfortable chair, he ordered red wine and wondered how long he would have to nurse it. He was rewarded by the return of the major shortly after 6:30. At 7:15, as Michael was getting very hungry and a little tipsy, the major reappeared and went into a French restaurant in the building next to his.

Thinking that he would have an hour at the very least, Michael ordered sausage and Russian-style cabbage. The sausage was good and the over-cooked cabbage was edible as it came smothered in excellent yoghurt. As he munched on, glancing occasionally at the restaurant door across the street, he heard a woman's voice from behind:

"Tut-tut, *Monsieur*, you should not eat alone in Paris. May I sit and keep you company?"

Looking up at the woman, Michael—a "veteran" of examining the prospective brides of GIs—instantly saw and smelled who she was: a still photogenic "professional" woman well into her thirties, wearing a bright-red blouse of questionable cleanliness, a tight skirt, and a rather over-powering perfume in her vain effort to compensate for the youthful bloom long gone.

Michael said apologetically: "Sorry, *Mademoiselle*, I am expecting a friend…she told me to start eating if she was late. I think she will be here soon…she would be mighty unhappy if she sees me eating with a beautiful lady."

"Well, then, some other time. I am Marcelle, and I would love to get to know you."

Shortly after "Marcelle" left, wafting a trail of perfume behind her, the major came out of the restaurant and returned to his building. That had been a quick meal for Paris, and Michael wondered if perhaps the major had an evening appointment. He dawdled over espresso, but the major didn't reappear nor did anyone else enter his building. Michael decided to repeat the surveillance on the following night. The second night was just like the previous with the major repeating the same routine. And so did the French prostitute, but this evening she was more persistent as she had figured out that Michael was alone.

Michael had had no more luck in the two nights he observed the major's building than he had in watching the older colonel's apartment, but somehow, he had a gut feeling that he should keep a watch on Major Osman. He wasn't sure if it was because the major lived in the Russian quarter, or because it somehow seemed unlikely the old colonel was his man.

On Friday evening, Michael returned to the same restaurant, hoping "Marcelle" wouldn't appear again. He would have liked to go to a different restaurant, but the other establishments on this side of the street were dry cleaners and small shops. Michael had barely ordered wine when the major arrived home, tonight with a long baguette under his arm and a number of bags, one of which Michael was sure contained a bottle of wine. Aha! Was the major expecting company? Michael now kept his eyes glued to the door.

Within minutes after the major returned, a fashionably dressed but unusually tall woman came to the same door and pushed the bell to be admitted. But as Michael watched the woman while she waited for someone to open the door, he became certain that this woman was actually a "he." Not only was this fashion plate extremely tall for a woman, her shoulders were wide and hips narrow. However, the giveaway was the way "she" put her handbag between her knees while she adjusted her wig with both hands. Michael was sure no woman would hold her handbag in such a way in public.

As the door opened, Michael caught a glimpse of the major. So the visitor was for the Turk! This discovery prompted Michael to suddenly recall that the major was not only single, his record showed that he had never been married. Could he be a homosexual? Michael decided he might be on to something, but that it wasn't worth a third Russian dinner as it looked like the visitor would be there for a while.

Michael was now eager to continue his surveillance of the major the following day, which was a Saturday. He knew that the major worked on Saturday, as did all military personnel, especially officers. But he thought it possible the major might leave early or not go directly home after work, so at 3:30, Michael went to a café across the street from SHAPE headquarters from which he could keep an eye on the front entrance. It was lucky he was in Paris where there were cafés everywhere and no one thought twice about someone reading a newspaper for an hour or more nursing one cup of coffee.

And Michael was in luck. Just before five, the major came out the front entrance and walked briskly toward the plaza and the bus stop used by USEUCOM and SHAPE personnel. Michael hurried to follow him. At La Defense, the major changed to the metro, and Michael got in the car behind his, standing where he could keep an eye on the Turk. Major Osman had a slightly worried look on his face and seemed deep in thought, seemingly unaware of his surroundings. *Where could he be going?* Michael wondered. He was slightly surprised to find that he was tailing the major to Place Léon Blum, his regular metro station. But when he emerged onto the street, instead of heading for his apartment, he entered a large corner café.

Should he follow the major in? Would it be safe? It was a large café, really a café-restaurant with a bar. Michael could see a number of people inside and decided to take a chance. First, he took off his regular glasses and put on a pair of rimless glasses often worn by the Vietnamese in Paris. Then, he entered the café from the opposite side the major had gone in.

Major Osman was already seated when Michael entered. He sat down at a table behind the major, where the major couldn't see him. He ordered an espresso, surprising the waiter who had expected someone at this time of day to order wine, but Michael needed to stay alert. The major nursed a glass of red wine, but kept looking at his watch. Some minutes later, a gaunt man in his forties entered, looked around, and spotting the major, came and sat down at his table. He was dressed like an office worker in a cheap, brown suit. Michael couldn't tell his nationality, except that he was a Nordic-looking Caucasian. The newcomer quickly ordered wine and, leaning over the table, began to talk to the major. Michael strained to hear the conversation, but the two were speaking softly, and all Michael could do was occasionally catch a word or two. What he was hearing was not Turkish and certainly not French...it sounded more like German. Michael recalled now that the major had spent a few years in Bonn.

Soon, the Turkish officer and the gaunt man began to argue, and when the argument became a bit heated, Michael caught some of their words. *"Nein, nein, das ist nicht richtig!"*—no, no, that's not right! That was the major. The other man yelled back: *"Ja! Wir müssen es haben."*—Yes! We must have it. Michael could easily understand their German when they yelled. And fortuitously, a noisy group nearby left the bar, which helped him catch more of the conversation.

As the café became quieter, the major looked around, and, in a quiet voice, said something Michael couldn't make out. The office worker replied in an almost normal voice that no one would understand what they were talking about because "these miserable characters in the bar" were all uneducated and "the Vietnamese guy behind you understands as much German as I do Vietnamese." Then a few minutes later, the Turkish major began to say something in a pleading tone. Because the major was speaking in a low voice, the only word Michael could catch was the name of a street, "Normannenstrasse," which the major repeated twice.

The conversation ended abruptly and the two got up to leave. Michael decided it was too dangerous to leave right away because the German had noted his presence. When he left the café a few minutes later, neither man was in sight. He looked at his watch. It was almost dinner time and too late to go back to USEUCOM to contact Jack using a secure phone.

Early Sunday morning, Michael went out to USEUCOM and put through a call to Jack in Berlin. As Michael expected, Jack did more than just answer his question.

"Michael, as you know, Normannenstrasse is the name of a street. It's the location of the HVA—Hauptverwaltung Aufklärung, the main 'reconnaissance' administration of the Stasi, the East German 'secret' police. The Stasi refer to the HVA simply as Normannenstrasse. From what you've said, I'm sure your Turkish major was talking to a Stasi."

The first thing Monday morning, Michael went to Col. Howell's office to report what he had seen and heard on Saturday and what Jack told him. Then he proposed to the colonel "a rather convoluted plan" he had hatched over the weekend. After hearing Michael out, the colonel took him to Gen. Bains' office to explain what Michael wanted to do.

The general asked Michael a lot of questions, then put his lips together and thought for what seemed a long interval to Michael. Finally, he said:

"I quite like your plan. It's certainly devious. Let's try it out. It just might work and it can't hurt."

That week, everything went according to Michael's plan. On Tuesday morning, all of the G2 NATO officers, including the two from Turkey, were called in for a briefing at which Gen. Bains informed them of a mobilization order he was issuing to move the 241st Infantry Battalion now in Ordu to Trabzon on the coast of the Black Sea. This order would move the battalion only sixty miles within Turkey, but it would take it much closer to the Russian border. The plan was for the mobilization order to be rescinded the day before it was to be carried out. It was likely the men would feel disgruntled for having gone to all the work that was required to move the entire battalion, but this kind of exercise wasn't unusual. This was one of the occasions when it was useful that the commanding general didn't have to give any reason for either issuing or rescinding an order.

After the general made his announcement, Michael had to try to find out if and how Major Osman would relay this information to the German he was sure was a Stasi agent. He "borrowed" Sgt. Mary Gilmann, a German-speaking WAC from the personnel office at NATO, and the two met at USEUCOM where Michael outlined what he wanted her to do. Though the circumstantial evidence led to Major Osman as the source of the leaks, Col. Howell had Col. Yilmaz watched as well because they couldn't set the same trap twice, and so they couldn't take any chances. But Michael was very certain the leak was through Osman, so he was concentrating on him. His only question was once his plan had been put into effect and the major wanted to get in touch with the German, how was he going to do it? In person? At the same café? By telephone? Or some other way, possibly using a "cut-out" or middleman?

Just before noon, Michael had Mary stand near the elevators at SHAPE as if waiting for a friend, while he went and sat near the rear of the ground-floor cafeteria in his army uniform and horn-rimmed glasses. He didn't think Osman would recognize him as the Vietnamese in the café, but he didn't want to take any chances. He didn't have long to wait. About 12:10, Osman came into the cafeteria looking slightly flustered and got into line. Mary came in a minute or two later and joined Michael.

"Sir, after the target came down in the elevator, he went immediately to one of the public phones. I followed him as soon as I thought it safe and heard him speaking in German. I'm sure I heard him say *'halb sieben.'* That means six-thirty....Sorry, Lieutenant, I forgot you know German."

He asked, "Was a place mentioned?"

"No, Sir. It was a very short conversation and I only caught the tail end."

Michael thought nothing would happen until the workday had ended, so he arranged to meet the sergeant at five back at the cafeteria, which was located near the entrance. He went back to USEUCOM to work. Having trouble concentrating, he got very little done that afternoon.

Michael had arranged for a car and driver from the motor pool, but when Osman left the building at 5:30, it was immediately clear that he was going to take public transportation. Michael waved the driver away and, with Sgt. Gilmann, he followed the Turk. Osman made straight for the café at Place Léon Blum. The major was going to meet the Stasi at the same café!

As Major Osman seemed so preoccupied, Michael didn't worry about being recognized by him, but he didn't want to take the chance of being seen by the German. He asked Sgt. Gilmann to follow the Turk and "listen to as much as you can when he meets the German." Michael went across the street and sat down by the statue of Léon Blum to wait, a copy of *Le Monde* open in front of him.

Half an hour later, Osman left the café, looking, Michael thought, very worried. He went off in the direction of his apartment. A few minutes later, the German came out, seemingly casual. However, over the top of his newspaper, Michael could see that he was carefully surveying the entire area. Then the man went down into the Metro, and five minutes later Sgt. Gilmann emerged and crossed the intersection to join Michael.

Michael was so eager to learn what had taken place in the café that before Mary could open her mouth, he demanded, "What did you learn?"

"Quite a lot, Sir." she replied with a pleased smile on her face. "They talked in such oblique terms that I wouldn't have understood what they were referring to if you hadn't clued me in, and had I not spent three years in Wiesbaden when my father was stationed there. Anyway, though I didn't see any note or paper passed to the German—whom the Turk addressed once as Herr Nadel—when I sat down, the German was thanking the Turk. Then he questioned him about *'der Grund'*—which I took to mean the reason for the mobilization order because he said something about 'only sixty miles,' but the major couldn't answer him and the German was annoyed."

Michael nodded. He was glad to hear his "plan" was working as he expected it would. The sergeant went on.

"Then the conversation turned a bit nasty. The major is clearly nervous about what he is doing and would like to stop, but Nadel said, 'You've got to continue…you know what'll happen if you don't.' I thought his tone rather threatening. Finally, the major abruptly stood up abruptly and left, while the German was still talking...I couldn't hear his words because the Turk was making noise pushing his chair back."

Michael thanked the sergeant heartily for her help, and she went off down the nearby Metro entrance. Michael sat and thought for a few minutes and then made his way back to SHAPE where he knew Col. Howell would be waiting for him. After Michael rather excitedly reported what had occurred, the colonel called Gen. Baines and relayed what Michael had told him. After Howell had hung up, he said to Michael, "Well, Lieutenant, thanks to the success of Phase I of your plan, we now know Major Osman is the man leaking NATO secrets. Gen. Bains just gave his okay to proceed on to Phase II of your plan. So, go over your plan for me once more in detail."

"Sir, the goal of Phase II is to use what we learned in Phase I to provide disinformation to the East Germans, and, possibly, even catch Nadel, Osman's Stasi contact. As of now, we don't have enough prima facie evidence to take Osman to court. But we know that he doesn't like passing information to Nadel. If he is promised that we, that is, NATO, won't tell anyone, including the Turkish Army, what we have found out...that he is leaking secret NATO information to the Stasi...I think we will get his cooperation."

Col. Howell jotted down a few notes as Michael went over the plan step by step. He concluded by saying, "Sir, I'm confident that the plan will work. The only thing we need to worry about is that we can't be sure how the East Germans will react. We can assume that there is more than one Stasi agent in Paris...and Nadel could call the HVA for help. In short, we may not be dealing only with Nadel." The colonel's response was very much what Michael hoped, "Lt. Koyama, I know we have to be careful...the Stasi are a nasty bunch. You'll get all the backup you need. Good luck and keep me posted."

The following morning, General Bains called Major Osman directly, bypassing Colonel Yilmaz, Osman's direct superior. When Osman arrived in the general's office and was told that NATO had two witnesses to his meetings with a Stasi agent and had learned that he was passing NATO information to the East Germans, the Turk's face turned ashen with fear. The general said that he suspected the major was being blackmailed, and if this was true, he had an offer to make to preserve the major's name, though, not his career in the Turkish Army. Michael later heard from Col. Howell, who was present at the meeting, that the Turk had nearly fainted, but that he readily agreed to help carry out Phase II of Michael's plan. In exchange, the general promised not to divulge Maj. Osman's crime to anyone, including Col. Yilmaz. The general said that all he had to do was arrange one more meeting with Nadel at the café on Place Léon Blum.

ON SATURDAY MORNING, MICHAEL SAT WAITING IN A PEUGEOT at Place Léon Blum. With him were two MPs, Sgt. Morales, a robust-looking sergeant in his early thirties, and Cpl. Noyes, a big, baby-faced man in his twenties. Both were armed, but in civilian clothes, prepared for anything, they hoped. Just after ten and right on schedule, the Turkish major appeared with a black attaché case in his hand and entered the café. Michael watched for the arrival of Nadel.

Neither Michael nor the MPs were prepared for what happened next. A large, black Mercedes came speeding down rue Voltaire and came to a sudden halt in front of the café. A man whom Michael had never seen before jumped out of the front, slammed the door, and ran into the café. Within moments, he came back out, towing Major Osman, who looked puzzled and rather anxious. The major tried to peer into the car, illegally stopped next to the Metro entrance, and when the back door opened, he moved to get in. As he bent down, a hand reached out and grabbed the major's attaché case while the man outside the car hit the major's face with full force. Michael could hear the distinct sound of the assailant's hand as it struck the major's face.

The major tumbled and fell backward onto the pavement, hitting his head on the curb. In an instant, the man outside leaped into the car, and even as the door was closing, the Mercedes shot out into the intersection and bore right, heading up Avenue Parmentier. Even though he got only a glimpse of the man in the back seat, Michael was sure it was the German who had met Osman at the bar.

As he opened the door of the Peugeot and jumped out, Michael yelled: "Follow the Mercedes! I'll take care of the major."

Sgt. Morales had the motor already started and raced after the Mercedes. As the Peugeot crossed the intersection, Michael could see two more unmarked sedans suddenly start up and follow the Peugeot.

A man and a woman, hearing the commotion, came out to see what was happening. From their bearing, Michael knew these must be the two members of the French police who he had been told would be waiting inside the restaurant. Frantically, Michael asked where there was a phone to call for an ambulance. The woman said she would do it and dashed inside. The undercover policeman was both trying to assess Osman's condition and keep a crowd from forming. Michael put a chair cushion under the major's head. He was unconscious, but Michael could see no blood. The ambulance arrived within minutes and bore Osman and the woman officer off.

As the crowd dispersed, Michael went into the café and rang Col. Howell to tell him that the meeting had not gone according to plan. Osman had asked to meet Nadel in the café with the promise of turning over a case full of classified documents in return for a payment that would be large enough to enable him to resign his commission and return to Turkey. When the transaction had been completed, Nadel was to have been arrested. Seeing what happened, Michael had to speculate that Nadel on his own, or the HVA, had decided to lose a "mole" who had become recalcitrant, in return for the mole's last valuable service—handing over highly classified NATO documents. But the Stasi had no intention of paying for them.

Michael felt that Osman's getting hurt and the plan going awry was his fault because the entire scheme has been his. He wondered if with three vehicles the MPs and the French police would manage to catch the very fast Mercedes, which had been heading in the direction of the autobahn that would carry them to Germany. Surely, the men would be stopped at the border if not sooner.

But at least the documents in the briefcase were either of common knowledge or false. Since they had thought it likely that Nadel would want to see what he was paying for, the top document was a table of the up-to-date, exact numbers of officers and soldiers in the fourteen largest U. S. Army bases in West Germany. The rest of the papers were fabrications made by Col. Howell and a G2 major—they looked authentic but were carefully designed to mislead the Stasi. All were marked "Top Secret" and had the two diagonal red lines on the top right-hand corner of each sheet that all "Top Secret" documents had. So either Nadel and his comrades would be caught, or else these documents would make their way to the HVA, which in the circumstances would view them as genuine.

After the ambulance bore off the still unconscious major, Michael went back to SHAPE and Colonel Howell. He was rather shame-faced, but the colonel reminded him, "You not only carried out the original commission of stopping the leak of information, you also uncovered a Stasi agent hitherto unknown to NATO forces or the French."

TWO WEEKS LATER, COLONEL HOWELL CALLED MICHAEL. "Lt. Koyama, this is not an order. If you can, could you drop by after work today?" Michael wondered what was up. But he quickly learned that Colonel Howell was being nice enough to tell him how the affair had wound up. Smiling, the colonel reported:

"Given the army's 'no need to know' rule, I couldn't order you to come in, but since you not only completed the assignment of learning who was leaking NATO information, but helped catch three Stasi spies none of us realized were operating in France, I thought I should let you know how everything ended."

"I'll admit I've been terribly curious," said Michael.

"Well, you'll be pleased to hear that Nadel was caught. The Stasi agents had gone north, but it would seem that in trying to evade their pursuers, they got caught up in the winding streets near the Canal Saint-Martin. Sgt. Morales reported that at this point, they all lost sight of the Mercedes, which indeed was faster than any of the military or police cars. Then, in a stroke of luck, Morales and Noyes caught sight of Nadel on foot, carrying the attaché case. Apparently, Nadel had gotten out of the Mercedes, assuming that his pursuers would follow the car while he made his way to some means of public transportation."

The colonel let out a guffaw and said," We got a real kick out of what happened next, but you must promise not to tell this story to your friends on a night out. Okay?"

"Agreed, Sir," said Michael. What had happened to make the colonel laugh so?

"I was told that Nadel saw that all three cars chasing the Mercedes had stopped. When he saw the MPs and the French police jump out of their cars and start after him, he was flummoxed. He had no place to flee; the cars blocked the street and the canal was at his back. Just yards ahead of his pursuers, he scampered down the sidewalk that ran above the canal to where there was a ramp going down to the water level. He ran down the ramp onto the path along the canal with the French police just behind him. But then Nadel came to a bridge support blocking the path. He tried to scramble around it on a narrow ledge but he lost his balance. He and the attaché case fell into that stinking sewer of a canal."

Michael laughed despite himself. "So you caught him?"

"We most certainly did. But that's not all. Nadel managed to scramble out and into the waiting arms of two officers who quickly handcuffed him and bound his feet for good measure. But the attaché case was still in the canal and sinking. Two French officers realized that in it was the evidence they needed to guarantee a court conviction of spying against Nadel, so without stopping to consult each other, both men dove in and retrieved it, spluttering and gasping. Sgt. Morales said it was quite a sight. And then the dripping French police had an argument with the drivers, neither of whom wanted to take three soaking wet men stinking of canal water in his clean sedan!"

"Was the Mercedes caught?"

"Yes, at the border when the two men in it tried to cross into Germany." The colonel continued, "All three men are East Germans who were in France illegally, using false passports. They are suspected of being 'Stasi operatives' and have been turned over to the French authorities to be deported to West Berlin, where the headquarters of the Bundespolizei—Federal Police—is located, for questioning and subsequent prosecution."

"What about Major Osman?" Michael asked.

"That's a rather sad story. He was released from the hospital a week ago and formally resigned his commission. We expected him to return home to Turkey. As you know, he had been told that because of his cooperation, he would not be formally prosecuted, nor did we even tell his superior why he was resigning. Of course, we really didn't want this affair to become public, and we had determined that Osman was telling the truth when he confessed, 'I swear on the Koran, I only handed over only Confidential or low-grade secret information but never highly sensitive "Top Secret" intelligence.' But after he resigned, he disappeared. Col. Yilmaz is, of course, dumbfounded. He doesn't know what is going on. He says Osman didn't return home, didn't even return to Turkey as far as he knows. He even checked the hospitals and the morgue. Negative. One of my staff suggested that Osman might have disappeared into St. Denis."

"You mean into the gay community here in Paris?" Michael said. Colonel Howell nodded.

Subsequently, Michael received congratulations from both Generals Lund and Bains for successfully completing the assignment and nabbing three East German spies in the process. But his satisfaction was tinged with sadness. A few days after he met Col. Howell, he had a phone call from Alissa from Gare de l'Est telling him that her mother had to have an emergency operation, and she was calling from the train station as she was leaving for Munich. The background noise was such that Michael could barely make out what she was saying. She promised to let him know when she could come back to Paris, and then she hurriedly ended the call. It was all most unsatisfactory.

Michael took the news with bleak resignation. He didn't have much time left in Paris. Would Alissa return before he had to leave for the States? In fact, Michael was increasingly concerned about whether he had a future with Alissa. She had become preoccupied with her upcoming recital and full of talk about possible summer plans back in Germany. Michael tried to bring up the subject of the future, but she refused to discuss it. "I can't tell where I will be or where my training and career will take me. Let's just enjoy our time together now, Michael, and let the future take care of itself," she would say.

Michael had fleetingly thought of staying on in Europe before he had applied to graduate school. If he were honest, he never seriously considered it because of the importance for his future of getting a graduate education in economics in the U.S. But that didn't prevent him from going through a lot of internal turmoil. What would his life be like if he stayed in France, he wondered. Michael was very much attracted to what France, especially Paris, had to offer—its beautiful language, the depth of civilization manifested in myriad ways, and the beauty of the city. However, France was still struggling politically and economically in the aftermath of World War II. And it was not difficult to discern that France, like Japan, had a vertical society, as could be seen in its education system, in the class consciousness of the French, and in the treatment of non-French—Vietnamese, Algerians, and other North Africans, and Michael as well. If one had to choose between the U.S and France, it was no contest.

And then there was the consideration that Alissa was German, not French, and who knew where her pursuit of a career in opera might take her. So in the end, Michael had to admit that Alissa's "selfishness" in pursuing her career in Europe was matched by his own "selfishness." However much in love they felt they were when together, the fact that they both intended to follow their separate career paths revealed that theirs was not the enduring, reason-defying kind of true love. But this was Michael's first experience with love, and he truly felt that Alissa was his love of a lifetime.

Alissa had promised to stay in touch with Michael. At the moment, he couldn't ask for more. He had treasured the thought of the last weeks he hoped to be able to be with her, and, now, even that had been taken from him. Feeling rather desolate, Michael threw himself into finishing up his reports for General Lund before he was mustered out. With Alissa away, he worked seven days a week. Late one Sunday afternoon, Capt. Burns found Michael still at work in his office and made him come for an impromptu sukiyaki dinner with him and his wife.

A few days before his departure from Paris, Michael called Jack and Tony who, he knew, were also leaving Europe. Jack told him he had been extremely busy assisting East Germans escaping to the American Zone because of the rumor that the DDR—East Germany—and the Russians might soon build a wall to stop the massive exodus of East Germans. But he was exultant that he was entering Harvard Law School in the fall. Tony in Rome was handing over to a newly arrived G2 captain a network of "contacts" he had built to "monitor the activities" of the Italian Communist Party, and was looking forward to Columbia. He couldn't reach Winston in Greece, but he knew that he had received an apprenticeship at *The New York Times.*

Michael said his goodbyes to a tearful Maman, his flat-mate Jean Luc, Prof. LaMont, who had taught him French, and many others Michael had met at Chez Maman. Sadly, Alissa was still in Munich. He did talk to her twice on the phone. In the final call, Alissa was exuberant at having just landed the role of Violetta in La Traviata in a summer opera company in Munich. She had originally been given the role of Violetta's maid, but the soprano who was to sing the lead part had had appendicitis, and Alissa had been offered the role instead. Even while talking to her on the phone, Michael felt that she had already parted from him. He didn't know how he could bear the sadness he felt.

On June 7, Michael left Orly airport on a MATS flight to the Azores and then on to San Francisco. The trip would take two days, and, possibly, as many as five changes of planes en route. He was carrying with him much, much more than when he came to Paris: the memory of all the reports he had written for Gen. Lund; the assignments he had worked on at USEUCOM—screening brides for GIs and assisting in court martial cases; the work he had done for Captain Logan on the Algerian independence movement; the investigations of the lost bacon, eggs, and ham in Foret d'Orleans; and his role in helping nab the Turkish officer who gave NATO secrets to the Stasi. And then there were the people: Maman, Prof. LaMont, his colleagues, and above all, Alissa. And finally, there was the City of Light.

Within a few minutes after Michael's plane became airborne, he saw Paris rapidly becoming smaller and the Seine reflecting the summer sun. His plane continued to climb easily under the blue sky despite the weight of Michael's memories.

Chapter 10

Burma, 1962

I N LATE APRIL, MICHAEL WAS IMMERSED in studying for his general examinations in economics, which he had to pass before he could begin to write his doctoral dissertation. Most students took these exams at the end of the third year, but Michael was determined to get his out of the way in his second. So engrossed was he in his studies that he gave barely a thought to the life he had led in Paris less than two years ago. He knew that Jack was finishing his second year at Harvard Law, Tony would receive an MBA in a couple of months from Columbia Business School, and Winston was now working for the *New York Tribune* and writing a book on "Greek politics and society."

Michael had another reason for completely submerging himself in his work. He had hoped that by completing his doctorate as soon as possible, it would enable him to go to Europe again to see Alissa. He had exchanged letters with her on a regular basis for the first year after he returned to the U.S., but gradually Alissa's had become shorter, and the intervals between them longer. And then, two months ago, after weeks without hearing from her, she had written a letter he would never forget. Alissa had decided that there was no future in their relationship and that it was best to end it. That she would have a career in opera was almost certain, and so she couldn't think of marriage now, and it would be unfair to

Michael to try to maintain a long distance relationship. The letter ended with a few lines that Michael could think of only as platitudes—"we had a wonderful time together in Paris...I will never forget you...I hope you'll soon find someone who can be with you all the time." It was a devastating end to the relationship that he so dearly hoped would be the lasting love of his life.

Like Werther, his love was doomed, but unlike Werther, he had no intention of committing suicide. He had a life to live and a future before him, and he would throw himself into the career that he had planned for himself since his undergraduate years at Berkeley. So he did his best not to think about Alissa, and pored over his economics books and lecture notes all hours of the day and night.

So focused was Michael on his coming exams that he was taken by surprise when he received a call from the Presidio, the large army base near San Francisco, with a request that he meet General Lund there on May 5. He hadn't thought about the general in...he couldn't remember how long. He wondered why General Lund wanted to see him now. Surely, it couldn't be just a social visit?

At ten sharp on May 5, Michael arrived at the Presidio. He found General Lund waiting in a G2 office from which Michael could see the Golden Gate Bridge. Now a major general, Lund looked even more imposing than Michael remembered him.

"Thanks for coming, Michael. I shall always think of you as my lieutenant, but now you are a civilian, let me try to remember to call you Michael."

"Congratulations, Sir, on your second star."

The general just waved his hand to brush off the compliment and continued, "Even though I am going to ask a big favor of you, the same rules apply as when you were on active duty. I will tell you only what you need to know, and I am going to use the term USG operations for all U.S. government operations without specifying the branch of government. All right?"

"Yes, Sir." Michael recalled what the general had said in 1958 when *Les Quatre Copains* were told they would be sent to Europe right after their G2 training: "We are making an unusually large investment in all of you, and, as you'll see, maximum freedom as to how you perform your duties. In return, we ask only that you do your level best in performing your assigned duties and, no less importantly, after you are discharged from the Army, that you help us from time to time for a short duration when we need your special capabilities. I hope you'll accept our requests both for the country and as a personal favor to me."

Suddenly hearing his name, Michael was called back to the present.

"...so as you can see, we have a lot going on now in Southeast Asia at the moment. But what I want to talk to you about today is not Vietnam, but Burma. Have you been following the news there?" asked General Lund.

"I know that on March 2, Ne Win staged a successful coup d'etat, overthrowing U Nu's government. He established a military regime he announced was to be based on nationalism, Marxism, and Buddhism."

"Yes, and our government finds that very worrying. I came here to attend an emergency meeting to discuss the situation. We need answers to such questions as: Will General Ne Win, supposedly a Marxist, be friendly with the Russians and actively help the North Vietnamese? Or will he be preoccupied with domestic matters and cause no trouble internationally...especially for the U.S.? And no less importantly, how stable is his government going to be?"

Michael must have had a rather puzzled look on his face because General Lund said:

"I don't blame you if you wonder where I am going with all this. The fact is that what kind of policy Ne Win adopts matters to us only if his government is going to stay in power, and how long he stays in power depends on how strong his political opposition is. So we would like to know who the opposition is. It is important that we know whether the opposition is communist, pro-West, nationalist or whatever, how strong they are today, and how much support they are likely to have tomorrow. So far, am I making myself clear?"

Michael nodded and sat up straighter.

"One branch of USG had a man in touch with a group of young Burmese, many of whom are recent graduates of Rangoon University, which I'm told is one of the best universities in the former British colonies. This group consists at present of eleven young people who call themselves the Committee of Young Burmese for Democracy—the CYBD. Some were elected by a large number of students and sympathizers, others were chosen by these leaders to work with them. The Burmese army, that is Ne Win's army, knows about them and has been hunting them. That's why this group is hiding out on the Shan Plateau, a rugged place across the border from northwest Thailand."

Michael began to get an inkling of what was to come when he heard the location mentioned.

"Our man who was in touch with the CYBD died two months ago. He caught malaria and some fever the doctors couldn't diagnose. His dossier—cover—was that he was an assistant professor of political science and wanted to learn what the CYBD is all about and whether he could help them in some way. He had a member of the CYBD sending him reports from time to time, a guy by the name of Ba Maw—

sounds like Burma, which makes it easy to remember. His reports are useful but we get the distinct impression that this guy writes what he thinks we want to hear, so that at times, he sounds as if he is a rabid anti-communist. My guess is that he is an opportunist."

Michael anxiously waited for what was going to come next as Gen. Lund paused, as if searching for words.

"Coming finally to the crux of the matter, we need someone to take over what the young man who just died was doing, and perhaps do an even better job...to serve as a contact with the CYBD, and also find out...assess, or evaluate may be a better word...who the people in the committee are...what they believe in...whether they are Marxist, pro-West, nationalist, opportunist, whatever. We want to know, we *have* to know, because of what is happening in Vietnam. I think you are the person for the job. When I described you to the brass attending the meeting, they agreed that we should ask if you would take it on. They conceded that you are a better candidate than the few they had in mind."

Michael nodded. He had thought this was what the general was going to ask of him, but he had some questions he needed to have answered:

"General, could you be more specific about what you want me to do? I'm scheduled to take my general examinations in June, and then I have a Ford Foundation grant to conduct my dissertation research in Japan."

"First, I think you could get the information you need for the report in a matter of weeks. Surely, you could take some time off from your studies this summer after your exams? We need to have you meet these people, and then write up a report—a good one, the kind you wrote for me in Paris—evaluating who the members of the CYBD are, and if we should support them actively with money, and, should we think it appropriate, even with some military hardware. Of course, depending on what your report says, we could just ignore them. In short, your report will be crucial in our decision-making."

"What kind of cover do you have in mind?" Michael asked.

"You don't need much of one. You can go in as a student interested in the Southeast Asian economy and history. So you can go as Michael Koyama, a grad student at Berkeley. You are a strong supporter of democracy in Burma, and know people in America who want to help groups such the CYBD and who are willing to help them financially."

"Can you give me the logistic details of the assignment? I mean how do I get to where the CYBD is hiding out?"

"We'll fly you to Saigon with our advisors now going to Vietnam. We can make the arrangements to fly you on to Chiang Mai, and from there you'll be driven to the Burmese border.

"How will I find the CYBD after I cross the border?"

"We're still in touch with Ba Maw. He will come to meet you near a town called Mae Hong Son, which is just inside the Thai border, and he'll take you where the CYBD is hiding out."

Michael was startled to hear the name Mae Hong Son, the town his father used as the base for his activities to help the British Army.

"Sir, I went to Mae Hong Son with my father when I was a child."

"Yes, I know. You told us that when you were debriefed for your security clearance. It's in your record."

General Lund changed the subject.

"If you take on my request to go to Burma, we'll deposit $10,000 in a bank in Chiang Mai—the same bank your predecessor used in sending money to the CYBD. You can tell them this is money you collected from supporters of democracy in Burma."

Then, looking into Michael's eyes, the general added in what was almost a pleading tone, "I know you can't start this assignment yet, but once your exams are over, could you read up on Burma and make the necessary preparations and then go, say around mid-July? I know this is a sudden request, but will you undertake this for us? We are prepared to give you the privileges and pay of a major, if that matters."

Many thoughts rushed through Michael's mind. Should he take on this assignment? Does the mention of Mae Hong Son mean karma is at work? Couldn't he delay his dissertation research for a month—or more realistically, two months? How could he possibly turn the general down? But he still had a few questions:

"You said, General, that the CYBD is being hunted. Does this mean that the Burmese army might attack or try to capture them?"

"Yes. I think the army is trying to capture them. It's also possible that the CYBD camp—their hideout—could be shelled or targeted by snipers. I can't tell you this job is without danger. But if anyone can make a run for it and get back across the border into Thailand, who else could do that better than you?"

"Sir. I am wondering, since local ties in that neck of woods are important, does the CYBD have any local support?"

"I am told the CYBD has contacts with the KNU—the Karen National Union—which is fighting the Burmese Army in order to create their own independent state, free of the Burmese. There are 20,000 or more in the Union, and they have a loose mutual aid agreement of a sort with the CYBD. The enemy-of-my-enemy-is-my-friend type of logic is at work here. After all, 7 percent of Burmese are Karen, and the percentage is much higher in the Shan Plateau. Your record says you have a bit of Karen blood."

"Yes, Sir. My grandmother on my mother's side."

"Speak any Karen?"

"Only a little, Sir. I can greet people and say a few things at the level of a small child. That's about all."

"Well, that's more than anyone else we have as a candidate can claim, and of course you speak Thai."

General Lund, feeling that Michael would accept the assignment, was responding easily to Michael's questions. But he suddenly looked solemn again and warned him:

"You may face another danger besides the Burmese army. Since your predecessor died from tropical disease, you definitely need to have all the preventive shots. And be very careful about mosquitoes. I hope that because you spent your childhood in that part of the world, you will have acquired some immunity your predecessor didn't have."

As Michael listened to the general's warnings, he realized that he had decided to accept the assignment. In fact, he had the distinct feeling that his mind was made up when the name Mae Hong Son first came up. He thought it was a good thing that the assignment involved Burma and not Vietnam. Like many at his university, Michael had very mixed feelings about the increasing American support of the very unpopular Diem government in South Vietnam, which could not have come to power had the plebiscite taken place, which had been agreed upon in Geneva in 1954, in both North and South Vietnam.

Finally, after another half hour of questions, answers, and suggestions, Michael formally agreed to undertake the assignment. He rescheduled his research fellowship to begin in September instead of July and, after successfully passing his exams, he began to focus his attention on reading the many reports sent by Gen. Lund as well as a dozen books on Burma. He found that many things—religion, customs, climate, and more—were the same as or similar to those in Thailand. But a few things were very different.

One of them was language. Although they shared some vocabulary from the ancient Indo-Aryan language called Pali, the Thai and Burmese languages had few similarities. Thais could not communicate with Burmese, a fact Michael decided not to worry about because he was told that the members of the CYBD were fluent English speakers. Another difference was their names. Unlike Thais, Burmese tended to have only a given name, usually consisting of two syllables, as in Ba Maw, but sometimes only one. Also, they changed their names often! And U was an honorific for males similar to Mr. in English, thus U Nu was really Mr. Nu.

Michael made a special effort to study the geography and topography of the Shan Plateau, the mountain range linking Mae Hong Son and Taunggyi, the largest Burmese town on the plateau, located 200 miles southeast of Mandalay. His other preparations concerned his appearance. He had to look like a Karen, or at least as though he was from northern Thailand. G2's "bag of tricks" department knew exactly what Michael needed: a sleeveless brown tunic top, hand-woven of coarse cotton and patterned with vertical stripes, plain blue or black pants, narrow in the legs, rubber thong sandals, and black Bakelite-framed eyeglasses.

MICHAEL LEFT TRAVIS AIR FORCE BASE near San Francisco on the evening of July 10 after he had received word that Ba Maw would be ready to meet him on July 14. He flew on a large cargo plane crammed with helicopter parts, a dozen helicopter pilots, and several soldiers who Michael guessed were mechanics. The flight was far from comfortable. He had a small hard seat and no one was allowed to get off the plane when it stopped for refueling at Hickam Air Force Base in Honolulu because the plane was to be on the ground less than an hour. After a long delay at Yokota Air Force Base in Japan, he finally arrived in Saigon. Because of the international dateline, it was now the afternoon of July 12, and his trip was far from over.

When Michael landed in Saigon, he was reminded that Southeast Asia was already fully into the rainy and extremely hot summer. Within minutes of his arrival in the crowded and noisy airport, the muggy hot air made his shirt cling to his skin. A sergeant who obviously knew who he was and was expecting him, greeted him and took him to a small room in a less noisy corner of the airport, where he changed from his fatigues to the "local" clothes G2 had provided and left behind his fatigues. He was told he would be put on a non-scheduled flight to Chiang Mai operated by "a government agency." He was a little disappointed at not going north via Bangkok, which he had hoped to see again, if only from the sky.

Michael left Saigon just forty minutes after he arrived. His small plane carried six men in civilian clothes in addition to himself. He guessed they were all either military or officers of "an agency" of the U.S. government, but the plane was too noisy for any conversation. When it landed in Chiang Mai, two of the men disembarked before Michael and hurried off. The plane immediately taxied off for take-off, as a slender young Thai with a smile that showed a gold-capped tooth, came up to him and greeted him in English:

"You must be Mr. Koyama, right? You'll stay over-night at my place and I'll drive you north to Mae Hong Son tomorrow. Come with me."

But Michael made sure the Thai was the man he should be going off with. *"Khorb koon. Glai mai?"* Michael asked in Thai, as prearranged. For thanking him and asking how far he was going, his contact was to say that his name was Kivet.

"Not far. My name is Kivet. Nice to meet you."

"Okay. You've identified yourself. What is your real name? Kivet was my Thai name."

"So I was told. My name is Htoo Lay and I am Thai-Karen. People just call me Htoo."

Htoo drove Michael to his place east of the center of the city in what was unmistakably an American jeep painted black. Michael was surprised to see how little Chiang Mai had changed since he first visited it around 1940. The city's main street, Chiangrai Road, was paved, but the other roads he could see were still covered with gravel. Most buildings were one story and in need of serious repairs. As on his first visit, he saw only a few small open-front Thai eateries and one large, garishly painted Chinese restaurant, possibly the one where he and his father had once had a meal. The people he saw on the street were simply clad in local dress such as he was now wearing, except for a few young people in western clothes.

Htoo's "place" turned out to be a two-room apartment on the second floor of a clothing store on the busy Chiangrai Road. After a simple meal of local beer and a bowl of noodles with a bit of vegetables and chicken, Michael was shown to an army cot. Michael wondered why Htoo was driving a disguised American jeep, and why he had an American army cot and blanket as well. But he decided not to ask. Fatigue from the long flights overtook him and he slept until Htoo woke him up at five the next morning. Outside, it was still dark and Chiangrai Road was deserted.

Htoo said: "It's a long drive to Mae Hong Son and I want to make sure we get there before evening—that area is dangerous." The trip proved to be arduous as well as long. The road was badly rutted in places, and in the open jeep, it was difficult to carry on a conversation. They were drenched in the usual afternoon squall of the rainy season, reminding Michael how much he enjoyed them on hot days in the rainy season back when he was Kivet.

Mae Hong Son was little more than a village, smaller than Michael had remembered. The province of the same name located on the northwest border with Burma was the most sparsely populated in Thailand, largely forested, and noted for its opium crops and smuggling. But the area was truly beautiful, and Michael recalled that his father had always referred to the town by its other name, Maung Sam Moke, for its frequent mists—Sam Moke meant "three mists." The breathtaking scenery in the early evening brought back memories of seeing the town in the morning mist rising above the river with his father. Michael suddenly felt bereft in the country he and his father had always called Siam.

Htoo clearly knew Mae Hong Son well and took Michael without hesitation to a small, very primitive guesthouse where they spent a rather uncomfortable night. Though the woman who ran the guesthouse fed them a simple but ample supper, the mosquitoes were out in abundance from sunset on. Michael was very glad that he had with him strong mosquito repellant and anti-malarial pills.

Htoo again awakened Michael before dawn. "I'll take you to where Ba Maw will be waiting for you, about fifteen kilometers from here. We usually meet at the same spot because that's as far as we can go in this jeep. From there, the road is impassable in any vehicle."

They left "Maung Sam Moke" in the morning mist as the sun was rising. They soon began to climb the narrow road to the ridge. "Road" was a misnomer because it was so narrow that a jeep could barely negotiate it. Htoo said the locals called it the Smugglers' Path.

As they steadily climbed, Michael could see the town 200 or 300 meters below. The air was still cool even as the sun rose higher and higher in the sky. After they had driven about ten kilometers on the ridge, Michael had a spectacular view: to his left, he saw a deep green-black valley at the bottom of which ran a river, still a stream at this point, with its water glinting in the morning sun.

Htoo said suddenly: "After the next bend, there is a place wide enough for me to turn around. That's where you'll meet Ba Maw."

When they rounded the bend, Michael saw a lone man standing at the side of the track. He was tall for an Asian, maybe 5'9". He wore a grey shirt and black pants. As soon as Michael jumped out of the jeep, the man thrust out his hand and said in English that was much better than Michael had expected:

"Mr. Koyama from Berkeley. A student of Southeast Asian history and a friend of Burmese Democracy!"

"Nice to meet you. Are we in Burma now?"

"Not yet. Not for another six kilometers. I hope you're a good walker. We won't stay on the ridge, which goes steadily up to 900 meters, at which point the Burmese army has a lookout near the border. Instead, we'll walk about 400 meters below the ridge on a smugglers' footpath and then descend to our campsite on the edge of the river. The footpath is safe because the soldiers don't want to exert themselves."

He paused briefly and then said, "Could I speak to your privately for a moment?" He drew Michael to one side, out of earshot of Htoo and whispered, "Did you bring the gift?"

Michael answered in a low voice. "Of course. You can confirm its arrival by calling the bank in Chiang Mai and you can access it anytime you want."

Ba Maw nodded and moved back toward Htoo. In a normal voice he said, "Now we'll say good bye to Htoo and be on our way."

Both men shook hands with Htoo, who jumped back into the jeep and started the engine. It sounded so loud on the quiet ridge that Michael hoped no Burmese soldier was anywhere nearby. Even before Htoo had turned around, Ba Maw had set out, and Michael hurriedly followed him. For almost an hour, the two men walked single file on a narrow path, both silent as they concentrated on their footing.

The sun was now higher in the sky, and so too had the temperature risen. Michael's shirt under his rucksack became uncomfortably wet. He frequently had to brush off from his face and neck the small, brownish bugs that Anna Wells had so hated—"horrible, just like chiggers!" Michael was sure he could never find the path alone because it often became no more than a barely recognizable trace of trodden grass. Ba Maw looked up towards the top of the ridge from time to time.

Suddenly, Ba Maw said: "Okay, we have only two kilometers to go. From here on, we'll turn off the path and slowly descend. You'll see more and more tall trees on your left, eventually becoming a forest, so by the time we get down to the river, no one on the ridge can see us. That's why we located our camp where we did—so we would have ready access to water, but be out of sight from anyone on the ridge road or the smugglers' footpath."

When the campsite finally came into view, Michael could make out a number of dark green tents and what looked like a wooden shed—also painted dark green—on the grassy bank on the other side of the river. Two people saw the pair approach and Michael could see them calling others in the group. By the time he and Ba Maw forded the shallow riverbed and crossed over to the camp, there were ten people waiting to greet them.

As soon as they reached the group, Ba Maw went to a man around thirty, handsome and with carefully combed hair, and whispered something in his ear. The man stepped forward to Michael:

"Greetings from us all, Mr. Koyama. I am Tun Aung and very glad to meet you. And thank you for the gift I'm told you've brought us. Let me introduce the others to you."

Tun Aung's English was, Michael thought, better than his own. It reminded him of the clipped English accent he heard when the Englishmen were coming to see his father at night in the summer of 1943. Michael could not remember all the Burmese names Tun Aung was giving him, but he noted they were all young, except one man who looked around forty. There were two young women in the group. One of them was very beautiful with bright eyes and a mop of long, black hair. Everyone was dressed in worn but clean dark-colored shirts and pants.

Michael thought he would stay a couple of weeks at most in the camp. But he ended up staying four weeks despite mosquitoes, Anna's "chiggers," leeches, and the unchanging diet of vegetable soup, rice, and fried dough containing only morsels of dried fish, shrimp, and meat. Once or twice a week, rice with grilled bits of chicken or pork was served. He missed coffee and disliked the scent of lemon grass that was invariably added to the soup. The only thing he liked was the squall that came almost every afternoon to cool the air and which seemed to refresh everything.

During the first two weeks, he just observed and learned. Michael was much relieved by the fact that everyone in the camp spoke English that ranged from passable to near native. He sensed that most of them were proud of being able to speak English so well, despite the fact that it was the language of their former colonial rulers. Tun Aung, a Rangoon University graduate in politics and government studies, was the leader of the CYBD and the camp. His father had been the minister of welfare in the U Nu government. The older man was The Hla, a former journalist who wrote the articles published in the CYBD pamphlets, which the committee distributed in as many cities in Burma as possible. The contents of the pamphlets were based on the discussions among the camp members and printed in Mandalay by a printer willing to risk imprisonment by the Ne Win regime.

For communication with the outside world, Tun Aung had only a WWII field wireless, which couldn't be reliably used for contact beyond about fifty kilometers, and, even within that range, it often didn't work because the camp was located in a mountainous area. This was why the CYBD had to use Thuanggyi and Mandalay as "focal operational centers" from where they could get in touch with Rangoon. Tun Aung claimed that his committee could mobilize "as many as 30,000 young men and women and older 'democrats' when the time comes." The two youngest members, who had just graduated from Rangoon University, took turns as "runners," making long treks on foot or in a jeep to exchange messages and deliver drafts of pamphlets as well as to bring in food.

One of the two women in the camp was Myint San, a short, plain-looking but affable graduate of English literature from Mandalay Teachers College. She was in charge of the "kitchen" and spent much of the day in the small building—

which Michael had thought at first was a shed—where meals were prepared. Myint San shared a tent with Khin Khin, the beautiful young woman with the mop of black hair. Khin Khin was thirty-two—older than Michael had guessed—and had a degree in linguistics from Rangoon University. Like Myint San, Khin Khin was a determined democracy-activist. In one of the earliest conversations Michael had with her, she told him: "I have a very personal reason why Burma has to become democratic as soon as possible. My husband, to whom I was married for only two years, was an army lieutenant who supported U Nu. He was executed shortly after Ne Win's coup."

The most important activity in the camp was the discussions—at times, very heated—about what could be or should be done against the numerous decrees from the government restricting various freedoms of the people, imposing longer conscription obligations, and mounting military operations against the Karen National Union and other smaller anti-government groups, including communist cells. The discussions were earnest because they determined what was written in the pamphlets that were distributed.

Michael just listened. Thankfully, the discussions were almost entirely in English. Since all of the members had been educated in English, and since Burma, like India, had a number of dialects, English was their common language. When arguments became really heated as happened occasionally, a few members would slip into their native tongue. Then, Khin Khin, who usually was near Michael, interpreted what she could for him. A linguist by training, she had an ear for languages and spoke Thai and some Karen as well as English and her native Burmese.

What Michael heard became the basis of an important part of the report he was to write for Gen. Lund. As the days passed, Michael began to form his evaluation of each member in the camp. Tun Aung was bright but too facile in his arguments and showed a lack of ideological conviction—ideological spine? He was a little too willing to tolerate the increasing encroachment by the government on the civil liberties of the people. Michael sensed that Tun Aung might conceivably accept some form of "accommodation" with Ne Win if he was promised amnesty and a position in the regime.

Ba Maw, Michael soon found, was an opportunist, as General Lund had suspected. He was a well-read young man with a facility for expressing himself, but even more than Tun Aung, he seemed to carefully choose his positions after judging from the direction of the argument what the majority seemed to favor. Michael thought that he would be a good politician in the parliament of an established democracy, but didn't think he belonged in the CYBD or that he should be writing reports to the Americans.

Three of the eleven were Marxists. All three wanted a leader who would nationalize all "the means of production" and make "Burma a part of the bulwark against Western capitalism." One of them, Lwin, often glanced at Michael as he attacked "the West," but Michael pretended not to notice.

Within three weeks after arriving in the camp, Michael was convinced that only four of the eleven—the journalist The Hla, the two women, and one young man, Myat, a handsome student of physics who left Rangoon University in his third year—were his idea of what the members of the CYBD should be: determined to bring about a democratic Burma; passionate against encroachments on civil liberties; and viewing the West, especially the U.S., as pro-democratic friends despite all their failings; and above all, firmly opposed to Ne Win, a "Burmese-style" leftist dictator.

As Michael grew more certain of what his assessment of the CYBD would be, he became increasingly eager to leave the camp as soon as he could. The primitive conditions and the unappetizing and monotonous diet were weighing on him. Then, at the beginning of the fourth week, when he was just about to ask Ba Maw to arrange his return to Mae Hong Son and Chiang Mai, something happened to make him decide to delay his departure. At the time, he didn't regret the delay because it would help make his report substantially better, more useful to Gen. Lund. But he had mixed feelings about how this came about, and, as it turned out, the delay seriously "complicated" his departure.

Khin Khin had been friendly toward Michael from his arrival. She seemed to be always nearby when he needed someone or something. As she told him with a smile, "Khin means friendly in Burmese, so I am a friendly-friendly woman." Though older than Michael, it didn't take him many days to realize she seemed strongly attracted to him. By the end of the second week of his stay in the camp, Khin Khin had become so possessive and openly flirtatious that Michael was glad that there was so little privacy in the camp. He didn't need the complications that would arise from entanglements of any kind while on this mission.

Khin Khin seemed to be aware that her flirtatious advances weren't getting her anywhere, so when she suspected Michael was about to leave, she tried another tack. While Michael was jotting down notes in the sun at the edge of the camp one morning, Khin Khin came and sat down next to him. She started talking in a quiet voice about the members of the group and her assessment of them. At first, Michael thought she was merely relating gossip, but he quickly realized she was telling him things that were important, things he could not have found out on his own.

Khin Khin was immediately aware that she had piqued Michael's interest, and so, when she was called away to help with lunch preparations, she promised Michael to tell him more, later. Michael decided to delay his plans to leave as Khin Khin continued to relay to him bits and pieces of information that would make his assessment of the CYBD considerably more negative than he had originally planned.

Khin Khin told him of a major debate the CYBD members had when Tun Aung asked that the content of the CYBD Pamphlet be "adjusted" by province to accommodate the local mix of ethnic groups and the degree of the strength of the opposition to the new regime. Michael also heard that "Lwin is a member of the Burmese Communist Party and keeps in touch with them." At another session she informed him, "There is no doubt that the figures for the number of pamphlets published and the amount of money supporters have contributed are very much inflated. The true number of supporters is closer to half the 30,000 claimed." She also told Michael that when Ba Maw spoke of money from America, his numbers changed unaccountably. "If I were American, I would send someone to see the banker in Chiang Mai and thoroughly audit the account."

On the third day after Khin Khin started "confiding," she suggested to Michael that since she would be busy all day, they should continue their session at night "in your tent since I have a tent-mate." Michael didn't answer for some time, avoiding Khin Khin's imploring eyes. Finally, he responded, "Okay, you know where to find me."

Michael was conflicted. Having listened to her over several hours, he knew that by now he had heard most, if not all, she had to tell him. He knew full well what her intentions were. But he had to admit to himself he had been enjoying this beautiful woman's flirtatious smiles and her "accidentally" touching his hands and knees. His young body was more than willing, regardless of what his mind was saying. Suddenly remembering the hours he had spent with Alissa in his room in Paris, he knew he was more than willing to let what would happen tonight happen.

At almost 9:30, Khin Khin slid into Michael's tent through the flap. The night was utterly quiet except for the murmuring sound of the river. Michael, sitting on his cot and reading his notes by the light of his oil lamp, put his notebook down and said, "A bit late, aren't you?"

She said nothing but sat down next to Michael, so close that their thighs touched.

Michael tried to be businesslike. "First, I've a couple of questions about what you told me yesterday."

"You don't need that lamp to ask questions. Turn it off and save the oil. I can answer them in the dark."

SOMETIME LATER, FUMBLING FOR HER CLOTHES IN THE DARK TENT, Khin Khin began to speak in a quiet voice. Her words surprised Michael:

"I will remember this for a long time. I know I forced myself on you. But you have to admit you were not entirely an unwilling participant." Then she knelt beside the cot and continued, her voice now faltering. "I wish this could continue, but I like you too much to put you in any danger. Tun Aung is looking into moving our camp. We've been here too long, and he's afraid we may have already attracted attention by all our comings and goings. I have told you everything I know that might be helpful to you. Please leave. As soon as you can. I want Burma to be free, and we must have support from outside. I told you things that are not flattering to the CYBD because I wanted you to know who we really are. But despite our flaws and differences, we all want to change our country. Please help us get our message out."

"Thanks, most friendly-friendly lady. I'll do that. And... thanks for being so *'khin khin'* to me."

The next morning Michael talked to Ba Maw and arrangements were made for him to leave in two days. Htoo was to pick him up at the spot where he had dropped him and drive him to Mae Hong Son.

THE SKY WAS BLUE AND THERE WASN'T A RAIN CLOUD IN SIGHT when Michael got up on August 11, just four weeks since his arrival. He was looking forward to relaxing and getting his notes in order during this, his final day. As he and several others were finishing breakfast, someone shouted:

"Hey, look up at the path...about 300 meters up. I saw something glitter and I think I saw the heads of a couple of people!"

Michael looked up and saw Lwin yelling excitedly and pointing toward the ridge. Tun Aung ran over to Lwin and shouted:

"It's a rifle...the sun is reflecting on the bayonet the soldiers attach to their rifles! I see two heads...no, I see more...at least four. It has to be soldiers. No one from the KNU is expected here until next week. We have at most ten minutes...possibly fifteen...before they get here. Plan Red! Grab what you have to. Get into the forest! Don't bunch up! Hurry!"

Everyone scurried. Michael rushed back to his tent and grabbed his rucksack. He dumped out his extra clothing to lighten it and quickly checked that his notebooks, passport, and money were in the small pocket. He emerged from the tent to see Khin Khin and Myint San running toward him. Khin Khin called:

"I know you don't know what do for Plan Red. Just come with Myint San and me. The Hla should be here any moment. We'll help him carry his papers."

They looked around anxiously. No sight of The Hla. Very worried, Myint San cried, "You two go ahead," and she dashed off toward The Hla's tent.

Khin Khin and Michael nodded and together ran toward the trees. They could see other groups of twos and threes also heading for the forest, still 100 meters away. The sun was now high enough that anyone running through the tall grass towards the forest was certainly visible to anyone coming down the path to the river. Khin Khin ran easily though her rucksack looked heavy, but Michael was panting.

Suddenly, he heard a rifle shot. The report echoed. Michael didn't know if he and Khin Khin were being targeted or some of the others. With only twenty meters to the edge of the forest, they picked up speed.

The pair dove into the woods and sheltered behind a large tree to catch their breath. Almost immediately, Michael heard a sound—something like "bitsh, bitshe"—as rifle bullets hit the tree trunk next to theirs. He knew, then, they were the targets. He grabbed Khin Khin's hand and the two plunged through the trees and into the forest as fast as they could. Finally, neither could run any further and they stopped.

"Khin Khin, do you know which way to go? We don't want to get lost."

"We studied this forest for Plan Red. There's an old smugglers' path to Mae Hong Son that runs through this forest, a path that cuts across the Thai border. It's the shortest way to Mae Hong Son, but the soldiers may know about it, so it's too dangerous to take. So we'll take a longer but safer route the KNU people showed me. "

"How far is it by the longer route to Mae Hong Son?"

"Give or take forty kilometers as the crow flies."

"Forty kilometers! twenty-four miles! Through this forest? We aren't crows...so it could be much further away." Michael was dismayed.

"Have courage. It's at most fifty kilometers. But we can make it in a day and a half. And this is no jungle. Look, you can see the sky in many places, and walking is not very difficult. If we spend the night in the forest, we'll be there by tomorrow noon. I have a canteen of water and a little food—two cans of tuna and something like what you call hardtack. Don't worry, I even have a little can opener in my Plan Red pack."

"But only a small canteen of water for two days in this heat?"

"If Mother Nature sticks to her routine, there will be a squall...count on it. It's the rainy season. Come on, let's go."

Michael and Khin Khin moved as quietly as they could deeper into the forest. The sun was visible in the east through the canopy of trees. They walked on and on in the hot and humid air. Michael's shirt became soaking wet from the heat and humidity. From time to time, they stopped to listen, but they didn't hear anything except the occasional flutter of birds nearby. They drank a few mouthfuls of water from the canteen and continued on.

The sun was now high above them. Michael's watch said it was noon. Exhausted, they sat silently at the foot of a large tree and had more water and a piece of hardtack that tasted more like flour than anything else. As they downed their snack, they became aware that they were not alone in this part of the forest. They could hear an occasional branch snap some distance away. Michael looked at Khin Khin. She whispered, "That's a person, not an animal. Stay low. I'm going to investigate."

Before he could reply, she had melted into the forest. Michael waited. Then he decided he had to follow Khin Khin. It could be someone from their group, but equally likely, it was a Burmese soldier.

After walking only a short distance, Michael heard voices. One was Khin Khin's and the other a young man's. He stopped and moved to the left so he wouldn't meet them head on. Their conversation became audible, and as he drew closer, he knew it was in Burmese. By now, Michael was barely moving so as not to make any noise. Peering around a tree, he saw a rifle pointing upwards and a khaki sleeve. He had no idea what was being said, and though none of the words sounded threatening, he didn't want to take any chances. He moved through the trees until he was behind the soldier and facing Khin Khin. When she saw Michael, her words started coming out in a torrent. He realized it was to cover any sound he made while approaching.

The soldier was no taller than Michael and certainly weighed less. Michael took several steps at a faster pace though as stealthily as he could, gathered his courage, and tackled the soldier from behind. He tried to follow his high school rugby coach's instructions: "tackle your opponent a little above his knees, wrapping your arms around him so he can't get away." The soldier fell forward onto the ground, his rifle flying away. Before he could get up, Michael jumped onto his back and twisted his right arm behind him. The soldier yelped loudly when Michael shouted, "Don't move. I'll break your arm!" Still with his face down, the soldier remained motionless, making Michael wonder if he understood English. But then Khin

Khin said something in Burmese. Both the soldier and Michael looked at her. She was holding the rifle with it aimed at the soldier.

Khin Khin said to Michael, "You can get off him now." As Michael stood up, the soldier sat up, rubbing his right arm. He was visibly shaking. Michael could see now that he was a boy of no more than seventeen or eighteen, and very scared.

"Congratulations," Khin Khin smiled at Michael. "That was quite a tackle. This guy got lost chasing one of our teams and his companion is nowhere in sight."

"What did you tell him?"

"That I was alone and totally lost. I asked him how many of them came down the path and how they knew where we were. He wouldn't answer and instead began to ask me where I was going."

"Okay, give me the rifle and translate." Khin Khin, looking at Michael quizzically, handed the rifle over.

"First tell him I am going to ask him some questions, and he better answer truthfully because I am the kind of a guy who shoots. Got it? Ask him again how many soldiers came with him and how they knew where the camp was."

Khin Khin translated. The young soldier looked at Michael but said nothing.

"Ask again," Michael demanded.

Khin Khin repeated her questions, but the soldier remained silent. Michael cocked the rifle.

"Tell him this is the last chance. If he doesn't answer my questions, I will pull the trigger. Tell him you have seen me kill Burmese soldiers before."

As the words were translated, the young soldier lost color. He swallowed hard and then mumbled something.

"What did he say?"

"He said six of them came down the path. He says a young guy came to the squad hut on top of the ridge on the border and told them exactly where the camp was."

"Ask him to describe the guy."

Khin Khin did and translated the young soldier's reply: "Just a young Thai, he didn't know him. But he was a dandy with a *shway* tooth and a beautiful white shirt—sorry, *shway* means gold or golden."

The only person Michael could think of who fit the description was Htoo Lay whom he had met in Chiang Mai. But why would he tell the Burmese soldiers where the camp was? As if reading Michael's mind, Khin Khin said:

"The only person I know with a gold tooth is Htoo, but why would he do that? I've got to find out what's going on. Let's get going."

"Okay, tell this soldier to leave his ammo belt, his canteen of water, and then get lost. Tell him to go north, back toward the river the way he came. The sun will be on his left. He can drink when he gets back to the river."

The soldier listened to Khin Khin relay Michael's orders with obvious relief. He unbuckled his ammo belt, handed over his water, and began to walk north toward the river as he had been directed.

"Do you think we can trust him to do what we told him to?" asked Khin Khin dubiously.

"I think so. He's young and scared. And what else can he do without water or a weapon? But let's get out of here fast. He could run into a soldier and they could decide to come after us. At least we now have a weapon."

Michael and Khin Khin walked on again in the opposite direction from the soldier. Eventually, they stopped to rest and Khin Khin opened one of her cans of tuna, which they ate with hardtack. Khin Khin's canteen was now empty, so they had a bit of the water left in the soldier's. The light was fading and mosquitoes began to annoy them. Khin Khin rummaged in her rucksack and came up with a small bottle of yellowish liquid, homemade mosquito repellant with the same smell as the incense Michael had used in the pine grove in Ashiya to ward off mosquitoes.

After their "meal," they continued on. The fading light made the forest seem denser and, soon, it became too dark to go on. There was no squall. This was good—they could stay dry—but bad, too, because they were becoming very thirsty as they had been sweating all day. They emptied the soldier's canteen.

They found a spot under a tall tree where they decided to spend the night. From her rucksack, Khin Khin pulled out a piece of water-repellant cloth large enough for both of them to sit on. As night descended, the woods seemed to become noisier instead of quieter. Michael could hear all around him rustling noises made by small animals as they disturbed fallen leaves. The two were exhausted and Khin Khin fell asleep immediately, her back resting against the tree. Michael found the ground hard and lumpy, and the night noises disconcerted him as well as the mosquitoes, which weren't daunted by the bug repellant. But even for Michael, a light sleeper, total exhaustion worked like a powerful hypnotic drug. He was in a deep sleep only minutes after he leaned against the tree next to Khin Khin and closed his eyes.

Feeling chilled and with a crick in his neck, Michael awoke to see weak light coming from the east between the trees. Realizing he had slept through the night, he looked to his right where Khin Khin had been when he went to sleep. She was gone. Alarmed, he jumped up and looked around.

He breathed a sigh of relief when he saw her coming toward him with an armful of long, thick grass stems.

"I have no idea what these are called in English, but if you cut the stems of this tall grass here, close to the roots, and suck...you get a little drinkable moisture. Such is the wisdom that comes from living in Burma."

When sucked, each of the stems yielded enough grass-tasting liquid to wet Michael's tongue. Khin Khin and Michael sucked hard on a dozen stems and had a breakfast of tuna and hardtack, and then they were on their way again. By nine o'clock, the sun was higher than the canopy and they had little difficulty seeing their way between the trees. Khin Khin kept looking at the shape of the low ridge in front of her and, after nearly as hour, she stopped:

"This is where we have to go a little more toward the northeast. We should soon come upon a little path."

They did come to a path, not "soon," but hours later, shortly after mid-day. The path became steeper. Finally, Khin Khin, smiling, turned to Michael and said:

"I think we've just crossed the border. Now we should be in Thailand."

"How do you know? This is just a narrow path with no signs of any kind at all."

"Nobody knows for sure where the border is. But about six months ago when three of us from the camp had to go to Mae Hong Son to consult with the KNU, the KNU guide told me that just about here, where you can see that big rock, is the border. They know—this is their country."

Another half hour brought them to the top of the ridge. Khin Khin pointed: "There...down this path...we will soon see Mae Hong Son. I'll call the safe house from the post office."

The descent from the ridge down to the post office took almost another half hour. Just before they came out of the path into the open, Khin Khin took the rifle from Michael and hid it in the underbrush by the side of the path. Then she walked to the small shack-like post office to make her call. Michael squatted on the ground to the side of the small building, trying to look inconspicuous but knowing how grubby he must look after their long trek and a night sleeping rough.

Within minutes, Khin Khin emerged with a panicked look on her usually calm face. "When I called the safe house, Htoo answered the phone. Htoo! He isn't even supposed to know it exists! I asked to speak to the owner—my KNU contact—but Htoo said he wasn't there at the moment. Htoo told me to get to the house right away as most of the others from the camp had already arrived and they were discussing what to do next. I asked him to let me talk to someone from the camp but he told me they're too busy. The lying bastard!"

Before Michael could ask any questions, the very agitated Khin Khin went on.

"Michael, I know it's a trap! We know from the young soldier that it has to be Htoo who told the army where our camp is. I'm not sure what I should do, but I have to get you out of here. I didn't tell Htoo where I was calling from, but where else could I be but Mae Hong Son? He pressed me to tell him who I was with. I told him I was alone, but I don't think he believed me."

"Why not?"

"I was so shocked to hear Htoo's voice that I'm sure I sounded as if I was lying. I don't know who may have gotten to the safe house. And if Htoo has any suspicion that you are with me—you certainly aren't at the safe house—he will alert the Burmese army. By myself, I can merge into the local population, but your Thai will give you away. They will want to get you at all costs, because if they catch you, they can 'prove' that the CYBD is just the running dog of American imperialism and Western capitalism."

Khin Khin, already looking very tired, was frowning. Michael racked his brains to think of the best way to get out of Mae Hong Son as soon as he could and back to Chiang Mai. He decided they were both too tired and hungry to think straight. He glanced at his watch and said:

"Khin Khin, I agree that I have to get the hell out of here. But I don't think anyone is going to come get me in next half hour. We've not eaten anything to speak of for over a day, and both of us are famished. Let's get something to eat and then make plans. I see a woman selling noodles from a cart over there. Here's some money. Please go get a couple of bowls, and then we'll decide what to do next."

Khin Khin agreed and purchased two large bowls of noodles with vegetables in soup. As Khin Khin was slurping noodles, she began to talk rather disjointedly about what was on her mind, as if to herself. She commented that it was a good thing that The Hla had given her a copy of the bank information that had been entrusted to him by Tun Aung "just in case."

Michael asked her where the safe house was, but Khin Khin replied, "It's safer if you don't know." Safer for whom, he wondered. If he didn't know where it was, he couldn't give the location away should he be caught by Burmese army agents. He tried asking her what she was going to do. But she wouldn't tell him that either, and Michael wondered if she had even decided yet. Her first thought seemed to be to get Michael to safety.

When both finished eating, Khin Khin turned to plans for getting Michael out of Mae Hong Son. "Don't call anyone from here. I mean your American friends. This is what you should do." She gave Michael directions to a small guesthouse on the north side of town—nowhere near the one where Michael had stayed with Htoo—and told him to say that she sent him. She warned, "Be sure to stay inside the guesthouse—this town is so small that you can't risk being seen. Tomorrow morning, take the first bus to Chiang Mai. The old lady at the guesthouse will tell you where the bus station is and she will know the bus schedule."

"If you can get to Chiang Mai, can you take care of yourself from there?" she asked Michael.

"Yes. We have a crisis ex-filtration procedure and I can speak enough Thai to get around. I'll call Bangkok when I get to Chiang Mai."

"Ex-filtration procedure?"

"Sorry, the procedure to get the hell out of Thailand."

Khin Khin went to return the bowls to the woman at the food cart and when she returned, she demanded, "Michael, kiss me goodbye—like they do in American movies."

Michael was a bit taken aback, but moved with Khin Khin to the shelter of the post office, put his hands on her shoulders and, softly but soundly, kissed her. When he let her go, he pleaded:

"You know how to write to me, so please do as soon as you can and tell me what happened with the people at the camp, the money—everything."

Without replying, Khin Khin stepped back, looked into Michael's eyes, and said, "Go, go! I will never forget you. *La gon.* Be well."

Michael, a little choked up, slung his backpack over his shoulder and replied, "*La gon.* Goodbye. Take care. And thank you!" Then he headed north toward the guesthouse.

When he looked back, Khin Khin was still standing in the same place and waved at him.

Michael's "ex-filtration" turned out not to be as easy as he thought it would be. He managed to find the guesthouse, where he hid out the rest of the day. He was fed more noodles for "dinner." That night, he got little sleep despite being so tired. He kept waking because he was afraid of missing the only bus going to Chiang Mai, "at 5:30 in the morning" according to the old lady at the guesthouse.

When it was still not fully light, Michael walked to the bus stop, hoping he wouldn't see anyone who might be looking for him. At first, he waited alone, but gradually, people began to straggle toward the stop, one man carrying a cage with two chickens in it, a woman trailing three small children who all looked under the age of four, and an elderly woman with a large cloth bundle, among others. Eventually a ramshackle bus chugged up, and they all piled in.

Michael didn't think he had ever before endured a more uncomfortable ride in any vehicle. The bus was rickety and the dirt roads heavily rutted. By the time they reached Chiang Mai, there were at least twice as many people as the bus could comfortably hold. The windows on his side of the bus were out, and if dust wasn't blowing in, the rain from the afternoon squall was. For lunch, he had a fried meat pie that he purchased at one of their many stops. But finally they pulled up in a main square in Chiang Mai and the passengers disgorged.

Michael found the post office and, at last, made contact with Bangkok. His call to the American Embassy went through immediately. When Major Bowden, the military attaché, answered, he seemed to be racking his brains over what the code words Michael was using involved. But after a delay of a good five seconds, he said, as if to himself, "Okay, I got it." Then, "Mr. Koyama? What's up? Where are you?"

"I'm in Chiang Mai and need transport back to the Land of the Free and would much appreciate a very quick getaway...it's a little too hot for me here, and Sir, I am not referring to the temperature."

"Understood. I'll get busy right away, but we can't send a plane up north until tomorrow morning. Can you rendezvous at 0800 tomorrow?"

"I'll be at the same end of the airport at 0745. I assume you are using the same charter service?"

"Yes. The best and the only one there is. Stay in one piece. I am not going to worry too much because I understand you speak the lingo of this country."

Then, Michael had to find a place to spend the night. Khin Khin had advised him to avoid the busy Chiangrai Road, which was Htoo's neighborhood, and also the bigger inns and the area near the airport in case someone searched for him. Taking back streets, he eventually found a small house about a mile north of the airport with a sign that it would take in guests. It proved to be dirty and full of bugs, but the elderly bent-over woman who ran it agreed to give him supper—more noodles. Though noodles were among his favorite foods and by now he was grateful for anything to eat, even he was getting tired of noodle meals. But best of all, she arranged for her neighbor's son to take him to the airport in the morning on his tuk-tuk, a three-wheeled vehicle that was a cross between a motorbike and a rickshaw. The ride to the airport was harrowing and Michael was charged what he knew was an exorbitant fare, but at least he arrived in time to meet the plane.

The pilot, who had been told to pick up an "American with the rank of major," gave Michael a funny look when he boarded. Michael realized the pilot hadn't expected his passenger to be an Asian who looked like an unshaven local in clothes that had been worn for three days. But the pilot must have had other filthy and strange-looking passengers and said nothing after Michael showed him his ID.

Saigon airport was a madhouse. Military helicopters were all over the runways and in the large hangers. More than a dozen among the almost thirty he counted were very large with a machine gun protruding from the left side. The sight of all the rotor blades on top of all these helicopters gleaming in the morning sun was beautiful and ominous at the same time. This seemed to Michael proof that the U.S. was now fully committed to the war in Vietnam.

A lieutenant at the duty desk carefully read the TDY order—temporary duty order—Michael handed him. Though full of Army-speak and codes, neither the order nor Michael's appearance fazed the lieutenant.

"Mr. Koyama, who is also 'status: pay grade, reserve major' with G2 priority. Gotcha. Since you are a G2 guy, I can tell you that we are now getting a lot of special forces guys, and more generals and colonels than I have ever seen are coming and going. This is to say that you won't get out here at the earliest...let me see...before Friday, three days from now. You can stay at the officers' transit barracks 300 yards down the road. They should also be able to outfit you in some clean fatigues."

Michael was told where he could pick up the bag containing his clothes and a few other things he had left behind what now seemed years ago. Then he went in search of a bed. Having no choice, he stayed three nights in the barracks between the airfield and the rice paddies, listening to croaking frogs, getting bitten by mosquitoes despite the repellant, and eating air force meals designed for nourishment rather than taste, alongside grumbling young air force and marine officers. He spent the remainder of his first day resting, and the following two days, drafting a report to Gen. Lund and reading newspapers he bought at the PX. The PX and a storage unit attached to it were the only sturdy looking, new concrete buildings around the airport. Michael wondered how long the U.S military was planning to stay in Vietnam fighting the war.

As the duty officer had predicted, Michael left Saigon on Friday, which he suddenly realized was his twenty-eighth birthday. His plane was full of soldiers and civilians who looked like reporters. He saw several soldiers who were carried into the plane on stretchers. During the long flight, Michael, sitting not far from the wounded soldiers, pondered on the seemingly never-ending fate of humans to wage wars. He wondered if Vietnam was about to become another Korea.

One young soldier died two hours before the plane landed at Hickam Air Force Base in Honolulu.

RAIN WAS FALLING AGAINST MICHAEL'S WINDOW as he looked up from his typewriter. He had been back in Berkeley for over two months now, furiously working to try to catch up on the preparations for his Ph.D. dissertation. With the encouragement of his principal advisor, he had decided on an ambitious, historical, and comparative study: to analyze quantitatively the relationships among the competitiveness of markets, the profitability of companies, and the growth rates of the economies of the U.S., Japan, and Germany since the 1880s. When Michael asked his advisor if he could also study why incomes were so unevenly distributed in the three economies, the advisor told him, "I always knew you were interested in that question. But your study is already too ambitious to add another topic. Do it later."

Michael had postponed his research trip to Japan until January. This enabled him to apply for jobs and, if need be, to attend the annual meeting of the American Economic Association in late December when many universities interviewed prospective assistant professors. He was also preparing for a presentation of his research at a faculty colloquium at the prestigious Buford University in San Francisco, considered by many to be the "Princeton of the West," just as Stanford was known as the Harvard of the West Coast.

Until this week, his five weeks in Southeast Asia had become like a distant memory, but then two pieces of mail brought his journey to Burma vividly back to him. A few days ago, he received a long letter from Gen. Lund. The general first expressed his appreciation for Michael's long and detailed report that "served as the basis upon which the Army decided not to maintain any further involvement with nor to provide any further financial assistance to the CYBD." Michael was pleased that his report had been taken so seriously, but what the general wrote next surprised Michael:

> Major Bowden, our military attaché in Bangkok, informed us that a day after you left Chiang Mai, a Thai by the name of Htoo Lay—a name the major recognized immediately because he had been long suspected of dealing in, even stealing, American goods—was shot and killed. The major specially asked me to tell you.

Michael was as sure as he could be that the weapon had been a Burmese army rifle that he had carried through the forest of the Shan plateau and was fired by a widow whose husband was executed by the Ne Win's soldiers. But what surprised him even more was what came next:

> A young Burmese woman, who spoke excellent English, contacted Major Bowden, asking him to meet her at a bank in Chiang Mai "to discuss the American money deposited in the bank." When the major arrived, she produced the code for an account, and demanded that the bank give the funds remaining in the account to the major. The major wrote that she threatened the bank manager: if he failed to comply with her demands, all the irregularities involved regarding the currency laws and nonpayment of interest on the deposit would be duly reported to the authorities. The bank manager had no choice but to give in to her demands.

After the major received the money, she argued with him to allow her to keep $1,400—just 10 percent of the total that she helped recover for the U.S.—to enable her to buy communications equipment, such as wireless field phones and a jeep, for local groups that were truly democratic and non-communist. Major Bowden was uncertain what he should do, but to his credit, he decided to give her the 10 percent she demanded because the large amount of money that he would be taking back to the embassy was an unexpected return of money no one thought would ever be seen again. Major Bowden wrote that 'she was a forceful and very smart young woman whom he could not help but like and respect.'

Thanking you again for all you did for us in Burma,
David Lund.

When he was putting the letter back into its envelope,
Michael found a U.S. government check for $3,800 attached
to a handwritten note from General Lund that read: "This is
the amount that anyone with the pay grade of major gets for
two months on special assignment and for writing an excellent report.

That was a few days ago. Then, today, he found a postcard
with a Burmese stamp on it in his mailbox in the economics
department. The only words on it were: "Hope you are back
safely and well. Setting up a new small group truly dedicated
to democracy. Much love, KK." No address of the sender.
On the back was a beautiful picture of the Shan Plateau with
the sun rising over the ridge. As Michael took his eyes off
the rain on his window, his glance fell once again on the
postcard on his desk, and his thoughts went back to the place
of "three mists" and the camp on the river.

Chapter 11

Cambridge and Elsewhere, 1967-69

I T WAS A PERFECT SATURDAY AFTERNOON IN SEPTEMBER as Michael walked across the Harvard Yard toward one of the oldest buildings on campus. After the publication of his first book, Buford University in San Francisco had promoted him to Associate Professor and given him a year's leave. Obtaining a research grant to spend a year at Harvard under the guidance of Professor Ross, the leading scholar of Japanese industrialization, he had come to Cambridge in July. With the Harvard libraries at his disposal, he was making good progress on his research topic: the role played in Japan's industrialization by the four *zaibatsu* or conglomerates—Yasuda, Sumitomo, Mitsubishi, and Mitsui.

Today Michael was on his way to a seminar held once a month for academics located on the East Coast who were interested in the Japanese economy. Still an avid baseball fan, Michael was listening to the Red Sox game on a small transistor radio held to his ear as he crossed the Yard. Carl Yastrzemski, the home run king, was coming to bat. Michael delayed entering the seminar room until he heard a clock strike three. For a moment, he toyed with the idea of hearing what Yaz would do, but then reluctantly switched off his radio and entered the room. As he took an empty seat near the door, he glanced down the table and was somewhat surprised to see two women at the other end. He hadn't seen any women at the past two seminars, and not many women seemed to be interested in the Japanese economy. One woman was a stolid-looking Japanese in her mid-thirties whom he had seen at the Faculty Club. The other was a young woman with short brown hair and a pretty checked dress. She was no Aphrodite, but he liked how she looked: large, intelligent eyes, a small, shapely nose, and lips red-rosy without the help of a cosmetic company. She gave him a curious look as he put his transistor down on the table. Michael wondered what she was doing in this group of middle-aged American professors, male graduate students, and a few sleepy Japanese economists always eager to visit an Ivy League university. He decided to find out.

At dinner following the seminar, Michael maneuvered to sit next to the attractive young woman and introduced himself. "I'm Michael Koyama from Buford. Are you a student in economics here at Harvard?"

"No," she said with a smile. "I'm Susan McCallum...a graduate student in Japanese history at Yale. If you are wondering if I am an interloper, Professor Hughes said I should attend these seminars. Since I'm going to do research on Japan's premodern history focusing on demographic change, he thought I'd learn something that would be helpful for my research."

Before Michael could respond, she added hesitantly, "Do you mind if I ask you a question? Your English has an accent, but it doesn't sound Japanese. What is your native language?"

Michael smiled and replied that he didn't think he had one. That started a lively conversation about how Susan had learned Japanese. Their conversation, in the midst of the clamor of the Chinese restaurant, was suddenly interrupted when a middle-aged Japanese professor leaned across Susan and, in heavily accented English, asked Michael:

"Professor Koyama, I have read your book comparing the industrialization of Japan, Germany, and the U.S. It's very good. Are you planning to publish it in Japanese as well?"

Talking across Susan, Michael replied to the professor's question, and then they had a brief conversation in Japanese. With the Japanese man ignoring the presence of Susan, it was all very awkward, and as soon as he could, Michael ended the conversation and turned back to her. She looked taken aback.

"You told him your book isn't as good as he said but was good enough to get you promoted to associate professor with tenure. I had no idea I was talking to a tenured professor who has published a highly regarded book!"

To Michael's regret, she suddenly became rather reserved. He was disappointed with this change in her demeanor. He didn't think he was much older than she was, but there was a sharp divide in academia between students and professors. Although he had also published three articles in top economics journals as well as the book to earn early promotion, he tried to downplay his achievements to Susan and remove the distance between them that she was now clearly feeling.

Michael, wanting to put her at ease, said: "I may have a book and tenure, but just a few years ago I was at the same stage in my career as you are now...a grad student working on a dissertation."

He didn't know exactly why, but as he talked to Susan, he realized that he was thinking something he always chose not to dwell on, the fact that he didn't have anyone in his life who could provide him with the warmth and security that only the closest of human relations—a spouse or a family—can provide. After he had been separated from his father, he had known many kind people in Japan, from the nurses in the orphanage, Konishi in Sannomiya, to many people in Ashiya. But Michael had always known that, despite everyone who had been kind to him, he was essentially alone and often lonely. His relationship with Alissa had been too fleeting and, as he had by now realized, too jejune to ever have lasted. Now that he was settled in his career, could he start to think about how wonderful it would be to have someone like Susan in his life?

The more he thought about her, the more he was aware that he really wanted to know more about Susan. He knew he could try to get to know her better because she was not his student with whom any romantic relationship would be frowned upon, even considered unethical.

Looking over at Susan who was now talking animatedly in Japanese with the stolid-looking Japanese woman, Michael decided to do his best to get to know her. He knew he already liked her a lot. But he wouldn't push or rush. He wanted to be cautious. The last thing he wanted was repeating what had happened with Alissa. Moreover, Susan was in the same small academic circle he was, and it could be awkward should things go wrong. Since she lived in a town over a hundred miles away, it wasn't possible to meet her casually for coffee or in the library. Well, he thought, he would meet her again at the October seminar and see what followed.

After the October seminar, Susan smiled at Michael as the group entered the restaurant for dinner, and he was pleased that he had no trouble getting a seat next to her. Michael started to find out more about her. He asked her about her family. She told him that she was the daughter of a war widow whose geologist husband had been killed on Okinawa. It puzzled Michael why anyone whose father had been killed in a war with the Japanese would be drawn to studying Japanese history and culture. Susan's answer was succinct, as her answers to his questions always were.

"Well, to me, the war is history. My father died just before my fifth birthday, and the war ended a year after that. To tell you the truth, I have no memory of World War II at all. So I don't feel as if I am studying an enemy nation. Besides, the war's been over for more than two decades."

Michael thought how very different their experiences in the war had been, though he was just five years older than Susan. How vivid was his memory of the day his father had waked him from a nap in his hammock when he was seven. His father had come to tell him that he had heard on the radio that Japanese planes had attacked Pearl Harbor. Michael could still remember his father's words:

"This means war between Japan and America, Bunji. But it won't last long...maybe a year or two. Japan cannot hope to win because the Americans can produce far more warships and planes than the Japanese can, and the Americans have petroleum and minerals."

Because the war had changed his life forever, he had to ask Susan, "Surely, your family suffered during the war, especially with your father gone?"

"We managed because my mother went back to teaching high school. I was too young to notice how much my mother grieved for my father. But Mom did tell me that the family was limited to a quarter of a pound of butter per week, and she thought my brother and I should have it, so she gave it to us, and she ate margarine. I understand gasoline was in limited supply, but that didn't affect me. I always had enough clothes, food, toys, and, of course, we weren't bombed—there was no physical danger to us."

Michael looked at Susan, thinking how nice it would be to have been able to go through the war without experiencing what he had. On the other hand, when she said that she didn't miss her father because she wasn't sure she could even remember him, he thought he was lucky to have known his father. By the time dinner ended, Michael thought he liked her even more, and he hoped she was beginning to find him friendly and likable.

Michael waited eagerly for the November meeting. That evening, he learned that after the December seminar, Susan planned to stay on in Cambridge to spend the holidays with an aunt. He asked if she would have dinner with him in Cambridge. She readily agreed with a pleased smile. Michael was delighted.

Then, on the first of December, he got a phone call he neither expected nor wanted.

The message originated with General Lund, but unlike on Michael's office phone at Buford, there was no scrambler on his phone at Harvard, so the message was very carefully worded. "Mr. Lund would appreciate it if you would come to his office for a meeting on Monday morning at nine. This is short notice, but would it be possible?" Despite the polite request, Michael knew this was close to a command. "I'll be there," he replied.

Sunday, Michael flew down to D.C. hoping that he would be back in Cambridge within a day or two, but given the news he had been hearing the past few months about the war in Vietnam, he had a dread in the back of his mind that this meeting could somehow involve him in this war. His heart sank when he walked into the small conference room on the fourth floor of the Pentagon to find with General Lund three officers: a brigadier general, a colonel, and a major, all just back from Vietnam.

General Lund made the introductions and then turned to Michael. "G2 is hearing a lot from their 'humint assets'—human intelligence sources—not only in Saigon but in Hué, Da Nang, and other places as well, about large-scale movements of vehicles and materiel, as well as increases in taxes on locals for food supplies. It looks like the Viet Cong is preparing for a major offensive, and with our forces already over-stretched, we are concerned about what may be in the offing. Our people need more information plus various other kinds of help only friendly people in the region can provide. That's the reason for this meeting today."

The brigadier general, the first near obese general Michael had met, took over the briefing. "The Hmongs—the hill tribes in Vietnam—are helping us, but we could use more help. I know many in the Karen National Liberation Army are well trained...so we would like to get their assistance. But our man in the field hasn't even been able to get a meeting with them because their leader, General Tin Soe, one of the few Karens who was made an 'honorary officer' in the British Karen Battalion during World War II, refuses to get involved with Americans. He says, 'white men do not keep their promises.'"

Michael knew what was coming next without being told. As far as he knew, G2 had few officers, active or reserve, whom they could enlist for any assignment involving Karens. Michael listened to the fat brigadier general with what he hoped was a poker face. When the general came to the point, Michael was not at all surprised.

"We know what you accomplished in Burma five years ago. We would like you to go again, contact the Karen National Liberation Army, which we understand has almost

20,000 soldiers, and try to get as many of their men as you can to agree to get us information on the VC's movements... to serve as our lookouts and guides...and to transport some of our supplies...including rations and ammo...anything short of becoming directly involved in combat. We're very confident that if anyone can succeed in this, you can...taking only a week, maybe ten days."

Michael didn't take to the brigadier general, whom he began to dub in his mind FBG for fat brigadier general. He didn't like what he was being asked to do, to get the KNLA involved in the Vietnam War, and he couldn't imagine how he could do this "in only a week or ten days." Since no one else had been able to even get in touch with the KLNA, he even suspected that the FBG knew how hard the job would be he was asking of Michael. And the fact that Michael had grave doubts about the American involvement in the Vietnam War didn't help. He had never been asked to do a project for G2 about which he had so many qualms.

Despite what was going through his mind, when Gen. Lund asked, "Michael, how about it? Could you do this for us?" he reluctantly agreed. He looked at Gen. Lund and said, "Sir, I'll do my best to assess the situation and write a report, and G2 can take it from there."

Very pleased, the FBG added, "We'll arrange for you to fly civilian as far as Bangkok, and you'll be a temporary lieutenant colonel for the duration of the assignment so that you'll have priority in transportation and get paid accordingly."

Michael was to leave as soon as possible, so the FBG said he would arrange for him to depart on Wednesday for Bangkok and, from there, "our people will fly you on to Chiang Mai." That was in only two days time, barely enough for Michael to get kitted out and read the documents provided by the FBG. On Tuesday, he took time to call his landlady in Cambridge, telling her that he would probably be gone ten days or so. He crossed his fingers that he would be back for the economics seminar on the sixteenth when he could arrange his dinner with Susan.

As things turned out Michael didn't return to Cambridge until December 30. During the New Year's holiday, he thought on and off about what to tell Prof. Ross and his colleagues why he had been gone all month. More importantly, what could he tell Susan for breaking his promise of dinner and having disappeared for so long?

For Michael, much of the past four weeks had been like having a very long nightmare. The nightmare started with the long flights to Chiang Mai with layovers and a time change that turned day into night. Exhausted with jet lag and lack of sleep, he had been met in Chiang Mai by a CIA man who, the FBG had said, "will give you useful information." But the CIA man turned out to be utterly useless. He had no idea where Gen. Tin Soe was hiding. His parting comment was, "G2 comes up with such hare-brained ideas. I'm glad you're on this assignment and not me!"

The nightmare just grew worse during the days that followed. Everyone he talked to in Chiang Mai was suspicious of who he was and what his true motives were in trying to get in touch with the KLNA headquarters. He heard rumors that Gen Tin Soe was in the southwest where a lot of Karens lived, but someone else said he was up north in Myitkyina. After a week, he decided he had to try something else and took the long bus ride up to Mae Hong Son, which was just across the border from Kayah, the Burnese state with the largest number of Karens.

The bus ride from Chiang Mai was no less grueling and miserable this time than when he had taken it in the reverse direction five years before. Once settled in a guesthouse that was flea-ridden and full of mosquitoes, he made a careful plan so that he would not repeat his failure in Chiang Mai. For an entire week, he went out for lunch and dinner at an eatery that could hardly be called restaurant, but the owner of the guesthouse had assured Michael that Thai-Karens frequented it. By the third or fourth day, several customers in the eatery felt comfortable enough to chat and even joke with this odd American called Kivet.

Finally, one night a shy young man, Kamron, who had first sought Michael out because he wanted to practice his English, said:

"Kivet, I've been thinking what you've told me about wanting to meet someone from the KNLA. It'll be difficult because they're being chased by the Burmese Army and, I hear, there are spies all over...but I have a cousin in Loikaw, the capital of Kayah...and he might know someone who can help you."

At last! Michael thought. Kamron told him this relative was an engineer who worked at Lawpita Dam, which had been built by the Japanese during the early fifties as part of their reparations payment to Burma. Kamron offered to contact this man, though he couldn't promise anything would come of it. Michael learned that the cousin was "a trained, sleeper reservist" who would join in battles against the Burmese Army if called upon by the KNLA, and he was willing to help. Michael had to meet two people, who he was sure were "screening" him, before it was arranged for him to meet someone who would take him to meet the KNLA and, he hoped, General Tin Soe.

Early one morning, Michael dressed in native clothing and set off to meet the KNLA contact named Paw Moo, who led him to a jeep hidden just outside town and frisked him. They drove to what Paw Moo said was the border. There, Paw Moo stopped to blindfold Michael and they set off again. This ride turned out to be an ordeal worse than Michael had expected. Unable to see made it almost impossible for him to keep his balance as the jeep followed a winding rough track. After what he thought was about an hour, the jeep made several turns. Finally when Michael felt he could barely stand the jolting, the jeep suddenly stopped. Paw Moo told Michael he could take the blindfold off.

His eyes blinking from the sudden glare of the sun, Michael got out of the jeep and looked around while Paw Moo lit a cigarette. The jeep had stopped in a clearing next to a wooded area, but Michael had no idea where he was. The place was very quiet.

Before Paw Moo had taken more than a couple of puffs on his cigarette, Michael first heard and then saw several armed men walk out of the woods toward them. As they moved out into the clearing, Michael could see that the leader was a wiry man in his forties. Just behind him were half a dozen armed soldiers wearing ragtag, dark green uniforms. Michael greeted the men with the traditional bow, his hands together in front of him.

The leader looked hard at Michael. Without identifying himself, he said in clear British English:

"You've been telling people in Mae Hong Son that although you are an American, you have Karen blood. Alright, take off your glasses."

Michael was more than a little surprised by the unexpected request—more of a command—but he obeyed. The spokesman approached him, and from a distance of about four feet, stared at him for the longest time. Then he said, "Turn around very slowly."

This request unnerved Michael but he did as he was told. When he was once again facing the leader, the man said to him, "Yes, you do have some Karen in you, or at least some Southeast Asian blood. Your eyes, your nose, and the shape of your head show me that."

Then the man said, "Let's cut to the chase, shall we? I heard you represent some people in America who are interested in helping us financially. I don't believe it. Why should they? So, tell me, who do you represent? The CIA?"

Michael was relieved by the question. He answered by telling the truth. When Michael finished outlining G2's proposal that the American Army provide a good salary and some advanced weapons in exchange for KNLA help in Vietnam, the spokesman for the soldiers launched into a tirade:

"Why should the Karen National Liberation Army help the Americans in their war against the Vietnamese? We aren't some kind of the mercenaries like the French Foreign Legion! You don't come with promises to help us win our independence. All you say is that the Americans will pay us and provide weapons if we help with their doomed war in Vietnam. The proposal you brought is insulting and stupid! It really grieves me to find someone with our blood becoming the messenger of such a proposal! I will relay this to the general."

The man turned away and led his men back to the woods. Paw Moo silently led Michael back to the jeep. This time he wasn't blindfolded. Several minutes later, when they were out of sight and sound of the camp, Paw Moo stopped the jeep and pulled out a small basket containing two large round *palatas*—flaky Burmese fried bread filled with curried vegetables and meat.

Although Michael was more tired than hungry, he accepted one. He knew that, among Karens, declining proffered food was extremely rude. The two ate the *palatas* and sipped warm water from the bottle Paw Moo produced from the side pocket of the jeep's door. Just as they finished their lunch, four young men wearing the KLNA's dark green uniform suddenly appeared. Michael hadn't heard them approach.

We're being ambushed by Burmese soldiers was Michael's first thought, but Paw Moo greeted the soldiers warmly by name. They were members of the KNLA who wanted to talk to Michael. As soon as they began to talk, Michael realized all four were bright and spoke excellent English. The clear leader of the group was Bo Tho, who was very blunt:

"We overheard your talk with General Tin Soe's man. We disagree with him. It's not a bad idea to work with the Americans." Bo Tho proposed that the four help the Americans in exchange for money and communications equipment—mainly short-wave radios. Michael didn't know how much he should trust him, or what his real motivation was. However, he told Bo Tho he would relay his proposal to his superior officers and made arrangements for staying in touch by short wave radio using Paw Moo as an intermediary.

On the long drive back to Mae Hong Son, Michael tried to find out more about Bo Tho from Paw Moo, but all he learned was that Bo Tho was a son of a Karen doctor and a top graduate of Mandalay Technical College. As they drove through the dry hills and grass land of Kayah, Michael's thoughts went back to his interview with the Karen general, and this made him think of his mother. He knew almost nothing about her—he thought of her as frozen in time and space from the framed photo of her that hung on the wall in his father's study. About all he really knew was that she was descended from the minority of Karens who were Christian and well educated.

How had she met his father? A child doesn't think to ask such questions. How did his parents communicate with each other? His father's Thai was rudimentary and he knew even less Karen. How would his mother know Japanese? Surely, they must have conversed in English, or could it have been German? How odd that Michael didn't even know what language his parents used with each other.

So Michael had to conclude that about all he was sure he had inherited from his mother was the shape of his eyes and his head! His father, looking at him, used to say to him that with his looks, he was lucky he had been born a boy. But Michael knew his mother had been beautiful, and he thought his father handsome with his sculpted moustache, so where did his own looks come from? His mind flitted from one subject to another during the long and uncomfortable drive.

Michael knew he couldn't do more. He knew now he couldn't meet the general, but he had "recruited" some of his men. He would leave tomorrow for Chiang Mai and hopefully home. He was physically and emotionally exhausted after his strange day, and the more he thought about the long ride back to Chiang Mai in an overcrowded bus with no springs, the more unbearable it seemed. He simply had to get a lift, whether in a car, jeep, even a truck. So far, he had spent very little money and he decided he would be willing to pay almost anything to get a ride in a private vehicle. He went back to the eatery and asked everyone he met there, he tried a shopkeeper a few doors down someone had suggested, he went back to the guesthouse and inquired around, but all to no avail. No one was going to Chiang Mai, few people had vehicles that could make the trip, and the round trip couldn't be made in a day. So Michael once again got up before dawn and endured the ride back with locals, crying babies, the inevitable chickens, and crates of produce.

As soon as he got off the rickety bus, he called the American Embassy in Bangkok and was patched through to the G2 office in Saigon where he was connected to the brigadier general in the Pentagon. Michael gave him a report of his meeting with Gen. Tin Soe's man and his success in getting some young Karen soldiers willing to "work with Americans." He had hoped that now he could return home, but no, this nightmare assignment wasn't over. The FBG told Michael to arrange a meeting between Bo Tho and his comrades and some people who would fly in from Saigon.

Michael went back to his guesthouse in Chiang Mai, which was only marginally better than the one in Mae Hong Son. He was so exhausted he couldn't make himself go out for a meal. The lady running the guesthouse took one look at him and offered to give him a bowl of noodles, which he gratefully accepted. He was so tired that he slept a full nine hours. But even after all this sleep, when he looked at his face in the mirror as he shaved, he was startled by the dark circles under his eyes. And he knew he had lost a lot of weight because he had had to poke another hole in his belt before he left Mae Hong Son. He had never taken to Thai food, and the quality of what was available in the poor northern part of the country certainly didn't help his appetite, nor did the hot and humid climate.

Michael now had to arrange for the meeting. This took four more days, but eventually Michael, a colonel, and a major met the four young Karens in a "safe house" in Chiang

Mai designated by Bo Tho. Michael agonized over what he had gotten himself into and worried about what would happen to the four Karens and perhaps other soldiers of the KNLA if they got involved in a war that did not seem to be going well. He was certain the Karens, largely hiding out in the forests of Burma, knew far too little about how the war was going, and he was dubious about how helpful they could actually be.

But things were now out of Michael's hands. He flew to Saigon with the colonel and the major. Still he couldn't leave for home. He was asked to stay to keep in touch with Bo Tho until a Captain Watson could arrive to be briefed by Michael, and then take over the handling of the Karens. So Michael had to hang around in Saigon a couple more days with little to do after he finished his short report. But even army mess food seemed tasty compared to what he had been eating in Thailand. Nothing had been worse than the fried bat he had been forced to consume out of politeness while in Chiang Mai. His stomach had been upset the rest of the day.

Finally, Michael had briefed the captain and the following morning, he headed back to the U.S. In Washington, he was debriefed by the FBG and a colonel. The only thing Michael learned about what he had rather unwillingly instigated was that twelve young Karen from the KLNA were going to Vietnam to help the American army. The colonel had revealed this when he thanked Michael: "Thanks to you, these guys are going to be very useful. Charlie won't know if they are friends or foes until too late. We hope we can get more of them." Michael found it hard to believe that recruiting a dozen Burmese was worth the expense, to say nothing of what Michael had had to endure.

At long last, on a snowy Saturday, the day before New Year's Eve, Michael arrived at Logan Airport in Boston and wearily made his way to his lodgings in Cambridge. The frigid weather was hard to bear after his month in steamy Southeast Asia.

ON THE SECOND OF JANUARY, Michael went back to Widener Library and threw himself into his work, trying to make up for the month that he had missed while on the G2 mission. But it was impossible for him to keep the events of the outside world from breaking his concentration. As the U.S. had expected, the Viet Cong launched a major offensive in January and February of 1968, known as the Tet—New Year's—Offensive. Even Saigon was attacked. Though the U.S. eventually repulsed the attack after hard fighting; it was clear that the army was in for a long, possibly losing, war. The only thing Michael could do was to hope that none of the Karens from the KNLA had been killed or wounded.

Michael had pondered how to explain his long and sudden absence to his Harvard colleagues, but he found that they readily accepted his explanation that he had gone back to the West Coast to clear up some business. After all, he was on leave with no duties at Harvard. He was still unsure what to tell Susan about why he hadn't attended the December economics seminar, even as he walked into the seminar room for the January meeting. But Susan didn't show up.

At the dinner following the seminar, Michael managed to ask Professor Hughes from Yale—casually he hoped— what his protégée was doing, and to his surprise learned that she had left for Tokyo at the beginning of January. "Her dissertation prospectus was accepted, and when she learned that her government fellowship could be used either in the U.S. or Japan, she decided it would be best to start collecting her primary materials." Hughes mentioned that she would be working with an economic historian at Keio University for the next year and a half.

Michael was crushed. He had never considered that she might disappear like that. The East Coast's miserably cold, damp weather, the nightly bad news from Vietnam, compounded by his disappointment at finding Susan gone, all made Michael mildly depressed. He continued to gather material for his research, but found his inspiration lacking. When the piles of white snow at the edge of the roadside began to turn dirty black, and the thaws that froze again at night made Cambridge streets treacherous, he decided to take action.

Michael hadn't been attracted to anyone as much as to Susan since his affair with Alissa ended, and who knew how or where he might meet Susan again if he didn't take some initiative now. After some weeks of dithering about how to contact her—he didn't want to become just a pen pal— he decided to go to Japan. In any case, he could use more primary materials for his project on Meiji entrepreneurs, and that would give him an excuse to track down Susan's where- abouts through the economic historians at Keio University.

As soon as he arrived in Tokyo, Michael went to Keio and quickly found that Prof. Hayami was Susan's Japanese mentor. Hayami told him that Susan had gone off to Kurashiki to "read some primary documents" in that city's library. He didn't expect her back in Tokyo for several weeks.

The next morning, Michael took the bullet train to Kobe and changed there for an express train to Kurashiki. There, he checked into the Kurashiki Kokusai Hotel where he left his small bag. Then he set out for the library. He found Susan in the stacks poring over an old manuscript with a frown on her face. She was astounded to see him, but he didn't think she seemed displeased.

"What on earth are you doing here?"

"I owe you a dinner. I had to be out of town in December, so I thought I would look you up and finally treat you to the dinner I promised you."

"No, really, why are you in Kurashiki?" Susan asked again. It seemed to Michael that she looked wary, so he decided to be honest...at least partially.

"I had to come to Japan for my research. I was at Keio to meet a friend and he introduced me to Prof. Hayami who happened to come by. In the conversation about his research, your name came up. He told me where you were, so when I came west, I wanted to look you up and apologize for not keeping my promise to take you out for dinner."

Wanting to change the topic, Michael added, "So have you found what you came for?"

Susan answered by showing him a handwritten document full of wormholes.

"This was written after the famine in the 1830s by a person who lived through it. It's a great source, but it's terribly hard-going for me." She handed it to Michael.

Michael agreed that it was difficult to read, but he thought he could make it out faster than Susan and offered to go through the contents with her. It was a fascinating first-person account of the terrible years when almost continuous rain caused the crops to fail and mushrooms to sprout out of season. Susan took notes as Michael went through the text, until a librarian came to tell them the library was about to close.

"So how about that dinner? I've checked into the Kurashiki Kokusai Hotel. Would you join me there for dinner tonight?"

Susan hesitated and then asked, "Do you like *tonkatsu?* I know a mom-and-pop store not far from the station that makes great pork cutlets."

As Michael and Susan sat at the counter of the small restaurant and drank beer, Susan began to relax with Michael. As they continued to chat, Susan suddenly asked:

"Didn't you tell me once your father came from a village in Okayama Prefecture? If you know where and if it's not far from here, it could be interesting to visit it. It might even have some population registers I could use. Do you know the name of the village?"

Michael, who had not thought of ever visiting his father's village, was surprised by the question. He answered almost stuttering.

"Yes...you're right...he did...it's not far. But I really don't want to go there."

"Why not?"

"I really don't think it's good idea. You see, my father was kicked out of his family—disinherited—and had to leave the village. I only know what he told me when I was just a child, and I suspect there's more to the story than what he told me. He said he refused to marry the daughter of a rich landowner, a marriage his father had arranged for him, nor did he want to take over his father's businesses—he was a sake brewer, as well as the largest landholder in the village. So my father left home in his late teens, went to Germany, became an international trader, and settled in Bangkok where he did very well up until the war. So you see, someone else will have inherited the family businesses, and the last person they want to show up now is my father's son."

Susan seemed satisfied with this explanation, which relieved Michael. He didn't want to reveal that surely his father's family had learned in some way that Michael existed. His guess was that after he had been repatriated to Japan, the army had contacted them. But if the family had been informed, they would have been too ashamed to let the world, meaning their village, know that the original heir to the most important man in the village had been executed for treason, leaving behind a child who was only half-Japanese. But all Michael really knew was that no one had claimed him. As an adult, he could understand why, but, still, he had absolutely no intention of ever looking these people up.

As Michael and Susan started in on their *tonkatsu,* Michael asked Susan more about her plans. She said that the next day being Sunday, she had an interview with the man whose family had formerly been the headman of one of the villages for which there was a rich collection of documents. When she invited Michael to accompany her, he accepted very gladly.

On Sunday, they took a local train running on the one-track line to Fujito, a village a little south of Kurashiki. The train made its way through paddy fields, barren now in early spring, and, every few miles, it stopped at a small cluster of wooden houses built a century ago.

The city of Kurashiki, though small by comparison with Japan's metropolises, was modern and bustling, but Fujito made Michael feel as if he had gone back at least half a century into the past. They found that the house they were looking for was one of the few new buildings in the village, but built in a turn-of-the-century floor plan with a western-style parlor just inside the front entrance. Here, Michael and Susan were treated to green tea and traditional sweets. The current head of the family could tell them little about the past, but he presented Susan with a history of the village, one of the few copies still extant. Then he suggested that they visit the ruins of his family's old home, which was soon to be torn down. He cautioned them to be careful as the house was in disrepair.

The old house was enormous by village standards and much larger than the family's current residence. It clearly showed the family's position as head of the village and the major landowner in the area. The house was unlocked, and so the pair went in the main entrance and started to wander through, room by room, though they had to take care as some of the flooring had given way in places. Had his father grown up in such a house, Michael wondered. Very likely was his conclusion. Today, seeing at first hand the kind of house and village his father had come from, Michael found that he could now fully understand what had led his father to flee the life laid out for him. His father's father had not only chosen his bride, but had determined that his son attend the agricultural department of Kyoto University where he would learn the science related to sake brewing. Michael concluded that his father had left Japan because he found life in his bucolic village stifling and unbearable.

This visit also shed new light on what his life might have been like had he been brought back to a village like this as a nine-year-old. How would his relatives and the villagers have treated him? Like some kind of cast-off that had to be fed but no one had to be nice to? Even if he had been welcomed back into the fold, could he ever have adapted to such a suffocating society?

Suddenly, Michael was brought back to the present by a cry from Susan. A seemingly sound floorboard had given way under her and she was in danger of falling through the floor, which was raised a couple of feet above the ground. He grabbed her arm and steadied her as she managed to step back onto a firm board. Susan decided that she had seen enough, and Michael was only too glad to leave the remnants of a dead past.

As Susan still had much work left to do in Okayama Prefecture, Michael returned to Tokyo, and after collecting research materials, he went back to Cambridge, happy with

Susan's promise to meet him in Tokyo when he next came to Japan. They began corresponding on thin blue air letters that flew back and forth across the Pacific every week. Michael was ever more determined to see her again as soon as possible, even if it meant spending months in Japan.

Michael had found going back to Japan difficult initially. He had returned several times since he had left to go to Berkeley, once on a fellowship to do his dissertation research, and, later, for research or conferences. At first, he had found it hard to return to the country where he had lost his father and where his life had been so difficult, to put it mildly. He would spend all his waking hours working because it helped smother his memories.

In fact, Michael had begun to find each return to Japan easier emotionally because Japan was changing so rapidly. Since the Tokyo Olympics in 1964, now when he flew to Japan, he could speed from Haneda Airport into the center of Tokyo either by the monorail or the new, elevated highway. No longer was the bus trip from the airport a tedious crawl along the old two-lane Tokaido, lined by small shops. In fact, the very mood of the Japanese had changed with the Olympics, and he felt the people themselves had recovered their pride as well as their economy. It was a different country from the one from which he had emigrated at the age of nineteen.

Now he badly wanted to see Susan again. So without the trepidation he had felt on his first visits to Japan, he booked a room at International House in Roppongi, a sort of club for scholars and home to visiting professors from abroad. Then, at the beginning of June, he bade farewell to his Harvard colleagues and made the long trip from Boston to Tokyo. He quickly settled into his spartan I House bedroom and the even more spartan office he had borrowed at Tokyo University.

Then he called Susan. She was living with a Japanese family not far from Michael's office. He suggested they meet at the Akamon, Tokyo University's "Red Gate," and from there he would take her to a nearby *unagi* restaurant for grilled eel. This proved to be the first of many evenings they spent together, and almost immediately, the two began to spend Sundays exploring Tokyo together as well.

Being with Susan changed everything. Michael realized that, for the first time, he was actually enjoying life in Japan's capital. Once the two were away from the hierarchy of academia, Susan relaxed with Michael and seemed to enjoy being with him as much as he did with her. For the first time in some years, Michael found himself engaging in silly pranks. When riding commuter trains, they would shake up the sedate and drowsing Japanese by entering a car by separate doors and then arguing over a seat, something Japanese would never do, and particularly not with a foreigner. The people around them would give them shocked glances, until one of the pair, usually Susan, burst out laughing.

Susan claimed that one of the nuisances of living in Japan was that even after more than three years in Tokyo, people still didn't think she could speak Japanese. "Watch and I'll show you," she claimed. Michael soon found she was right. The next time the pair went to a restaurant, Michael pretended he couldn't speak Japanese and told Susan in English what he wanted to eat. To their amusement, the waitress looked at Michael while Susan ordered the meal for both of them, as if Michael was a ventriloquist. The pair could be silly and then at the next moment seriously discussing their research.

To Michael's great pleasure, this summer, he was at last able to renew his friendship with Yasusuke Murakami, who had lent him money when Michael was a freshman at

Tokyo University and too broke to eat. Michael had tried to contact him on two earlier research trips, but each time Tokyo University had informed him that Murakami was out of the country. This time, Michael reached him by phone immediately and invited him and his wife, Keiko, to dinner at the Imperial Hotel.

Michael was waiting near the entrance of the hotel when a bespectacled man of Michael's age walked in the front door with an attractive woman by his side. Michael recognized Murakami immediately from his lopsided smile. When the convivial dinner ended and coffee was served, Michael turned to the subject of his debt to Murakami. "I borrowed 2,000 yen from you in 1953 when I was cheated out of my wages and had no money to eat. I agreed to pay you back with interest, but then I left for America. How much do I owe you now?"

"I need a pencil and paper to give you the amount. But I suspect the total is about the same as what you are paying for a steak dinner for us at the best hotel in Tokyo, so let's call us even. I'm sure you ate student fare for many days on what I 'loaned' you all those years ago, but I have blown your repayment on dinner tonight. I am only glad things have worked out so well for you."

That evening was the start of a long friendship with Murakami, one that spanned the Pacific and resulted in each spending research stints in the other's university, plus organizing conferences together, and most pleasurably for both, long hours discussing their research.

But that summer in 1968, Michael spent nearly all of his waking hours either doing research or with Susan. In the conversations he had with her during the summer, he was beginning to tell her things he had never told anyone, including some of the shameful things he had done in

Sannomiya and Tokyo. He knew he was telling her every-thing because he had become very serious about her, and he wanted her to know everything about him. And one impor-tant thing he had to tell her was what he had done in the army.

So one evening, as Michael and Susan sat in a tiny restaurant eating bits of chicken on skewers, he told her he had been an officer in G2.

"What's G2?" Susan asked blankly.

"Military intelligence."

"You mean you were a spy? Like James Bond?" Susan, fascinated but unbelieving, asked him with a smile.

"No," Michael said shortly. "Only the enemy has spies. Americans have agents and G2 officers. I think you've been seeing too many movies."

"I knew you served in the army—you said that's how you were allowed to go to graduate school and then become a citizen. But," she added rather disbelievingly, "you were in intelligence? I hadn't realized that foreigners could serve in such a capacity."

"I had to go through a rigorous clearance, and that's why I became a citizen when I did. One of the strengths of American intelligence is that the government can call on people who speak so many of the world's languages like a native."

Susan seemed fascinated. "Wasn't it dangerous?"

Michael laughed. "People in military intelligence mainly write reports. Though I'll admit I came close to getting killed at least once. But I want you to know I've never killed anyone."

Susan looked downright shocked at the last statement. "I've never known anyone who would be in a position to have to tell me that he had nearly been killed or had never killed anyone!" She hesitated. "But you're out of the army. So what you did in the army is history, isn't it?"

Michael had to answer her question carefully. He wanted to reassure her but he didn't want to lie. "True, I am out of the army, but it's not quite accurate to say I have nothing to do with G2 anymore. I do get called occasionally—not often, mind you—to help G2 out. I'm still in the reserves on an unofficial basis. Don't worry, G2 considers me too old to do anything that might be dangerous."

Given Susan's concern, he was relieved he could never tell her about his trip to Southeast Asia at the end of the previous year. He hadn't realized before that G2's prohibition to discuss these projects without express permission could be useful. However, despite his reassurances, he learned decades later that for years, Susan had lived in fear of Michael disappearing on a "project," never to return, and she would never learn what happened to him.

From his conversations with Susan, Michael was becoming aware how little Americans who had never served in the military knew about it. Susan might know a lot about one of his cultures, the Japanese, but she knew virtually nothing about the part of American culture he was so familiar with and what had made him an American, not merely someone foreign-born who was living in the U.S. But except for Susan's lack of knowledge about the military, Michael discovered that he could talk about virtually anything with her. As they revealed their thoughts to each other, Michael became sure that he'd found the person with whom he wanted to share his life.

Susan was no Charlotte, but Michael had come to realize that he didn't want an elusive beauty to dominate his life, as Charlotte had Werther's. He wanted a companion, a warm human being, someone who loved him back. He knew he was still wary of marriage—yes, he could admit he was thinking of this. But he had lost so many people in his three decades of life, his father first of all, but also his amah, Mama Cheung, even Iguchi Sensei who got him admitted to Ashiya High. He wanted someone dependable, someone he could count on. Susan was all that and more. She was inquisitive, curious about so many things—he would sometime kid her about being "an information hound." She would just laugh—he liked her sense of humor as well.

And while she was very serious about her studies and wanted a career, she seemed adaptable and willing to consider various possibilities. Michael had been terribly unhappy when Alissa wouldn't consider anything other than pursuing a career in opera wherever it took her, but hadn't Michael been equally "selfish" in insisting on returning to graduate school in the U.S? He now realized that his love affair with Alissa was more "the passion of youth" rather than the enduring love of a lifetime.

As the weeks passed, Michael became very certain he wanted to marry Susan. But she planned to stay in Japan for another year, possibly two. He didn't want to lose her. Would their love last if they had to communicate across the Pacific via air letters? Each took at least five days to arrive, so if he asked a question, he wouldn't get an answer for ten days, if not two weeks. He felt panicky. Look what happened when he moved a continent away from Alissa. And he was about to turn thirty-four and Susan had just had her twenty-ninth birthday. He knew that not only did he not want to wait for another year or two to marry her, he felt it might prove fatal to their growing love to tempt it. He didn't want to wait now that at last he had found the woman with whom he wanted to share his life, his "anchor in humanity" as he thought of her.

He broached the subject of a future together in a round-about way, commenting as he walked Susan home one evening that he would really like to marry and possibly have a family. He could feel Susan turn to look at him, trying to read his expression by the light from a nearby street lamp. She said nothing. But what could she say to such a statement, he realized. So he bravely said, "Susan, I'm asking you to marry me."

As he had expected, Susan looked rather startled. After a lapse of several seconds, she said quietly, "Thank you for asking...but, please let me think about it...for a while."

Michael was very disappointed but not surprised because he knew Susan had planned a future of her own and he was rushing her—they had been seeing each other in Tokyo for less than two months. Moreover, their friendship had started out as one between a senior colleague and a junior one, at least on her part, Michael presumed.

For the next two days, Michael found himself rather despondent. Susan hadn't been able to meet him on the day after he had proposed, but he called her at her office at Keio on the afternoon of the day after that to suggest dinner. They met at a quiet, upscale Japanese restaurant near the American Embassy. At shortly after six, the restaurant was still quiet. Soon after they were seated, Susan looked at him and beamed: "I asked you to give me a while to answer the question you asked me two days ago...well, the 'while' has passed. And my answer is...Yes, yes, I would love to marry you. I'm sure I can manage some kind of career, but I can never find another man like you... an orphan, a 'hunter,' a spy, and a professor!"

Michael was overwhelmed by her answer. He was now determined to marry her as soon as possible. He didn't want to risk her changing her mind. He told her that he was already in his mid-thirties and Susan would turn thirty on her next birthday, they had missed out on a lot of years together, and his father had died at only a decade older than Michael was now, Susan's father, too! What they should do was to get married as quickly as practicable...besides, he didn't want her to live in a tiny, unheated Japanese apartment through a Tokyo winter, making a long commute in crowded trains.

"You've made your point! Michael. I'll think about it. But what if I'm not allowed to use my fellowship in California? And there's my dissertation!"

Michael said that he would get her permission to use the Buford Library, and there was a small room in his house overlooking the garden that would make a perfect study for her. And his salary was more than sufficient for the two of them to live on. He knew he was being very insistent. Susan gave him a long look and bit her upper lip. He didn't know what she was thinking, but at the end of the week, she said she could collect all the materials she needed by the end of the year and finish her dissertation in the U.S. He felt relieved, exhilarated, and slightly panicked at letting another person into his life. But at last he was to have what he thought of as his own family.

SUSAN HAD AGREED WITH MICHAEL that a simple wedding would be best. She looked into getting married in Tokyo, but she learned that the only way for two Americans to legally marry in Japan was to sign papers at the American Embassy. Even Michael, who had so disliked ceremony of any kind since childhood when his father had dressed him up and made him sit through long formal dinners, thought that such a momentous occasion should be more than signing a document.

So Susan sought the advice of her uncle who was a retired minister. He arranged for them to marry at a church in Kailua, a town across the Ko'olau Mountains from Honolulu. Four days before the wedding, Susan flew to Hawaii from Tokyo, Michael from San Francisco, and Susan's family from Minneapolis. The following day, they all drove to Kailua to see the church, meet the minister who was to marry Michael and Susan, and discuss the ceremony.

The first question the minister asked Michael and Susan was, "What religion are you?" Susan replied that she had grown up in the Congregational church, the same denomination as that of this minister.

Next he asked Michael the same question. "Southern Baptist," Michael announced. He saw Susan's mouth open, but she shut it again without saying anything. The minister seemed slightly surprised, but he wrote down Michael's answer.

Later when the couple was alone, Susan said, "Knowing your views on religion, I expected you to say that you were an atheist, or perhaps a Buddhist. Why did you say you were a Southern Baptist? And why pick that denomination? It's one of the most conservative and fundamental."

"Well, it seemed more appropriate when talking to a minister than telling him I'm an atheist. And I really was baptized—full immersion."

"What!" Susan was startled. And so Michael had to tell her about his week at a Bible camp while he was an undergraduate at Berkeley.

"All week we were pressured to be 'saved.' I thought I understood what it meant, an experience similar to the *satori* of Zen Buddhism, which you seek through meditation or pondering impossible riddles. But I didn't experience any epiphany...no voice from God. One by one, other people at the camp stood up and said they had 'found Jesus.' There was to be group baptism on the last day of camp. I had accepted free room and board for a week from these people, and I thought I owed them something. And I thought that maybe if I were baptized, I would at least have the physical sensation of what people experience when they are saved... maybe that could even trigger an epiphany. Of course, nothing happened—except that my head was pushed under the water before I expected it and I came up choking. But I was baptized—it's on record," Michael insisted.

Susan thought this hilarious. "Well, I promise not to tell the minister what *kind* of a Southern Baptist you are!"

When she had stopped laughing, Michael commented, "You know, I'm still surprised by how much religion seems to color so much of American life without Americans being aware of it."

"What do you mean?" asked Susan, clearly puzzled.

"Religion seems to be lurking behind art displays, in books and in conversation, even on money. It isn't that Americans are basically more religious than Thais or Japanese, but they seem to find it necessary to act as if they are. I'm not accusing them of being hypocrites, but, rather, that there is a cultural standard out there to which they have to conform or adhere to."

Susan responded thoughtfully, "I'm not sure if most people are pretending to be religious or are serious about following religious precepts. But I agree with you...it's odd that anyone running for public office has to announce that he is a Christian and attend church services at least occasionally."

The conversation ended when Michael said, "Well, you're going to have an American husband...because I think it's a good idea to have a church wedding."

THE COUPLE WAS MARRIED ON SUNDAY, DECEMBER 15, in a simple ceremony with Susan's mother and her brother, John, serving as witnesses. Susan's aunts and her friend, Ayako from Tokyo, attended as guests, along with a few acquaintances from Hawaii. The wedding dinner was held in the Maile Room of the Kahala Hilton, with its famous coconut cake for their wedding cake. When the couple retired to their room, they found a bottle of Dom Perignon, a gift from *Les Quatre Copains*.

"So your army buddies are with us in 'spirit' if not in body," smiled Susan. Michael agreed, more pleased than he wanted to admit.

The following day, the newlyweds flew to Kauai for a five-day honeymoon. When the couple checked into the sprawling two-story Sheraton Kauai, Michael was amazed. He felt as if he was back in the Siam of his childhood! His earliest memories were of his father's house on the outskirts of Bangkok. The rooms opened directly onto the garden and to covered walkways with polished wooden floors. Everywhere was the fragrance of tropical flowers.

He exclaimed to Susan, "This hotel really reminds me of my father's house in Bangkok! The flowers here are different—here in Kauai the flowers are bougainvillea and plumeria rather than frangipangi and night-blooming jasmine, but the effect of being surrounded by tropical flowers in an open architecture is just the same." Michael thought how wonderful it would be if someday he could once again live in a warm, tropical climate, preferably near the ocean, and surrounded by fragrant blossoms.

A week after the wedding and just two days before Christmas, the newlyweds boarded a jet bound for

Minneapolis from San Francisco to spend the holiday with Susan's family. Susan had agreed to Michael's wishes for a simple ceremony—almost an elopement, she said—but she insisted that Michael had to meet her family afterwards. So far, he had focused on Susan alone. He thought of her family as her widowed mother and her one sibling, her brother John, both of whom had attended the wedding. What was this "family" he was going to meet?

Christmas dinner proved to be a confused ordeal for Michael. Susan's mother had invited her father's brother and his wife, a half-aunt, a couple of her friends who were "almost family" as well as John's fiancée, who to Michael's astonishment arrived with her parents, her sister, and an aunt. The party was noisy with everyone talking at once and Michael couldn't keep people straight. He couldn't even go outside to sit quietly for a few minutes because there were two feet of snow on the ground and more coming down. Everyone was tactful and tried to welcome Michael and say nice things about Japan, but it was clear to him that the fiancée's aunt couldn't tell the difference between China and Japan.

Michael found this kind of gathering, where no one had anything in common except a blood or marital relationship, hard to endure. He wondered why Susan had been so insistent that they spend Christmas with her family, particularly since she didn't often talk about them, and it seemed to him that she had little in common even with her mother and brother. It took him a while to realize two things. First, in marrying Susan, he was joining her "tribe," as he called them, much to their amusement. And too, it dawned on him that Susan was trying to give him the family he had never had. It took time to make her understand that not ever having had a "tribe" of his own, he didn't miss one. He was rather relieved that he would be living half a continent away from his in-laws.

But now he knew why during the past summer Susan had teased him about his lack of knowledge or experience of family life, either Japanese or American. She had found it ironic when they were in Tokyo that she, an American from Minnesota, was sleeping on futon on *tatami* matting in a Japanese house, while Michael was sleeping on a bed with sheets and blankets and living in I House, essentially a Western-style hotel. The fact was that during his decade in Japan, he had never lived with a family. He had slept on a cot in an orphanage dormitory, on the floor of a black-marketeer's shack, on the beach at Ashiya, and then for four years in an oven. Only during his few months at Tokyo University had he slept the way most Japanese did, and even then the futon his landlady provided were so thin that Japanese referred to them as *sembei buton,* or "rice cracker quilts."

Michael had seen glimpses of family life only when he occasionally visited classmates' homes in Ashiya as a guest. Had he ever had a real family-style meal before this past summer? After he and Susan had become engaged, her mentor invited the couple to lunch at his home. Professor Hayami said that his wife wanted to know what they would like to eat. Since Michael was eating all his meals in restaurants or at the university cafeteria, Susan suggested a "simple, home-style family meal—treat us just like your family."

Mrs. Hayami complied with this request to the letter. After a delicious lunch of grilled fish, various vegetable dishes, and homemade pickles, Mrs. Hayami brought in a pot of tea and proceeded to pour some into each of their empty rice bowls. Michael couldn't remember having had a meal in Japan at which tea was drunk from a rice bowl and not a teacup, but Susan said this was how family dinners without guests ended.

Just as Michael was now puzzled by the family life Susan seemed to expect him to become involved in, so was Susan intrigued by Michael's background. She pestered him with questions he couldn't answer. She had never met anyone who not only had no relatives, but also not a single memento, not even a photograph of himself when he was young. Michael finally found a picture taken when he was twenty-eight, but that was only six years ago. The only thing he had from the past was the small, blue suitcase with broken locks that he had brought with him to the U.S. and which Miss Heath, a former teacher living at the Hotel Ivanhoe in Berkeley where he had worked, had kept for him while he was in the army. He couldn't travel with it anymore but found it useful for storing things so, somehow, he never threw it out. When Susan saw it, she was surprised by how small it was, and she was even more surprised when Michael told her that it hadn't even been full when he left Japan.

Michael had little interest in possessions, and found Susan's attachment to "things" puzzling and constraining. She had such a long family history on both sides, family homes filled with antiques handed down from great grandparents, and cupboards full of family photos dating back to daguerreotypes. Susan and her family felt these must be preserved as part of the family's history. The family also had numerous possessions of all kinds. Susan had grown up as the daughter of a war widow who had initially struggled to maintain her middle-class life style. She had learned as a small child that if a toy broke or if she lost a sweater, they would most likely not be replaced, or not anytime soon. When she became upset when a possession broke, Michael would remind her of the Buddhist saying, "Things with color fade, things with shape lose it, living things die." She was surprised that Michael placed so little value on "things" unless they were immediately useful. He explained why.

"At a number of times in my life, I lost everything I owned. I learned that what I really needed could be replaced or I could live without it. For me, possessions are a kind of shackle, or at the very least a nuisance—stuff you have to worry about taking care of, losing, or packing when you move." Susan and he may have shared the same ideas about politics and religion, but the difference in their attitude toward "things" was to remain unchanged throughout their married life.

Michael was amused at Susan's attempts to figure him out. Just as she hadn't been able to tell what his native language was when she first met him, she couldn't seem to grasp what his basic socio-economic and cultural reference was. After months of trying, she said, "I really think you act more like a rich man's kid, an *o-botchan*, than a boy who lived for years in an orphanage and was homeless in his teens. I've heard that the first decade of one's life are the formative years, the years that determine what you become as an adult. So your life in Bangkok when you didn't have to worry about anything seems to have been more important in determining your personality, than your years of deprivation in Japan. But whatever you are, you sure aren't middle-class, either Japanese or American!"

Though Michael lacked experience living with a family, he determined to be a good husband. Sometimes, he found it wasn't easy to live with another person when he had lived essentially alone since he was a boy with only himself to think of.

His first problem was that it was expected that a married couple would keep the same schedule as much as possible. Meals were no problem, but Susan required at least eight hours of sleep, and Michael slept far fewer hours, as he had since he was a teen. There was no way he could stay in bed for eight hours. But he managed to solve the problem quite simply. He would to go bed with her, and when he could tell by her breathing that she was asleep, he would slip out to his study and work on a project for a few hours. Then in the small hours of the morning, he went back to bed, and there he would be in the morning when Susan woke up.

Michael knew that Susan was aware that he got up in the night for a few hours, but she had no idea what he did. But almost two years into their marriage, his secret was found out. Susan was at home alone when a large package arrived from Harvard University Press marked "manuscript." She was brimming with curiosity when Michael finally arrived home and took out the contents.

"Galley proofs for a book manuscript? *Samurai Without Swords*? When did you write that book? I thought you were at work on articles on the contemporary economy!"

Michael admitted to her astonishment that he had written it at night while she was asleep. So began the years when Michael lived two academic lives in terms of his research. He taught statistics and economic theory and published theoretical articles, but, at the same time, he began to delve further and further into Japan's economic history, eventually publishing articles on the *shoen* (Japan's manors) and every period from the formation of Japan as a state in the seventh century to the present day. And after Susan completed her dissertation, they wrote a book together. Although it was published by Princeton University Press, they vowed for the sake of their marriage never to write another book together. Neither wanted to again go through the experience of fiercely arguing over every sentence.

MICHAEL FELT CONTENTED WITH HIS LIFE WITH SUSAN. They didn't agree on everything, but on important issues, they hardly ever disagreed. Like Michael, Susan was a liberal who almost always voted for the Democratic Party. She was an agnostic, while Michael said he was "an agnostic leaning toward atheism." And both would rather save than live to the limit of their income. That she was familiar with the culture of his youth and loved Japanese food made their life together go even more smoothly. In fact, he had to request that they sometimes have spaghetti instead of rice. But he thought he had finally gotten the hang of living with another person, and it certainly was convenient and comfortable, even if he sometimes had to do things he certainly wouldn't have on his own.

He discovered one benefit to marriage that he hadn't thought of: it was now possible for him to indulge in small luxuries that he could never have enjoyed on his own. The couple started visiting restaurants in San Francisco on week-ends, enjoying everything from seafood on Fisherman's Wharf to sumptuous meals in Chinatown. What with the home cooked meals they ate the rest of the week, Michael soon gained five pounds. He so enjoyed giving Susan treats that she hadn't been able to afford on her graduate stipend, that he started making grandiose plans for when she had finished her dissertation.

"I'll show you Paris, we'll dine at Maxim's, and we'll order you some *couturier* dresses," he offered magnani-mously. He was taken aback when Susan laughed.

"Me in French designer clothing? I only have to look at silk for a stain to appear. And since you don't dance and hate formal occasions, where would I wear it? But I would love to visit Paris with you and eat at Maman's. I want to see *your* Paris!" She gave him a big hug.

"Ah, we do have the same tastes," he thought, rather relieved at her suggestion when he thought more about it.

Michael knew Susan worried about his G2 activities after he told her that he had continued to take on projects even after his discharge from the army. Then for several years after they married, Michael heard nothing from G2. Susan kidded Michael about how boring his life had become after he married her. But after surviving all the "excitement" of getting shot at and falling on his velo into the cellar in Paris, plus all of the G2 "projects" he couldn't talk about even with Susan, he told her he was only too content to live the "boring" life of a university professor with "a wife as dependable as the sunrise on a clear day."

Chapter 12

Tokyo, 1973

IN AUGUST 1973 WHEN MICHAEL WAS PUZZLING over how long it had been since he had heard from Gen. Lund, as if by telepathy, he received a message that he suspected originated with the general.

He and Susan were in Tokyo for the summer doing research. They were staying in Roppongi at the International House for foreign and Japanese scholars. It was affordable even after the value of the yen had shot up almost 20 percent with the ending of the fixed exchange rate regime in 1971, and its amenities included a large library and a beautiful garden off an elegant restaurant. The couple now had less than two weeks left in Japan, and both were spending long hours trying to finish up their research projects.

Returning to I House from a day at Tokyo University, Michael was greeted by the assistant manager who handed him his room key.

"Professor Koyama, this phone message came in for you an hour ago."

Michael looked at the slip of paper. He was asked to call an extension at the American Embassy as soon as possible. He realized that G2 must have caught up with him again. He wasn't surprised because he was still reporting his whereabouts to the general's office whenever he traveled abroad. But he wondered what was up now.

Michael fished in his pocket for coins and went to use one of the public phones located just off the lobby. He didn't want the possibility of an I House operator overhearing this conversation.

His call was answered on the first ring. The man on the other end of the line asked, "If possible, can you come to the embassy tonight to take a secure call at nine?"

Michael agreed and hung up, and as he turned toward the entrance, he saw Susan come in. She waved at him and waited for him to catch up with her, then asked, "Why were you using a public phone instead of the one in our room?"

Michael told her about the message and the request that he be at the embassy by nine to take a call. "I really don't know what it's about, but I suspect it's from G2 and I wanted to avoid any risk of the operator hearing anything. Sorry, this means we have to grab a bite here instead of going out for noodles as we'd planned."

Susan asked, her face clouding, "G2? Why would they be calling you here in Tokyo?" But Michael couldn't answer her question.

MICHAEL ARRIVED AT THE AMERICAN EMBASSY AT 8:45 and was escorted by the military attaché, Major John Thomas, to a "bubble room"—one that was "bug-proof." When the call came through, Michael wasn't surprised to hear General Lund's voice.

"Michael...thank you for giving up your evening for me, and congratulations. I hear that you received early promotion to become a full professor." Before Michael could respond, the general said, "I apologize for bringing you out on such short notice, but I have a rather unusual favor to ask of you. This is not the kind of request I've made in the past. See what you think of it. This is about loaning you to one of my good friends."

"*Loaning* me?"

"Yes. Let me explain. Several years before I first met you, I spent ten months at the War College in Carlisle, Pennsylvania. There I met Randall Tobin. He was one of a half dozen civilians who were selected to attend the college that year. Randall is now Under Secretary for International Affairs at Treasury."

Michael knew of Randall Tobin. He was an economist who had once taught at Princeton, and Michael had read his work. The general went on:

"Well, I ran into Randall again this week and he mentioned he has a major problem. We are now seeing a steady increase in our trade deficit with the Japanese, and a good chunk of this is because we buy, Randall tells me, several hundred million dollars more of Japanese machine tools than we sell to them. But as an economist with an interest in Japan, I'm sure you know this."

"Yes, Sir, I do."

"Well, Randall and his people in the Bureau of Economic, Business and Agricultural Affairs, along with relevant people from Commerce, the International Trade Commission and the FTC—the Federal Trade Commission—they've organized a task force to look into the complaint made by our companies that make machine tools. Most of these complaints involve dumping—selling products at below the cost of production—in order to gobble up the American market and force American companies into bankruptcy. I understand several have already gone under."

"Yes, Sir. I know about it." Michael was amused at getting a lecture by the general on the major trade issue between the U.S. and Japan, one he knew well. But he listened politely, waiting for the general to come to the point.

"The task force has very good people, but no one on it is knowledgeable about how Japanese companies do business. Of course, I immediately thought of you...so I told Randall about you. He said he knows your work on the Japanese economy well, and asked me if I would contact you immediately. I know you're busy and won't be in Japan much longer, but could you hear him out?"

Michael was definitely interested. The Japanese economy had grown because of the rapid growth of its exports, so all aspects of international trade interested him. And how could he say no to General Lund? He responded, "I'll be happy to talk to him, Sir."

As Michael waited for a call from Randall Tobin to be put through, he realized he was most likely getting involved in a case that was an inevitable outcome of the Japanese policy to increase exports to the U.S., even by resorting to dumping.

He had not long to wait. After the briefest of pleasantries, Dr. Tobin explained the problem in a tone that was cordial but almost beseeching.

"Professor Koyama, the complaints we have concern the machine tool industry. Many of Japan's product lines sell at 30 percent below the American price. Our problem is primarily with the two major companies in that industry: Tokyo Machines and Osaka Machines. I know you know that they were created in 1947 by the American Occupation when it forced the prewar Japan Machines Corporation to divide into two. Given this history, we strongly suspect these two companies are colluding, but we don't have the evidence. The data that Tokyo Machines have sent us—that's the major exporter—indicate that the company is not dumping, it's just more efficient than American firms."

"Dr. Tobin, I take it that you suspect these numbers are 'cooked,' that is, inaccurate. Is that correct?"

"That's right. Since the domestic and the export prices are essentially the same, Tokyo Machines argues that no dumping is involved. But we know that the prices of many other products they produce and sell in Japan, but which are not exported, are much higher. I'm sure they would argue that these are very different products from what they sell to us. If we impose a countervailing tariff...a punitive tariff...on their exports, they are sure to challenge it in court...this means we would have to fight a case that I know would drag on for years, costing us millions of taxpayer dollars. And we can never be 100 percent sure we will win such a case because Tokyo Machines can afford to hire top American anti-trust lawyers."

"So, you want me to find out how reliable the data are that they sent you? That is, are they dumping their products in the U.S in clever ways that we can't pin down using the data they've sent us?"

"You've summarized it very nicely. Would you be willing to look into it? This is a confidential investigation—we really don't want the Japanese to even suspect we may be investigating. We don't want MITI and the companies involved to cover their tracks. But if you look into this as a scholar interested in general trade issues, no one in Japan should get riled up."

Michael was intrigued and agreed to make a preliminary investigation. He was told that copies of the documents pertaining to this case would be sent by special courier to the military attaché at the Tokyo Embassy, courtesy of General Lund. When Michael told Major Thomas to expect a packet for him in two days, the major said that he would leave a message at I House when the documents arrived.

Michael arrived back at I House just before 10:30. Susan was waiting anxiously to learn what was up. Michael told her, "I was asked by a friend of Gen. Lund in the Treasury to do some investigating on a dumping case. This is not for G2, so it's nothing dangerous, I assure you. But the Treasury wants to keep the investigation very confidential so you mustn't let anyone know what I'm doing. Okay?"

LATE FRIDAY MORNING, MICHAEL CALLED I HOUSE from the Tokyo University Library to find out if he had any messages and was informed that "Professor Thomas' secretary" had called to say the manuscript was ready for him to read. Michael immediately left for the embassy where he collected a thick packet of papers. He returned to I House, had a quick lunch in the coffee shop, and got to work.

Michael spent the next few hours going over the data he had been sent. He quickly learned that the machine tool industry produced more varieties of lathes than he had thought possible, plus milling, grinding, metal forming, boring, drilling, and other types of machines. Even among the same kind of machines, the quality and function, thus prices, differed widely. It was so very complex that he wondered what he could possibly find of value to Tobin in the little time he had left in Japan.

He suddenly realized it was getting late. He managed to make an appointment with the Japan Fair Trade Commission for Monday morning, but he found it too late to set up an appointment with anyone else until Monday. But the JFTC would be a good start. He knew he would have to ask his questions very carefully, but if anyone could help him get started in his investigation, it would be the JFTC.

After an enjoyable weekend with Susan and their friends, Michael set off on Monday morning for Kasumigaseki. Finding the JFTC's five-story building, hidden among the taller and more impressive buildings of the major ministries, was not easy. To Michael, the Commission's dingy-looking building bespoke what the Japanese government thought of the anti-trust law bequeathed to them by the occupying Americans.

Precisely at ten, Michael arrived at the office of the section chief of the Sixth Investigating Section of the Japan Fair Trade Commission, which was in charge of the machine tool industry. He was here ostensibly as an American economics professor wishing to study the role of the JFTC in promoting competition in Japanese markets.

A young woman wearing a clerical smock led Michael to a chair next to the only empty desk in the room. Facing it were a cluster of desks at which six men of various ages bent over their work. The woman informed him that the section chief would be back shortly and gave him a cup of green tea. The small room was quiet except for the whispers between two young men. Michael could smell the lingering odor of cigarette smoke although no one was smoking.

Within a few minutes, a shrewd-looking man in his early forties—every inch a Japanese bureaucrat—walked in wearing a dark suit, a subdued necktie, and a grimace that he didn't succeed in transforming into a smile.

"Sorry for the delay. Meetings. Always more meetings. You must be Prof. Koyama of Buford University. My secretary said you told her we can talk in Japanese." He switched to Japanese as they exchanged business cards. The card Michael received informed him that Yukio Fujita was Chief of the Sixth Investigating Section.

Michael, after apologizing for asking for an appointment with so little notice, began to ask the questions he had carefully prepared. He asked about Tokyo Machines only as an example of a company that was now seen by the U.S. as an important contributor to the increasing trade deficit it had with Japan.

Fujita answered Michael's questions easily. To Michael, all his answers sounded as if he was repeating well-rehearsed statements that Michael would have expected to hear had Fujita been appearing as a defense witness for Tokyo Machines in an American court.

"Tokyo Machines' costs are low because of its productive efficiency, so the company is clearly not dumping in the U.S. market." "Some machines sold in Japan are priced higher than many types of machines sold in the U.S. because they are functionally and qualitatively different from those sold in the American market."

And to Michael's last question regarding the data that he had heard had been submitted to the U.S. authorities by Tokyo Machines, Fujita answered.

"Yes, I know about the data. I've absolutely no doubt they are accurate. The American machine producers and the government are questioning the data because they are unwilling to face the fact that these American companies are not competitive with Japanese producers. What's happening is that the Americans are losing an economic war...sorry, Professor...and what has been happening in the trade balance of machines is the most recent evidence of how the war is going these days."

Fujita kept peeking at his watch, and as soon as he answered Michael's last question, he stood up and dashed off "to another meeting" without even ushering Michael out of the office. Michael followed him more slowly, nodding to two men who looked up as he made for the door.

Although Michael had expected Fujita to be somewhat defensive, he was quite taken aback by Fujita's answers, which all sounded like those an executive of Tokyo Machines could be expected to make. Michael knew that he had to get to a phone and try again to make appointments to see someone in both of the machine tool companies and also MITI. As he left the JFTC building, he wondered if he was really going to be able to help Randall Tobin, or would everyone at both companies and MITI stonewall or even counter-attack as had Fujita.

Michael had gone only a few hundred meters before it began to sprinkle. As he grappled with his umbrella, he heard someone softly calling him from behind in English:

"Prof. Koyama. Don't look back. Please put up your umbrella and keep walking. I'm one of the men from Fujita's office....I've something very important to tell you about Tokyo Machines. I'm going to pass you by. Please, follow me."

In his peripheral vision, Michael saw a young man on his right. Surprised by the young man, Michael asked in a low voice:

"Where are we going?"

The young man said as he passed Michael:

"I'm going down that subway entrance on the corner. Please follow me, buy a ticket to Ginza, get on the same car I do, but don't talk to me. And please get off when I do."

Michael was a bit leery, but he had to hear that "something very important" about Tokyo Machines. It didn't matter if he tried to make his appointments a little later.

The young man got off at the first station, and began walking at a rapid pace down a long underground passageway to one of the exits. Michael followed, climbing the stairs onto the street behind him. Without looking back, the young man made a sharp left. Michael was some fifty feet behind him but managed to follow him as he went another block and abruptly turned right into a narrow street where he entered a small coffee shop. Michael went in after him. It was 11:30, and the shop was empty. The young man went to the far end of the shop and sat down at the last table, facing the back wall.

Michael sat down opposite him: "Why this cloak and dagger stuff?"

"Professor Koyama, my apologies, but I can't take the chance of anyone seeing me talk to you."

"Why not?" Michael was puzzled.

"I'll explain, but first let me introduce myself. I am Tadashi Imai...my friends in Ann Arbor called me Tad."

"Your friends in Ann Arbor? Did you go to the University of Michigan?

"Yes. I received a competitive government grant to get an M.A. in economics from Michigan, and I returned just two years ago. By the way, I read your book on the industrialization of Japan, the U.S., and Germany. It's an excellent study."

"Thanks, Tad. And, please, call me Michael. So you came back and got a job at the JFTC?"

"No, I was already with the JFTC. I went to Michigan for two years on leave from my job. I always wanted to work with the JFTC to clean up a lot of things going on in our economy that I didn't like...practices that should be changed."

"Okay, let's get back to the cloak and dagger stuff. Why are we talking at the back of this small coffee shop?"

"It's going to take a little time to tell you. I've got to get back to the office by one, so let's get a sandwich and then talk."

After giving their orders to the waitress, Tad began his tale, and what Michael heard was nothing short of astonishing.

For some time, Tad had wanted his section to initiate a formal investigation into what he believed was the price fixing of more than a dozen product lines by Tokyo Machines working in collusion with Osaka Machines. And then, six months ago, Tad had learned that Tokyo Machines was submitting a large amount of data to the American Department of Commerce and the Federal Trade Commission with regard to possible charges of dumping.

Tad had no doubt that the two companies had agreed that Osaka Machines would "specialize" in the domestic market and Tokyo in the American market. The large profits made in the domestic market by Osaka Machines, which could fix its prices, would "subsidize" whatever loss Tokyo Machines might incur by dumping in the American market. Tad explained:

"Michael, their strategy is simple. Tokyo Machines is dumping their products in the U.S. in order to increase their sales volume. The increased sales will soon justify their building a new, large factory, which will reduce their production costs. At this point, Tokyo Machines will stop dumping because its production costs will have been lowered. It will be able to outsell its American competitors and still make a profit. At present, Osaka Machines is covering the loss Tokyo Machines incurs while dumping, but when Tokyo Machines begins to make a profit after increasing its capacity, Osaka Machines will more than get back what they contributed. For example, Osaka Machines owns a lot of shares in Tokyo Machines and these will rise in price."

This explanation didn't completely satisfy Michael. He said, "I think you must be right. But your analysis doesn't completely explain why the unit costs of the products that Tokyo Machines sells in the American market are so low... at least so it appears from the data the company submitted to the American government. It's hard to believe that Osaka

Machines is fully 'subsidizing' Tokyo Machines out of the profits they make by fixing prices in the domestic market."

Tad confirmed what Michael had suspected.

"You're right, of course. The exports of Tokyo Machines to the U.S are too large for that. So they have to 'cook the books.' The numbers Tokyo Machines gave the U.S are junk. The company has valued the cost of land they use at the book value in 1921, not at the current, much higher, value. This is allowed under Japanese accounting rules and significantly lowers the so-called 'fixed costs.' Moreover, their subcontractors—three layers of them, about 320 sub-contractors in all—are asked to submit phony invoices for payment that are far below what they are getting paid. And all the wage data are based on normal working hours of 40 to 45 hours per week, when in fact the employees of Tokyo Machines, like those in many large Japanese companies, do a lot of overtime, often working up to 60 hours per week if not more. For these reasons, the data submitted to the U.S. greatly understate the real production costs of the machines."

"If you know all this...I assume you've told all this to your section chief. Why hasn't Mr. Fujita done something about it? "

"If you graduate from Tokyo University, like Mr. Fujita and I have, you can expect to become a bureau chief...if lucky, even the chairman of the commission...*if* you don't make waves. Or, as you say in the U.S., if we keep our noses clean and are quiet...do as we are told. The politicians of the Liberal Democratic Party, who as you know have been in power now for almost two decades...they have ways of pressuring the chairman of the commission, and he, in turn, everyone below him. Mr. Fujita is ambitious, and he knows that the highest officers of Tokyo Machines and Osaka Machines are some of the biggest supporters...with wads of

10,000 yen notes.... of the current prime minister and many LDP Diet members...do I have to go on?"

"No. I get the picture. Are you saying you don't mind ruining the chance of becoming a bureau chief by whistle blowing?"

Tad answered with a determined look on his face.

"Michael, we live only once. If I don't do my job as I should and let the price fixing and dumping go on, how proud can I be even if I become the chairman of the commission? Yes, I know. I might end up paying the price...and retire at fifty-five as a section chief. But I've decided that I will pay it if necessary."

Ted paused and looked back toward the front of the shop to make sure no one could hear him. Seeing no one close by, he went on in an even quieter voice.

"I have what are essentially the real numbers, the numbers that should have been sent to the U.S. I calculated the real unit costs of the products being exported to the U.S. using the current price of land, 'real' invoice values I obtained from the sub-contractors, and my estimates of total wage costs."

"Tad, I am impressed. You said you 'have' these data. Where do you keep them? From what I saw, you certainly couldn't hide them in your desk at work."

"No, certainly not. I don't even keep them in my apartment. They're like holding dynamite. I was hoping to eventually meet someone like you so I could hand them over."

"Why couldn't you give them to a newspaper?"

"If I did, they would most likely be suppressed by an editor or someone higher up. Unlike in the U.S., news sources are not always kept secret here. So I would like to give you these data. However, I'm not sure you really want to have them. It could be dangerous."

"Surely not. Why do you think so?"

"If anyone ever finds out you are in possession of my figures, you can't rule out the possibility that someone will come after you to get them. And if this happens, they won't hesitate to clobber you in some dark alley. You could suffer more than a few cuts and bruises."

"But this is Tokyo and not Saigon, or even New York."

"Michael, you don't understand. What I have could get you killed. I'm not exaggerating. Large companies like Tokyo Machines and Osaka Machines take these things very seriously."

"Tad, I can't believe these big, well-known companies are going to send someone after you or me...to get me hurt or even killed...just to obtain your data. The president of Tokyo Machines says to his underling, 'Go and maim the JFTC guy or knock off that American professor'?"

"That isn't how it happens. The president of Tokyo Machines knows nothing about this sort of thing. But he knows everything."

"You've lost me, Tad. You're talking like a Zen monk!"

"What I'm saying is that the president doesn't say anything directly, but makes it clear that he doesn't like something. He goes to someone below him—often the section chief of the general affairs section, which is in charge of all the odds and ends that must be taken care of. The section chief 'reads' between the lines as it were what the president wants done. The section chief 'intimates'—is that the right English word?—to a *sokaiya* that his company would be grateful if such and such person was 'punished'— either gently or severely. Then the *sokaiya* goes out and does the punishing. If this comes to the public's attention, the president expresses his extreme regret for what happened. He swears publicly that, had he known anything about such a thing, it would never have happened."

"Wait. The *sokaiya*...I thought these were the guys who show up at the annual shareholder meetings to make sure no stockholder objects to the slate of executives who are being proposed by the management. That's the reason why, I've read, the annual shareholder meetings end in ten minutes or even less for 99 percent of the largest companies in Japan. Do they 'punish' people on the side?"

"The *sokiaya* get paid by the general affairs section of big companies. Sometimes in cash. But that's rare. Usually, the *sokaiya* sell subscriptions at an exorbitant price for the so-called business magazines they publish a few times a year, or else they ask for large donations to 'charities' or a miniscule 'political party' they have created."

"Okay, so they 'punish' people to express their gratitude for the money?" Michael was not convinced.

"In a way. See, the majority of the *sokaiya* are themselves yakuza or connected to yakuza groups...."

"I've read that, but I thought it was gossip."

"No, it certainly isn't. Two years ago, a Ministry of Construction officer investigated a huge contract given to a large construction company to build a dam in northern Japan. He was sure too much gravel was being mixed into the cement. But before he could make his report, he died by falling into the dam. The local police said he was drunk and stumbled into the dam. His wife said he was a teetotaler, but nobody paid any attention to her."

"Surely, you don't think he was murdered by yakuza, do you?"

"You don't think so? Last year, one guy in the third investigation section of the JFTC was looking into label switching by a big meat wholesaler...one of the biggest in Japan. The wholesaler was passing lower-grade American and Australian beef off as high-grade domestic beef. The guy investigating was a high school graduate but a very able and upright guy. Soon after he had started his investigation, his seventeen-year-old daughter was beaten up by a couple of guys...she now has ugly scars. One of the guys told her that, unless her father stopped meddling in how imported beef is labeled, the next time, he was going to 'enjoy' her instead of just bruising her. The father quit his job, and I hear is now driving a taxi."

"All right, Tad. I got the message. But I would still like to have the data. And I promise to be very careful until I leave Tokyo."

"Fine. I'll give them to you. But I have to tell how you can get it, and explain how I calculated the figures, and how they are to be interpreted." He glanced at his watch. "I have to get back to the office. Can you come to my apartment at eight this evening?"

Michael nodded yes. Tad quickly wrote out his address, and as he drew a crude map, he said to Michael, "I'm not far from Yotsuya Station on the Chuo Line. Give this map to your cab driver and keep your eye out for a three-story building that has a big sign that falsely advertises the run-down apartments as 'Yotsuya Mansion.'"

Michael said he would pay for the lunches and, thanking him, Tad dashed out of the coffee shop. Michael looked at his watch and wondered how he should spend the afternoon. He decided not to try to make any appointments until he had talked to Tad again. It was unlikely that he would have much time for his own research in the week he had before he left Japan, so Michael decided to go to his office at Tokyo University and pack up his books to send back to the U.S.

When he left the university, Michael got caught in rush hour traffic and was late in returning to I House. He suggested to Susan that they have a quick supper in the coffee shop as he had an appointment that evening. As they ate their curries, he told Susan about his appointment with Tad. She immediately asked:

"May I come with you? I want as many first-hand observations as possible for my last chapter in my study of historical changes in Japanese housing. It's hard for me to get to see the inside of Japanese apartments."

Michael thought about her request. He remembered Tad's warning. But Tad had said the data weren't in his apartment. So how dangerous could it be for her to go with him to Tad's apartment? And if Michael took Susan, their visit would appear purely social. This could be very useful on the off chance Tad was being watched. So after a long minute, he agreed.

Despite Tad's map, their taxi driver had trouble finding Tad's address and they arrived a few minutes past eight. Tad was right: the building was definitely shabby and old-fashioned with its outside corridors and staircases. Michael and Susan climbed to the second floor where they were surprised to hear someone yelling in crude Japanese.

Then Michael heard Tad say, "I tell you, I don't have anything from work here. I don't know what you are talking about." His voice was high-pitched and sounded panicky.

Michael put a finger on his lips and gently shoved Susan back toward the staircase. The pair climbed up to the third floor and quietly conferred, just out of sight of the staircase. Michael told her that had been Tad's voice.

Susan, who had not been told by Michael about Ted's warning how dangerous anything to do with Tokyo Machines could be, was all for finding out what was going on. Thinking of possible yakuza involvement, Michael argued that he shouldn't be seen because he might be recognized by whoever was in Tad's apartment and his investigation was confidential. Susan countered that she could casually walk by the apartment as if on the way to visit someone. No one would worry about the presence of a foreigner who wouldn't be expected to know Japanese. She would listen and try to find out what was going on.

Before Michael could object, Susan dashed out of his reach and descended to the second floor. *What a spunky wife I have*, thought Michael, though at the same time very worried.

But before Susan had gone more than halfway down to the second floor, Michael heard heavy footsteps walking down the corridor to the staircase. So had Susan. She turned around and ran backed up to where Michael was hidden. Both heard a gruff voice command, "Move! Down the stairs" and sounds of the heavy, uneven steps of someone being shoved down the stairs.

"I'm going. Stop pushing!" yelled Tad, as if he wanted to sound an alarm.

Susan and Michael remained frozen until it was clear that the men—Michael was sure there were two besides Tad—had reached the ground level and were walking away from the building. Michael said, "We'd better check Tad's apartment."

When the couple reached the door of #242, it was closed, but Michael could see through a window that the lights were still on. He touched the knob, then turned it slightly. The latch gave. So the men who had "abducted" Tad hadn't given him time to lock his door.

Michael was not sure what he should do. Should he enter or just leave? What would he do in Tad's apartment if he went in? Maybe he had better check; this could be a case for the police. While he hesitated, Susan pushed the door open and stepped into the entryway.

As soon as Susan was inside, she stopped and took a step back. Michael looked over her shoulder. From the entry, both rooms of the small apartment were visible. The place was a mess. It was clear that a search had been made, and from the looks of it, a rather hasty one. In the front room, books had been pulled off the shelves of the small bookcase, cushions had been ripped open, and a cup of tea had been knocked over onto the *tatami* matting. In the back room, everything had been pulled out of the cupboards. Michael thought it was certainly wise of Tad to have kept the data elsewhere.

Michael was very worried about Tad. He no longer doubted what Tad had told him at lunch. Michael suspected that someone at the JFTC had already known that Tad was surreptitiously collecting data on Tokyo Machines and today, when Tad hurriedly left the office immediately after Michael, that person had reported it to someone at the company. But since it was unlikely that the gangsters had found any evidence on Tad, they would probably just rough him up. Michael decided that if Tad didn't contact him by morning, he would go to the police.

Susan was clearly upset by the condition of the apartment. She asked Michael to stack books that were strewn about while she mopped up the spilled tea and otherwise tried as best she could to tidy up the rooms. When order had been more or less restored, Michael turned off the lights and they left the apartment. They found a taxi near Yotsuya Station and were back at I House in twenty minutes.

"What's going on?" Susan demanded of Michael as soon as they were in their room with the door closed. "I'm of course correct in assuming that what happened to your new friend, Tad, is connected to your investigation for Randall Tobin. Right?"

"Yes. But I'm almost as surprised as you are about what happened."

"Why 'almost'?" asked Susan, picking up on the qualifier.

"Well, when I met Tad Imai today, he warned me that these big Japanese companies could play rough. Not anyone in the company, mind you, but they are connected to *sokaiya*, and he says the *sokaiya* have yakuza connections. I didn't believe him at the time. Now I do. I'm worried that he might be in big trouble. I'll try calling him in the morning, and if he doesn't answer, I'm contacting the police."

"Why don't we call the police now?" Susan was visibly upset.

"No point, Susan. We don't know where they took Tad... so what can the police do at this point? I don't think these guys will do serious harm to Ted. After all, he is a government official. Since they don't have any evidence, the worst they'd do to him would be to beat him up in such a way as not to leave visible bruises."

"The worst is his getting beaten up? Had you gone to see Tad on time, you too could have been beaten up! You told me," Susan said accusingly, "that you were just going to just do a bit of research for Tobin and it wouldn't be dangerous at all!"

Michael slept fitfully that night and woke up before six. He thought about calling Tad, but hesitated because it was still early and, more importantly, there was a possibility Tad's phone was tapped. While he was dithering, the phone rang, waking Susan. Michael picked up the receiver on the first ring.

"Michael?" Michael was very relieved to hear Tad's voice, but before he could say more than "yes," Tad hurriedly went on, "I didn't dare call before this. It's a good thing you didn't arrive at my apartment at eight. Was it you who mopped up the tea and picked up and turned the lights out?"

"Yes. We were late—we nearly ran into you and the two guys who took you away."

"We? Who were you with?" Tad asked anxiously.

"I came with my wife, Susan. I thought that if she was with me, it would just look like we were making a social visit."

"Well, it's a good thing you were late. I don't know what they would have done if they had seen us together."

"Are you all right? Who were those guys? Where did they take you?"

"I'm fine but I can't answer your questions now. I'm using a public phone near Yotsuya Station. But I have to ask you about a couple of things that are important. First, can you find a reason to go to Hitotsubashi University tomorrow? You know it, don't you? Out in Kunitachi?"

"I know it well. And I think I know why you want me to go there. I'll make an appointment with a professor I know."

Tad hurriedly went on: "Excellent. Second question, did you tell my section chief yesterday where you're staying? What does he know about you beyond what's on your business card?" Tad sounded very concerned.

"He doesn't know where I'm staying. Let me think. I may have told him I was doing research at Tokyo University while I'm here."

"So he knows your full name and he probably knows you're doing research at Tokyo University. Since he has a pretty good network—contacts all over—I think he can easily find you. Can you move to a different lodging and use a different name?" Tad's voice took on a very insistent tone. "Please take me seriously. If you saw what those thugs did to me last night and had heard all the questions they asked about you, you'd know I'm not being paranoid." Tad now sounded rushed. "Look, I'll get in touch with you again. This evening? Can you tell me how I can reach you? Some trusted friend who will know where you are?"

Michael took Major Thomas' card out of his wallet and gave Tad the number at the American Embassy. "Ask for Mr. Thomas. Identify yourself by saying you are Tad, a friend of mine when I was at the University of Michigan. Okay?"

Tad said, "Got it," and abruptly hung up.

Michael looked over at Susan who had been listening with concern on her face. Michael summarized what Tad had said so she could understand what the conversation was about.

Michael was very silent at breakfast because he was trying to think what to do. In the end, he decided that he had better take Tad's advice and move. On his own, he might have chanced it, but he didn't want to risk Susan's safety. So as soon as they finished breakfast, Susan, who readily agreed with his decision, went upstairs to pack while he made some phone calls.

Michael went to the public phones and called Major Thomas. When he finished explaining his need to move to a new "safe" lodging as quickly as possible, and asked for his suggestions and possibly his assistance, the major quickly responded:

"No problem, Professor Koyama. We'll put you up in one of the secure rooms we hold for special visitors at the Hotel Okura. It's convenient as it's right across from the embassy. What name do you want to be under?"

Michael was going to give Susan's last name, but then thought better of it. "Just a minute," he said and racked his brains. It took only seconds before he came with Yamamura, the name of the actor who had played Admiral Yamamoto in the movie "Tora! Tora! Tora!" which he had seen only recently.

"How about Yamamura? Yamamoto is fine, too."

The major replied, "I prefer Yamamura over the name of a World War II admiral. I'll make the necessary arrangements with the hotel, and send a Japanese car to pick you up. Just give me a time. The driver's name is Koji Morita, a guy we use in situations like this...he used to be a cop."

At ten, Michael and Susan apologetically checked out of I House, saying only that their plans had changed and they had to return home sooner than expected.

Morita was waiting for them in a black Toyota Corolla. After telling Michael that he hadn't seen anyone suspicious near I House, either on foot or in a car, he drove the couple to a back entrance of the Okura where they were checked in as Mr. and Mrs. Yamamura.

Michael had once stayed at this hotel, but only in a rather small though lavishly furnished room. Now he found himself in a suite—Major Thomas said he had booked one so the couple wouldn't feel too much like they were under house arrest.

Michael had been assured by the major that it would be safe to make calls from their suite. He first phoned Hitotsubashi and made an appointment to meet Prof. Nohara in his office at eleven the next day, Wednesday. Then the couple discussed what to do next. Michael didn't want Susan wandering around Tokyo, and she reluctantly agreed. "I would have liked to visit some bookstores again, but *c'est la vie*."

And since she wasn't to go outside the hotel, Susan also agreed to leave Japan sooner than planned. She said with a wry smile, "To cancel the meetings I've scheduled for the rest of this week, I'm going to tell people this hot and humid weather has gotten to me and I'm not feeling well...instead of that the yakuza are after my husband."

Tad called a little before seven that evening as Michael and Susan were finishing a room service dinner. "I'm calling from a pay phone but inside a lobby, so I can talk. Did you do what I asked you to?"

"Yes. I did. We moved to the Hotel Okura. I'm registered under Yamamura. And I have an appointment at Hitotsubashi at eleven tomorrow with Professor Nohara in Economics. Now please tell me what happened last night."

"Those thugs came to my apartment just after 7:30. I thought you might be early, so I opened the door when I heard the knock without looking to see who it was. They burst in and shoved me in a corner. One guy with a knife watched me while the other guy ransacked my apartment. When they didn't find what they were looking for, the older of the guys told me they had more questions but they weren't going to ask them in my apartment. I think he didn't want my neighbors or someone else coming by because of the rumpus they were causing. I admit I was petrified. They took me by car to the sports ground of the women's college not far from my apartment."

"What kind of questions did they ask you?"

"The older guy said he knows I chased after you when you left the JFTC....that you were nosing around about Tokyo Machines under the guise of doing research on U.S.-Japan trade issues. He wanted to know why I chased after you...did I know you before...exactly what did we discuss and where am I hiding whatever information it is I've been collecting on Tokyo Machines. He knew a lot to ask such questions."

"Wait, Tad...how could he know so much...that I talked about Tokyo Machines with your section chief and that you came after me when I left the JFTC building...?"

"The thug was guessing about some of it, but someone in my section must have told Fujita when he returned from his meeting that I had left the office immediately after you. This fact plus your conversation with Fujita must have made him suspicious, and I think he must have called Tokyo Machines who then contacted the yakuza."

"So you think it's just Fujita who suspects you or your colleagues as well?"

"I really think it's just Fujita. He must have returned sooner than I expected and asked where I was. No one else has any reason to rat on me, but Fujita wants to become a bureau chief as quickly as he can. My guess is that he didn't call specifically to tell them about you, but he called under some other pretext and mentioned that an American professor came and asked him questions about Tokyo Machines. And he might also have told them that it was likely I spent time talking to you about Tokyo Machines."

"Tokyo Machines sent those two guys to rough you up just because you talked to me?"

"Yes, but I'm afraid that the chief of general affairs had already heard from someone that I've been nosing around. I almost got caught once when I was asking one of their sub-contractors about an invoice they had sent to Tokyo Machines. I suspect the sub-contractor mentioned that someone from the JFTC who looks like me was asking odd questions. It was clear the guys last night were looking for something on paper. The older of the guys who came to my apartment kept asking me where I kept my papers with 'the numbers.'"

"Do you know the guys who came to your apartment?"

"No. I might have seen the older guy somewhere in the JFTC building before I went to the U.S. The other guy, the younger one, I never saw before and I think he is just hired muscle."

"Why couldn't you call me before this morning? Surely you weren't with those guys all night!"

"No, they let me go after about an hour and half. They hounded me with their questions, and when I didn't give them any answers, the young guy roughed me up. I'm really bruised but I don't think I have any real injuries. Anyway, then they told me to get out of the car and drove off and I had to walk back home. But I didn't dare call you because someone might have bugged my phone while I was gone. And I didn't dare go to a public phone because they could still have been watching."

"What an ordeal you've gone through. Are you sure you're all right? You don't need to get checked up by a doctor?"

"Thanks, but I'll be okay in a few days...nothing is broken."

"That's good." Michael waited a second and asked, "What next, Tad? Where are the figures you calculated? My guess is out at Hitotsubashi."

Tad hesitated and then asked, "Are you sure you still want them? Knowing how dangerous it could be to possess them?"

"Yes, Tad, I'll take that chance. Your thugs probably think I have them anyway. They're at Hitotsubashi. Am I right?"

"Yes. A friend of mine from my Tokyo University days is teaching in the Business faculty there. He has hundreds of books and several large filing cabinets in his office, so he can stash my envelope somewhere safe."

"I made an appointment to meet Prof. Nohara, a good friend on the Economics faculty, at eleven tomorrow in his office. Are you thinking of asking you friend to bring the papers to Prof. Nohara's office while I'm there?"

"That's correct. As I said, they are yours. I'll call and ask my friend, whose name is Akira Naito, to make a copy of the papers and drop them by Prof. Nohara's office shortly after eleven. When you turn them over to someone in the American government, give them with my compliments, but please leave my name out of it."

"Excellent. It's a deal. But aren't these guys going to continue to hound you? And couldn't your section chief make your life difficult?"

"Yes to both questions. But I will survive. You see, I passed the Upper Class Bureaucrat Examination, which makes me an elite in the bureaucracy and not easy to fire. And I'm sure they wouldn't dare harm me any more than they did last tonight."

"Except when you walk around the edge of a dam or get married and have a daughter they could beat up on?"

"Those are chances I'm willing to take. As I've said, I will survive. In fact, Michael, I am more worried about you at this point. Please don't walk anywhere alone, don't get in a taxi that is trolling and trying to pick you up, don't get on a crowded train. Remember that if someone whispers to you in a crowd that he'll stab you with a knife unless you hand over what you got, there's nothing much you can do. And, it may be a good idea to tell your wife to be careful...we never know how the minds of the gangsters work. I see my friend coming...I'd better get off the phone."

The line abruptly went dead before Michael could offer his thanks for the indispensable help Tad was providing in his effort to help Tobin's task force, and for Tad's concerns for his and Susan's safety.

WEDNESDAY MORNING MICHAEL LEFT FOR KUNITACHI, more than a little uneasy at taking the long train ride. To minimize the risk of being seen by someone like the two thugs who had gone to Tad's apartment, he took a taxi from the hotel to Yotsuya Station on the Chuo line. He stopped at the public phones in the station before boarding his train in order to try to contact Professor Nakagawa, his sponsor at Tokyo University, whom he so far had been unable to reach. He phoned the professor's office, but again there was no answer, so he asked to be put through to the secretary.

"Professor Koyama, I'm so glad you called. Professor Maeda's office, the one you've been using, has been broken into and ransacked." She sounded very agitated. "I opened the office yesterday morning so your boxes of books could be taken to be mailed, and I locked the office again afterwards. But last night, the security man thought something was wrong with the door and when he checked it, he found the lock had been jimmied and the office was a mess. Books and papers everywhere. Was anything important of yours still in that office?"

Michael was shocked. "Nothing," he managed to get out. "Everything was in the boxes you mailed for me."

"Then I'll inform security that you had nothing stolen. But what are we going to tell poor Professor Maeda who's in England till the end of the year? By the way, there was a strange phone call for you on Monday afternoon. The caller wanted to know where your office was located and when you were likely to be in, but when I asked for a name so I could leave a message for you, he said it wasn't necessary and hung up. And he didn't talk like any professor I know. I wouldn't be least bit surprised if he was the man who ransacked Professor Maeda's office. Do you have any idea who he was?"

Michael could truthfully say, "No, I don't know who the caller was."

But he now knew that the people responsible for roughing up Tad had traced him. Though he was thankful that he had moved from I House, here he was now in a busy station about to take a train out to the suburbs to collect the very item the thugs were so desperate to get their hands on. Had he known about the break-in earlier, he would have asked Major Thomas to have him taken out to Hitotsubashi University by car, but he would have had to leave much earlier to allow for traffic. Pressed for time, Michael had no choice now but to take a semi-express train.

Michael bought a ticket and quickly boarded the next train. He had never before been so uneasy on a Japanese commuter train. When he felt wary while riding a train without a ticket back in his impecunious youth, he had worried only about the conductor catching him. Today he didn't know who he was looking for.

However, Michael arrived in Kunitachi safely, and when he left the station, no one seemed to be following him. He suddenly realized he was using "the tricks and tactics" of watching out for "a tail" that he had learned at Fort Dix. On his walk to the university, he saw no one but students on bicycles and mothers with small children. He breathed a sigh of relief as he knocked on Professor Nohara's office door.

MICHAEL DIDN'T RETURN TO THE OKURA UNTIL LATE AFTERNOON. He knocked three times on the door and Susan let him in. He plopped down on a chair and let out a huge sigh.

"What a day!" he exclaimed. He winced as he tried to straighten up.

"What happened to you? Are you hurt?" Susan was suddenly tense.

"Don't worry. I'll be all right."

"But what happened to you?" she persisted.

"Wait, let me tell you. Everything was okay until I got back on the train in Kunitachi. There were hardly any people on the platform—it was before school let out. The train was rather empty, but I managed to get onto a car with a group of women. I sat down on a seat at one end and started to relax. But when we got to the next station, the women all got out. I looked down the car and the only other people were a woman at the far end with two small children and a man nodding off over a newspaper."

Michael sighed again, and again winced. "And?" prompted Susan.

"As the train pulled out of the station, the door to the next car opened and three yakuza swaggered in. Two guys with short haircuts, dark glasses, leather jackets, and one guy with long disheveled hair who looked like a bartender. Two of them shoved in next to me, one on each side, and the 'bartender' sat down directly across from me. I tried to stand up, but the guys sitting next to me grabbed me and pushed me down, and one of them on my right poked something hard into my ribs, like a gun."

Susan, inhaling audibly, said, "How frightening!"

"I tried to bluff my way out. I told the guy to get that thing out of my side, but he said, 'No. What you called that thing happens to be a gun. So, just sit still and keep your mouth shut. We'll get off at the next station...but you stay on. If you do anything–scream or come after us—I know how to pull the trigger.' When the train slowed for the next station, the 'bartender' grabbed my briefcase. It was pretty stupid, but I tried to grab it back. The guy on my right hit me hard in the solar plexus. I was so winded I was nearly knocked out, and the next thing I knew, they were gone."

"Oh, Michael, he could have had a gun and shot you!!" Susan was aghast.

"I know I took a chance but I doubt the guy had a gun."

"But...Omigod, they got Tad's data?" Susan's voice rose in a screech.

For the first time since his return, Michael smiled. "I haven't forgotten quite everything I learned in G2. No, what they got were two of today's newspapers. Oh, and I'm afraid you're going to have to buy me a new folding umbrella. Luckily I was carrying that plastic portfolio case I was given at a conference, and not my leather briefcase."

"But where are the data? And if you weren't carrying it, why did you risk your health and possibly your life trying to keep them from taking that cheap plastic case?"

"Part of it was instinctive, but also, I didn't want to risk letting them realize before they got off the train that they hadn't gotten Tad's data."

"They didn't get the data? Why not? What did you do after they got off the train?"

"To answer your last question first, I just stayed on the train to Yotsuya. I couldn't be sure that someone in another car wasn't watching me. It could even have been the guy at the other end who was supposedly asleep. Then I did what any good American would do if attacked—I took a taxi to the American Embassy."

"Is that what they taught you in your army training that was so secret you could never tell me about?" Susan laughed, but then asked with wifely concern: "Do you think you should see a doctor about your injury? You wince every time you take a deep breath or move."

"There's nothing any doctor can do. Major Thomas insisted a nurse at the embassy look me over. She decided I hadn't suffered any internal injuries so all I need to do is take it easy for a day or two."

"Wait a minute...you said they didn't get the data. If it wasn't in the portfolio case, where is it? Did you get it when you were at Hitotsubashi?

"I got it all right. And even after taking a cursory look at it, I could tell it's something Tokyo Machines would kill for."

Seeing the shocked look on his wife's face, Michael hastily added, "Just an expression. Anyway, by the time it was delivered to me in Professor Nohara's office, I was terribly nervous about bringing it back on the train with me even though it's a copy. So I asked Prof. Nohara to take it to the local post office and send it to Major Thomas at the American Embassy by special delivery. So the copy—all of Tad's data—is safe, thank heavens. I'll have the major make a copy of my copy, so there'll be one for me to carry home and another set to be mailed via diplomatic pouch to Randall Tobin."

Michael hadn't wanted to tell Susan everything, but he now realized he had to be completely honest, if only to make her fully aware of the dangers they would continue to face after whoever sent the gangsters found Michael's bag didn't contain Ted's papers. So he went back to the beginning of his trip and told her about the ransacking of his office at Tokyo University. He also related word for word the major's reaction to what Michael and Tad were facing. The major had said:

"You know, in the two years I've been in this post, I don't think I've ever felt safer on the streets, and the Japanese people are the most law-abiding I've ever met. Then your FTC friend was given a going-over and his apartment torn apart, as well as your university office. A week ago, I might have said you were being a bit paranoid for wanting to be spirited into the Okura, particularly for a man of your background and training. But not after what you've just told me. I can believe a big company would go to great lengths not to lose tens of millions of dollars. Yes, Professor Koyama, the company must be desperate to make sure those figures won't get into the 'wrong hands,' like the U.S. Treasury. But we'll make sure they do," and he had winked at Michael.

Then Major Thomas had again gotten permission for Michael to enter the hotel from its service entrance. With Michael crouched down in the back seat of an unmarked embassy car, the same driver had driven him to the hotel's loading dock. From there, Michael went back to his room via the very busy kitchen where a couple of *sous-chefs* stared at the man in the suit who looked totally out of place.

Susan had been skeptical about this assignment from the start, and after hearing what Michael had been through, she was visibly shaken. "Well, now you have what you need, how soon can we leave?" she asked.

"The special delivery packet Prof. Nohara promised to send should arrive at the embassy tomorrow, so I should think on Friday. I really have to see Tad one more time so he can explain the data.

Michael finally got in touch with Professor Nakagawa, whom he wanted to thank in person for all he had done for him during the summer, and to apologize for being the probable cause of the office having been ransacked. Michael used the back entrance of the hotel in both going to and returning from lunch with Professor Nakagawa at a private room of a Japanese restaurant in nearby Shimbashi.

When Michael returned from his lunch, Susan handed him a thick envelope. "Major Thomas himself delivered this half an hour ago." Michael was puzzled why the envelope was unstamped until he read Prof. Nohara's note: "As secure and efficient as the Japanese postal system is, I thought it would be better if my wife drove in to deliver your package directly to Major Thomas." Michael was very relieved to have it in his hands at last, and now he could discuss the data with Tad with the figures in front of him.

Tad arrived at the Okura shortly before eight that evening, slightly hot and disheveled. He claimed he felt like a secret agent. He had taken three rush-hour trains a few stations each, getting off just as the doors were about to close. At Shimbashi, he grabbed a cab. He was certain he hadn't been followed. He apologized for arriving so late, but Fujita had stayed on and no one could leave until the section chief did. "That's Japan," he said, looking at Susan. When she learned that he hadn't had anything to eat, she ordered a Japanese box lunch for him from room service and then retreated to the bedroom to let the two men get to work.

Michael pulled out his set of the copy—thirty-odd pages of data—and Tad took him over the figures page by page, emphasizing the areas the Americans should focus on to prove that the Tokyo Machines data were falsified. When he had finished, Tad said, "Remember: land prices, over-time, and the sub-contractors' invoices. I'm very sure you can break some of the sub-contractors and get them to admit their invoices aren't accurate."

Michael told Tad how enormously grateful he was to him, and he was sure that the officials in Washington would be, too, but "not to worry. I won't give anyone your name."

MICHAEL AND SUSAN'S DEPARTURE FROM TOKYO the next day went smoothly. The major had arranged for an embassy car to take them to Haneda, so they enjoyed the luxury of a ride in a comfortable American sedan instead of the usual trip on the monorail or in an airport bus. Once at the airport, they were whisked into a VIP lounge where they were given their tickets. They had even been upgraded to first class. A young marine who had accompanied them stayed with them until they went through the departure gate. Michael relaxed and enjoyed the luxury since Major Thomas had informed him that Treasury was paying for all of the expenses from the day he and Susan moved into the Okura.

As Susan sat back in her first class seat and sipped a glass of champagne, she commented to Michael, "That was some experience! And never again will I believe you when you tell me you are just collecting a bit of economic data for someone and it certainly won't be dangerous!"

Three weeks after Michael and Susan returned to San Francisco, Randall Tobin called Michael:

"Professor Koyama, I'm calling to tell you that something very interesting has happened. We sent Tokyo Machines the letter you suggested, although we changed the wording a bit, responding to our lawyers' advice. But the central points were the ones you suggested: we said we had a group of specialists go over the data they submitted and these experts expressed serious doubts about the accuracies of their data regarding the fixed costs, especially the prices of land, labor costs that included no overtime work, the effective prices paid for the products supplied by the sub-contractors, and six other costs. We informed the company they had thirty days to either submit a new set of data or to desist with their current pricing practices. Otherwise we were contemplating dispatching a team of experts to Japan to make our own inquiries and we were quite confident that several ministries of your government would provide all necessarily assistance to our experts in the interest of maintaining a harmonious relationship between the U.S. and Japan."

Michael said, "I'm not sure Japanese officials will be terribly happy to cooperate with the experts you send...."

"I agree. So to make sure Tokyo Machines took our letter seriously, we also threatened them by saying if we do find the data had been falsified, we would consider prosecuting the head of their New York office, who submitted the initial data, with felony charges for submitting false data to the U.S government. It worked! Tokyo Machines didn't respond to our letter, but last week, it raised the prices across the board for the machines they sell in our market. And the American companies that had petitioned us to impose a surcharge on the import duties for these items have just withdrawn their petition."

"Really!" Michael responded. "Very wise of Tokyo Machines. And now that the dumping has ended, it is most unlikely we need to worry about the goons, whom Tokyo Machines would deny ever hiring, doing anything to my JFTC whistleblower. I'm relieved. Everything seems to have worked out."

"Right. So let me thank you on behalf of our task force for all you and your wife have done. Please tell your wife that the unpleasant and scary experience she had in Tokyo helped end a serious dumping case and has saved a lot of money for our taxpayers because there will be no expensive trial. Thanks again....Oh yes, I told David... General Lund... all about this—he was delighted. And Professor Koyama, if you ever need some data from Treasury for your research, you have my promise that you'll get it uncooked."

Chapter 13

Maui, 1989

"How would you like to go to Hawaii in February?" Michael casually asked Susan as he came back to the breakfast table after taking a long phone call.

"What! We just got back from spending the holidays there!"

Michael grinned. "I thought you might like to get out of cold, damp San Francisco and you could take your research with you. After all, you're on sabbatical."

"Since when have you taken two vacations only weeks apart? Something's up. I don't think it could be a G2 project. You're going to turn fifty-five this year, though you can still swim a mile in the ocean when you've a mind to. Come on, who was it?"

"You're right, it's not G2. It was Miles Anderson, the head of the Office of International Affairs in Treasury. It concerns the work I've been doing for him to try to find out who, if anyone, is rigging the bid prices of the Treasury's thirty-year bonds."

"You've been flying to D.C. periodically on that investigation. So why Hawaii now?"

"To tell you why Hawaii, I have to tell you about the investigation, but remember, it's all strictly confidential though nothing dangerous."

"You mean nothing dangerous like the dumping case you investigated in Tokyo back in the early seventies?" Susan asked with irony.

Without responding to Susan's justified dig, Michael went on: "Miles has been working with people in the Office of Financial Crimes Enforcement to investigate whether some bankers, who are major players in the bond market, are colluding to rig prices for the sales of long-term bonds. They're only sold twice a year, in February and August, so Treasury had to hold its investigation in abeyance until the next sale in February...Susan, this could take a while...." Michael looked unhappily at his cup of coffee, by now stone cold.

"That's okay. I'm on sabbatical and my historical documents aren't going to get out of date. If I make you some fresh coffee, will you tell me what's going on?" Michael laughed as she went over to the coffeemaker, but began to explain the problem.

"Well, you know some of this, but let me start from the beginning. Miles became convinced that some banks are fixing bid prices as low as possible in order to earn the highest possible interest on the long-term bonds they buy for themselves and their institutional clients. He says the prices in recent auctions have been appreciably lower than what Treasury expected, and he isn't buying the argument made by some in Treasury that the low bids are the result of our steadily rising budget deficit, which has forced Treasury to sell more and more thirty-year bonds...."

"Wait a minute," Susan interrupted. "If there's some doubt there's even a problem, how much money could be involved?"

"Billions! If colluding banks succeed in buying bonds even by a tiny bit less than at the competitive—unrigged—

price, it costs the government a huge amount. If the bid-price is lowered by just 0.01 percent, the interest rate rises by 0.01 percent. So if we sell 100 billion dollars of long-term bonds, a 0.01 percent rise in the interest rate costs 100 million dollars per year—year after year. For a thirty-year bond, this adds up to three billion bucks. And who pays? You and me, us, the American taxpayers! At the rate we're going, we may be selling more than 100 billion dollars' worth of the long-term bonds every year."

Looking at Susan who was clearly surprised by the amount of money involved, Michael continued, "So, anyway, Miles began an 'unofficial' investigation and called me in to help because he's convinced it's foreign banks doing the rigging. He knows my research on capital flows to the U.S. from Japan, recently one of the biggest buyers of our long-term bonds."

As the espresso machine began to hiss, Susan turned her head to look at Michael and asked, "Why foreign and not American banks?"

"For a couple of reasons. First, no American bank buys as much of these bonds as do several foreign banks, so it would take a lot of American banks to be able to affect the price. And Americans know they would be breaking the law and risking huge triple damage, anti-trust penalties if they got caught, so it's extremely unlikely that enough of them would agree to collude. Recently it's been the Japanese, other Asian, and German banks who have been the largest buyers, so Miles thinks it has to be some of them. But it's extremely hard, if not impossible to prove any price-fixing, as the Justice Department has learned in trying to prosecute the price-fixing of gasoline by oil companies."

As Susan put a cup of coffee down in front of Michael, who was starting in on a croissant lavishly spread with strawberry jam, she asked, "This sounds like searching for the proverbial needle in the haystack. What makes Miles Anderson think that you, an economics professor, can find the culprits?" asked Susan.

"It's not quite that bad, Susan. Although billions of dollars worth of the long-term bonds are sold, these bonds are first purchased by thirty-two primary dealers, who buy them on behalf of other banks and securities companies. The big buyers make their bids via the primary dealers, letting them know how much they are willing to pay for what amount. The highest price, yielding the lowest interest rate, is what the Treasury likes, so it allocates the bonds according to the bid-prices, that is, first to the highest bidders and so on down the bids until the bonds are all sold."

"So how is collusion possible?"

"I can imagine some of the biggest Japanese and German banks, along with a few East Asian banks, deciding to fix the bid prices. Together these banks buy upwards of a third of the bonds sold. The booming Japanese economy is flooded with cheap money and the Japanese, who already own 650 billion dollars of T-bonds, would like to buy a lot more. Germans and Chinese in Hong Kong and Taiwan also have a lot of money to invest. So it wouldn't surprise me if a Japanese bank buying for other banks as well as its own clients has considered organizing a bid-rigging cartel."

"Okay, that means you only have to figure out which among the largest foreign buyers are fixing the price and catch them red-handed, with evidence that will stand up in court. I guess it makes the haystack smaller, but I still wonder how you and Anderson think you can find out who is doing it and, if you do, catch them at it. Or am I being too pessimistic?"

Michael swallowed his last bit of croissant, wiped his sticky hands on a napkin, and replied, "Ordinarily, you'd be right, but we think we have found where the needle may be hidden. I brought Tony Blando in on this because his firm has a T-bond specialist who knows the people involved in bidding for T-bonds. A guy named Steinberg. Most of the primary dealers are American, but Steinberg suggested we look at two foreign primary dealers: a German Bank called NDB—Nord Deutsche Bank—which buys T-bonds for a lot of European and some Arab banks, and a Japanese bank, Nihon Credit, which buys the bonds for Japanese banks and large investment funds. Steinberg knows the chief traders of both banks quite well, Peter Beck and Koji Osumi, because he often runs into them at the auctions."

"I bet you've already looked into Osumi."

Michael laughed. "When I was in New York in October, I went to the office of Nihon Credit hoping to meet Osumi, just to find out what kind of guy he is. I knew he should be there because there was an auction of short-term T-notes earlier that day. He wasn't in the office so I said I would wait. Finally, the ditzy blonde receptionist called out his Japanese secretary to talk to me. I think the Japanese secretary intended to just get rid of me. She said Osumi was tied up with appointments, but when I told her I had a Japanese-American friend who is thinking of buying about ten million dollars' worth of T-bonds, she became a bit less icy and said she didn't expect her boss back that day and to phone for an appointment just before the next sale of T-bonds. When she went back to her office, the blonde made a face and said, 'Yeah, he's always wiped out after the auctions even when he doesn't fly in overnight from Hawaii on the morning of the auction.'"

"So what did you do next?" Susan was hooked.

"I called Tad."

"Tad Imai? The nice young man who had helped you in the dumping case years ago?"

"Yup. It was in 1973. He's not so young anymore....He's now the chief of the Administration Bureau of the Japan Fair Trade Commission. I asked him to find out all he could about Koji Osumi of Nihon Credit. A couple of days later, Tad called back to tell me what he had found out from his University of Tokyo classmate who works at Nihon Credit."

"And?"

"He learned a lot—that's Japan for you! Our Mr. Osumi is a Keio grad and the chief T-bond trader for Nihon Credit. He's pretty high up in the bank. Fukui, Tad's friend at Nihon Credit, told Tad that his boss is jealous of Osumi. He's especially annoyed that Osumi goes to the bank's newest 'acquisition,' a posh condo in a brand new oceanfront development on Maui, while Fukui's boss has never been offered use of either the old condo in Hawaii or this new one. He's groused at after-work drinking sessions, wondering what Osumi could be getting up to in Hawaii."

Susan nodded, "Interesting. Definitely sounds worth investigating."

"Right. So when I learned all this, I asked Tony what he could find out about Peter Beck who trades T-bonds for NDB. His guy Steinberg, who's originally from Germany, called NDB to try to find out Beck's whereabouts prior to the auction on February 13, pretending to make an appointment with Beck just prior to it. He was told Beck would be 'out of the office from February eighth to the fourteenth for business in Asia and New York.'"

"So, you have information that Beck will be in Asia for business and then in New York. That's not much help, is it?"

"You're right, but I decided to find out Osumi's schedule for the same period. I remembered that woman we met in Switzerland who thought the Hawaiian Islands were located somewhere in Asia."

"You called Tad again?"

"No. I used a variation of Steinberg's ploy, and I was told that Osumi would be in Hawaii for a short vacation and then in New York on business. And then I called Tad and asked him if his friend Fukui could get me the name of the place where Osumi goes on Maui. Tad learned that it's a place called Wailea Point in the resort area of Wailea located south of the town of Kihei. Anyway, I reported all of this information to Miles, and Miles called me just now to ask if I would go to Hawaii and see what I could learn."

"Isn't it rather a long shot for you to go to Maui?"

"Yes, it is. It could turn out to be a fool's errand and we end up only having a nice paid vacation. But all of us involved think something smells. It isn't credible that a banker with the responsibility that Osumi has would be on vacation just prior to one of the half-yearly T-bond auctions. Particularly not a banker from Japan where no one takes more than a day or two of vacation at a time. We really don't know what Beck is going to do, but none of us will put money that Osumi will go to Maui just to relax."

"But why are you suggesting that I come along? You've never done this before."

"Well, partly cover. Middle-aged men vacationing alone really stick out. And Tony will be coming, and I'm going to suggest that he bring his wife with him. Since Liliane is from Honolulu, I suspect she'll be happy to join us. You really don't want to turn down an all-expenses-paid week with friends in a tropical ocean resort in February, do you?"

"Put that way, no, I don't. And I can imagine that it could be useful for your investigation to have on board Liliane, who is part Asian and can talk with the local Hawaiian lilt." Susan grinned.

"You always arrange for our travels, so it would be more natural if you call our travel agent and find out which hotels are nearest Wailea Point and book us into the most likely one for bankers to stay. Oh, one more thing. Miles is sending along a young woman...a Jessica Ostmann. She worked for 'an agency' before moving to Treasury—I'm assuming it was the CIA or NSA. She's an expert on security—telecommunications. Miles thought she could be useful, and he's having her take special eavesdropping equipment with her."

Susan left to call their travel agent, and Michael picked up the morning paper. Burma was in the news again. Aung San Suu Kyi was still making speeches around the country in defiance of the military leaders. What a spunky woman! Was she incredibly brave, a bit crazy, or maybe a bit of both?

Michael leaned back in his chair and thought back to his first trip to Burma. When was it...over a quarter of a century ago. Then he had been sent in to assess Ne Win's opposition and the chances of a democratic movement. It was hard for him to imagine that Ne Win had stayed in power until last summer, but it didn't look like Burma was any closer to becoming democratic. Briefly, he wondered what had happened to Khin Khin, and then he settled back to read the rest of the news before going to work on the book on bilateral trade and capital flows between the U.S. and Japan, which he intended to finish while on leave. He had just finished a stint as department chair, and he was way behind on the research project he wanted to complete. This Treasury business wasn't helping.

ON FEBRUARY 5, MICHAEL AND SUSAN FLEW TO HONOLULU on a 747 and there changed to a 737 for the inter-island flight to Maui. While they waited at the luggage carousel at the airport in Kahului, enjoying the scent and warm humid air of the island, a petite brunette in her early thirties with a perky face came up to them and introduced herself as Jessica Ostmann. She handed Michael a manila envelope of photos and other information on the bankers from the primary dealers who usually attended the auctions. Then, she took the couple to her rental car and drove them down to Wailea. "It takes the better part of an hour as most of the way is on a two-lane road between sugar cane fields," she explained.

Jessica said that she was booked into the Intercontinental along with them. "I arrived last night and scouted out the area. Most of the hotels and condo complexes in Wailea are strung out along the shore. Our hotel is just a short walk north of the Wailea Point complex, which has about 100 units and is gated with round-the-clock security. But security is rather a joke.... While there's a gate and guard at the main entrance, which vehicles have to use to enter the complex, there are three gates to enter via footpaths from the walkway that goes along the shore. All you have to do is lift the latch, push open the gate, and walk in. The gates are not in sight of any of the condos in order to give the owners privacy. I guess the rationale is that burglars will arrive only by vehicle. Pretty silly security, if you ask me!"

"Thanks," Michael said. "That's useful information. Have you found out which unit Osumi stays in? Or if Beck is scheduled to stay at any of the hotels?"

"You're in charge of this project, Professor Koyama, so I thought I would wait and see how you wanted to handle it."

"Call me Michael, please. We're a team so let's all use first names...Okay, let Susan and me get checked in and settled and then let's meet for dinner. Could you make a reservation for the three of us at the hotel's restaurant for say, 6:30?" Michael asked while looking at his watch.

Michael saw that Susan was delighted with the location of their ocean-front room on the third and top floor of the spread-out hotel, which made up for the cookie-cutter chain hotel decor. They had a view of the ocean across an expanse of grass. The only disappointment was that the shore was rocky in front of the hotel, but Jessica had assured them that there were good swimming beaches just a short distance from either side of the hotel grounds.

The trio snagged a corner table away from other guests so they could quietly confer after their main courses had been served. Michael assigned Jessica the task of visiting the half dozen hotels located along the coastline from the Maui Prince on the south to Stouffer's at the northern end of Wailea to find out if a Mr. Peter Beck was on the guest list. "Don't tell any lies," he said. "If you can't get a receptionist to give you the information, then ask to see the manager and show him your Treasury ID."

Jessica agreed, but Michael could tell from the look on her face that she thought he was telling her the obvious.

The three agreed they had to find the condo Osumi was using without alerting him. So they couldn't use a ruse to find the number by asking at the gatehouse. After discussing various possibilities, Michael concluded, "We'll just have to keep an eye out for him. But from what Tad said, I concluded that it's an oceanfront apartment so it should be visible from the path. Tomorrow morning while Jessica looks for Beck, Susan and I will suss out Wailea Point."

At noon the following day, Jessica joined Michael and Susan at a patio table in the small Wailea Shopping Center, and as the three unwrapped their sandwiches, they began to report what they had found out since they had parted the evening before. Jessica was rather glum.

"I went to every hotel you asked me to, and when I couldn't find Beck registered or expected at any of them, then I went to the condo complexes in Wailea, the ones that make weekly rentals. I drew a blank at these as well. I stayed away from Wailea Point, and in any case, you have to rent an apartment by the month there."

"Did you have to show your ID?" asked Michael.

"At about half. But I played it very low key, said it was a Treasury investigation the nature of which I couldn't disclose—it's very convenient having Treasury 'creds.'"

"Okay, so we've drawn a blank there. Susan and I are now familiar with the area around Wailea Point—we walked to the end of the shore path and came back via the highway, but we saw little. Certainly no sign of Osumi. Susan went into the complex through one of the ocean-front gates and walked through the condo grounds to another gate. Amazingly she met no one, neither a guard nor another resident. We both think that possibly a majority of the units are currently unoc-cupied, either unsold or the owners are using them just for vacations."

"What next?" asked Jessica.

"We can hit the beach this afternoon. Tony and Liliane arrive this evening, and if we are going to find out which condo Osumi is using, it will almost certainly have to be after dark when lights are on. We won't be able to reliably tell which units are occupied and by whom in daylight hours. And we need to study those photos of likely suspects Miles had you bring."

"I'm sure you've seen they are of uneven quality. Most of them were taken by Mr. Steinberg of Blando Securities at a reception after the last auction, and a number were taken with a telephoto lens, but they're good enough to see what each person looks like."

"But remember," said Michael to Susan and Jessica, "there could be bankers in on the collusion who aren't primary dealers, so we have to keep our eyes open for anyone who might possibly be involved." He tried to keep an optimistic tone in his voice, but in truth, he was worrying that they were behaving like a team of teenagers about to undertake a made-up, pointless assignment, rather than a team of serious investigators trying to catch international bid-rigging malefactors.

For the next two days, Michael's fears seemed justified. On Tuesday and Wednesday, he played tennis with Tony, swam with Susan, and all five of them spent hours hiking up and down the beach walk trying to see if they could spot Osumi or any of the other men whose photos they had memorized in any of the condos or anywhere else they might run into them.

And then on Thursday, Jessica reported that Osumi had arrived. When she took an early morning jog, she spotted Osumi and a middle-aged woman, presumably his wife, having breakfast on the patio of a ground floor unit on the oceanfront. She rushed back to tell Michael. His spirits lifted immediately.

Michael had another piece of luck. A few hours later, he was sitting in the lobby of the Intercontinental reading a newspaper when a pair of middle-aged Chinese men checked in. Michael took a good look at them. He didn't recognize either from the packet of photos, but neither looked as if they were coming on holiday. Both were dressed in business suits, though they had taken off their neckties and were carrying their suit jackets. He went up behind them as they signed the registration forms and was in time to hear the clerk hand a key to what sounded like a "Mr. Chen."

Michael had another job for Jessica.

IN MID-AFTERNOON, WHILE MICHAEL AND SUSAN WERE RELAXING in chairs on the hotel lawn, Jessica came to tell them who the two men were.

"You were right, Michael. They're both bankers. One is registered as a Mr. Julian Cheung from Hong Kong. His business affiliation is listed as the Hong Kong Long-Term Credit Bank. The other man is Wan Chen from Taiwan, and he gave his business affiliation as the Taipei Investment Bank.

"Mr. Cheung and Mr. Chen? Sounds more like a comedy team than bankers," laughed Susan.

"And they look like it, too," agreed Michael. One is tall and lanky—must be five foot ten or eleven. He has short salt and pepper gray hair and his thin face is lined. Whereas the other is short and rotund, maybe five foot five. He has a pudgy face and is balding, combs long strands of hair over his pate. When they are together, you should be able to recognize them even if you haven't seen them before."

He turned to Jessica. "Did you learn anything else?"

"They are booked in until the twelfth, Sunday." She added, "Do you know these names and banks?"

"I recognize the names of their banks. They are both big banks that I've no doubt hold huge amounts of T-bonds. As far as I know, their representatives don't go to the auctions, but these guys could well be in on any bid rigging. So the fact they are here, I think means they must be colluding with Osumi." Michael paused. "But I don't think these Asian banks alone could affect the bond price. I would have bet money that Beck would show up, given his travel schedule and the amount of bonds his bank bids for. But at least we have some evidence now that Osumi isn't here for a few days' rest with his wife!"

Michael called Tony and they arranged for the five of them to meet at Hakone, the Japanese restaurant in the Prince Hotel, to discuss what to do next. Michael thought it safe enough because he was almost certain the bankers would not want to meet as a group in public, and in any case, none of them knew anyone in Michael's group.

After a large serving of sushi was put down in the middle of the table, Michael summed up the problem. "We know Osumi and the two Chinese bankers are here just prior to the auction next Monday, we know where Osumi is staying, and I am sure that for the sake of privacy, his condo is where the group will meet. But we don't know when they will meet, and the real problem is how to get the evidence we need."

They organized a rota to start that evening to check who was in Osumi's condo. The grounds of the complex ran down to a four-foot-high retaining wall, at the bottom of which a path followed along the shoreline, so there was no way they could manage a stakeout. Instead, they would have to take turns walking along the shore path. They arranged for the Koyamas and Blandos to reconnoiter in pairs and Jessica by herself. Michael felt the bankers wouldn't find couples or women suspicious should they be seen.

Tony and Liliane took the first turn. When they returned to the Intercontinental, Tony remarked, "The living room of the condo is dark, but there are lights on in the kitchen and in the hall. I could see an Asian woman working in the kitchen, but no sign of any men." Tony complained to Michael not entirely in jest: "Here I am...the president of a securities company, walking back and forth on the path acting like a peeping Tom. Michael, the things you make me do!"

Michael laughed. "Too bad Winston isn't here. He'd love a caper like this, even though he's now a best-selling author and the proud possessor of a Pulitzer!"

Michael and Susan went out next. When they reached the edge of Wailea Point, Michael took Susan's hand and they slowly sauntered in front of the condo, which was now lit up. Michael stopped and leaned against the rail, his back to the ocean and pulled Susan toward him putting his arms around her, like lovers stopping for a cuddle. With her face against his shoulder, Susan asked in a muffled voice, "Can you see anything?"

"A woman—Mrs. Osumi, I presume—has just brought drinks into the room and has taken them over to serve to someone? Two people? Out of sight. Wait! Two men have just come in from the hall. One is Osumi, and yes! Just behind him is Beck! So he's here! He must be staying with the Osumis...Oops."

Michael suddenly turned and gave Susan a long kiss. When he released her, he put his arm around her shoulder and turned her back the way they had come.

"What happened? What did you see?" she asked excitedly.

"When Osumi came into the room with Beck just behind him, he said something to his wife and pointed to the window. She hurriedly put the tray down and came and closed the curtains. I didn't want her to see me looking in so I acted like a lover."

"And did a pretty good job of it," murmured Susan. "So, now what?"

"Now we go back to our room and have a pow-wow about what to do next."

When Susan and Michael got back to their room, they found Tony regaling the two women with stories, but the laughter quickly ended when Michael made his report.

"I am very sure the group is meeting to discuss bid prices. There could even be one or two others who will join them. Now we have to try to listen in to what they say. Jessica, we are going to have to resort to the eavesdropping device you brought with you. Can you get it for us? I'm not up to date on that kind of technology any more, and I suspect Tony isn't either."

Jessica nodded and went to her room down the corridor and returned a few minutes later with a yellow beach bag from which she took out a black metal box the size of a shaving kit.

"As you see, this is a compact German-made 'bug,' one of the most advanced. Despite the size, this is a highly efficient transmitter-receiver with valuable 'accessories.' One is a small, thin metal disc that serves as a 'bug,' which can be inserted into the mouthpiece of a telephone or hidden easily anywhere else. Another is a directional receiver, a very small funnel-shaped metal piece that catches any sound from where it is pointed...it's good for up to almost 100 meters."

After Jessica gave a five-minute explanation of how to use the bug, the other four felt confident they, too, could operate it.

Michael said with a worried look on his face, "The question is, where can we use it to listen in on the conversations in Osumi's condo? They have to conclude their negotiations during the next two days as Osumi and Beck have to fly out on Sunday, and that's the day the two Chinese are scheduled to depart. We certainly can't stand on the path and point the directional receiver with people passing by us constantly. And I don't see how we can plant the bug inside the condo."

"One of us women could dress up as an employee and scout out the condo—see if we can somehow plant the bug on the low louvered window of the living room," suggested Susan.

"That would have to be me," Liliane said immediately. "Since when have you seen a pretty haole—I mean white woman—in a housekeeper's uniform? And I can still talk like a local. If I run into a security guard, I can fake it."

Tony wasn't crazy about the idea, and Michael too had his doubts about the wisdom of this, but eventually Liliane convinced them it was their only option. Michael had never asked what the ethnic concoction of Tony's second wife was, but whatever it was, this dark-haired beauty was the typical mixed-race woman found in Hawaii.

THE FOLLOWING MORNING, FRIDAY, TONY DROVE HIS WIFE up to the town of Kahului to get outfitted as a housekeeper, while the other three took turns timing the guard's rounds at the ocean end of the complex. Shortly after ten, Michael returned from his stint and joined Susan on the sandy beach next to the complex. He found Susan trying to hold in her excitement. She whispered to Michael:

"Look at those two Asian guys down to the right, the ones in dark swim trunks. Aren't they the Chinese bankers? They sat down a few minutes ago and have been talking to each other since, almost as if they are arguing about something. We're so far away that I can't even tell what language they're speaking. Let's get Jessica to come down with the gizmo to see if she can hear anything."

Michael agreed and hurried back up to the shore path. When out of sight of the beach, he started to sprint and arrived out of breath at the Intercontinental just as Jessica was coming out of the hotel to take her turn monitoring the security rounds at Wailea Point. He hurriedly told her to get the listening device, and within ten minutes she was on her way to the beach carrying her beach bag and a beach umbrella. Michael hoped the pair would still be there after all the time that had lapsed.

Michael and Susan went back to checking on the guard rounds. At noon, they went back to their room, and within minutes, Jessica came in to report.

"This bug is amazing. I was sitting about 100 feet away from those guys. Hiding it behind my beach umbrella, I aimed the directional audio-receptor at them. Their conversation came in clear as a bell."

Susan interrupted her. "What did you learn?"

Jessica laughed. "Not much from the conversation because it was entirely in Chinese. But I'm sure I caught the names Osumi and Beck, and more than once. However, I gathered a lot from the tone and from their body language. They seemed to be having a discussion that bordered on an argument. So I would guess that something isn't going smoothly with our conspirators."

Michael sighed. "We still don't have enough to go on. I'm wondering...." But before he could finish his sentence, there was a knock on the door. Michael opened it to find a housekeeper who asked if she could make up their room.

Michael started to say that their room had already been done and then did a double take. "Liliane?" he gasped.

Tony's wife was almost unrecognizable. Gone were the stylish shift, the dangling earrings, and the elegant French twist. She had taken off her make-up and scraped her hair back into a ponytail. The uniform was ill-fitting and added some fifteen pounds to her weight.

"You could be an actress!" Susan exclaimed.

Tony followed his wife into the room and shut the door. "Have you figured out the security rounds?" he asked, clearly apprehensive about what his wife proposed to do.

Michael replied, "As far as we can figure, the guards come by only once an hour." Then he said to Liliane, "So if you wait until the guard is seen going down the driveway toward the Osumi's condo and then go into the complex, you should have nearly an hour to snoop around. But you will look strange walking into the complex from the shore in that get-up...."

Susan piped up, "I've got a long caftan Liliane can wear to cover her uniform. One of us will go with her carrying an empty tote to stow it in, and then wait until she comes out."

Susan was eager to be the person to accompany Liliane, but Michael insisted that Jessica go. "She's got the training and experience needed for this kind of job. I'd like to have Jessica plant the bug, if possible. But first we need to have Liliane scout out the condo and see what the possibilities are."

Mid-afternoon, the five set out from the Intercontinental and headed south. Michael, Tony, and Susan spread out their towels and set up umbrellas on the beach between the Intercontinental and the Wailea Point complex. Jessica and Liliane continued on, crossed the little bridge over the gulley next to the complex, and were soon out of sight. None of the three on the beach said much while they nervously waited. Time crawled. Finally, Liliane and Jessica slid down the sandy hillside and joined them on the beach. Michael could hear Tony's audible sigh of relief at seeing his wife once more.

"What happened? What did you learn?" Susan got in first with the question the two men also wanted to ask.

"Quite a lot," said Jessica with an excited edge to her voice. "I think I may have discovered how we can collect that evidence we need. But Liliane, this is your story," she said as she turned to her companion. With quiet composure, Liliane related what had happened.

"The reason it took so long was we waited until we saw the guard do his rounds. Then I went in through the gate and walked to the Osumi's condo. There was no car parked either in their parking space or in the guest space, so I assumed the condo was empty. I went through the service area where the garbage cans are stored and went to where I could see the lanai. I didn't want to take any chances, and it's a good thing I didn't, because Osumi was on the lanai. Luckily, he was facing the ocean and didn't see me. He was concentrating on typing on a funny-looking black box and wearing earphones...you know like the ones we use to listen to music on planes. There was a long wire extended from the black box in front of Osumi and, at one end of it, there was an odd-looking small ring-like looped wire dangling from the edge of the patio. If I hadn't been looking for something, I'd have missed it."

Liliane paused and then said, "That's all I saw and then I got caught."

"What? By Osumi?" Tony was aghast.

"No, by a security guard as I was leaving the way I came, through the walled area where the trash cans are kept."

"Is that why you were gone so long?" asked Tony, very agitated.

"No, no, it was really no problem. The guy greeted me and made the comment that he hadn't seen me working here before. I said the Osumis had important guests and needed extra help. He wasn't in the least bit suspicious. I guess we didn't have the rounds figured right, or the guy was on an errand. Anyway, I went back out and told Jessica what I'd seen, and she tried to get a glimpse of Osumi's equipment from the path."

Jessica responded. "I have binoculars. I was surveying the landscape and obscured by some bushes, I got a good look at the patio. I'm pretty sure from the looks of it...the black box in front of Osumi and his talking on that mouth piece...that the telephone is attached to a SMART and they are sending spurts to Tokyo or somewhere with access to a computer and a lot of data. I've seen a unit almost identical."

Susan asked, "Jessica, what is a SMART and what do you mean by sending spurts?" Both Michael and Tony knew what they were from their G2 work, but they nodded for Jessica to explain because they thought it would be useful for Susan and Liliane to know as well.

"SMART is an abbreviation for 'spurt message alphanumeric radio terminal' which sends and receives spurts— an electronic radio message in a highly condensed form. A longish radio message that, say, takes a full two minutes to send in the usual way, is sent in a few seconds. If you have a lot of data to send, you can spurt them in less than ten seconds instead of taking almost four or five minutes. My guess is Osumi is using is a terminal-cum-PC with a telephone attached...the kind made in Bangalore, India, where you find a dozen excellent high-tech upstarts. I'm sure these terminals are still very expensive, maybe about 25,000 to 30,000 dollars per unit."

Michael observed: "Nihon Credit can afford them." Then, as if talking to himself, he asked, "The question is why use a SMART and spurts? Osumi has just come from Tokyo...so why does he still have so much to communicate with the head office of Nihon Credit? Why not telephone? Do they have to send a lot of last-minute data? Or get some

kind of very long, detailed instructions after they have nego-
tiated the quantities and prices in Hawaii?" He turned to
Jessica. "Am I correct in thinking that the NSA can catch
these spurts coming and going from the SMART?"

"Yes, and in this case, it will be easy because we know
where the SMART is located. And I'm sure that in this area
no one else is using a SMART that the NSA doesn't know
about....not like in D.C. or the New York areas. But neither
of these agencies will help you unless it involves national
security."

Michael countered, "We can say anything that affects
the U.S. economy by billions of dollars every year and also
involves foreigners is a national security issue."

Jessica was politely skeptical. "That's not the usual definition of national security. And so far as we know, the countries directly involved are our allies."

"We can let someone high-up decide that," Michael
said firmly. "I think this is important enough to see if the
NSA might be willing to, let's say, flexibly interpret the
definition of national security?" But then he considered and
commented, "But I can't ask Miles to call in other agencies
on the basis of the kind of circumstantial evidence we have
so far: four bankers meeting on Maui, and one of them while
by himself using what we guess is a SMART. We've got to
have some confirmation that they are conspiring before we
get the NSA involved."

"They weren't meeting this afternoon, so it's probable
they'll meet again tonight," Tony surmised.

Michael said immediately: "I agree, Tony, particularly
since the Chinese seem to be unhappy about something so
they'll need to iron things out. I'm going to go over with
Jessica's German gadget and try to pick up a conversation.
Jessica, I know you're the technical expert, but I am familiar

with the jargon bond traders use, and I might be able to pick up any German or Japanese that's spoken."

"I'll serve as look-out for you," volunteered Tony. Michael tactfully forbore from commenting that with the thirty pounds Tony had gained since leaving the army, this was a better task for him than climbing over the wall. He only said, "Thanks, Tony. Now, Jessica and Liliane, tell me the best way to listen to a conversation in the living room of Osumi's condo. We can't think of planting a bug until we are sure everyone has gone to bed, and I want to try to get evidence before tomorrow."

Jessica replied, "Well, first of all, you're going to have to be near the living room. The device will work through glass, but not through metal and not through brick walls, for example."

"That means," said Liliane, "that you can't hide in the most obvious place, the walled off trash area. The walls are made of brick."

"So that means I'll have to be on the oceanfront side, on the lawn above the sea path so I can be directly in front of the living room. How am I going to get there? What do you think, Liliane, from your foray into the complex?"

"I don't think it's going to be safe approaching as I did from the driveway. If anyone should see you sneaking around the building, whether Mrs. Osumi or the neighbors, you would be taken as a burglar. I think you are going to have to get onto the lawn from the sea path."

Tony suggested, "How about if I boost you up from the pathway when no one is in sight? If last night is anything to go on, the curtains are going to be drawn. You won't have to worry about being seen from the living room, only being heard. And I'll take Liliane to help create a diversion if necessary, since you are going to have trouble remaining completely out of sight. Jessica could stand watch near the bridge where she can see the driveway to keep an eye out for a guard or anyone else she thinks we should be concerned about."

"Good idea!" said Jessica. "I brought some pagers we can use. I can alert you if I see a guard coming down toward the waterfront."

"What about me? What do you want me to do," asked Susan.

Michael thought quickly. "I think it would be best if you stayed in the lobby of the Intercontinental just in case the Chinese aren't already at the condo. And with a pager so you can alert Jessica if need be." He didn't really think this would be much use, but with Susan's lack of training and experience, he didn't want her anywhere near the field of operations, as he thought of the Osumi's condo unit.

After a quick meal, the five prepared for their venture. Michael dressed in black pants and a navy blue T-shirt. The other three who were to serve as lookouts dressed in what they hoped would be taken for ordinary resort wear but on the dark side. Susan had to be taught how to use a pager.

When it was fully dark, the four set out. Luckily for them, the sky was covered with clouds and it was on the chilly side for Hawaii. They didn't find many people out for a stroll. When no one was about, Michael stood on Tony's knee and was boosted up over the wall and onto the lawn at the edge of the Osumi's unit. He scooted over to where there was some cover with a few low shrubs, but though he lay flat on his stomach, he knew he could be seen by anyone coming from the south if they were looking closely. He could see the lighted living room behind the closed curtains, but heard nothing.

Silently he set up the listening device, pulling out the antenna in the direction of the condo. He heard nothing. Was the device on? Yes, the little red light was lit. Was no one in the living room? Then he realized he could hear clicking noises, as if someone was tapping into a machine. After a few minutes, he heard the murmur of voices but he couldn't distinguish what was being said. Was this entire undertaking going to be a waste of time?

Suddenly, he heard a door open and a light went on in the patio. Oh, oh! Someone was coming out! Hurriedly, Michael put his head down on the grass, his face toward the ocean so light couldn't glint off his glasses. Metal chairs scraped on the patio and he thought at least two people sat down. He caught a few words. Not English. Chinese! He heard what he knew must be a cigarette lighter. So the Chinese bankers had come out for a cigarette break. He lay as still as possible, the side of his face uncomfortable on the damp grass.

Michael could feel his heart beating fast as he tried to concentrate to hear the conversation between the two Chinese. All he heard was the sound of waves. The two men seemed to be focused on getting nicotine in their bloodstream as fast as they could.

Finally, he heard a chair leg scrape again on the patio. A few moments later, he heard the loud click of the sliding glass door to the living room close. As he was breathing a sigh of relief, he realized that the gizmo was picking up voices, now in English. He couldn't catch everything that was said, but enough to make him immediately aware that they were discussing the rigging of bids.

A lot of what he caught was disjointed, and it was clear to Michael that the men were looking at numbers. A voice said in a Japanese accent, "Mr. Chen, your bank will get its shares in this price range...here." The reply in Chinese

English was something about having to check with his superiors. After some conversation he couldn't catch, he heard loud German-accented English. "Great. The president of my bank will be pleased...six billion for us and our clients." More conversation in low voices he couldn't catch, and then Michael clearly heard in Chinese-accented English, "Our clients on the mainland may not be happy. I'll call them and discuss this again with you tomorrow."

Michael was wondering how long he should continue to listen in, when he heard Tony and Liliane start what sounded like a lovers' quarrel on the path. Someone must be coming and they were trying to create a diversion to make anyone on the path hurry past them, but not loud enough to be noticed in the condo.

Again Michael lay flat. A group of people, obviously quite happy from an evening out, passed by. Then Michael heard Tony say in a low voice, "Let's get out of here. My pager went off and there are more people coming—I can hear them in the distance."

Michael handed over the German device for Tony to dismantle, rolled over, and jumped down onto the path. Then the trio set off toward the Intercontinental. Jessica was waiting for them at the bridge. "I paged you because I saw two guards head south on the driveway and I didn't know why. Did they see you?" she asked Michael.

With suppressed excitement, Michael responded, "No, and I got the goods!"

When the four got back to the Intercontinental, they quickly told Susan what had happened and then Michael said, "I'm going to call Miles. We have enough for him to get the NSA to pick up the spurts they're sending. We have to act fast as there's only one more night before Beck and Osumi have to leave for the auction.

Miles did not appreciate being awakened at three a.m. East Coast time, but by the time Michael finished describing what he has found and what he wanted Miles to do, Miles' attitude had changed. Michael told him that he couldn't accurately predict when, or even if, Osumi would send messages, but he reported that today Osumi had used the machine at three in the afternoon, and again between eight and nine in the evening.

Miles sounded almost elated that Michael had gotten some evidence, though it was nothing that would stand up in court. He told Michael that if he could manage to get the spurts read, he would want Michael to fly to Washington immediately to tell him what was in them as they would almost certainly be in Japanese. "I'll be in touch. Get some sleep," he said and hung up.

Fat chance, thought Michael. He went to bed and lay there, wide awake. He could feel Susan's deep breathing beside him, but he couldn't relax enough to fall asleep. But after some time he felt drowsy and finally slept.

Suddenly Michael was jolted awake as an alarm screamed all around him. Jack yelled, "Run! We've tripped an electric beam. Out the door to the left. Follow me!"

Michael ran as he had never run before. Jack was zigzagging between buildings and down alleys to the harbor, hoping to avoid the guards and almost certainly the Stasi who would certainly be after them as well. Michael was breathing hard, but though his legs were shorter than Jack's, he managed to keep up.

They finally reached the river and ducked behind the remnants of a wall that Michael thought must once have been a bunker. Even crouched down with his arms around the pile of documents he had gotten away with, he was freezing from the wintry wind coming down the river from the Baltic Sea.

What a miserable refrigerator of a city, and still not fully rebuilt from the Allied bombing that took out its airplane and V2 rocket factories.

"Where's Anna?" Jack wondered aloud. "She should have been here by now. I hope she didn't get caught by the Stasi who were looking for us."

"And I wonder what went wrong," said Michael. "Everything she told us was totally accurate, but she must not have known about the beam—too low level a clerk to be allowed to know what the security was?" He mused on Anna, an attractive, young East German woman with the same name as Anna Wells, his father's English mistress, but so very unlike the sophisticated, well-educated Anna he had known. He shivered in the cold. Even thoughts of Siam couldn't warm him up. And he was having difficulty maintaining his footing on the narrow strip of land atop the icy bank of the river.

Simultaneously, he heard a soft but desperate female voice call, "Wo sind Sie?" and, over the top of the broken wall, saw the strong headlights of a vehicle approaching. Who could be out at three a.m. other than the Stasi?

"Anna!" Jack raised his head over the wall and called in a low voice, "Wir sind hier. Macht schnell!"

Anna got behind the wall just as Michael heard the vehicle come to a stop. Where was the boat?

Michael looked at his watch. Five minutes now until pick-up time. He shivered violently. He was sure his sweat from running was turning to ice. Neither he nor Jack was dressed warmly enough for a winter night on the Baltic Sea because really heavy jackets would have hampered their movements.

Michael could hear car doors open, and then silence.

*In the silence came the faint sound of oars splashing
through the water. It had to be their rescue boat approaching
with its motor cut. It drew closer to them. Jack whispered to
Michael and Anna:*

*"We've got to take a chance. If we quietly slide down
the bank, we won't be seen." Michael was already slith-
ering down the icy embankment in a sitting position, one
hand tightly holding one of Anna's hands. Jack was at the
top, holding Anna's other hand, trying to steady her descent.
But Michael couldn't break his slide, and he slipped faster
and faster down the icy bank toward the fast-running water,
water he knew was nearly freezing cold.*

*And then shots rang out, and Anna screamed and her
hand jerked out of his. He felt her body pushing down on his,
pushing him ever closer toward the icy river. More shots. He
tried to brake, but there was nothing to grab onto. He was
almost at the water's edge....*

*"Michael, Michael," someone urgently called in a low
voice. Who was it?*

"Michael, wake up. You're having a nightmare again.
And you're so cold. You've kicked off all the covers.

Michael struggled to waken. A light came on and he saw
Susan peering at him.

"Okay, okay, I'm all right." He rubbed his eyes and sat up.
It was that old dream again, as real as if it had just happened.
Would he never be rid of that recurring nightmare?

He got himself a glass of water, and curled up next to Susan
to get warm. Finally he fell into a fitful sleep only to be awakened by the phone ringing just after five a.m. It was Miles.

Miles had contacted the Secretary of the Treasury, who,
in turn, had successfully persuaded the Director of the NSA
to "pick up" the spurts being sent and received by a SMART
on Maui. The Secretary had used the "national security"

argument in making his case. Miles had been told that picking up the spurts to and from Maui would be relatively easy because of the "non-congestion" of radio traffic "in the middle of the Pacific ocean."

"I'm sorry to wake you," Miles finally apologized, "but I need to have you in Washington as soon as you can get here. The spurts are going to be monitored, but we will only have tomorrow to read and interpret the contents before the auction on Monday. If you have any problem getting a flight, give me a call and I'll have our people in the Criminal Division get you a seat. We'll pay for First Class. Let me know when you will arrive and at which airport—National, Dulles, or Baltimore."

Susan was not surprised when Michael said he had to leave Maui immediately. She got up and started to pack his carry-on, remarking that he would certainly be cold in D.C. in February with only the light windbreaker he had worn from San Francisco.

Michael smiled and replied, "Don't worry, Miles will have someone meet me."

Michael flew out of Kahului on the second flight of the day. The other four followed in mid-morning, Jessica to return to the East Coast, Tony and Liliane to spend a few days with her family in Honolulu, and Susan to get a flight back home to San Francisco.

SUNDAY MORNING JUST BEFORE SEVEN, MICHAEL ARRIVED at Miles' office in the Treasury building not far from the White House. He had flown nearly halfway around the world, had five hours of jet lag, and two nights with little sleep. He was glad that, when as keyed up as he was now, he could still function on so little sleep.

Miles greeted him with the news Michael expected. "Morning, Michael. Yes, the NSA got it. I was handed it forty minutes ago. I haven't had time for breakfast." Yawning, Miles handed Michael a brown file containing the printout of the spurt.

"Great. And good morning, Miles," Michael said, already starting to scan the first page of the print out in the file.

Miles said, "The NSA guy who brought the file said that it first came out in gibberish. But since we told them it would be in Japanese, he and his colleague had no problem in getting the whole thing printed out in Japanese. There are a few multiple regression equations...beats me what they are for."

Michael was now flipping through the pages, glancing at each briefly. The last page was numbered twenty-two. The printout was single-spaced and in Japanese, and included a dozen or so tables and, as Miles had said, a few equations. After re-reading the first few pages slowly, Michael said to Miles, who was watching him closely:

"This is quite something. Hard to believe...I'll tell you what...why don't you go have breakfast and come back in an hour. By then, I ought to be able to give a rough summary of what's in the spurt. And could you bring me some coffee and a Danish, please?"

Miles nodded and left. Michael poured over the entire printout, scribbling notes as he read. After what he had thought was only a few minutes, he found that Miles had returned with a paper cup of coffee and a small box containing two Danish pastries.

"What's in it?" Miles asked as he handed over Michael's breakfast and sat down. Rubbing his eyes with the palm of his right hand, Michael took a sip of coffee and said:

"I need a lot more time to tell you everything that's here. Some of it is pretty convoluted. But I can give you the gist.

First, this is a record of the final tweaking...making very fine adjustments in the prices each of the participants in the collusion is to bid. Because the first few pages often refer to 'the new inputs from the developments on February 10,' it's obvious that the author...someone writing this for his superiors at Nihon Credit...is sending new numbers, reacting, I am quite sure, to what was happening in the capital markets in the U.S. and elsewhere, as well as to the demands made by the German and the two Chinese bankers, and possibly others. The author says more than once, 'given the reactions at this end,' which I think refers to the Japanese banks in collusion with Nihon Credit. The author proposes newly revised narrow ranges of the prices and amounts the participants are to bid."

"Okay, I'm following you. Now we know why they had to meet....Go on," Miles prompted Michael.

"It took two pages for the author to stress to the guys on Maui that the suggested bid prices are determined primarily by up-to-the-minute macroeconomic numbers as well as 'political developments.' He added the equations to show them that the data .... as of eighteen hours before the calculations were made...include the long and short-term interest rates prevailing in the major markets, which he said are also critical in determining the bid prices. The big boys at Nihon Credit clearly wanted to let the guys on Maui know they know best and what they know is as up to date as possible. And there's something else that's very important."

"What?" asked Miles impatiently.

"The printout reminds the guys in Maui to get busy immediately in following up on what they call 'the usual whisper campaign' aimed especially at 'our trusted friends in the City and the Desert Princes.'"

"I don't believe this!" Miles exclaimed. "They are to let pliable English and Arab bankers know the bid price range!

What they are after is a tight collusion among the Japanese, Chinese, and the Germans, and a 'soft' collusion with some British and Arab bankers!"

"Do you want me to translate this?" Michael asked. "It could take a while."

"We don't have time," replied Miles. "Not only is the auction tomorrow, but I have to return this printout to the NSA as soon as I can. Officially speaking, the interception of the spurt never took place. And neither you nor I have ever seen this document." He looked at Michael. "What would you do, if you were handling this?"

Michael bit his lower lip as he thought, and after a moment replied, "I'd threaten to make it all public, since we don't have the evidence to go to the Justice Department and more important, we don't have even twenty-four hours in which to act."

"Like minds, Michael. That's my thought as well. The problem is time. I think the only solution is to threaten to go public with all the details without telling how we got them. That we will give the whole thing to *The New York Times, The Washington Post,* and other major papers. Ideally, the Secretary of the Treasury should call the presidents of Nihon Credit and NDB. We need someone with that kind of clout. But I can't reach him this weekend. And I can't risk some other higher up telling me the calls shouldn't be made for legal or diplomatic reasons. And I can't believe the bank presidents would take someone with my title seriously enough to stop the big rigging for tomorrow." Miles let out a sigh and sagged in his chair. "I've already been getting some flack. Some people think these foreign bankers will say, 'Okay, go public, we won't buy your bonds; instead we'll invest our money at home, and see how you like it!'"

"Miles, I really don't think that will happen, though there's always the possibility. But Japan has been adopting a very easy money policy; the interest rate the Bank of Japan charges banks is only 1.5 percent to 2 percent for long-term loans. It's a historic low in Japan, so the country is awash with cash. If they stop buying Treasuries, they can't invest all the money they have at home to earn anywhere near what they can by buying T-bonds. The Germans, too, have more than enough low-cost money even though their economy is now growing at a decent pace. And both Taiwan and Hong Kong have very large trade surpluses accumulated in U.S. dollars, so they need to invest these. Even if they have to pay a bit more than they were planning to bid, they will still come way ahead by buying T-bonds...Say, I've an idea!" Michael exclaimed.

"I'll consider anything. What is it?"

"Some weeks ago, your deputy, Bennett Sands, called me regarding this investigation. When he first started speaking, I was almost shocked. He really sounds exactly like the Secretary of the Treasury. The secretary's voice is well known because of all the TV interviews he does plus all the testifying before Congress. What if Bennett made the phone calls? He wouldn't have to lie and say he was the secretary, but given the timbre of his voice and the message he is giving, I think the presidents of NDB and Nihon Credit would assume it was the secretary calling. And they will be so shocked by the message that I don't think they will question who the caller is."

"Michael, why didn't I think of that? Whenever Bennett calls me, for a moment I think it's the secretary on the line. It's brilliant! Bennett wouldn't have to lie or even prevaricate. He can just come right out with the message and end the call quickly without small talk!"

Miles looked at his watch and said he had to get going and get hold of Bennett. He told Michael he'd call him later. Michael knew this was the equivalent of "Dismissed, Lieutenant," and got up to leave. He looked at the coffee, by now cold, and the box of pastries, but just left them on the table. He took an elevator down and left the Treasury building to walk to the Hay Adams where Treasury had booked a room for him. Once outside, the icy wind gave him the shivers, making Michael regret not having an overcoat.

Once back in his hotel room, Michael felt exhausted. But he decided a hot breakfast would revive him so he ordered room service and *The New York Times*. After getting through most of the bulky Sunday edition, he looked at his watch and decided it was late enough to call Susan in San Francisco. He reported that they had "gotten the goods on the guys" and it would be taken care of. He couldn't say much more about that on the hotel phone, but he would fill her in when he got back to San Francisco, "probably tomorrow."

At noon, Miles called him and said he would meet Michael in the Hay Adams dining room at one to report. Michael could hear the excitement in his voice. And when they met, Miles could hardly wait until they had ordered their meals to report:

"Michael, we did it! Bennett called the presidents of both Nihon Credit and the NDB himself. He started both conversations by asking if each happened to know the other. Both presidents told him, yes, for many years and were good friends. Then 'the secretary' dropped the bombshell."

"I bet all 'the secretary' said was, 'I have reliable information that....'"

"Right. He said that he had been 'reliably informed' that their employees met in Maui with a few Asian bankers to discuss the prices they were to bid, and he named Osumi and

Beck. Both presidents were indignant, said they didn't know what he was talking about, but would immediately investigate. Bennett told me, chuckling, that neither banker asked who he was—they just assumed he was the secretary. When he told them that he could either start a legal inquiry or go public...give the information he has to the newspapers, both said they would check into what their employees were doing right away. So, we shall see tomorrow morning what these colluders bid and at what price the bonds will sell!"

The next morning, Michael waited for the call from Miles who had promised that, "I'll call you as soon as I know the results of the auction. I get the numbers even quicker than the *Bloomberg* does."

Just before 10:30, Miles called.

"Done. We sold all eighty billion. The bid prices were definitely higher than in the auction this past August, and even the lowest bids were 0.04 percent above the lowest price we thought we might get. This means that we saved 0.04 times 80 billion times 30....That comes to what?...320 million times 30...9.6 billion dollars...compared to the lowest prices we were afraid we might get. We'll find out who bid what in a couple of days, but it's safe to assume the colluders abandoned their scheme."

"I'm glad the bids came in high enough to save close to ten billion dollars from the worst case scenario you were expecting. But, Miles, there is no objective way we can say whether the colluders decided the lowest bids, or whether the colluders gave up because the presidents of NDB and Nihon Credit told them to."

"I know some of the guys in Treasury will say the same. We'll almost certainly never know for sure, but I'm going to think you guys did a fine job in Maui to save us 9.6 billion dollars. You'll be hearing from us."

TWO MONTHS AFTER THE FEBRUARY AUCTION, Michael received a check from Treasury covering all his expenses plus a $40,000 honorarium.

"It's very good payment for what we did in Maui...but it's a pittance too, given how much we saved the taxpayers. Don't you think we should send half of this to Tony? Then we'll think about what we'll do with our share," suggested Susan.

Michael suspected that Tony had also received an honorarium, but called him to ask. "Yes, I received expenses plus $20,000 for not doing very much and having a nice vacation. I ought to say that I'm sorry if I bitched about you suckering me into the Maui caper. I've no idea how Treasury figured the amount, but I'm grateful. I'm using it as seed money for the Blando Foundation I'm starting to promote economic literacy among high school kids."

Michael liked the idea of donating the honorarium. Susan and he didn't need the money, though he knew from the way his buddies treated him last year when they all met to celebrate General Lund's retirement that the other three considered him the "poorest" of the group. True, he didn't run an investment firm like Tony, he wasn't a highly paid international lawyer like Jack, nor was he a best-selling author like Winston. But he was a senior professor of economics at a major university and Susan was a tenured professor of history. So they had good salaries, no children, and very little time or inclination to indulge in what he thought of as frivolous luxuries. So he thought about what to do with the money for a couple of days, and then told Susan what Tony planned to do with his honorarium.

"Donating ours would be a great idea! But you earned it. What do you think?" she asked Michael.

"I'll admit that I've thought about it. What would you think about using the money to promote democracy in Burma? The generals who took over from Ne Win have stated they will hold an election next spring, a year from now."

"And I'll bet you want to donate the money to Aung San Suu Kyi, that beautiful woman who has gone back to Burma after some twenty years, when she could live comfortably with her husband and sons in England. I really admire her! Yes, I think it's a good idea!"

Michael couldn't tell her about his two trips to Burma for G2, but looking at Susan's face, he realized she was probably thinking about his Karen-born mother and his ties by blood to that part of the world.

Chapter 14

San Francisco, 1990

I N June 1990, Michael received a telephone call from
Paul Lo, a lawyer in San Francisco, who wanted to
consult him about a case involving soy sauce.

"Soy sauce?" Michael asked with some surprise. He
had served as a consultant or expert witness on a number
of legal cases, ranging from the dumping on the American
market of Japanese products, such as machinery and TVs, to
tax evasion cases by Japanese and other foreign firms doing
business in the U.S. He found himself in demand because not
only were there almost no other American economists who
were fluent in Japanese, but he came with the added bonus
of having a high security clearance. But a case involving soy
sauce?

Paul Lo explained. The plaintiff was a second-generation
Japanese-American, David Tada, who imported a wide range
of Japanese food products, which he sold to retailers who
catered to Japanese and Japanese-Americans on the West
Coast. He was suing a large Japanese maker of soy sauce.
After hearing the basic facts of the case, Michael agreed to
help. This case stood out in Michael's mind from the many
others he'd worked on, not only because of the unusual way
in which it was eventually solved, but because it also got
Michael thinking about national and ethnic identity, something he wasn't usually concerned with.

Michael met David Tada in Lo's office in the Embarcadero district in San Francisco. Tada was a very near-sighted, but robust and easy-going man of around sixty. He explained what had happened rather ruefully. Almost two decades earlier, back in 1971, he had received a visit from the president of one of Japan's soy sauce producers. Gihei Sasaki had come to San Francisco to explore the possibility of exporting his soy sauce to the United States. The two largest Japanese soy sauce producers were already selling their soy sauce in increasing quantities, and Sasaki was confident he, too, could get a share of the American market by promoting his "gourmet" soy sauce, well known to "the better restaurants and more discerning customers in Japan." Because Sasaki spoke almost no English, he had stayed in a small hotel run by a Japanese-American. In chatting with the owner, Sasaki learned that Tada was an importer of Japanese food products who spoke Japanese. Without looking further, Sasaki had hired him. Tada said they "hit it off immediately"; he found Sasaki to be "a real samurai gentleman."

Tada was to market the gourmet soy sauce of Sasaki's company—Nada Shoyu—for expenses plus 5 percent of the net profit of sales in the U.S. He was to travel throughout the U.S. in search of new customers, which wouldn't be easy because in California and Hawaii, where there was the largest potential market, the big Japanese companies and a couple of local producers were already in the market, and few people outside the West Coast were familiar with soy sauce.

For the first five years, the going was extremely tough. But the sales of Nada soy sauce began to grow, at first very slowly and then steadily. Tada received an annual commission that rose from $18,000 in 1973 to almost $50,000 by 1989. During all those years, Tada never asked how his commissions were calculated, let alone to see "the books" of Nada Shoyu. He felt what he was getting was "good enough."

Then in 1989, without consulting Tada, Nada Shoyu built a factory in Iowa that could produce the soy sauce at a lower cost than shipping it from Japan. In late April of 1990, Sasaki invited Tada to dinner at one of the best Japanese restaurants in San Francisco, as had become "an annual tradition." The accounting year ended at the end of March in Japan, so Tada always received his commission at this dinner. However, this year, Sasaki handed Tada a check for $75,000, the largest commission he had ever received, and then came the shocker.

Sasaki went into a long monologue, mystifying Tada with phrases of extreme politeness along with difficult, classical expressions Tada couldn't fully understand. But finally, the message got through: Sasaki no longer needed him, and this check was to be his last. Tada had just been dismissed and, henceforth, was no longer the agent of Nada Shoyu in the U.S.

Tada said that he was boiling inside but his relationship with Sasaki was such that "I just couldn't make a fuss at the restaurant." Instead, he determined to get what he deserved "in the American way" by suing Sasaki. He firmly believed that, had it not been for all his hard work, Sasaki could not have built the factory in Iowa. "If I hadn't worked as hard as I did for many years staying at cheap motels all over the country and kowtowing to the store managers so they'd stock the pricey Nada gourmet soy sauce, Noda Shoyu wouldn't have gained a foothold in the U.S."

"And Professor, I can tell you all the things I did to help market Sasaki's gourmet soy sauce. Outside of Hawaii, the West Coast, and a few big cities like Chicago and New York, most Americans had never heard of, let alone tasted, soy sauce, even in the 1970s. Believe it not, as late as in the mid-1980s, some people in the South called it 'bug juice.'"

"*Bug juice*?" Michael was surprised.

"Yeah, bug juice. They said soy sauce looked and smelled like the juice that came out of squashed bugs! Believe me, it was never easy to sell soy sauce in any quantity—there were some days, especially in the earlier years, I couldn't even find anyone who would talk to 'Tada from Nada.'"

As Tada told story after story of the difficulties of marketing Sasaki's soy sauce, Michael could feel how angry and frustrated the man was, and he realized what was really at stake in the case. To be sure, money was involved, but no less important was Tada's conviction that he had been betrayed by Sasaki, who had played on his "weakness" of wanting to be a "real" Japanese who were, Sasaki often alluded, superior to Japanese-Americans. Listening to Tada, Michael thought how devious Sasaki had been and how complex the inner feelings of a Japanese-American could be towards Japan.

"Looking back," Tada went on, "I made a fool of myself because I wanted to behave the way Sasaki said 'a samurai would,' not like a sensible Japanese-American. Funny, isn't it? My family immigrated from an impoverished village in Yamaguchi Prefecture nearly a century ago. Such a numb-skull I was...a grandson of a poor farmer wanting to be like a samurai! But you have to understand that Sasaki made me feel we had become good friends, and as he always said, a friend wouldn't cheat a friend. I couldn't start asking him for a contract and rights to see the books after our friendship had developed. No way!"

So Tada had come to Lo. His case would go before the Federal Court for Northern California in three months. And Lo had come to Michael for help.

Lo explained the problem: "Michael, those guys didn't sign a contract. They agreed on everything orally. Tada said he was a bit uneasy, but since Sasaki always said that in Japan business is based on trust because 'samurai never lie,' he thought he had no choice. Tada says he was convinced that asking for a written contract would jeopardize the trust on which their relationship was based. Sasaki had told Tada that 'Americans are contract-and-lawyer happy because they don't trust each other. American baseball players sign contracts of many, many pages when Japanese players are happy with a three-page contract. We Japanese are honorable, so we don't need the lawyers and contracts the way Americans do.'"

Michael was puzzled. "But how can Tada win when he didn't have a contract?"

Lo replied, "In some cases, U.S. law views oral contracts as valid as a written one. I think I can make a good case for Mr. Tada, but I need help in figuring out how I can get what he wants, which is a commission from the future earnings that Noda Shoyu makes from selling its soy sauce in the U.S. Any thoughts?"

"I'm no lawyer, but I think Mr. Tada has a case for future commissions. Since Sasaki couldn't have built his factory without Tada's years of groundwork, I would think that he should either continue to get a commission or else much more 'severance pay,' certainly more than the $75,000 dollars he received. I know that increasingly Japanese companies doing business here and elsewhere are writing contracts that allow for access to the books. Mr. Sasaki sounds old fashioned; either he really believes in what he says or he is very shrewd and guileful."

Lo talked to Michael about the strengths and weaknesses of the case. The strengths were the sales data of

Nada Shoyu, which made it plain how effectively Tada had helped increase sales from 1973 on. And under contract law, the fact the "contract" between Sasaki and Tada was "oral" and not "written" was not a weakness per se, though written contracts were far easier to enforce. Also, Tada had scores of letters written by the two men that showed the close nature of their relationship.

In contrast, the biggest weakness was that Tada had admitted in a deposition taken from him by Sasaki's lawyer that he had received commissions on an annual basis, accepted them without once complaining about the amount, and had had no discussions with Sasaki about the long-term future of Nada Shoyu in America. Moreover, Tada had unfortunately admitted that his importing business was not as prosperous as it had been and he was nearing retirement and had been counting on the Nada commissions.

Michael agreed to make two important calculations. First, he had to determine whether Tada had received the commissions he should have, using the data in the Sasaki's company's annual financial reports to the National Tax Bureau of Japan. He also had to make a projection of the profits Sasaki's company would likely earn in the U.S. during the coming decade, at the end of which it could be assumed Tada would retire.

To make sure he had the facts straight before he started his work, Michael read all the documents in the case, including the deposition Lo had taken from Sasaki in the initial "discovery." What he read was very was revealing. Sasaki had stated with apparent confidence:

As a Japanese, it never occurred to me that we needed to have a written contract. After all, Tada-san has Japanese blood, why should I expect him to question me about the correctness of the commissions I was paying him? I am very grateful for what he had done for me over the years but he had nothing to do with the factory in Iowa.

Michael found Sasaki condescending and arrogant in his attitude toward Tada. In the disposition Sasaki had said, "I realize now that Tada-san isn't as Japanese as I thought. I am convinced that he is greedier than Japanese would be and litigious like all Americans."

When Michael examined the financial data, he was quite sure Tada had been underpaid, even grossly underpaid, and that the amount of underpayment had increased as time passed. But proving it turned out to be extremely difficult. The company's financial reports included an entry called "the costs of overseas market development," but this was of little use because the entry lumped together all the costs incurred in Japan with those in the U.S., European, and Asian markets. And the "net profit from exports" was not even disaggregated by country. Also, like most Japanese companies, Sasaki's used a variety of accounting techniques to make its "net profit" seem substantially smaller than it actually was. These techniques were legal in Japan, but American accountants would consider them to be sleight of hand. Even so, using the data he could get and applying standard American accounting procedures, Michael estimated that Tada had received only 60 to 70 percent of the commissions he should have had during the 1973-77 period, and no more than 50 percent since 1978.

A month after Michael made his complicated calculations, a preliminary hearing on the case was held. The presiding judge rejected the motion made by Sasaki's lawyer to dismiss the suit and set the trial to begin in sixty days.

Now knowing he had less than two months to acquire any new evidence to strengthen Tada's case, Michael made more searches of his university's East Asian Library for any publication that might help win the case. Michael was vaguely hoping to find some data he could use or an authoritative projection of the future sales of soy sauce in the U.S. Just when he had about given up hope, he came across an item in a newspaper that led him to the magazine, *Gekkan Zuihitsu* (Monthly Essays). Here, to his surprise, he found an essay by Sasaki entitled "Making Inroads into the American Market: Challenges and Rewards." Michael felt his heart rate increase.

Before he had read very far into the essay, Michael realized that what Sasaki had written could affect the outcome of the trial:

> The difficulties encountered in trying to enter the American market were far greater than I had first anticipated. A very large majority of Americans had never heard of soy sauce, let alone a gourmet one. To overcome these difficulties, I carefully chose a Japanese-American who could assist me in the daunting task of selling our gourmet soy sauce in the American market. The fact that he understood our culture not fully, but sufficiently, helped. At times, we even spoke in Japanese. He was a hard-working man, like all who have Japanese blood, and I might even go as far as to say he played a pivotal role in opening up the American market for us in the most difficult first few years and also in laying the foundation for the continued growth of our business in America.

The essay went on, very similar in content and tone, never mentioning Tada by name. But, whenever he wrote about his "American agent," it was clear to whom Sasaki was referring because Tada had been his only agent in the U.S. And equally if not more important, Sasaki had written at length about how he had been able to do business with this agent in the Japanese way. Then near the end of the essay, Michael found a long paragraph he reread three times because he couldn't believe that in the midst of a legal case against him, Sasaki would actually write what he had:

I am convinced our initial success and our bright future with the help of our new factory in Iowa owe in a very fundamental sense to our Japanese way of doing business. The Japanese way, based on mutual trust instead of contracts written by lawyers charging high fees, will, I am very sure, continue to help the growth of our business in America. Thus, I believe it may be quite accurate to say that our Japanese-American agent, who understood our ways, was able to play an indispensable role both in helping us establish our company in the U.S., and in enabling us to continue to succeed in the American market in the future.

Michael was astounded. Did Sasaki think no one but Japanese would ever read his language? Didn't he know many American universities and others subscribed to this publication? He translated the relevant paragraphs and faxed them to Lo's office. Within minutes, he had a phone call from a very excited Lo.

"Michael, Sasaki has impeached himself! I am going to call his defense lawyer and inform him that his case has just been lost. Not only did Sasaki say Mr. Tada was crucial in getting his exports to the U.S. started, but he also said he did business in the Japanese way...putting honor and trust as the basis of his business. For Sasaki, not having a *written* contract does not mean there's *no* contract! And best of all, what he says leaves little doubt to any objective reader that the future success of his company with the Iowa plant is based on the past success in which Mr.Tada played 'an indispensable role!'"

The case was immediately settled. The lawyers dickered about the amount of the settlement, but the final offer from Nada was $300,000 for Tada and $62,000 for his legal costs. The former was just about the amount Lo was hoping to get in the final settlement of the suit, and the latter fully paid what Tada owed to Lo. Lo accepted the offer with the consent of the delighted Tada.

For Michael, who had left Japan at least partly to escape from the suffocating social mores of the country, it was surprising that anyone who had been born and educated in the U.S. would want to take on those same traditions, many of which were as outdated as the samurai. He now knew for certain that there was no way he could classify himself as a hyphenated Japanese-American like those born in the U.S.

Though Michael had been surprised by Tada's attitude toward Japan, he had long known that he was a different kind of Japanese-American from Tada. In fact, the Japanese-Americans in the Bay area didn't let him forget that. He wasn't sure whether they viewed him as an ordinary American or as a Japanese immigrant, but in any case, he wasn't accepted into their community. They had subtly but clearly rejected Buford University's nomination of Michael to serve on a committee to select the student to receive the annual scholarship donated by local Japanese-Americans.

It didn't help that Michael didn't participate in any of the various traditional celebrations held at New Year's, O-Bon in summer, and other dates important as a reminder of their roots for the descendents of Japanese immigrants. Michael thought these a waste of time and knew the celebrations would seem quaint and, by the 1980s, no longer authentic to Japanese in Japan.

The soy sauce case made Michael wonder if the Japan he had left in 1953 still existed—a country where "insiders" could decide how much or how little "outsiders" are allowed to be participants in society, especially in business and politics. Though Mr. Tada may have participated in Japanese cultural activities and spoken Japanese, he was essentially unaware that he was "an outsider" in Sakaki's Japan. Michael thought it possible that underneath all the high rises and elevated highways that had been built on the war-torn ruins of Japan, the country hadn't changed all that much.

Several months later Michael was again made aware of how little the Japanese attitude toward themselves and foreigners seemed to have changed since he left Japan. He was in New York helping to negotiate an out-of-court settlement in a breach of contract case involving a Japanese steel producer and an American importer of steel products. He had been called in as an expert witness by the American legal team. During a break in the negotiations, he sat in the ornate lobby of the hotel where the meetings were being held. As he reviewed his notes, a Japanese lawyer in his late sixties who was working for the Japanese steel manufacturer approached him.

"Koyama Sensei, you made a good presentation." Both the form of address and the rather smarmy tone irritated Michael, who thought it inappropriate to be addressed as *sensei* as if Michael was the man's senior. *What was this obsequious man trying to do*, he wondered.

The lawyer went on with a smile on his face, "Permit me to ask a question that came to me when I was listening to you speak. As a Japanese—I mean someone who has Japanese blood—wouldn't you rather be defending a Japanese firm instead of 'attacking' it...of course, only in the legal sense?"

"I'm an American and my blood has nothing to do with this case," replied Michael rather shortly.

"Ah, but it is your blood that makes it possible for you to read Japanese, and that ability helped you make such an effective presentation this morning. So, in a sense, you are using an advantage due to your blood against a Japanese company...."

"If 'by blood,' you mean I had a Japanese parent, you are right. But, the fact remains that I am an American who happens to be able to read Japanese. My wife is an American born in Minnesota, but she learned to read, write, and speak Japanese. It could have been my wife who made the presentation I did...blood has nothing to do with the ability to read Japanese."

"I'm not going to press you, but I think you know what I mean. I've been told that Japanese-American soldiers from Hawaii were sent to fight in Europe so they wouldn't have to fight against their own blood in the Pacific theater."

Michael chose not to respond. He realized the man was goading him out of his resentment against Michael's presentation, which the American firm's lawyers believed had weakened the core of the defense being offered by the Japanese firm.

Michael did think it rather ironic that this Japanese lawyer had accused him of acting against his blood, when he knew that in Japan he was no longer considered really

Japanese. He had been slightly shocked the first time he had published an article in a Japanese journal and found that his name had been written in *katakana*, the syllabary used for foreign words instead of the Chinese characters for Koyama. It was a clear signal to the reader that the author was foreign, not Japanese.

Had the Japanese attitude toward race, blood, and who was Japanese never changed at all? He made yearly trips to Japan for conferences and research, but he hadn't lived there since he left Tokyo for Berkeley on his nineteenth birthday. When he visited Japan, he stayed at International House in Tokyo, in a hotel, or at a conference center. He spent his time in libraries or with other academics who accepted him as an economist. When in Japan, he wasn't quite a foreigner, but neither was he perceived as fully Japanese. So it was hard for him to say how much different the Japanese attitude toward outsiders was now, in 1990, than it was in the 1950s.

He did know that the attitude toward foreign countries, particularly the U.S., had changed as the Japanese recovered from the war and began their remarkable period of economic growth. And the younger generation had a very different view from their elders who had experienced World War II and its aftermath. This was brought home to him one day in the summer of 1988 when he and Susan were in Tokyo on a research trip.

Susan had arrived back at International House fascinated by what her taxi driver, a man in his sixties, had said to her. "He asked me if I was an American," she said. "When I admitted I was, he then said, 'You're too young to remember the war, but still I want to thank you. A lot more of us would have starved after the war without the food you Americans gave us. Even though you won the war, still you fed your former enemy. I've always wanted to meet an American to tell you how grateful I am.'"

Hearing this, Michael remembered saying, "How ironic!" Only that morning, he had interviewed a young officer at the Ministry of International Trade and Industry who couldn't have been more than thirty-five. The officer had boasted that the Japanese owed their strong economy to no one but themselves. And that Americans had nothing to teach them. "In fact," he had bragged, "we agreed to sign the Plaza Accord to raise the value of the yen vis-à-vis the dollar, but even with the higher value of the yen, we will still be able to export to the U.S. because American industries are steadily losing their international competitiveness."

When she heard this, Susan had commented, "Your MITI guy must have been born in the 1950s, well after the end of the war, and he grew up in the decade of the Olympics when Japan had recovered its self-respect and its economy was growing rapidly—what, nearly 10 percent, wasn't it? He didn't live through any of the suffering of World War II or the immediate postwar years. Amazing how different generations of Japanese view the world so very differently!"

What about the attitude of Americans toward him? How had that changed? When he had arrived at Berkeley, he was most definitely considered a foreign student. There were other Asians on campus, though not a lot as he remembered, but they were almost all foreign students, not Asian-Americans. In Chicago, in the army, in Paris, he realized that he had been almost the only person with an Asian face outside of the Vietnamese in France. And then he had gone back to California and spent the decades of his academic career in San Francisco, the American city with the largest Asian-American population outside of Honolulu. So he saw Asian faces on the streets and in his classes all the time, but his social life revolved around his university, not the local Asian or Japanese-American community.

Although the Japanese considered Michael more a *gaijin*—an outsider or foreigner—than a Japanese, he was also occasionally reminded that Americans didn't always take him for one of them. He remembered the time he had been asked to go to the White House to attend a meeting of the Council of Economic Advisors to the President. He had walked up to the gate, and after Michael told the guard why he was there, he was asked for his identification. He hadn't been prepared for this. He pulled out his wallet and took out his American Express card and his university ID. The guard took a look at these and then a long look at Michael. "No driver's license? I need an ID with a photo." Michael explained that living in San Francisco, he didn't drive and he hadn't thought it necessary to bring his American passport to gain admission to the White House. He knew the guard was now suspicious because he could tell Michael spoke English with a foreign accent.

The guard went to the gatehouse telephone. Michael stood waiting while the guard seemed to be on hold. Finally, after a good five minutes or more, he came over to Michael and said that he could go in. Michael was embarrassed at being late for the meeting, but the CEA chair just laughed at Michael's problem gaining access to the White House.

Now that he considered it, Michael realized that there had been a definite change over the years in how Americans treated people who weren't Caucasian and a greater acceptance of minority groups. He was seeing the effect of the Civil Rights Act of 1964 and the new wave of immigrants from Asia from the mid-1960s. Following these came a wave of "political correctness." Though the term wasn't new and was used as a pejorative and sarcastically by both the left and the right, it encompassed a general movement not to offend anyone by using terms perceived as negative by any minority group. Michael had felt the effects of this in a couple of ways that he thought of as humorous or sometimes annoying.

His friends all got a chuckle out of Michael's experience when he flew to Idaho to give some talks on the Japanese economy. He flew into the small airport outside Moscow where he was to be met by someone from the university who said he would pick Michael up in his yellow sports car. A yellow sports car pulled up, Michael got in, and they set off. The driver made small talk for a mile or two. Then he said in a rather puzzled voice, "You don't look much like someone with the name McNeil."

It turned out that there were actually two people with yellow sports cars who were picking up visitors arriving in this small university town on the same day. So Michael was taken back to the airport where he got into the right yellow car whose driver had been anxiously wondering what had happened to his guest speaker.

And then there was the reception at Buford that someone in the administration had gotten the bright idea of holding in honor of "faculty of color." Michael was so disgusted at what he considered a truly racist expenditure of money that he threw the engraved invitation into his wastebasket without responding.

However, Michael couldn't think of many incidents in his life in the U.S. involving his racial, ethnic, or national identity. If he looked way back, there was that incident at the Durham railway station way back in the late sixties. He had gone to North Carolina to attend a conference at Duke University. At the station, he looked for a restroom and found two for men, one marked "White" and the other "Colored." Michael went up to the station agent and asked which he should use. The grizzled, gray-haired agent looked at Michael and then in a tired voice said, "I don't care. Whichever you like." Michael had been shocked that in the late sixties, there was still segregation in public places, even in a university town like Durham. Though Michael was both Asian and an immigrant, he never had to undergo any of the kind of discrimination that African-Americans suffered daily. He remembered his old friend, Rufus, from the Chicago florist and what that intelligent man had endured throughout his life.

Michael truly felt that he had never felt discriminated against in his profession or even in his personal life. Rather, he had become gradually aware that as a woman, his American-born Caucasian wife faced far more discrimination than he did in terms of employment, salary, and membership in various organizations.

But most of the time Michael never thought about his ethnic identity. He didn't remember having explicit conversations about it in Ashiya, at Berkeley, or in army training.

However, the subject of ethnic or national identity had surfaced while he was in France. One such occasion was when he was recovering from the broken ankle he had suffered from falling into the cellar on his velo in Paris. While he was laid up, a stocky, gray-haired man with a large nose came to clean the floor of Michael's room. The first morning he came into the room, the janitor paused and peered at Michael.

"You don't look like an American Army officer," the man said in French with a strong Russian accent.

Michael told him that he was an immigrant and had just recently become an American. The janitor smiled broadly.

"Ah...you are lucky, too. You can enjoy your life 200 percent, just like me."

"What do you mean 'enjoy life 200 percent.?"

"*C'est simple.*" The cleaner leaned on his mop. "Me, Igor Smolenski, an émigré from Mother Russia, enjoys a Russian life with my Russian wife, Russian newspaper and good vodka...not the sour French wine...and I enjoy my French life in the world's most beautiful city, no commissars telling me that I have to believe in communism. I can go to my church and eat all the *coq au vin* I want. And my children got an education and can do whatever they like. No collective farms. No conscription. My daughter's a registered nurse here," he said proudly. "*Monsieur*, a good Russian life and a good French life...that adds up to 200 percent!"

With his foot in a cast, Michael had had a lot of time to think. What the Russian had said got him thinking, "Who am I anyway?" He hadn't been sure of his nationality even as a child in Bangkok, though he had taken his strange status as normal. His father considered him Japanese, and so he assumed he was, though he felt more at home in the kitchen talking pigeon Cantonese with Mama Cheung and the local Thai dialect with the boys in the neighborhood than when speaking formal Japanese with the tutors his father hired for him. They made him feel as if he was learning a foreign language.

But when he was little, he did think he must be Japanese. He had a Japanese father and he was being taught to speak and read Japanese. He recalled a long ago conversation with Gong-Suk who called him Kivet. They had been playing by the river, and suddenly he had told his playmate he had to go.

"Why do you have to go already, Kivet? It's nowhere near dinner time," protested his friend.

"Because the lady who teaches me Japanese is coming. If I'm late, Mama Cheung will scold me," he had answered.

"Why do you have to learn Japanese?"

"Because my father says I'm Japanese...so I have to be able to speak Japanese."

"I don't understand. You live here...and I heard your mother was Thai. Why does your father want you to be Japanese?"

"Because someday he wants to send me to Japan to study...and become a real Japanese."

"Do you want to? I mean...to go to Japan and become a real Japanese?"

Michael couldn't answer him. And he remembered that when he was taken to Japan as a nine-year-old, he had felt like a stranger in that cold, war-torn country. The children in the orphanage had laughed at the old-fashioned Japanese he had learned in Bangkok, and he wasn't familiar with the food or the lifestyle. Even after a decade in Japan, he hadn't felt completely assimilated, though he had managed to pass the entrance exam to Tokyo University. This meant he had known the Japanese language better than most Japanese students, at least for the purpose of passing a university entrance exam. But this hadn't made him feel comfortable with many Japanese customs and ways of thinking that most Japanese took for granted. Thinking about it, it seemed rather as if he had learned a part in a play so thoroughly that people saw only the successful actor and not the real him.

But if national or ethnic identity hadn't played much of a role in his life during his first years in the U.S., this question surfaced again after he met Alissa. Michael was only too aware that they had different racial, national, ethnic, and religious backgrounds, not to mention their native languages.

One Sunday evening, as they were eating dinner at Chez Maman, Michael asked Alissa: "How do you think of yourself? Are you Jewish first, or a German who happens to be Jewish? "

"Neither. I'm European," she blithely answered, surprising Michael. "I'm happy here in Paris, I'm happy at home in Munich, I could easily live in Salzburg or Vienna if I joined an opera company in either city. Michael, I'm trying to tell you I'm an aspiring European opera singer. I really don't like to think of myself Jewish or even German...not after what we saw during the war. How about you? Do you feel like a Japanese who became an American? Or have you become so thoroughly American that you rarely think of having been Japanese or Thai-Japanese?"

"I'm not sure. One thing I know is that I've become more and more American and less and less a Thai-Japanese."

"I think I understand your feeling. Of course, no one can just switch over from being one kind of person to become another kind of person. Besides, what you start with is only a biological and geographical accident...like I was born German to Jewish parents in Munich. Michael, there isn't much point in fretting over our own nationality and ethnicity, which were decided by chance, is there?"

But the conversation about national identity that Michael had found the most thought provoking had taken place with strangers in southern France. Michael had gone to Aix en Provence on an assignment during his last months in France. He had completed the assignment within hours of his arrival, but since it was Friday evening and he wouldn't be expected to be back at his desk in Paris until Monday morning, he decided to spend the weekend in Aix. He had found a small *pension*, and the *madame* who ran it recommended a nearby brasserie to Michael. He so enjoyed the Mediterranean-style cuisine with its olive oil, garlic, olives, tomatoes, and herbs that he returned on Saturday.

But on Saturday, the popular brasserie didn't have a single empty table. A couple seated near the door must have seen the disappointed look on Michael's face and had taken pity on him. The man leaned over and touched Michael on the arm, "*Monsieur*, if you would like, you are welcome to join us."

Thus began a conversation about identity with a professor of political science and his very attractive companion, a sociologist, both from the University of Provence. Professor Karim Nizami had been very curious about his background.

"Let me guess, you are from somewhere in the northern part of Vietnam, Hué perhaps?"

"No, I'm not Vietnamese. I'm an American lieutenant on vacation here."

"*C'est tres drole*. You don't look American and you sure don't look like any American officer I've ever seen. Pardon my rude question, but what are you anyway?"

Michael told Nizami he had been born in Thailand, gone to school in Japan, and then immigrated to the U.S.

"So are you Thai or Japanese?"

"Neither. I'm only half Japanese because my mother was Thai. But in the U.S. I'm known as Japanese-American, mostly because my name is Japanese.

"So you must be Japanese-American like I am Algerian-French."

"What do you mean by that?"

"Biologically Algerian and legally French...an ethnic Algerian who has a French passport but who belongs neither to Algeria nor to France."

"Why do you belong to neither country?"

"My Algerian friends think I have become French because of my doctorate from the University of Lyon, because I never go to a mosque, and because I am seeing a French lady, Danielle here. But my French colleagues and landlady...and yes, the mirror I see every morning too...never let me forget I am an Algerian."

"I see what you mean. But I think I belong to America. Of course, it depends on what you mean by 'belong,'" Michael had replied.

"It means who in your heart of hearts you identify with...I am not a Frenchman but I no longer think I am an Algerian. Ergo, I belong to neither. I live in an imaginary space called Algerian-French."

"I think it's different for me. I am American, as all immigrants past and recent call themselves. But, by your mirror test, I am still Asian. So why shouldn't I say I 'belong' to both!"

"*Mon ami*, that is not possible. It is your subjective illusion. If you go to Japan, I bet Japanese are going to think— even though they may never say so to your face—'He is an American, with an American education, mannerisms, and tastes in most things...he's not one of us.' In the U.S., with your appearance, accent, and...yes, your mannerisms, and tastes again...you will never be accepted as a real American; the Americans in the country clubs, the boardrooms of the largest companies and in all other kinds of 'inner circles.' Hence you belong to neither!"

Danielle spoke up. "I don't really agree with Karim. Nationality on paper means little. Where one lives and how one feels are the most important things. I lived in London for a dozen years, and the longer I lived in England, the more English I became. *Mon Dieu*, I even began to like those greasy fish and chips! I know Karim will be even more French by the time he becomes an old man. And when he is seventy-five and white-haired, he will see a very old Frenchman in the mirror! Don't you know all very old people look alike?"

Then, they all laughed and a most enjoyable evening followed. That took place shortly before Michael was mustered out of the army, so it must have been late in the spring of 1960, but even three decades later he could remember the conversation well. And then Michael recalled a conversation he'd had with his wife after they'd been married about a year, so that would have been at the end of the sixties.

Michael had been thinking about how comfortable he was with Susan, and he knew that one reason was that she treated him just like an ordinary American. When he first met her, he was pleased that she understood his Japanese background. But Michael had neither expected nor wanted Susan to act like a subservient Japanese wife. In fact, the last thing he wanted was a submissive woman who kowtowed to his every wish without speaking her mind. And as he had come to expect, he found her always forthright. If she offered him something and he said no thanks, she didn't ask again. He didn't expect her to show *enryo*—reserve or self-efface-ment—toward him, as a Japanese wife would be expected to do. He had once asked her why she invariably treated him as an American. She had replied:

"Michael, you may think you've been away from Thailand so long that you no longer think or behave like someone who spent his childhood there, in a culture I know virtually nothing about. But you often count from one to ten in Thai, saying '*Soong, neon, song, samu,*' and so on—don't laugh at my pronunciation! And quite ridiculously, you consider refrigerators and rocks to have feelings. If you kick a rock, you say 'Ouch,' not because you hurt your foot, but because the rock might feel pain. Every time you open the fridge to look for something and I tell you it's on the left side, you ask me if I mean left from 'my point of view or the refrigerator's point of view.'"

She went on: "And I can think of dozens of ways that you aren't Japanese. You talk to people you don't know in elevators and in restaurants, usually joking with them. You even talk to almost everyone without first greeting them, not even saying hello. You are completely straightforward with people. You can't stand what you call 'ceremony,' by which you mean almost anything formal, such as receptions, dinners in honor of someone, award ceremonies, even funerals. You even say that the only funeral you are going to attend is mine! No well brought-up Japanese I know would say or do these things! So how could I possibly think of you as culturally Japanese? We are going to have no end of problems if we try to follow all your different cultural traditions—Thai, Japanese, and American, plus the French and military customs you like to talk about!"

Michael had just listened, rather amused by her outburst. But she had made him think about himself. However, what she said next quite surprised him.

"And I really think you must be American because you are so 'liberated.' You treat me as an equal partner, you don't expect to be waited on, and you do your share in keeping up the house and garden. From what you say, you were waited on hand and foot by your amah until you were seven, and from the age of nine, you lived in Japan for a decade, a culture where the man of the house usually rules the roost, at least nominally. How did you get this way?"

Michael had had to think before he could begin to answer this question. He had always had to be independent and stand on his own two feet, even back in Bangkok. This was how his father had taught him to be, and after he ran away from the orphanage, he had had no one to rely on but himself. He explained this to Susan, adding, "It never occurred to me to discriminate by sex! It's not being American or liberated—it's just the way I am."

On the rare occasions when the question of his identity came up, Michael looked back and realized that Susan was right when she had said some years ago, "It's amazing for someone with your background not to have any identity problems." He had countered with the declaration: "It's because I am 110 percent. American." And both had laughed.

Now, in 1990, looking back on his life, Michael realized that he had followed his own advice. He lived in the U.S. and felt American, so he considered himself American. He did realize, though, that Nizami had been half right: when he visited Japan, he was reminded that he was now a *gaijin,* a non-Japanese in the eyes of many. It wasn't just editors who wrote his name in the Japanese syllabary used for foreign names. As a professor in an American university and traveling on an American passport, he was viewed as an anomaly by many of the Japanese he met, though he spoke natural, very educated Japanese. And then he realized that he had really always been an anomaly in Japan, and now was no different than during his decade in Japan as a boy.

Chapter 15

Back to Ashiya, 1999-2003

W HEN THE NEW MILLENNIUM APPROACHED, Michael found himself becoming increasingly reflective. In August, he had turned sixty-five, an age he had never expected to reach, mainly, he guessed, because his father had died in his forties. But here he was in good health and likely to live well into the next century. He was not unhappy with his current life of teaching, writing, consulting, and conferences, but he had been hearing a voice from somewhere in his head saying: "Change your life to make the most of the years you have left!" He hadn't said a word to Susan because he feared she would laugh and say, "Michael, you're just beginning to think of your own mortality."

But he felt in a rut, and he wanted to spend the years he had left doing what would mean most to him. He would also like to spend time in other countries, not just fleeting trips to conferences or for short vacations. He certainly wouldn't regret not having to spend hours each week in committee and faculty meetings, plus what seemed to him ever increasing administrative paperwork. Finally he broached Susan with his idea of working less or even retiring. Somewhat to his surprise, he found her supportive.

"If you want to travel and you don't want university duties, you'd be better off retiring than going half-time. You know, I rather like the idea. I can retire too. But Michael, what on earth are you going to do with yourself?" Knowing how her husband was still actively engaged in research and enjoying teaching, Susan was genuinely surprised by what seemed to her Michael's sudden decision.

"I want to continue to write, and maybe it's indulgent, but I want to travel. Will Rogers said something to the effect that traveling is the best cure for firmly held misconceptions and prejudice. And if truth be told, I think we should spend time abroad because we always enjoy it. I don't mean take short trips, but live in other countries so that we can really understand other places and peoples."

"You know I like traveling even more than you do, so I'm game. But what do you have in mind? Travel part of the year? Or for a year or two? Can we afford to live in another country and maintain our house here?"

"I've already thought about some of the things you've brought up. I don't want to do yard work for the rest of my life. If we sold our house and invested the money, what with our pensions and savings, yes, I'm sure we can afford to live abroad for long periods of time. And also Hawaii—we regret leaving every time we vacation there. If we rent, we can decide what we want to do year by year, and just see how things go."

The more Susan thought about it, the more she liked Michael's idea. What she hadn't anticipated was that the months before they both left their university posts would be the most frenetic either had experienced. They put their house up for sale, donated their academic libraries to a German university with a new Asian program, got rid of most of their possessions, and stored the rest. Then there were their university offices to clear out before they could become what Michael called "homeless." Their friends and colleagues told them they were crazy, but Michael also thought many were a bit envious at the lifestyle the couple planned.

Susan wondered what Michael was going to do with his time. "You don't like to sightsee or go through museums. How are you going to write when you're giving away your library?" she asked him.

He was ready with an answer. "I'm going to write books that I can write on a laptop and using the web for information I need."

"Essays on contemporary economic issues? Or the autobiography of Michael Koyama that everyone's been telling you for years you ought to write?"

"Neither. I'm thinking of writing a novel...an international thriller that involves something economic...like an attempt by an international group of greedy high officials and bankers to cause a sudden collapse of the dollar in order to make billions. There will be murders, betrayals, love affairs....How about helping me?"

Their first year of retirement, Michael and Susan spent the summer traveling in Switzerland, the country they had visited several times already and had come to love; lived for a couple of months in Montpellier, a charming Southern French city with the cobbled medieval streets and large parks where Michael had economist friends; spent the year-end holidays on an atoll in Fiji so small they circled it on the beach on foot in ten minutes; and then Susan taught at Canterbury University in Christchurch, New Zealand for a semester. During the year, the couple often spent hours dreaming up and discussing the novel Michael was seriously beginning to outline. There was no end to the discussions of the subplots to be added, the refinements to be made to the characters, and motivations of the protagonists, and "the local color" they wanted to include.

By the second year, they decided they would travel around the world always going west because it was easier to cope with jet lag, and buying round-the-world airplane tickets significantly reduced the cost of flying. They wintered in Honolulu where Michael had long wanted to live, visited Japan in May, traveled on to Europe where they spent three or four months in the Swiss Alps, visited cities in France and Germany, and then, each year, returned to Honolulu via different American cities.

Working on it wherever he was, Michael's novel made enough progress to make him wonder if the story was publishable. Susan kept saying, "This story is better than a lot of thrillers I read. There ought to be a publisher." Michael's standard reply was: "Maybe. When I finish, we will try to get one. I know it's going to be difficult because I hear so few manuscripts by first-time authors get published. But it really doesn't matter if the book is published or not because it's already done what it was supposed to do. It keeps my head occupied and I enjoy writing it."

Susan would invariably make a face and say, "That's not why I'm working on it with you! I want to see it in print!"

IN SEPTEMBER 2002, JACK LANDAUER AND WINSTON TAYLOR, two of Michael's old army buddies, visited Michael and Susan in their mountain summer home in Grindelwald. Jack had lost his wife to cancer four years before, and Winston had never married. Tony Blando, the fourth *copain,* and his wife, Liliane, had planned on joining them, but the crash of dot-com companies had forced Tony to cancel their trip. On the last evening of the visit, the four sat on Michael and Susan's terrace, which faced the north slope of the Eiger. All were mellow after a dinner with underrated but excellent

Swiss wine at the Hotel Kirchbuehl just down the mountain from the chalet.

Michael was in high spirits because, just that afternoon, he'd received an email that his "economic thriller" had been accepted for publication by a Japanese firm. Winston was the professional writer in the group, and even he admitted to being impressed that Michael could switch from publishing "dry economics articles to books people actually want to read. But then, you always had creative ideas—'resourceful' you called them."

"By the way," Winston asked, "how did you find an agent? It's not easy. I was about to offer to help you get an English version published because the draft you sent me was so good. But you have already arranged for a Japanese translation. How did you find a Japanese publisher?"

"That's quite a tale," Michael replied. "I got lucky. Before I even got as far as thinking about an agent, a few months ago, when I was sitting on the beach reading over a chapter, a Japanese guy came up to me and started chatting. He asked what I was doing, and when I told him I was writing a thriller called *The Kyoto List*, he said he had friends in the publishing world in Tokyo. So I sent a draft of the English manuscript to his friend who had it translated so it could be evaluated. I didn't hear a thing for months, until I got the email today that it's been accepted."

"To use one of Michael's favorite words, I was flabbergasted!" said Susan. "Michael hadn't said anything to me because he couldn't see how a retired banker could get a book published, even if he is descended from a famous *daimyo* family. But connections count in Japan!"

"So what's your next project, Michael?" Jack asked.

Before Michael could reply, Susan jumped in. "I'm trying to get him to write his autobiography. In fact, I've been pressing him to do it almost since I met him, and he promised to do it once he retired. But I can't get him to start."

"Who would want to read about my life?" protested Michael. "Millions of people have had more interesting lives than mine. Even if I did try to write my autobiography, there are a number of problems. I can't verify anything about my childhood in Bangkok, so all I have are my childish memories. I know so little about even my parents."

Michael didn't want to mention the fact that dredging up his memories of his years in Japan in order to write about them would almost certainly be extremely painful. He had never looked back, always ahead in life. That's how he'd gotten on.

But the other three were speaking at once about how much they would like to read about his extraordinary experiences. So Michael added, "Jack and Winston, you know I can't write about what I did as a G2 officer. So what's left? I spent most of my adult life as an academic, and while I like to think my work was important in some small way, people can read my academic publications. Nobody wants to read the boring details of my everyday university life."

"Hmm, I see your point," commented Jack.

Michael addressed his two old friends. "Has either of you read *Dreams from My Father* by Barack Obama? He's a law professor who's now a senator in the Illinois State Legislature."

Simultaneously Winston said "yes" and Jack "no."

"So you have been thinking about writing your autobiography?" added Winston.

"Clue me in. Why did you bring up a state senator's book?" demanded Jack.

"Well, the subtitle of the book is *A Story of Race and Inheritance*. Obama's an interesting guy. His mother was a white woman who lived in Hawaii and his father a Kenyan foreign student, a black man. So Obama has a complex international and interracial background, and I wanted to see how he would write about himself. It's a very perceptive book, and he writes extraordinarily well, though I think he could have used an editor to pare it down a bit. But the point is that I could never write an introspective book like that. I've never spent a lot of time worrying about my identity, though of course there have been incidents that have reminded me of who and what I am. But you know me—I can't write a 'bare my soul' kind of book, and I'm a dry economist, not an eloquent writer, so how could I write an autobiography, given all the problems it would entail?"

Winston, who had been listening to Michael with a thoughtful look on his face, spoke up.

"Michael, why don't you write an entirely different kind of book? A fictionalized autobiography? Or put the other way around, a novel based on your life, if you prefer. And you can write it in the third person. That way you can write what you want to write, leave out what you consider boring, and write about things similar to what you did in the army without worrying about violating the secrecy agreements we all signed."

Michael laughed. "So you're saying that if I call what I write 'fiction,' I can put in all sorts of real stuff that the other people involved wouldn't want to have made public. And without getting in trouble with G2 and the law. But what I write would have to be more fiction than fact because most of my life has been ordinary by any standard."

"Being sent to Japan with your father and his getting executed is 'ordinary'? Running away from an orphanage in Tokyo to live with a black-marketeer in Kobe is even less so. And getting admitted to one of the best high schools in Japan without even going to middle school is extraordinary!" Jack was emphatic.

"That's all when I was young...." Michael demurred.

"But then you became a G2 officer...and what you did in Paris...a lot of things you did there you can write about. If you remember, we caught a Captain Baum in a base near Munich. That would make a pretty good chapter," Jack added.

"And I know what Michael did in catching a bunch of thieves at the base near Orléans...young girls stealing eggs and ham...and getting shot at by Algerians in Paris. These are great stories and all true," Susan said.

"Again, all many years ago. They may amuse some people but that's all," Michael responded.

"No, Michael, I really don't think so." Susan said with conviction. "If you write these stories, I think it will remind readers what a war does to people. Your story could even inspire a lot of young people. And what we did in Tokyo on that dumping case and on Maui to catch those bankers who were fixing the bid prices of the Treasury bonds....These are very revealing of what really happens in our economy but which few people know about. Besides, these stories would be great fun to read. A lot of the things you've really done are truly fascinating but also moving. And I especially want you to write about how you became American."

"Michael," Winston said, "if you write about the things we've talked about as well as you did in your economic thriller, it will make a very readable story that also tells people what you want them to know about what you went through without offending anyone alive. I've read an awful lot of autobiographies, and so many of them were self-serving. If people had told the 'real truth,' I doubt a lot of these books could have been published."

Michael said slowly:

"Winston, I have to admit that your suggestion of writing a fictionalized autobiography intrigues me. I haven't really been considering writing my story because I can't write about my G2 experiences. Nor can I write about a lot of things I did or that happened to me because they involved other people who would be very unhappy to see these incidents in print. But if I write a novel about my life as you suggest, I can write the facts and things that happened if I change the names and dates and some specifics. That could actually be a truer autobiography, one that reveals what I consider important without pussy-footing around to avoid making other people mad, or even incurring lawsuits. And writing a novel about a fictitious character—even if all my friends and I know it's me—wouldn't be as painful as trying to write about myself. I think that's been the main reason why I didn't want to write my autobiography despite Susan's entreaties."

Michael knew that the more he thought about it, the more taken he was with the idea of a fictionalized autobiography. He was silent for a moment and then added:

"And if I were to write my autobiography as fiction, it would also get around the problem of my not knowing the facts of my early years and also the lapses in my memory. I can't remember the names of so many people, or the exact years when things happened. For example, when Susan wanted to see the cellar in Paris that I fell into with my velo when I was chased by the Algerians, I couldn't locate it even though the memory of that chase, the shot, and my jarring fall into that concrete hole is still so vivid. Not only that, my memory of the name of the statue in the Jardins des Tuileries near the bench I used as a dead-drop and its location turned out to be incorrect. It was a bit of a shock."

"Michael, your memory's not that bad," asserted Susan. "When we were in Paris last year and went to the Jardins des Tuileries, we found you remembered most of the details quite accurately. And you proved a lot of your memories were accurate when we went to Place Léon Blum and that café where you eavesdropped on the conversation between the Stasi and the Turkish major who had been spying for East Germany. Amazingly, the same café was still in business. We even had a rather bad lunch there."

She thought a moment and added, "And Michael, you found where Maman's restaurant had been located on rue Laplace, even though the street had completely changed and many of the buildings were boarded up and empty."

"Yeah, that was a bit of a shock. But I only located the building where I had a room because there was still on the wall across the street one of the large metal Chinese characters of the name of the restaurant that used to be there."

Winston had been thinking and now spoke up.

"Be sure you don't make up some goody-two shoes character for your protagonist! I suspect you won't want to tell quite all the nefarious things you've done, but no one wants to read about a Pollyanna. Be sure to put in all your quirks."

"Quirks? I don't have any quirks," protested Michael rather unconvincingly.

"Yeah, sure," said Winston with a laugh. "Who else do you know who carries around an electronic dictionary so at any moment he can check on the etymology of a word in some foreign language? Or who else sits outside in all kinds of weather listening to the news halfway around the world on a shortwave radio?"

"And you shock the Europeans," commented Jack, "by always having Susan pay, whether it's for bus tickets or dinner at a restaurant. It's like you enjoy what money can bring you but can't bear parting with it."

"Nah, that's not the reason. Money is boring. And, anyway, samurai don't deign to deal with money," Michael proclaimed grinning.

"That's because they never had any," chimed in Susan. "But you're getting off the track. It's how Michael coped with the horrendous situation he found himself in as a child, what he made of his life that's so interesting. And he can write about what he remembers about what happened, what formed him, without worrying about names and dates if he follows your suggestion, Winston. And, Michael, just think, you won't have to worry about footnotes."

Michael laughed at the last comment and then fell silent. Though the idea of writing a fictionalized autobiography was very enticing, still, he was highly dubious he could bear to write what had happened to him, even fictionalized. He knew he wouldn't enjoy dredging up the many terrible memories he had.

Everyone looked at Michael who seemed lost in thought. The momentary silence was broken when Susan said, "Well, do think about it, Michael. In the meantime, I'm freezing. Look, we're less than a couple of miles from the snow-capped Eiger. Let's go in and I'll get you three *copains* some brandy."

Some six months later, Michael sat in front of his laptop on the lanai of his Honolulu apartment, pondering how to end his autobiographical novel. With the help of Susan, he had written a first draft that went up to the end of the twentieth century. As he sat with his chin in his hand staring out at the palm tree outside his fourth floor apartment, Susan burst in the front door with the groceries and the mail.

She dumped the groceries in the kitchen and came out to where Michael was slumped in a chair.

"What's up with you? You're usually pounding the keys of your laptop when I come back."

"I'm stuck," Michael admitted. "I don't know how to end the book. I'm still alive and I don't want to kill off my character. But now that I'm retired, I spend my days sitting in front of a laptop pecking away and then take a late afternoon swim in the ocean. What's there to write about? Any ideas?"

"I see your point. If this were a biography, it would end with your funeral, but your doctor says you're in enviable health. I'll think about it. But I can't solve your problem right now, I'm too hungry. I'm going to make us some lunch. By the way, there's an interesting letter from Japan for you in the mail, something personal from the looks of it. It was forwarded from Buford University. Here." Susan handed him a thin airmail envelope and disappeared into the apartment.

Michael looked at the name on the envelope. He couldn't think of anyone he knew by the name Kinoshita. He tore one end off and extracted several sheets of thin paper filled with beautiful calligraphy.

Fifteen minutes later when Susan came out onto the lanai to set the table, she found her husband staring at the letter.

"Susan, you won't believe this! This is an invitation from a former classmate at Ashiya High. It's for the fiftieth reunion of my high school class. Kinoshita is the married name of Asako Matsuda, a very artistic girl who was in *A-gumi* with me. There were about forty of us in that group, and since we had all our required classes together, I got to know everyone well. Funny, I hadn't thought of her in years—can't imagine what she looks like now."

Susan broke into his reminiscences. "Your fiftieth reunion? When is it?"

"This weekend. Tomorrow, in fact. So obviously I can't go. But what's surprising is how they found me. Remember that conference I attended in Cologne at the end of last year? When Wolfgang persuaded me to come out of retirement long enough to serve as the senior commentator? There were several journalists attending as observers, and I had a chat with a young guy from the *Asahi* at lunch one day. Turned out he also graduated from Ashiya High, though years after me. I mentioned that I graduated the year that the baseball team won the national championship, and when he wrote up the conference, he mentioned me and that fact."

"Strange you never saw the article when you read the *Asahi* every day."

"The article was printed only in the edition of the newspaper that's circulated in western Japan, and I read the international edition. But my old English teacher, Okuda Sensei read it—he's the teacher who took me to see *Gone with the Wind.* Although the article gave my name as Michael and not Bunji, he thought the name Koyama and the year of my graduation couldn't be coincidental. When he met some of my classmates over New Year's, he mentioned it to them and one of them began an Internet search, according to Kinoshita-san's letter. They traced me to Buford—I have no idea why it took so long for the letter to be forwarded here."

"That's too bad. It would have been interesting to attend your fiftieth reunion! And the reunion is missing an important person without the president of the student body."

"The letter did say that if I couldn't attend the reunion, could I meet with members of the class at a later date."

"Michael! We're going to be in Japan at the end of May. Do go!"

"I dunno. Who was it who said, 'You can't go home again'?" Hoping to distract Susan, he said, "I'll think about it. Let's have lunch."

MICHAEL'S INITIAL REACTION TO THE LETTER WAS AMBIVALENT. He had had many opportunities to visit Ashiya when he had been in Japan for research or conferences. But he had purposely stayed away, mainly because he had learned that rekindling memories of his early years in Japan when he had suffered so many sorrows and miseries gave him a strange feeling he didn't like. He knew his feelings were not altogether rational, but something had always prevented him from going back to Ashiya.

However, for some years now as he had grown older, he had been curious to see how Ashiya had changed. He had no desire to go back to either the orphanage in Asagaya or to Sannomiya in Kobe because neither held happy memories for him. But Ashiya was different. He had spent a memorable five years of his life there, it was where he had realized his dream of going to high school, and he had had many friends, both in the high school and among the townspeople.

But somehow, Michael had been reluctant to visit Ashiya. He told himself it was because he wanted to cherish his memories of that city. There was the beautiful beach and the nearby grove of pine trees where he had spent his first summer, there was Ashiya High and the school grounds where his conversation with Iguchi Sensei had led to his being admitted to high school, and of course Mrs. Nitta's bakery and the baker, Mr. Maekawa. But whom would he contact if he went back? Surely many of the people he had known were dead or had moved away. He was sure that many of his high school friends would no longer be in Ashiya, and those who were might not even remember him.

Despite this, Michael found that in recent years when he read Japanese newspapers in the East Asian Library at Buford, he'd started looking for references to Ashiya. He came across one article that sadly reported the beach in Ashiya and its neighboring cities no longer existed. Construction of concrete walls, built to protect the shoreline that was rapidly eroding due to the changes in the patterns of ocean currents, had destroyed the lovely sandy beach. If there was one place Michael had been certain would stay the same over the decades, it was his sandy beach in Ashiya, and now he'd learned that it was gone.

When Michael had finished reading the letter, he had put it down and closed his eyes. After fifty years...fifty years!... he could still see the faces of many of his classmates and hear the loud cheers and feel the excitement as "his" team won the national baseball championship in the Koshien Stadium on a very hot August day. He recalled his classmates. There was Ohta-kun who had pitched during the championship series. And Okagami-kun with whom he had so often studied, and many others.

Why go back now and risk spoiling his memories? Michael had never been one for looking to the past, but rather lived in the present, looking to the future. Now, for the first time, Michael was really thinking about returning to one part of his past. He was not sure why. Maybe at his age, he wanted to assure himself that he too, like everybody else, had roots. He couldn't go back to Bangkok. He would never find his boyhood friends with whom he had chased elephants— what were their names? Monyakul and Gong-Suk? And he was sure Mama Cheung was long dead. He had no doubt that the prewar foreign settlement and his father's house, too, had disappeared in the building boom of the past few decades. Ashiya was different, and Kinoshita-san's letter had reminded him of that. Michael could still remember most of the forty-some classmates who had been in the "A Class," a group that had remained virtually the same during his junior and senior years. The practice of his high school was, like that of all other public high schools of his day, to place students in groups according to the academic performance of each student the preceding semester. This was to help college-bound students prepare for highly competitive entrance examination to the best universities. The system had its cost: students in "lower classes," such as F or G, could not help but feel inferior. But the students in the top class, especially, became a tightly knit though competitive group of friends.

For the next few days, Susan kept harping at Michael to write back to Kinoshita-san and to put a visit to the Kobe area on their Japanese itinerary. He knew that Susan was terribly curious about Michael's high school days as well as concerned that he did not discard his entire past. She was well aware that he had never gone back to any of the places he had ever lived in, and the only people from his youth that he still kept in touch with were his army buddies. He had to admit that he was curious about all these people he had known so well, and from the letter, he knew that his classmates, at least some of them, did remember him and had gone to considerable lengths to invite him to the reunion. At long last, he emailed Kinoshita-san who was delighted to hear from him, and within a few days, a date had been set for a May meeting in Ashiya.

Michael and Susan flew from Honolulu to Kansai International Airport and took the long, tedious bus ride to Kobe. When they checked into the Hotel Okura, Michael was handed a note with the reunion schedule. Instead of one, there were to be two meetings, the first, a lunch at an upscale Chinese restaurant in Ashiya, and the second, a small dinner at a Japanese restaurant in Kobe.

Michael set out alone for the lunch meeting—in Japan, wives don't attend reunions. He underestimated the amount of time it would take to get to the restaurant and arrived twenty minutes after the lunch was scheduled to begin. By now, he was distinctly nervous at what he was about to get into. He walked into the private dining room to find twenty of his classmates along with his English teacher, Okuda Sensei, already seated. As Michael entered, everyone clapped, quite to his surprise.

His English teacher, now in his early eighties, was as lucid as Michael remembered him from fifty years before. Okuda Sensei told the gathering how "Bunji" had been found and welcomed him back, saying, "You are one of a small number of students in my thirty-two years of teaching whom I've never forgotten—the student who argued with me that the plural of house ought to be 'hice,' because the plural of mouse is mice!"

During the following hour, Michael went to all four tables and chatted with each of his classmates in turn. He learned that seven of his classmates had died, and six of his female classmates were widows. One of those who died in February was Morita-san who, Michael was told, "had been hoping to see you again." Michael felt a sense of sadness at hearing that he could never thank the classmate who had given him a brand new pair of sport shoes, saying her brother had bought them by mistake. He had trouble recognizing a distinctly rotund, white-haired man who greeted him effusively. After a discreet look at his nametag, Michael realized that this was the skinny boy who carried an empty lunchbox, and whom

Michael had sometimes given some bread, saying he had too much.

The reunion ended at three. His biggest impression was how much he had enjoyed talking...reminiscing and joking... with his old friends, as if only a few days had passed since they had last met. He had come to Ashiya with a feeling of trepidation, but now, he was very glad that he had worked up the nerve to meet his classmates once again.

The next evening, Susan and Michael took a short taxi-ride from their hotel to the restaurant where a private room had been reserved for the second reunion group. Susan had been specifically invited to join this smaller gathering, but since she knew this wasn't normal practice, today it was Susan who was nervous about the reunion. This time, Michael made sure they arrived on time. As his nine class-mates—three women and six men—walked in, Michael knew immediately who each was. After Asako Kinoshita had introduced everyone for Susan's benefit, they all sat down around a large table.

As Michael looked around, it became clear to him why this group had come to this smaller get-together and not the reunion in Ashiya. They had been his closest friends, and he suspected Kinoshita-san and others on the committee had somehow engineered to split the reunion into two parts.

Susan had worried about being the only spouse and the only "foreigner" at this dinner, so Michael was glad to see her chatting with two women: Noriko Nakano, who had pushed Michael to run for student body president, on her left; and Kinoshita-san on her right. Unlike the reunion in Ashiya, the atmosphere and the feeling of the gathering was more like long-parted siblings meeting, rather than a reunion of old classmates. Everyone was open and uninhibited...willing to confess his or her own foibles and even to boast a little.

Among the three women who had come to this reunion dinner, Noriko Nakano had become a lawyer. Michael knew to become a lawyer in Japan meant to pass a national examination with a passing rate of 3 percent or less. She must have been one of only a handful of women who passed the exam prior to 1960. Asako, married to an importer of Canadian lumber, was an accomplished painter. And Yoshiko Tobata had become the first female senior executive of a major department store, accomplishing what must have been the extremely difficult task of breaking through the gender barrier in these male-dominated Japanese firms.

The six men in the attendance had also made something of themselves. One was an internationally known physics professor, another, the president of a large trading company in Kobe, a third, a vice president of a good-sized producer of home-electronic appliances in Toyonaka, still another, a retired surgeon from a large hospital in Osaka. Noboru Ohta, the pitcher who had won games to make the Ashiya High the national champion, was the president of a company producing a product he had invented, "a sensor mechanism" that measured "everything you have to know about the inside of a gasoline tank." And Shinzo Mita was the speaker of the Ashiya City Council. It was a group that Susan later characterized as "smart, ambitious, and successful, as well as interesting, friendly, and entertaining."

Though they had not met Michael for half a century, their former closeness returned immediately, and they teased him. Susan, who had only known Michael after he became a tenured professor, now had an opportunity to learn what he had been like as a teenager. She turned to Noriko.

"What was Michael like in high school? I know he had to have been a very serious student, but what did you and his other classmates think of him?"

Noriko didn't hesitate with her reply. "We called him a *yancha-bozu*. But," she hastily added with a smile, "he's now a real gentleman."

Michael could see that Susan was unfamiliar with the term so translated for her: "A *yancha-bozu* is a rambunctious boy."

Susan grinned. "*Yancha-bozu* seems an apt description for a boy who threw stones at a baby elephant and got chased by its angry mother back in Thailand." "Wait a minute! Threw stones at an elephant!? " exclaimed Noriko. "That's something I never heard about."

So Michael had to tell the story of how he nearly lost an eye more than sixty years before.

The conversations, Michael thought, differed little from those he would have had with a group of Americans who occupied similar positions. As the evening progressed, Michael realized that, in sharp contrast to 1953, the United States was a very familiar country to his classmates. It was no longer a far richer and very distant country either in miles or in psychological distance. All of these classmates had been abroad, some of them many times. Two had daughters married to an American, one living in California, and the other in New York. How the distance between Japan and the U.S. had ceased to exist for Michael's classmates was, Michael thought, neatly encapsulated when the pitcher-inventor of "the sensor mechanism" joked at the end of the memorable evening: "Let's hold our next meeting...ten years from now...somewhere in the U.S. Hawaii would be my choice, assuming I can still swim when I'm seventy-nine."

The success of the two reunions gave Michael the courage to do something he thought he would never do: revisit Sannomiya where he had spent the better part of a year in 1947-48, a year during which he had nearly starved, had worked for a black-marketeer, and had engaged in the devious and dubious business of selling "American coffee" and "salted salmon."

Sannomiya, of course, was nothing like he remembered. He had been afraid the visit might bring back painful memories, but there remained nothing he could recognize of the Sannomiya where he had lived. All the black-market stalls were long gone. The stores were now all ordinary shops found anywhere in large Japanese cities, brimming with all kinds of legal merchandise, in stark contrast to what had been sold in the decade after the war. Michael stood for a long moment in front of a women's clothing shop that he thought might be where Konishi's stall had been, and fondly recalled the black-marketeer who had saved the three boys from starving after they had run away from the Tokyo orphanage. He remembered wolfing down the large bun Konishi had given him when they first met. But it all seemed a lifetime ago, almost as if it happened to a different person, Bunji, not Michael. That world was long gone. The only thing that had not changed was the loud noise of the trains running overhead.

Michael decided to take the mile-long walk to Kobe Station along a busy street paralleling the train line. He was now asking "what if" questions. What would have happened had he married Kazuko Noda? Not that he had really considered it, but he would have spent his life as a banker, at least until her father's bank was taken over by a larger one when the economic "bubble" burst. What would his life have been like if the Japanese army hadn't sent him back to Japan from Thailand on the *Bungo Maru?* At this point, he couldn't even begin to imagine what kind of a life he would have had in Thailand. What if he hadn't run away from the orphanage... what kind of apprentice job would the *encho-san,* the head of the orphanage, have found for him when he turned thirteen? What if a high school teacher hadn't seen him behind the fence at Ashiya High and come to talk to him? What if he hadn't met Mr. Siegrist who gave him the scholarship to go to America? What if...what if...the questions were as endless as the answers were impalpable.

How lucky he felt he was to have no regrets at how his life had turned out. At any number of times, something could have occurred—or not occurred—that would have changed the course of his life. But here he was nearly seventy and very happy with his life. He wished his father could have known how he had followed his advice and accepted so many challenges.

And he now knew how he would end his book. This fiftieth reunion was the perfect place to stop. He smiled at the thought that readers would think the beginning and the end of his autobiography were pure fiction, when in fact they were among the parts of the book that were most true in every detail.

Acknowledgments

O ne ordinarily does not thank someone who has importuned him persistently over many years. But there are always exceptions and this is such an instance. Had it not been for the constant prodding by my wife, Susan B. Hanley, to write the story of my life, this book would not have been written. And had she not become the de facto co-author, it would not have evolved into this fictionalized autobiography, which I believe is more readable and "truer" in essential ways than a memoir written by me alone. Susan also shouldered the added responsibilities of verifying countless details and defending the beauty and the grammar of the English language, which her husband, a non-native speaker, is prone to besmirch. For all of this, I express my heartfelt thanks by adding the middle initial 'S' to the author's pen name.

Wishing to be as accurate as possible in regard to all the details of each location, local color, and other facts described in this book, we had to impose on the kindness and patience of many friends and acquaintances (as well as some strangers) in those cities in Asia, Europe, and the United States where the events in this book unfolded. To all of these people, too numerous to list their names, we are most grateful.

We express our deep appreciation to Bennett Hymer, who agreed to publish this fictionalized autobiography, a genre of books for which a good publisher is hard to find. Like many of the truth-is-stranger-than-fiction stories in this book, when I approached Bennett's firm, I was unaware he had been a graduate school classmate decades earlier! And we most sincerely thank Jane Gillespie, the production director of Mutual Publishing, for all she did for this book with top caliber professionalism and her sunny aloha.

Honolulu, 2011

About the Author

B orn in Bangkok in 1934, Michael came to the United States on a scholarship in 1953 after living for a decade in war-torn Japan. He earned a B.A., completed a tour in the U.S. Army, and went on for a doctorate in economics. During his career as an economist, he served as a chaired university professor and also as a consultant to the Departments of Treasury and Commerce and the Council of Economic Advisors to the President. Under his own name, he wrote and edited more than twenty books in his field, and then began to write novels under the pen name of Michael S. Koyama. These have been published in English, Japanese, German, and Chinese. He is married to Susan B. Hanley, and they now divide their time between Honolulu and Switzerland.

Michael S. Koyama's novels

Hard-landing Sakusen (Operation Hard-landing),
   co-authored with Jay Rubin and published under the
   pen name Jason Kozol, in Japanese in 1989, in German
   in 1990.

Doru-Teikoku no Houkai (The Collapse of the Dollar),
   2008.

Tamashii no Ryuboku (Journey Against the Current,
   Japanese version of *The Boy Who Defied His Karma*),
   2010.

The Kyoto List, expanded version of *Doru-Teikoku no
   Houkai*, published in English and in Chinese in 2010.